SHADOWS OF HOPE

A SCIENCE FICTION & FANTASY ANTHOLOGY

SHADOWS OF HOPE

A SCIENCE FICTION & FANTASY ANTHOLOGY

GLYNN STEWART

FAOLAN'S PEN PUBLISHING

faolanspen.com

This is a work of fiction. All the characters and events portrayed in this book are fictional, and any resemblance to any persons living or dead is purely coincidental.

This edition published in 2023 by:

Faolan's Pen Publishing Inc.

22 King St. S, Suite 300

Waterloo, Ontario

N2J 1N8 Canada

ISBN-13: 978-1-989674-39-0 (print)

Illustration by Roman Chalyi

Faolan's Pen Publishing logo is a registered trademark of Faolan's Pen Publishing Inc.

Read more books from Glynn Stewart at faolanspen.com

CONTENTS

INTRODUCTION

Greetings!

Welcome to Shadows of Hope, a print collection of my novellas and short stories released from 2020 to 2023.

In these pages you'll find everything from an experiment with dieselpunk knights (*Fire, Steel & Petroleum*) to a distant prequel to the Castle Federation series, showing how the first war with the Terran Commonwealth began (*A Question of Faith*).

Two of the stories (*Pulsar Race*, in the Starship's Mage Universe, and Excalibur Lost) tell the stories of people picking themselves up and rebuilding after failing completely. Two more (*Balefire* and "Blue Lancer") tell stories of more questionable protectors of the innocent, like dark knights and vigilante superheroes.

Last and by no means least, *Mage-Queen's Thief* (the source of our gorgeous cover art from Roman Chalyi) tells the story of an attack on the Mage-Queen of Mars and how a fluke of fate puts her fate in the hands of a petty criminal.

When putting together this collection, it took me a minute to realize there was a commonality beyond just "this is three years of novellas and shorts." My novellas tend to be more experimental works, often with a darker touch than my full-length novels. Not everyone lives. The prices paid for victory are high.

Maybe even too high.

In all of my work, the focus is on the strength of humanity and hope for our future and growth. In these shorts, I hope that message remains, but that more of the shadows creep in.

After all, it's only in the darkness that you find the true measure of a hero.

Happy reading,
  - *Glynn Stewart*

EXCALIBUR LOST

A SPACE OPERA NOVELLA

CHAPTER
ONE

33rd Year of the Interregnum
Alpha Centauri System

Gerard Arkanis shook his head swiftly to clear away the kaleidoscopic lights of phase emergence. As his vision cleared, the gaunt dark-haired man checked over the screens surrounding his station on the bridge of the salvage ship *Likira*.

"Phase emergence complete," he reported, the liquid syllables of an alien language rolling off his tongue smoothly after years of practice. The Medari trade tongue unified many worlds and had been the main language of the planet he'd spent his formative years on.

Likira's Captain belonged to the same race as the language, a tall and slim Medar with four long riblike structures rising from his shoulders and dark green and gold feathers covering his body. Salish K'tet fluffed those membranous shoulder-vanes as he regarded his own screens, only vaguely acknowledging his human first officer's report.

"Confirm our location," K'tet ordered.

The screens surrounding Gerard could provide that information—

but then, so could the screens surrounding K'tet. Gerard glanced sharply at the only other human on *Likira*'s cramped circular bridge.

Harold Newell was oblivious to Gerard's glance but not, thankfully, to K'tet's instructions. The younger human bore the long-term marks of childhood malnutrition in his face and gaunt shoulders, but his eyes were focused as he ran through the reports and scan data on his screens.

He looked up at K'tet after about twenty seconds.

"We are on target," he said slowly. His Medari was rusty to Gerard's ears, but that was expected. They'd only picked up their new junior navigator a few months earlier, plucking him from a rusted-out aircab in the human ghetto on Sameria.

Like the rest of the human crew, K'tet had brought Newell aboard because the human refugees that had escaped the fall of the United Nations were desperate…and desperate meant cheap.

"We are thirty-two-point-one light-minutes clear of Alpha Centauri B," Newell continued, his slow speech never quite reaching the proper intonations for Medari but clear enough in meaning to everyone. "Well clear of all phase boundaries."

"Good, good," K'tet shrilled. "Now, let us pray and give thanks to the One God for His grace and aid today."

The four nonhumans on the bridge immediately bowed their head. Gerard hesitated for a moment to check on Newell, who met his gaze and rolled his eyes.

Gerard's sharp headshake made its point, however, and Newell bowed his head in at least the pretense of prayer. Gerard did the same, shivering against the anger in his soul.

Salish K'tet was a priest of the One God, fully committed to the gentler and compassionate side of that faith. He was, however, *completely* blind to the fact that anyone would have a problem with joining in his worship—K'tet had been raised in the Council, where the One God was the state religion.

A state religion that humanity had refused to adopt—and a state religion that had ordered humanity's destruction for that refusal.

Gerard recognized that the old bird didn't even realize the demons he was taunting or the distaste the human crew felt for his religion.

Part of that, of course, was that Gerard made *damned* sure none of the human members of the crew *let* K'tet realize.

Likira's human crew members were refugees to a one, either evacuated from the United Nations as children or born to evacuees later on. They and their parents had ended up in slums and ghettos on the worlds around the old UN stars and had traded at least surface conversion for survival.

Salish K'tet had pulled them out of those slums and given them a chance at a decent life. He had saved them from poverty and starvation—and if he wanted to pretend he'd saved their souls as well, Gerard would make certain his people gritted their teeth and went along.

Even if it was a virulent acid on his own soul to do it.

EVEN K'TET DIDN'T EXPECT his people's silent prayers to last more than a few minutes. Once the Captain had lifted his head and started to go through the initial sensor reports, it was safe for Gerard and Newell to return to work as well.

Most of the real work at this point came through Gerard's station. *Likira* was functionally unarmed and would have no use for a tactical officer, so sensors fell under the first officer's authority.

Gerard had worked for K'tet for almost ten Terran years now—six Medari years—and he and his team had a smooth pattern and practice to their work now. Dots and data labels started updating across the maps around him, and he regarded them with scant favor.

He was pragmatic enough to admit that the immense supply of refined metals and potentially salvageable technology there represented an asset that couldn't be ignored—and that harvesting that asset kept *Likira* going and him aboard her.

But each of those dots represented a warship or a significant piece of a warship, one destroyed in the brutal battle across Alpha Centauri that had marked the penultimate action of humanity's defiance. There were hundreds of those dots—*thousands*, even. This wasn't his first salvage mission to the ruins of the Terran-Council war, but this was the first time they'd come to Alpha Centauri and he'd never seen quite this much debris before.

The old human stars were regarded as vaguely cursed by the subjects of the Medari Sacred Council. That hadn't stopped scavengers like *Likira* from picking through their bones, but it had slowed the process and limited it to border systems. Alpha Centauri, at the very heart of the old Terran stars, was clearly still almost untouched.

Gerard couldn't help but note that the majority of the hulks had the reflection patterns of complex alloys and hypertensile ceramics, the armor of Council warships. The Terran fleets had been advanced enough, certainly, but their armor was visibly cruder compared to their enemies...and yet, far more of their *enemies* had died here than them.

Centauri had seen fleets of thousands of warships clash, humanity's true final chance, and they'd very nearly carried the day. Now trails of wreckage crossed Gerard's screen, and he could guess at what particular sections represented.

There was where the Centauri Orbital Fortress Command had relocated their battle stations, moving the battle platforms into deep space to ambush the Council Fleet. There was where the massed fleets had made their stand...and that path of wreckage, leading away from the crush of the main battle, had to be where Admiral Kawa of the Japanese Self-Defense Force had covered the final set of evac transports.

Gerard had met people who'd *been* on one of those transports. Admiral Kawa's heroism was one of the tales the human refugees warmed their bones with...and it had damned Earth, for those same evacuation transports had carried a deadly bioweapon to the human homeworld.

"Set a course for that zone," K'tet ordered, dropping a highlight on the trail of debris Gerard was eyeing. "If the Terrans withdrew along that line, they would have been less thorough about scuttling their wrecks."

The bridge was silent and Gerard sent a ping to Newell's console. The navigator jerked as if stung, catching up with the reality of now instead of the shadows of the dead.

"Yes, Captain," Newell replied, as if he hadn't been lost for half a minute. "Dialing in the course."

Gerard wanted to argue that the concentration of hulls around the Fortress Command ambush would provide the greatest density of raw material to salvage, but the words died unspoken on his tongue. K'tet's words had already given away his hope.

"Scan the debris fields for any active power signatures," K'tet told Gerard. "Flag anything intact to have salvageable hardware. Systems sell for better rates than titanium, and we will serve the One God better there."

"It's been almost twenty Council years, Captain," Gerard said quietly. "There won't be any intact power sources."

Thirty-three years. He could remember his own flight from New Athens, a year before the Battle of Centauri. He'd been ten years old then, but he'd been old enough to understand what was going on.

"The One God may bless us with a clue, Arkanis," K'tet replied. "The Terrans used a number of fission and decay-style power plants that may guide us to more-intact ships—and it is in the more-intact ships that we may find great worth."

Gerard ground his response and emotions under a practiced mental heel. The intact systems on the Council warships would be worth more than those on the Terran ships in the main, but he knew the *great worth* K'tet was hoping for.

The UN had realized early on that they had a single advantage over the Council Fleets, and they had protected that advantage ruthlessly, with self-destruct charges and a willingness to fire on their own wrecks. Somehow, they'd kept the technology of the two-point phase transmitter out of Council hands, and three decades of effort hadn't duplicated it.

If *Likira*'s crew could find a working two-point phase transmitter in the wreckage, the Council's scientists would finally be able to duplicate the phase cannon that had very nearly saved humanity. The reward for that discovery would set every one of the salvage ship's crew up for life, even with the relatively miserly shares the human crewmembers had.

And Gerard was absolutely certain that if he ever laid his eyes upon one of the unique devices, the one technological advantage his people had had over the Council, he would destroy it—and he knew that any human aboard *Likira* would do the same.

TWO HOURS of travel brought them to the space where Centauri's defenders had made their last stand. The wreckage of the battlespace looked like a comet's tail to Gerard. It started thin and scattered where the Council warships had first drawn into range of the Japanese fleet, and grew thicker as the faster Council ships had closed the range.

As *Likira* drew close to the cluster of debris where the Council Fleets had finally reached the range of their own weapons, something flickered across Gerard's screens.

It wasn't particularly near to them—he eyeballed the ghost as orbiting Alpha Centauri B's farthest gas giant, over half a light-day away—but *Likira*'s sensors were more sensitive than the battered old salvage ship's appearance might suggest.

"Lirrow, can I get a second set of eyes on this?" he asked his second.

Lirrow was a Rowwlan, a tailed alien race with short fur and sharp-edged ears that reminded Gerard of pictures his mother had shown him of Earth's foxes and cats. Lirrow herself had a night-black pelt that gleamed under the ship lights as she turned her own attention to the data anomaly.

"I'm not sure what I'm looking at," she admitted, her ears flicking forward in agitation as she answered. "The distance is immense and we lost the trace almost as soon as we had it. But it *could* have been a power core on standby."

"We can pick that up from this far away?" Gerard asked.

"We can," K'tet interrupted, the Medari's shrill voice high with interest. "Newell, reverse course. Arkanis, flag the location where we picked up the signal."

Gerard did, an uncomfortable itch poking at the back of his neck.

It took the salvage ship almost ten minutes to shed velocity and reverse course, and Newell kept their velocity low as they drifted through the zone where the anomaly had pinged their scanners.

This time, Lirrow and Gerard were watching for the ping.

"There," Lirrow barked, a moment before Gerard could say anything. "Hold this position."

Gravitic engines allowed *Likira* a lot of flexibility, but that was still a big ask. Without knowing the exact course of the anomaly, Gerard knew that Newell couldn't keep them motionless relative to it.

The navigator did his best, though, and Gerard turned his own years of experience into ripping apart the sensor data they were getting.

"Range is eleven light-hours," he told K'tet. "It... It's definitely a power source, but if these are standby readings, it might be one of the biggest ones I've ever seen."

"Not *that* big," Lirrow mewled, wrinkling her nose at him. "Check your resolution. We have more data now."

Gerard increased his digital zoom and nodded grimly.

"I see," he confirmed. "Looks like five to seven power sources in close proximity, all producing standby emissions. Fusion cores in idle maintenance mode."

"Big cores," the Rowwlan agreed. "In very close proximity." She leaned into her console, ears flicking again as she went over the data in detail. "Two ships, maybe one, but the patterns are weird.

"They're Terran, I *think*," she told Gerard and K'tet. "The overall pattern is right, but the frequencies and emissions aren't what I'd expect. Without getting closer, I can't say for sure, but some of these metrics are almost at Council levels—and these are *big* power plants."

A chill shivered down Gerard's spine as the description niggled at the back of his mind. Multiple very large, extremely advanced Terran power cores...on one ship. There was *one* ship that fit that description —but that was just a legend.

"A Terran warship?" K'tet demanded.

Gerard ground a spike of anger down and looked over at the Captain. K'tet's shoulder-vanes were vibrating, a clear sign of interest in a Medar. A Terran warship with intact power plants would likely have *other* intact systems.

Maybe even intact guns, though the phase cannon had additional fail-safes built in.

"Possible," Lirrow admitted, then raised her hands in a defeated shrug. "We're too far away. I think it *has* to be a warship—probably more than one, just at a weird angle. The signatures don't match up to anything I know of, but it *could* be two or three of their final prototype ships."

K'tet's shoulder-vanes were now shivering to the point of being audible from Gerard's station. It was almost *obscene*—if the Medar had been human, he'd have been openly salivating.

"Set a course for the anomaly," K'tet ordered.

"We're nearly twenty hours' travel away," Gerard objected. He knew it wasn't an argument he was going to win, but part of him wanted to try and find an *easy* answer to the struggle he knew was coming.

"What does it matter?" K'tet demanded. "The One God has blessed our efforts with a greater prize. All we must do is reach out a hand and take what He has given. Set your course, Newell."

Gerard couldn't disagree. The power sources alone, even if there was nothing else there, were worth far more than the fifty or sixty thousand tons of metal and ceramics *Likira* could extract from a wrecked fleet.

He was just afraid of what they might find.

CHAPTER

TWO

Gerard limped slowly into the mess reserved for the ship's human crew. A long time ago, a much-younger Gerard had convinced K'tet that if the Medar was going to keep recruiting humans, it made sense to give them their own space.

Now, as the ship's first officer, he knew the only monitoring on the ship was for audio and that K'tet had never bothered to spring for the translation software that could handle human languages. All of the humans spoke English, which gave them a measure of security.

Somehow, he wasn't surprised that there was a crowd gathered in the mess as he walked in. He looked them over and sighed, limped over to the nearest table and gestured for someone to pull out a chair for him.

An injury in his teens had shattered Gerard's knee, and there had been little charity or medical attention for another injured boy in the refugee camps. He hadn't walked straight since, but his self-taught skills at electronics and computers had earned him a spot on *Likira*.

He didn't need to move quickly to help keep a salvage ship running.

"So, who talked?" he said drily as the crowd gathered around. There were two hundred and thirty-six humans among *Likira*'s five hundred and nineteen–strong crew. Given that a third of them should be asleep and a third should be on duty, he was pretty sure there was a *reason* there were a hundred people in the mess.

He heard at least four different names in the murmurs that answered him, and snorted. There were ten people on *Likira*'s bridge at any given moment, so he guessed he couldn't blame Newell.

"All right, someone get me a coffee," he ordered. He was going to need caffeine tonight. "And someone tell me what you all *think* is going on."

The group was silent for a long moment, and then one of the engineering techs, a young woman named Milian Caro, passed him a cup of black coffee. As he took the cup and met her gaze, she swallowed and mustered the courage to speak.

"Rumors are flying," she admitted. "Nothing clear...but someone said we found *Excalibur*."

Her voice was soft and touched with awe. Gerard shook his head at her and took a long swallow of the coffee.

"We've sure as hell found something interesting," he agreed, looking past Caro at the rest of the human crew. "But I doubt it's the incarnation of an old myth."

"The ship, not the sword," Caro clarified. She had to know the correction was unnecessary, but it still got a chuckle from the crowd.

"Honestly, my friends, the myth is about the same," Gerard warned them. "If Earth *had* a superbattleship, if it had existed, they would have acted. Wouldn't her Captain have done *something* in thirty-three years?"

The crowd was silent, and Gerard grimaced in pain as he adjusted his leg. His own understanding of even the Battle of Centauri was second- and thirdhand. What little he knew of the final Siege of Sol had come from the handful of evacuation ships that had fled the system at the end.

His crew knew about the same. They were children of the refugee camps, not the arkships. And yet...they all knew the story. That the combined scientific and engineering minds of the United Nations' warring powers had assembled a massive battleship, as large as—or even *larger* than—a Sacred Council fleet carrier. That the UN had believed that single ship could turn the tide…and yet it had somehow failed.

"*Excalibur* the ship is a myth, told by arkship survivors to make themselves feel they *could* have won," Gerard said quietly. "We want to believe it was the Plague and fate that robbed us of our independence, but the truth was we could never have won. One magical story about a battleship doesn't change that."

The crowd shuffled, but Caro stayed standing next to him, looking at him with wide and hopeful eyes.

"But what if it *is* true?" she asked him. "What if it *is Excalibur*?"

"Then the situation changes," Gerard told her, his voice clear enough that he was sure the entire room full of humans could hear him. "Lirrow raised another option, one I think is more likely: that we may be looking at several of the late-era cruisers in close company. Likely, their crews were Infected and their Captains tried to hide—or even destroy!—the ships."

Caro nodded, her hope turning to determination—and he could see the same look in many of the others behind her as they caught his meaning.

"Even a *single* fully functional phase-cannon-armed cruiser is something I do not wish to see in the hands of the Sacred Council," he admitted, keeping his voice soft enough that the crowd had to be silent to hear him.

"We are entering a situation where we will need to act quickly and decisively. Can I count on you all to follow my lead when the time comes? Instantly and without question?"

There was, after all, only one way they could *stop* a cruiser falling into the Council's hands if K'tet found it.

Newell stepped out of the crowd to stand by Caro, the two younger humans almost a matching set. Both had the gaunt faces of once-malnourished youths. Both had the fiery drive of refugees for the home they'd never seen.

"We've always followed you, Gerard," Newell murmured. "We won't stop now."

Gerard nodded grimly and slugged back the rest of his coffee. He'd been the first of K'tet's human *strays*, the example that had led to the old Medar recruiting from the human ghettos for cheap and reliable crew. He was the ship's first officer—and he was *also* the senior human aboard by any measure.

"Good. Then be *ready*," he ordered.

～

THE TINY NEEDLE pistol he'd tucked away in his pocket weighed down on Gerard like an anvil as *Likira* slowly approached the gas giant. The bridge was thick with tension and anticipation, and he hoped that he was the only one to whom it felt like a ticking time bomb.

Even he didn't know what would follow the crew learning the details of their target. They'd lost the anomaly as they closed, but in the process, they'd learned why no one had seen it before. Not only was *Likira* the first ship to visit Alpha Centauri in years, but the anomaly was in a very low, very fast orbit of Alpha Centauri B-VI. With the gas giant's own heat and radiation signature helping shield the ship or ships, *Likira* had needed to be in exactly the right spot at the exactly the right time to see anything.

But they had been, and now the salvage ship was in orbit of ACB VI. Soon, the anomaly would crest the gas giant's horizon and *Likira*'s crew would know what they'd found.

Gerard shifted painfully, trying to get his leg comfortable as he glanced around the bridge. His gaze settled on the unusual sight of K'tet's Shiz'ke bodyguard. A tall, red-scaled amphibian named Cor, the man didn't usually accompany the Captain around the ship.

The Shiz'ke had the unusual distinction of evolving on the same planet as another sentient species—in their case, the Medari who ruled the Council. Slow and steady by nature, with an average intelligence most species would regard as childlike, they'd long served the Medari as heavy labor, bodyguards and shock troops.

Cor's presence on the bridge was a complicating factor, an additional weight on the tension aboard *Likira*. The Shiz'ke had six-centimeter claws and the strength to rip most adult sentients in half. He might just be there to see what the ship had found—certainly, enough other crew were huddled around monitors throughout the ship—but his presence made Gerard worry.

"We clear the horizon in thirty seconds," Lirrow reported, and Gerard glanced away from Cor, back to his workstation.

"On the screens," K'tet ordered.

Gerard tapped a command and relayed the main optical pickup to the central display. The image of Alpha Centauri B VI shone beneath them in a mix of blues and whites, and the pickup was focused on a particular part of the horizon.

Gerard joined the rest of the bridge crew in watching the central display as Lirrow's thirty seconds ended, inhaling sharply as a metal peak emerged over the horizon. Several of the crew cheered as that peak continued to rise, revealing itself as unquestionably the prow of an intact ship.

And the ship *kept* coming over the horizon. All of them were familiar enough with the data on the display to recognize the scale and realize that each passing moment brought a full *kilometer* of starship up over the horizon—and still the ship continued to rise. It was a sharp, serrated triangle that looked like a giant monster tooth in orbit around the gas giant, highlighted against the massive planet's lights.

"What in the name of the One God have we found?" K'tet breathed.

"I don't know," Lirrow replied, ears flickering in confusion and awe. "Twelve kilometers in length. Four wide at the stern. Mass just over a billion tons…"

Her voice faded off into silence. The numbers she'd just given made no sense to anyone. It was twenty times the size of *Likira*—and the salvage ship was larger than many warships. It was four times the size of a Council fleet carrier, the largest warships the Council had *ever* built.

Gerard was riveted to the screen with everyone else, if for very different reasons. He *knew* what he was looking at, and he couldn't help but take in the incredible beauty of the ship in front of him. The lines were those he'd seen before on wrecked Terran cruisers but on an almost unimaginable scale.

It was *Excalibur*. The last great military and technological achievement of his species lay floating in space in front of him—more than just intact phase cannon, intact examples of *every* Terran technology.

And combined, a dream of hope for a race that had almost forgotten the word.

Gerard's leg might mean he couldn't stand quickly, but he'd made up for that with a dozen different types of practice. He drew the needle pistol from inside his jacket in a practiced motion, turning his seat to face where K'tet had risen to his feet, the Medar's shoulder-vanes audibly clicking in anticipation and greed.

Likira's Captain never had a chance to say aloud what he was thinking. A five-round burst of high-velocity ice needles tore Salish K'tet's head apart and sent his body crumpling to the floor.

Gerard continued to move, levering himself out of his chair as he turned to bear on Cor. The Shiz'ke was reacting quickly—*far* too quickly. He was already charging toward Gerard, the claws on his left arm extended forward as his right hand fumbled for the big pistol at his waist.

Cor didn't make it before Gerard fired again, hypervelocity ice needles tearing apart the amphibian's torso before they shattered against the wall behind him. The big Shiz'ke only made it halfway across the bridge before his body hit the floor and slid across the metal, leaving a trail of dark red blood.

"I suggest," Gerard said sadly, sweeping the weapon over the rest of the bridge crew, "that none of you make sudden movements."

Newell was the only person on the bridge crew who wasn't frozen in terror, the navigator's hands busy on his console as he maneuvered *Likira* toward a holding orbit near the massive warship.

"Get me an all-hands channel," Gerard ordered the navigator in English, keeping the bridge crew covered with the needler.

The young navigator paused and tapped a few new commands into his console before looking back at Gerard with a nod.

"You're on," he answered in the same language, a tongue that *should* keep their secrets for a few more minutes.

Gerard leaned into the pickup at the first officer's station, making sure his voice would carry before he spoke—still in English.

"It is *Excalibur*," he told his friends. "Seize the ship."

Salvage ships like *Likira* were the ones most likely to stumble on an intact two-point phase generator or Terran ship. The human portion of the crew had long since made plans for that situation—and today, Gerard doubted he was the only human who'd armed himself.

The off-duty humans would seize armories using Gerard's command codes and then move on Engineering and the bridge. Without K'tet to countermand the first officer's codes, the ship's security systems wouldn't slow them.

Gerard and Newell controlled the bridge. There were a dozen humans on this watch's engineering shift, so he'd shortly control life support, engines and gravity.

With those at his command, resistance by the nonhuman members of the crew would be resolved *very* quickly.

CHAPTER

THREE

The main staff conference room felt sparse with only the human officers in it. The English conversation added to a sense of surrealism for Gerard, who'd attended hundreds of meetings in the room with its big table...and every one of them had been held in Medari.

Thanks to close range and *Likira*'s capable sensor suite, they now had a detailed image of the exterior of *Excalibur*. A hologram of the Terran capital ship floated above the conference table, holding every eye in the room.

Gerard had added *Likira* to the hologram for scale. The salvage ship was a blocky horseshoe shape eight hundred meters long and two hundred and fifty wide. The hologram of the salvage ship was only forty centimeters long...versus the just-over-*six-meter-long* image of *Excalibur*.

"What do we have on her?" *Likira*'s new Captain asked his crew, sweeping the gathering with his eyes. Everyone in the room had been an officer before the mutiny, and now they were the command crew.

What, exactly, they were the command crew *of* was still in question.

"She is fucking huge," Hillary Beck said with a broad grin. The Black woman with the short-cropped hair had been the third watch sensor officer, one of Gerard's personal trainees. Now she headed the sensor team…such as it was. "We're close enough in that we've got exact numbers on everything we can from the outside.

"She's twelve-point-two kilometers long. Three-point-five klicks wide and one-point-three high at the back. Her hull has some passive sensor baffling built into it that I've never seen before, so we've got nothing on her innards."

Beck shrugged.

"Given that the only *weapons* I see look like antimissile lasers, and the fusion drives we're picking up couldn't push her past maybe ten gees, I'm guessing that means both her guns and engines are internal— which means phase cannon and gravitic drives."

The gravity-based engine used by *Likira* and the rest of Council space was extremely efficient and had no visible external components. Similarly, the phase cannon relied on two-point phase generators that didn't need line of sight to their targets.

That lined up with what the stories said about *Excalibur*.

"What about power sources?" Gerard asked. "We detected those from a long way away."

"We did," Beck agreed. "And that is because a power plant *has* to radiate. It doesn't matter how baffled the hull is when your design will intentionally vent to outside. The armor prevents us from getting a detailed look at the plants beyond the emissions workup that Lirrow already did, but…"

She shrugged again.

"What I can say at this distance is that Lirrow underestimated the size," she told them. "There are eight power plants over there, all of them on standby…and on *standby*, they're pumping out more power than *Likira*'s main power plant."

Several people around Gerard whistled softly. *Likira* was a salvage ship, which meant she produced almost ten times as much power as a ship her size normally needed. Assuming the Terran plants had the same five percent standby that they were used to, those eight fusion cores produced over three hundred times as much power as their ship.

"What is she *doing* with it all?" he asked. "Even on standby, that's a lot of power, and we're not even seeing running lights."

"There might actually be *more* power plants over there," Newell reminded the council of war. "We're only picking up the ones that are running, and that ship hasn't been refueled in over thirty years."

"She has low-level phase shielding up," Beck told them. "Not enough to stand off any kind of weapon, but enough to keep out meteorites and give us a pain if we try to drill through the hull."

"Hopefully, we can avoid those, but that's assuming we can get the main boat bays open," Gerard said grimly. "But she's undamaged?"

He'd looked over the data himself, but he wanted confirmation from the sensor techs who'd been deep in it from the beginning.

"Apparently," Beck confirmed with a nod. "I can't guess about what thirty years of neglect have done to the inside or her systems, but she seems free of outside damage. The drives, though… That's the big question, isn't it?"

Gerard grimaced. There were gravitic-drive techs among his human crew, but none of them were the real experts he'd want for reactivating a drive that had been inactive for longer than many of the crew had been alive.

"That's the *second* big question," he told his people, though, letting his tone quiet their excitement. "The *first* big question is why she's still sitting here. She would have had a crew of what, ten thousand? What happened to them?"

The room was deathly silent, but Gerard already suspected the answer. His gaze slid across the room to meet that of Dr. Giang Tran. The attractively petite dark-skinned woman wasn't *technically* a doctor, since she'd learned her trade by apprenticeship to *Likira's* Medari physician, but the human crew gave her the title out of respect for what she'd learned.

"There's only one possible reason, isn't there?" Tran asked rhetorically. "Someone aboard was Infected."

The already grim silence turned bleak. The bioweapon that humanity's survivors called the Plague had been the Sacred Council's idea of an *efficient* solution to the "human problem." It had killed any human it infected—eventually. With a three-month-long asymptomatic contagious period, it had been almost impossible to tell who was Infected until the last week or so before death.

The Council's doctors had a countermeasure for any human who surrendered—they couldn't risk it mutating and spreading to other races from the refugee camps, regardless of how small that chance was, and they wanted to show their *mercy*—but the Plague had burned through the colonies like wildfire. Delivered to Earth by the Centauri evacuation ships, the Plague had done as much to end the Siege of Sol as the Council's fleets.

Rumor had it that there were entire evacuation convoys, anchored on the *Excalibur*-sized arkships, floating dead in space because a single Infected refugee had been accidentally allowed aboard. In the self-contained environment of a starship, even one as large as *Excalibur* or the evacuation ships, it would wipe out the entire population.

"It's the only possible reason," Gerard agreed. "Will it be safe?"

"Yes," Tran confirmed before Gerard could speak. "The Plague was designed to die off once it eliminated its hosts. It could only live a few weeks in a dead host, let alone with no hosts at all. Plus, they almost certainly had enough warning for the Captain to order the computers to sterilize the ship once they were dead."

Gerard let the gloomy silence hang over the room for a few more seconds, letting the weight of the past settle onto his crew, then cleared his throat.

"The past is dead," he reminded them. "All we can control is the future. Newell, Beck, start putting together a scouting party to go over with me. While you're doing that, I'm going to go talk to our prisoners."

"Is that wise?" Newell asked, apparently the only one willing to challenge Gerard even that much. "After all, with what we did, they are—"

"Our shipmates and friends," Gerard cut him off. "They deserve to know *why* we betrayed them, if nothing else." He sighed. "They have a *right* to know. Can any of us deny them that?"

He swept the officers in the room with a level gaze that none of them met. He doubted there was a human in the room who didn't have friends stuffed into the hold they'd converted to a mass jail. None of his people objected.

Even if any of them disagreed, they'd followed him this far. They'd follow him the rest of the way. Gerard Arkanis was their Captain now.

❧

THE DOWNSIDE of being unquestionably his people's Captain was that his crew refused to let Gerard enter Hold Six, the hold they'd converted into a prison, alone. A dozen techs had appointed themselves as the ship's security detail, and all of them went in ahead of him.

When Gerard stepped into the cargo hold, those guardians lined the walls in powered battle armor, stun rifles at the ready. If that wasn't enough of a threat, the two troopers flanking Gerard and the door both held heavy battle rifles.

His attention only lingered on the guards for a few moments before he regarded their prisoners. *Likira*'s brig could only hold a dozen people at best, far short of the almost three hundred nonhuman crewmembers. The cargo hold was a crude solution but a working one.

It was not, however, a comfortable one. Gerard's conscience twinged at the sight of the cots and rough pallets scattered through the space. They'd raided the ship's survival supplies, but that hadn't been enough to provide beds for everyone. There were more than a few simple piles of blankets on the metal floor, and his knee ached to look at them.

The presence of the armored humans had drawn everyone's attention, and the crowd was already pushing toward him—hesitating at the sight of the armored guards but starting to shout questions as they approached Gerard.

Most of the questions were some variation of "Gerard, what the hell is going on here?" He'd been their first officer as well as the humans'.

Finally, he raised his hands and voice.

"Quiet!" he bellowed in Medari.

To his surprise, they were. Then the crowd split as Lirrow pushed her way to the front and stepped out to face him. Her sable-black fur was in disarray, her careful grooming lost to the limitations of the prison hold.

She was Gerard's closest friend among the nonhumans other than K'tet—and she'd watched him *kill* K'tet. He'd hoped to avoid having to face her, but he'd known that was a vain hope.

Lirrow glared at him, her ears flat to her skull as she met his gaze and spread her hands. Her claws glinted in the light, their extension almost certainly an unconscious reaction to her mood.

"Gerard, what the hell is going on here?"

"That's what I came here to explain," he told her, sticking to the Medari everyone understood for now. He sighed, trying to lean against his knee brace without drawing attention to it. "I thought you'd have guessed, Lirrow," he admitted. "You saw it, after all. I don't think everyone did."

"I saw *something*," the Rowwlan replied, her fur rippling in anger. "All I really managed was *big* and *Terran* before you *shot our Captain in the head.*"

From the ripple of surprise and horror that spread through the crowd, *that* part of the mutiny hadn't made its way through the entire rumor mill yet. Gerard was surprised.

"Big and Terran," he echoed with a small smile. "That does describe it, doesn't it? What we found, people, is the United Nations Starship *Excalibur*, the only battleship ever built by humanity. She was built to turn the tide at the Battle of Sol—but for reasons that didn't survive the evacuation, she was nonfunctional and did not fight in that battle."

Gerard sighed, studying his former shipmates.

"I don't expect you to understand what she means to us humans. She was the ultimate technological achievement of our people, the last chance to keep our freedom. She is our dream and our hope, and she is *here.*"

Lirrow was still staring intently at him but there was a different edge to her eyes now. Not anger... Something else, something just as sharp but not directed at him.

"You were my shipmates and *are* my friends, but I cannot see that ship fall into the hands of the Council. That ship represents my people's only hope. If I must choose between my species and my friends, I will choose my species.

"That is why we took the ship," he explained as he met his friend's golden eyes. "I could not permit Captain K'tet—or any of *you*—to send a message to warn the Council about *Excalibur*."

With *Likira*'s resources, Gerard had a chance to salvage the ship, but he wasn't going to tell the nonhumans that. Even *that* depended on her being more intact that he'd dared hope—and the humans having an answer to whatever had failed the ship decades earlier.

"You do not understand what *Excalibur* means," he repeated, "because you are not human. Let it suffice, then, to understand that whoever commands *Excalibur* will restore humanity's hope. She will be our unifying banner, the call for Terra's scattered children to raise arms once more against the enemy."

"*The enemy?*" someone demanded. Gerard twisted sharply to see Loran Tel'ken standing at the edge of the crowd. The Medar's right arm was broken, marking him as one of the few injuries in the seizure of the ship, and he leaned on another Medar as he glared at Gerard. "The Sacred Council of Races spared your pitiful life out of mercy. If anyone here is an enemy to the people, an enemy of *peace*, it is *you* and your xenophobic race."

Gerard met Tel'ken's glare with a barely concealed snarl.

"Do not speak of the Council's mercy to *me*," he growled. "I was ten years old when Council assault troops landed on Serenade, Tel'ken. I *remember*. I saw fire falling from the sky at anyone who resisted. I *remember* the deaths of cities—and the *murder* of my parents as they tried to protect others."

His entire body vibrated with rage as he held Tel'ken's eyes. He caught himself with his hand on the needler he openly wore, and exhaled, slowly controlling his anger as he glared at the Medar.

"I saw the results of the Edict of Excommunication firsthand," he finally finished, his voice cold as helium ice. "I *remember* and I will never forgive the voices that ordered the death of my species. No one, person or race, is without fault—but *my* people are innocent of *xenocide. Medar*."

Humanity was not the first race the Council had pronounced

Excommunication on, after all. The Medari word didn't *quite* have the same meaning as Excommunication, but it was close enough. Every planet belonging to humanity had been bombarded into uninhabitability. Only children and those willing to swear conversion to the One God had been allowed to live.

An Edict of Excommunication had been pronounced only twice before—and one of those races was completely gone, wiped from the face of the universe by Medari orders.

With a final exhalation, Gerard restored his calm and turned to the rest of the aliens.

"I apologize for what we have done," he told them, his voice level and controlled, "and I regret the betrayal of our friendships. But realize I would do it again in an instant. I see no other way to serve my species and do what we must."

He turned to leave, but Lirrow's soft voice interrupted him.

"That, my friend, is because you lived too long among Medari," she told him. He turned back to find her grinning at him, long fangs bared. "Medari like Tel'ken would tell you the Sacred Council is an equal body—the *Sacred Council of Races*—but there is a reason *we* call it the *Medari* Sacred Council."

She gestured dismissively at Tel'ken.

"The Council is a tool for Medari rule, and your people are hardly alone in your hatred or desire for freedom," she told Gerard. She spat at the broken-armed Medar's feet and then stepped forward into the clear space between him and the prisoners.

"If you're going to pull together a fleet and give the Council a clawed awakening, I'm in," she told him. "I volunteer."

Gerard stared at the elegant black-furred woman in front of him and found himself speechless for a moment—and in that moment, the other ten Rowwlan crewmembers stepped forward to join her.

Others followed, until over three-quarters of *Likira*'s crew of misfits and troublemakers had separated themselves. The fourteen surviving Medari of the crew stubbornly pulled away from their crewmates, as did some of the crew Gerard had known to be the strongest believers in the One God.

But there were at least a hundred and fifty people of a dozen or more species surrounding Gerard, offering their services. He coughed away his surprise as he met the concealed gaze of the man leading his guard detachment—and saw the man's partially concealed thumbs-up.

"Thank you," he said quietly. "Give us time to make arrangements… We didn't expect this. At all. So…thank you."

~

"NEWELL, Beck, I want you to set up Deck Five for our friends," Gerard ordered his people. The former navigator and third watch officer were the senior members of the human crew—and they were doing a lot of the organizing for him.

"How are we defining *set up*?" Beck asked. "I mean, they *are* our friends, but…"

"But this is also a human show and we can only trust them so far," he agreed with the Black woman. "So, I want the Deck Five living quarters wired with every damn bug and surveillance system you can fabricate. *Likira's* built-in surveillance is audio-only, and I want more than that."

He shrugged.

"Privacy is all well and good, but over ten percent of the crew is still locked in Hold Six," he reminded them. "Until we are one hundred percent certain, we take no chances. We'll need to do a lot of the surveillance with software, but I want people on the cameras as well.

"Understood?"

"We can do it," Beck confirmed. "Might take a couple of hours."

"Take the time to do it *right*," Gerard insisted. "I don't want to have gone to the effort of seizing the ship only to lose it again a day later. We *need* everything to go right. The moment any of the Council military knows what's going on, we are in serious trouble."

"I'll get it done," she told him with a vague salute-like gesture.

"Newell, where are we at on *Excalibur* herself?" Gerard asked, turning to the younger man as the three strode toward the bridge.

"We're prepped for the first flight whenever you're ready," Newell replied instantly. "Four shuttles ready to go with the standard salvage teams—or as close as I can manage with just the humans."

"Good, good," Gerard said. "We'll use our volunteers—none of us are gravitics experts and I suspect we'll need one—but the first boarding team is going to be human. *Excalibur* is our heritage.

"The first feet upon her decks today will be the same as the last feet on them three decades ago: human."

"Makes sense to me, boss," Newell agreed. "If you're ready, I can have the teams on the shuttles in five minutes?"

"Do it," Gerard ordered. "Let's get this show on the road."

CHAPTER

FOUR

The heavily-armored hull of the immense warship was a frustrating wall of metal, a firm denial to any desire of Gerard and his people to enter *Excalibur*. The shuttles swept across her surface, using visual scanners to attempt to locate any access points.

"I'm starting to reconsider the drills," Gerard said drily as he looked at the square kilometers of armor. *Excalibur*'s surface was far from featureless, with sensor blisters and automated laser turrets breaking the smooth lines of the armor, but nothing he saw suggested entrances.

"Would be a waste of time," the salvage team leader told him. Alexandra Vollan was a large blonde woman with a ready smile. She held her space suit's helmet in one hand as she eyed the same video feeds as Gerard.

"That armor is at least ten meters thick, with multiple layers of everything they could think of," she told him. "It's not Council fleet armor, but there's still *ten meters* of it—and the phase-interface shield would play havoc with our drills' energy systems."

She shook her head.

"We need a door. Most Terran ships use literal doors, too: big bulkheads that slide open to let shuttles in."

"And Council ships use phase-interface shields, I know," Gerard reminded her. He kept his gaze on the screens as he spoke, and held up a hand before the discussion could continue. "But speaking of bulkheads, do you see what I see?"

"I do indeed," Vollan agreed. "Jackpot and open sesame!"

Two massive bulkhead doors, each a square thirty meters on a side, had finally swung into view on the side of the ship. They were locked together and twice the size of what Gerard was used to, but the pattern was what he was looking for.

"Heckler, bring us in," Gerard ordered the pilot, a Vietnamese man who had somehow acquired the very white name of Alistair Heckler.

The refugees had sufficiently chaotic backgrounds that Heckler was hardly the only one with an incongruous name, and he tossed Gerard a vague salute as he brought the shuttle to a halt in front of the big doors.

"Transmitting opening commands," Vollan announced. The teams had a stockpile of those that should work on most Terran ships. The codes varied, depending on the ship's builder and the time period the ship was from, but *Likira* and the other salvage ships had opened up a *lot* of wrecked Terran ships over the years.

This time, the codes did nothing, and the two bulkheads remained resolutely shut.

"That's not good," Gerard said. "I'm guessing forcing the bulkheads isn't much better than drilling through the hull?"

"That depends," Vollan replied. "They're somewhere between five and seven meters thick, and *I* would have built them of the toughest materials I could find." She shook her head. "But there *should* be a set of manual controls...*here*."

She tapped a point on the screen and sighed.

"We've got zero-gee mobility units aboard," she told him. "I'll take two of the team out and see if we can tickle the doors open."

～

GERARD HAD FAKED a lot of things over the years. Worship for the One God. Gratitude for being pulled from the slums. On one spectacularly memorable occasion, sexual attraction for a female Medar.

Patience was high on the list of things he had practice faking, and he was using a lot of that practice as he watched Vollan and her team jet over to the shuttle bay's manual control panel.

"You know," Heckler said quietly, "it kind of makes senses that the doors are ignoring us. All of our Terran codes predate this ship—and we're using *Council* communication hardware. They'd have known how to recognize that by the time *Excalibur*'s security systems were designed.

"If we have a marginal code, the computers will reject us for using Council hardware."

"Lovely," Gerard muttered. "So, the computers can definitely hear us, but they're not going to *admit* it."

"They probably think we're a Council boarding team," Heckler said faux-cheerfully. "Vollan is prepped for defenses, right?"

The man in charge of humanity's tentative hope for freedom shook his head grimly.

"She knows this drill as well as any of us," he told Heckler.

Before he could say anything else, one of the massive bulkheads suddenly started moving. It slid smoothly away from its counterpart to reveal a matching set of bulkheads on the other side of a forty-meter-long passageway.

More than enough space for the shuttle, but the black void was nerve-wracking.

"We're in," Vollan reported redundantly. "But...we didn't *do* anything, boss. I linked my suit hardware in and the doors opened before I could send a single command. I think... I think it ran a bioscan and recognized us as human."

"That makes sense," Gerard agreed. "Move in and set up to control the airlock from inside, Vollan. We're bringing the shuttles in."

"Shouldn't we leave someone outside?" she asked.

"Are they going to be able to do more from the outer hull than you can do from inside the airlock?" Gerard said quietly.

There was a long pause.

"No. Moving my team in."

Gerard nodded and looked over at Heckler.

"Once Vollan is through the first set of doors, lead the way in," he ordered.

It took a couple of minutes for Vollan to get her team set up. Then Heckler took his shuttle in, slowly and carefully. Three other shuttles followed, seeming to drift on their gravitic engines.

Once the last one was in, the outer door started moving again.

"Please tell me you did that, Alexandra," Gerard said grimly.

"I did not," she replied. "I'd say it's an automatic system, but a fully automatic system wouldn't have waited for all of the shuttles to be in."

The principle of the massive airlock was crude, but it had been built well. It took less than ten seconds for the outer doors to slide shut, and for just a moment, Gerard wondered if even *this* was a trap.

"I have atmosphere venting," Heckler reported suddenly. "Multiple vents opening up and the airlock is filling. Standard shipboard air, oxygen, nitrogen, C-O-Two." He paused. "Give it sixty seconds, from the rate I'm seeing."

That was...actually fast, given the volume of the space. It was longer than Gerard *wanted* to wait, but it was still impressive.

"Vollan, get back onto the shuttle," he ordered. "We're either being welcomed in or we're in a trap. Either way, I think you're better with us."

The salvage team lead snorted—but she obeyed, jetting back up to the lead shuttle as the air around her thickened.

She'd barely made it aboard when one of the lights on Heckler's consoles flashed green for breathable air—and the inner doors started to open, sliding just as smoothly as the outer doors had.

The airlock was both functional and somewhat cooperative. That was a good sign, and Gerard allowed himself to feel a bit more optimistic about their chances of reactivating the massive battleship.

As the boat bay itself came into view, however, the state of its decks dispelled much of his optimism. The neat storage racks of small craft were still intact, with their contents tucked away safely, but the main floor was a disaster zone.

The wreckage of a forty-meter-long phase-capable pinnace was strewn across two-thirds of the hangar bay floor. From the blast pattern, Gerard guessed someone had put a handheld antiaircraft missile into the craft as it tried to flee the ship.

The explosion and crash had almost certainly killed everyone aboard the pinnace—and, almost certainly, everyone in the shuttle bay. Whoever had fired the missile had killed themselves, too.

"Land us clear of the wreckage," Gerard ordered, keeping his voice calm.

"What in the God's name happened here?" Heckler demanded, unconsciously using the English form of the Medari invocation of the One God.

It would be a *long* time before that particular indoctrination fully cleared their heads.

"At a guess, the Captain ordered quarantine and someone panicked," Gerard said grimly. "Marines probably tried to head off the deserters before they made it to the shuttles or off the ship, but the end result was…well, that."

His gesture took in the wreckage strewn across the boat bay.

"Poor bastards," the pilot said quietly.

"I would not have liked to be on this ship in her crew's final hours," Gerard replied. "But that is the past and we *must* look to the future. Let's move."

Gerard Arkanis looked over his initial survey team as they gathered in the boat bay in front of their shuttles. Forty human salvage techs, a good portion of his really reliable crew. He could call them a hand-picked crew, but the truth was that he had every human salvage tech from *Likira*.

The boat bay they stood in was huge, almost four hundred meters deep and sixty wide. If he remembered the scans correctly, the ship had to have at least two of these bays. That would give the battleship a small-craft capacity to rival many space stations he'd seen—but then, the ship was *bigger* than some space stations he'd seen.

Each side of the bay was lined with individual cells holding regular shuttles, similar to the ones they'd arrived in. Splitting each side of the bay into thirds were the larger bays for the phase-capable pinnaces, each barely small enough to fit into the massive airlock.

There were three of the pinnaces left—there had been four, but one was spread across the deck—which was two more of the expensive small craft than Gerard had ever seen in one place before.

"All right," he said loudly, bringing his people's attention back to him. "We could sit here and stare at this one boat bay all day, but that's not getting us anywhere. If we were still salvagers, the pinnaces alone would make us rich."

He grinned.

"We have *much* bigger goals today," he reminded them. "Move in teams and keep your weapons to hand. It's pretty clear that the computers have some active programs paying attention to us, and we don't know what will set them off—or what *else* might still be on the ship."

The groups began to divide into teams, and Gerard gestured for Heckler and his team to join him.

"Where are we headed, boss?" Heckler asked.

"The bridge," Gerard told the pilot. "I want you to go over the nav consoles, but *I* want to get at the AI access links."

He'd done a lot of things for K'tet aboard *Likira*, but almost all of them fell into the bucket of "systems specialist." He could run a salvage op, but he could also make computers sing.

"Any idea where the bridge *is*?" Heckler asked.

"So far as I can tell, this ship is basically a United States cruiser multiplied by fifty," Gerard pointed out. "So, yes, I'm reasonably sure I know exactly where the bridge is. Follow me."

THE TRIP toward the bridge provided disturbing evidence of the chaos of the final hours of the original crew. It was obvious that the ship's maintenance bots were still active—they saw a few of the drones scuttling around, searching in vain for dust to vacuum—and they'd done their best, but there were limits. The largest of the drones were barely forty centimeters tall, and holes blasted through interior bulkheads were beyond their abilities.

Commanded by the ship's computers and central artificial intelligence, the bots had cleared away bodies and returned armor and weapons to their armories, but they could do little to fix the wreckage of what appeared to have been a full-fledged battle through *Excalibur*'s corridors.

The damage grew worse and more omnipresent as they approached the bridge. When they reached the location where Gerard expected to find their target, he found the access cut off by a massive blast door.

"I'd suggest we send someone back for explosives, but it appears that's already been tried," Gerard noted as he studied the door. The armored surface was visibly cratered and blackened where explosives of some kind had struck it.

There was a control panel to one side of the door. It looked like smaller explosives and a vibroblade had been used to remove the panel at one point, but the maintenance bots had replaced it. Ugly scarring covered the wall, but the control panel appeared intact.

If the maintenance bots could fix a control panel, wiring and all, Gerard found it hard to believe the bulkhead holes were beyond them. Outside their programming, perhaps, but potentially not outside their abilities. That suggested *some* options, at least.

He tapped on the panel to activate it, looking for the best place to get into its wiring to override it—and to his surprise, the blast door slid open without further prompting. The damage from the explosion created a nasty screeching sound that penetrated through his space suit's helmet, but the bulkhead retracted fully into the wall.

As Gerard stepped back in surprise, he saw the inner door of the security barrier slide open as well, revealing *Excalibur*'s central control center.

"Now, *that* was creepy," Heckler said.

Nodding in agreement, Gerard nonetheless stepped forward into the bridge and looked over what he hoped to make his new domain.

Compared to the cramped control center of *Likira*, barely able to fit a dozen souls, *Excalibur*'s bridge just went on and on.

He stood on a raised balcony at the back of the bridge, with curving ramps sweeping downward on either side to provide access to the lower pit. Two more levels of balconies swept off from the ramps, creating a three-level space forty meters long and twelve wide.

Every level had neatly arranged consoles, all collected in pods of six to eight and all facing toward an immense fifteen-meter-high display at the front of the bridge.

At the center of everything was a central platform with a single chair, surrounded by screens on what looked like mobile arms. Gerard guessed that the platform could raise or lower to match the level of any part of the bridge—which, combined with the array of individual controls, meant he was looking at the Captain's chair.

He hesitated a moment, aware that Heckler and the other techs were waiting behind him, and then walked down the right-hand ramp and approached the central seat.

There were no visible controls around the Captain's station, and as Gerard looked around, he realized there were no visible controls *anywhere* on the bridge. For all of the Terran ships he'd helped dismantle, he hadn't been on an intact warship bridge before.

Likira, for all of the relatively advanced technology built into the salvage ship, used physical controls to avoid issue with different race's physiologies. *Excalibur*'s designers hadn't had that worry and had equipped the bridge with touchscreen systems and haptic interfaces.

On the other hand, they still should have been functional. The panel for the security system had been online, after all. Instead, every screen on the bridge was dark, and he glanced around again.

There was *one* screen that was online. The screen on the right-hand side of the Captain's chair had a slowly flashing dull green light, the only indication that anything on the bridge was working.

"Arkanis, it's Vollan," the salvage tech said over the radio. "We're in Engineering and everything is shut down. There's power and the systems *should* be online, but I think we're looking at some kind of complete system lockdown."

She paused.

"I can probably work around it, but without the ship's brain, this becomes a whole lot harder," she admitted.

"We're on the bridge and it's much the same," Gerard told her. "But I do have a flashing green light that I suspect is meant to be a 'push me' button."

He exhaled.

"Let's not do anything irrevocable just yet," he instructed. "I'm going to see what happens up here."

"If it kills you, can I have your shit?" Vollan asked.

"No," he told her. "Because if it kills *me*…"

He didn't finish the thought before he took a seat in the Captain's chair. Taking a deep breath, he reached out and touched the flashing green light with a single finger.

For a few seconds, nothing happened and he began to wonder if they could lobotomize both *Excalibur* and *Likira* and use the salvage ship's computer to get at least partial function from the battleship.

Then the entire bridge visibly brightened as the main screen lit up. Gerard's attention was drawn to the light, and he grimaced as he realized he was looking at a five-times-life-size version of the chair he now occupied—and this version was occupied by an olive-skinned and dark-haired man with tired eyes.

If the chair hadn't been enough of a clue, the stranger wore the surprisingly plain black uniform of the Provisional United Nations Space Force, the unsteady alliance assembled to guard Earth at the very end, with the markings of a United States Space Force Captain.

He stared blankly into space for a moment, then coughed into a cloth and faced the camera. At five times magnification, it was blatantly obvious he was coughing up blood.

"This is the final log of Captain Tiberius Mikos of the United States Space Force and the Provisional UN Space Force, commanding *Excalibur*," Mikos said flatly. "As I record this, the bridge bioscanners are reporting that I am in the later stages of infection from the Council bioweapon. Physical deterioration began some hours ago, and I expect the mental effects are already in play. I apologize for any lack of coherency in this message."

He paused to cough into the handkerchief again, looking at the bloody cloth with distaste before returning his focus to the visual pickup.

"My crew has panicked, and the effective result is mutiny," he said in a tired voice. "To maintain quarantine, I have ordered the Marines and crew still following orders to shoot to kill. Since the bioweapon is now in its active state in *all* of the surviving crew, I doubt they will last much longer.

"To both keep the location of this ship secret and protect anyone who might try to save us from the bioweapon, I have put into place security protocols to contain my crew.

"Those protocols will also trap anyone accessing the ship after we are dead." He shrugged. "Both fire control and navigation have been rerouted to the departmental control centers, and those centers have been sealed. The automated defenses are programmed to terminate anyone entering those rooms.

"The fire-control computers have been programmed to use any remaining functional weapons to destroy any vessel departing *Excalibur*," Mikos said calmly. "I cannot permit my crew to escape, and so whoever is watching this message will be trapped inside that defensive perimeter."

Gerard swore aloud, swallowing further curses as he realized Mikos was continuing.

"I doubt any of my crew have more than the forty-eight excruciating hours I estimate I have left, but I cannot take any chances." He shrugged. "And because there are other chances I cannot take, the command you touched to activate this message will have taken a microscopic sample of your flesh for analysis.

"If you are not human, I am sorry, but that analysis has triggered a silent self-destruct countdown that should end about now."

Gerard *heard* the techs behind him inhale sharply, but he kept his gaze on Tiberius Mikos's face. He did, after all, *know* that he was human. He was glad, though, that they'd decided against waiting to have the nonhuman members of the salvage teams join them.

"If you are still viewing this message, you are either human or the Council is more capable than I fear," the Captain said. "My duty to humanity requires that I leave this ship intact. I will do all I can to keep it out of Council hands, but…if my measures have failed, we are doomed."

The dying man leaned forward in a hacking coughing fit. He didn't get the handkerchief up in time and bloody spittle was visible on his hands as he faced the pickup again.

"You will need to deactivate my security protocols," he said, his voice hoarse now. "The commands to do so are stored in the computers of the command dais, activated by the verbal command to shut down all automated defenses. To give that command, *Excalibur* must recognize you as her commanding officer."

Mikos straightened his spine and for a moment, Gerard saw the proud and confident officer selected to command humanity's last hope.

"Now, therefore, I, Captain Tiberius Mikos of *Excalibur*, activate security condition Omega. I relinquish command. Reactivation code is nine kay kay twelve."

As he relaxed from his moment of attention, another coughing fit overtook him. This time was definitely worse, and Gerard reflexively checked the pickup to make sure the droplets of blood Mikos had sprayed over it were gone.

The man raised his head slowly and Gerard could clearly see him draw his sidearm with a hand speckled with his blood.

"I have done all that I can," Mikos said in a hoarse and pained voice. "May God and the righteous preserve my people, because *I* sure as hell failed. Captain Tiberius Mikos, signing off."

The image faded, but Gerard still saw the pistol rising from Mikos's lap as it did. He understood *exactly* what the man had done next—and why. He knew just how bad the Plague's final hours had been for its victims.

"What now, boss?" Heckler asked, the pilot's voice loud in the grave-like silence of the bridge.

"Now I follow his last orders," Gerard replied. None of the screens lit up and the green light had faded. There was no sign at all that the system was awake. He had to assume that the computer was listening.

"*Excalibur*," he said aloud. "Activate Omega security condition protocols. Reactivation code is nine kay kay twelve."

The screens flicked awake instantly, shifting from black to a gray haze. A small *LOADING* sign appeared in the middle of the screens around him—but the other screens on the bridge remained dark and Gerard sighed.

The *LOADING* text flicked over to *READY*. No other text. No operating system. Just a single word flashing—and only on the screens around the command chair.

Mikos's instructions had been clear enough, Gerard supposed.

"*Excalibur*. Shut down all automated defenses."

The screen flashed.

EXECUTING PROGRAM: MIKOS-1189.

...

PROGRAMS MIKOS-1185, MIKOS-1186, MIKOS-1187, MIKOS-1188 DELETED.

SYSTEM REINITIALIZING.

The screen flickered and an artificially generated voice echoed across the bridge as iconography began to fill the displays around Gerard.

"Omega reactivation complete. Genetic sample acquired. Please identify."

"My name is Gerard Arkanis," he told the computer.

"The record shows that Gerard Arkanis has assumed command of *Excalibur*," the voice replied. "Welcome aboard, Captain Arkanis."

CHAPTER

FIVE

Gerard stood at the head of the conference room table aboard *Likira* again but with a far better idea of what he'd got himself into—both with *Excalibur* and with the salvage ship's nonhuman crew. While most of the people in the room were human and there was no question the humans were running things, three of the nonhumans had joined them: Lirrow from the sensor teams, Shel—from a squat and red-skinned race called the Kitni—from Life Support, and Kralnir, a Blust from the gravitics team.

No one except maybe the ship's doctors knew what Kralnir looked like. One of the few non-oxygen-breathing races in Council space, the Blust traditionally wore all-encompassing cloaks that concealed both their forms and their heavy life-support equipment.

Given some of what Gerard knew about the Blust, he didn't begrudge them their secrets. One way or another, though, Kralnir was the best gravitics engineer on the ship.

Which meant Gerard *needed* him.

"All right, everyone," Gerard said, pulling everyone's attention to him as he gestured to the schematic of *Excalibur* that once again filled the room. Unlike last time, the schematic now covered much of the internal workings of the warship.

41

His people had rigged up enough of a translation program for the others that he was still speaking English, trusting the earbuds provided to everyone to convey his meaning in their native tongues.

"Our initial survey is complete and we have a pretty good idea of what we're looking at," he told them all. "The good news is that *Excalibur* is fully intact and many of her systems went into standby without problems. The mixed news is that we have a lot of minor damage throughout the interior and exterior of the ship from multiple causes, and we can't be certain of the overall effects until we start bringing systems online."

He shrugged and spread his hands to stave off excitement from the people who didn't know the survey's results.

"The *bad* news is that we now know why *Excalibur* is here," he told them. "She has one severe problem that will require all of our efforts. So far as we can tell, none of her gravitic drives ever functioned."

That sent an appropriate chill through the room. The Terrans hadn't realized there was a *reason* the Council didn't build ships as big as *Excalibur*, and had erred on the assumption that bigger was better. That had resulted in a ship that couldn't really move without gravitic engines…and whose gravitic engines didn't work at all.

That error had killed Gerard's homeworld, and it stuck in his throat. It was hard to swallow that such a minor-seeming mistake had doomed his species.

"Presumably, there were tests of the concept as they were building her up, but this was one of the first gravitic drive units humanity built and far larger than any other they worked on," he said quietly. "The designers might have been able to fix it, given time, but they didn't *have* time.

"Once they phased here from Earth, well…" He shook his head. "Alone, stranded and dying, the crew of *Excalibur* couldn't fix her."

Gerard's gaze settled on Kralnir's shrouded figure. It was hard to tell if the Blust was looking back at him, but he suspected the man was.

"We, on the other hand, have far more expertise in all the varieties of gravitic engines and the ways they can go wrong than the crew of *Excalibur* did," he reminded them. "Kralnir, if we can get you in there, do you think you can fix them?"

"It depends on the problem," Kralnir said precisely, his voice artificially generated in *any* language, which meant changing his vocoder had been easy enough. "The size alone would lead to several errors. There are reasons that drives of this scale are not built, but those issues *can* be overcome. If they made the expected errors along the way of their development process, the work may be time-consuming but it will be straightforward.

"Given the scale and your people's creation of other unusual technologies, they may well have achieved something more esoteric," he warned. "That may take more time to fix…but we should be able to do *something*."

"So, our next priority is to get Kralnir and a gravitics team over to *Excalibur*," Gerard concluded with a nod. "We'll probably want to assemble and move over repair teams for everything else at the same time. Newell, Beck, can we do it?"

"Yes," Newell confirmed instantly. "We spent the time you were doing the survey putting together the lists of who we needed to go," he explained as he checked a data slate in front of him. "Fair warning, though. If we send all of the repair teams over, that puts most of our reliable people on *Excalibur*. We'll have a skeleton crew to run *Likira* and watch the prisoners."

"I know," Gerard conceded. "But we have battle armor and weapons, and they're on the wrong side of the heaviest doors we had. That said, I'm almost *more* comfortable having our people on *Excalibur*. She is a battleship, after all, with shields, armor and heavy guns. *Likira*'s sole advantage over her is that she can move."

"What about you?" Lirrow asked, the Rowwlan wrinkling her nose in amusement.

"I have to be on *Excalibur*," Gerard said instantly. "Right now, the only person the ship's main computers are recognizing as *crew*, let alone an officer, is me. She thinks I'm her Captain, and with a warship's systems, well…that means I'm her Captain.

"We need me over there to talk to the computers, authorize overrides and convince it to accept our people as officers and crew."

Lirrow made a swallowed meowing noise, but she didn't object as she leaned back in her chair and studied him.

"Anything else?" he asked. "Newell, I want you to stay aboard *Likira* and coordinate things from there. Get all of the teams set up with times to move over—we only have so many shuttles."

"Understood, boss," Newell said. "We also serve who stand and wait. I'll mind the shop, but I hope I'll get over there soon enough!"

"We all will," Gerard promised. "You have my word."

Six hours later, Gerard watched the shuttles making the transfer flights on the tactical display he'd *finally* managed to convince the bridge computers to give him. There were holoprojectors hidden throughout the bridge that allowed him to fill the open space between the balconies with a three-dimensional image of the space around Alpha Centauri B VI, but the computers had taken a while to admit that.

That was representative of his general experience with the computers. *Excalibur* had a pretty good idea of what was broken and why for a lot of her systems. When Gerard could get the computers to *tell* him that, he was passing it on to the repair teams.

The computers were all linked together into an artificial intelligence that had about the intuition and independent thought of a moderately clever pet. That *pet* hadn't decided whether to trust him yet, which meant he had to use his authority as Captain to force it to disgorge information and lower-level authorization codes on a regular basis.

He sighed, rubbing his temples and studying the shuttles again as his com beeped. He eyed the device sitting next to his abandoned space-suit helmet—they'd confirmed there were no contagions or other threats in the ship's air a while earlier—and then grabbed it.

"Arkanis," he said crisply.

"Boss, this is Vollan," the salvage tech told him. "We're about to open up the gravitics section to let the team get in, but I can't find Kralnir. He isn't answering his com—and when I started asking, no one remembered him grabbing the transport over.

"I'm worried he might be up to no good on *Likira*, Arkanis!"

"Unlikely," Gerard said slowly. "*Shit.*" Regardless of what Kralnir was up to, he wouldn't have missed his flight over to *Excalibur*.

"Understood, I'll deal with it," he told Vollan. A quick set of commands on the cylindrical communicator closed the channel from Vollan and switched him to the link to *Likira*.

"Newell, come in," he ordered. "You there?"

"Yeah, boss," Newell replied instantly. "What's up?"

"We have a problem. Kralnir missed his transport and isn't answering his com," Gerard told him sharply. "If he's still aboard *Likira*, I need you to find him. Now."

He paused as a grim idea struck him.

"Check the prison hold and have all of the hands still aboard *Likira* check in," he ordered.

"You think Kralnir's up to something?" Newell asked, his voice grim.

"I don't think so," Gerard replied, "but *something* is going on. Deal with it!"

"Newell!" someone on the other end of the com shouted, their voice shocked. "No response from the brig guards. Cameras are live and…"

"And what?" Newell barked. He'd been listening to Gerard too much, the older man figured.

"They're dead," the other tech said flatly. "We had four people there and they've all been shot. Someone ambushed them."

"*Shit,*" Gerard repeated. "*Handle that,* Newell," he ordered. "We'll secure *Excalibur*, but we can't do anything for *Likira* from here."

"Understood," Newell conceded. "We'll be in touch."

SIX

Harold Newell wasted at least five seconds staring at the silent communicator, mentally running through swear words in three languages. The *last* thing they needed was a breakout, but he'd accepted responsibility for *Likira*.

This was his problem…and much as he respected Gerard Arkanis, he suspected he was better qualified to deal with a knife fight in a starship corridor than his boss was.

"All right," he said aloud, looking at the half-dozen people in the cramped bridge with him. Only three of them would be worth anything in a fight, he judged, so he smiled grimly.

"Karina, Praveen," he addressed two of the humans. "Get into the lockdown systems and seal *everything*. Power, internal security gates, everything—but especially the external airlocks and the small-craft bays.

"You should be able to remotely shut down the pinnace so it won't launch without an authorization from here. Do it."

Likira only had one of the phase-capable small craft, and K'tet had been paranoid about losing the expensive ship.

"Srroow." He turned to the one Rowwlan tech on the bridge.

"You're software overwatch. For things to have gone this bad already, we're looking at people who are in the ship's systems. Kick them out."

"On it," the silver-furred tech confirmed.

Harold rose from his chair and grabbed the gunbelt he'd slung over one arm. While the ship had been under K'tet's control, he'd let the habit of going everywhere armed lapse—but he was glad he'd decided to pick it up again.

At its highest power settings, the heavy gauss pistol on the belt was capable of punching through almost any personal armor. At its lowest setting, it relied on its heavy steel slug more than its velocity—but it was a simpler weapon with more easily acquired ammunition than a needler with its magnetized ice.

Gauss guns were *very* popular with gangs…like the ones Harold Newell had run with from the age of eleven. That time gave him an eye for the right kind of thug to use for a problem, and the three people on the bridge he hadn't given tasks to yet were the ones for this job.

"Jun-ho, Michel, Ionela, you're with me," he told the three humans. "Get weapons; we're going to check the prison hold and brig for survivors—and see what we can find out."

As the three produced weapons of their own, confirming his assessment, he turned back to Karina Hanssen.

"Karina, don't let anyone back through this door except me," he ordered grimly. A thought was niggling at the back of his mind, warning him that he'd missed *something*. A shake of his head didn't break it loose, and he turned to his impromptu team.

"Let's go," he said, leading the way out of the bridge with the gauss pistol at the ready.

The corridors were eerily quiet, and it wasn't just that most of the crew was on *Excalibur*. He knew the feeling that permeated the space— he'd felt it a dozen times in the past, in the ghettos of the Medari world he'd been born on.

Most of the time, that eerie quiet had been because the gangs had been about to throw down. People learned to take cover when the swaggering gangsters had stepped out with intent.

Harold was supposed to be in control of this ship, but every instinct from the gang struggles of his youth was screaming he was in danger. He'd abandoned his gang for Arkanis's offer to get away from this kind of moment.

His senses were pushed to the limit and he heard a strange shuffling around a corner, still near the bridge. He gestured for his team to pause and listened.

Someone was moving, but it didn't sound right. Instead of footsteps or the slithering sounds he was used to from the Council races, it was more of a shifting, lurching sound.

With his pistol in hand, he charged around the corner—in time to watch the cloaked form of Kralnir crumple to the floor, a dozen meters short of the bridge.

"Shit," Harold swore. He holstered his pistol as he knelt by the Blust's side. "What happened?"

A high hissing noise answered him. For a moment, the lack of translator left Harold thinking that was Kralnir trying to respond—and then an equally high-pitched buzz came from the man. That buzz was more modulated, more divided.

That was his speech—and the combination of the hissing noise and lack of a translator told Harold exactly what the problem was. Ignoring a feeble gesture from the alien, he tore open the enveloping cloak.

If he hadn't been panicking about a friend's health, Kralnir's appearance might have given him pause. The Blust was a gelatinous blob with dozens of tentacles that would normally hang down and move him across the floor. Glove-like garments covered several of the tentacles to allow him to interact with the world—and a carefully fitted helmet-like apparatus surrounded his upper torso and eyes.

That apparatus had multiple holes in it. Kralnir didn't have any visible injuries beneath those holes, but he'd tried to block the gaps with his own flesh—and his final collapse had shifted his body away from the damage.

"Medic," Harold snapped into his communicator. "Kralnir is down, Bridge deck. His breathing apparatus is damaged and he's clearly injured."

One of the techs had produced a roll of sticky tape while he was on the com. The black tape tore apart in chunks that *should* hold in the atmospheric mix Kralnir needed to survive.

As Harold started to apply the tape, a gloved tendril grabbed his shoulder. Kralnir lifted himself slightly, enough to make a more intelligible—if still inhuman—sound.

"Shel… transcei…"

The effort was too much. Kralnir collapsed back to the floor, the palpitations of his translucent chest growing weaker as much of the remaining color faded.

A familiar old feeling filled Newell. *Shel* was obvious enough—the Kitni had done this—and gangsters knew how to handle betrayal.

But *transcei*? No. *Transceiver*.

That niggling thought of forgetting something slammed back into him as he realized what he'd missed. *Likira* had a phase transceiver, capable of interstellar FTL transmission. If Shel and the escaped prisoners reached the transceiver, they might manage to raise a Council fleet.

The transceiver was one of the secured sections of the ship, but everything could be overcome, given time and determination. If Shel had come this far, she was *definitely* determined.

"Stay with him," Harold ordered Jun-ho. "You two, with me."

He hit a command to switch his com to the security channel.

"All available hands to the phase transceiver!" he barked. "Someone is trying to call the Council. *Everybody* with a gun to the phase transceiver!"

Despite the general order, Harold and his impromptu team were the first to the transceiver room. It had been one of the few places on the ship with a regular guard, but the woman was crumpled against the wall in a pool of her own blood.

She hadn't been wearing armor, and her upper torso had been minced by the characteristic small wounds of a needler. One of the women with Harold started to kneel to check on her.

"There's no time," Harold snapped. "We can't let them transmit."

The other tech was already at the door and looked back at him with fury on her face.

"Sealed and severed from the main system," she told him. "It's rejecting my codes."

Shel was one of only a handful of people on *Likira* with the skill to do that—and Harold wasn't one of the ones who could undo it. Fortunately, he was one of the people who understood the structure of an internal ship door *intimately*, and he was holding a *very* powerful sidearm.

He cranked the gauss pistol to maximum power and targeted the locking mechanism. Three slugs, powerful enough to punch through even *Likira*'s outer hull, smashed into the security lock and shattered it into a dozen pieces.

There was a decent chance the slugs would continue on and breach the outer hull, but most importantly right now, the destruction of the locking mechanism activated a safety mechanism no warship would have tolerated.

A civilian ship couldn't risk being cut off from help. If the control mechanisms for the security door on the transceiver bay broke, the door automatically opened—allowing Harold to charge into the room as he cranked the power back down on his gauss pistol.

There was no time to assess threats in detail, and he opened fire as he charged forward, taking advantage of what little surprise he had. His first shots were targeted at the transceiver station more than the person standing at it, but they slammed into Loran Tel'ken regardless. The injured Medar fell forward over the console, likely dead before he'd even realized he was being attacked.

There wasn't much cover in the room, but Harold's focus wasn't on his own survival at that moment. Another Medar was covering the door with a gauss rifle, a rapid-firing version of the pistol in his hand—and he shot the shoulder-vaned alien before they could shoot his own companions.

Gunfire filled the room now and Harold dropped behind a console, an extremely expensive piece of cover that rattled as two needlers opened fire at him. A second later, the console gasped its last as someone fired a gauss round into it—and another round punched clean through it, missing Harold by a finger's breadth.

He sprayed the room with bullets as he tried to get to the main transceiver console. One of the mutineers dropped, but gunfire drove him back behind another console. Practice let him assemble a mental sight picture, one that he took a second to review.

One of his people was down, wounded but probably still breathing. There were still at least four mutineers up—and Shel was heading right for the console.

And his gauss pistol indicator told him he had one bullet left. There was no time to reload, and he rose up over his impromptu cover to locate the mutineer leader.

Shel had grabbed a pickup and was taking cover behind the console itself. Harold knew he couldn't afford to miss and took a critical second to aim before he fired—and heard her gasp into the microphone.

"We're in Centauri. Humans mutinied. Old huma—"

He might have only had one bullet, but one bullet was enough to silence Shel forever.

A moment later, the entire room was silent. Harold slowly turned to survey the space, sliding a new clip into his gauss pistol as he shut down the transceiver.

One of his people was wounded but alive, leaning against the wall as she covered him with her gauss carbine. The other… The other had taken a full needler burst to her face.

They'd stopped Shel, but Harold already knew that too many people had died today.

～

TWENTY MINUTES LATER, Harold Newell was in the sickbay, standing next to an atmospherically sealed tank intended for injured crew who couldn't breathe a normal oxygen-nitrogen mix.

The tanks could be sealed for privacy, but right now, a window was open to allow him to check in on Kralnir. The Blust was very still, but his torso was moving with breath. The odd air in the tank gave him a slightly red tinge, but Harold could also see that there was some level of color to the jellyfish-like alien's skin again.

"How is he?" he asked Dr. Tran.

"He'll be fine," she told him. "We have some pretty detailed records on Kralnir, though very little on the Blust in general. Flesh injuries heal quickly for him, and the needles managed to miss his actual organs.

"The damage to his breathing system was rapidly poisoning him when you started sealing it," she continued. "If you guys hadn't taped up the holes, he might have died before we got him in the tank.

"As it is, he'll be back to normal in a few days."

"Thank you," Harold told her. "I owe him an apology."

In the aftermath, he could assume Kralnir's innocence and guess what had happened. Kralnir had run into the mutineers after they'd broken into the prison hold. Whatever discussion might have happened had ended in Shel deciding he was a threat, so the Blust had eaten a needler burst.

The mutineers had figured he was dead and left him—after which Kralnir had tried to reach the bridge to warn them all.

"We all owe him an apology," Harold admitted. "We thought he had betrayed us and he might just have saved us all from an even worse fate."

What they were going to face was likely bad enough. He'd checked the coordinates Shel had plugged into the transceiver. Her garbled and cut-short message had been sent directly to the nearest Council fleet base.

Hopefully, Shel's death had prevented the fleet from having enough information to move in force, but the war against humanity had been ugly, messy…and only thirty years earlier.

Even a *hint* of mutiny by a human crew was going to bring an armed response. The only question was whether it was going to be an armed response *Excalibur* could deal with in her current state.

CHAPTER
SEVEN

am E'tek, Great Wing of the Ninth Grand Talon of the Security Fleet of the Sacred Council of Races, woke from his nightmare with an undignified screech. His shoulder-vanes quivered with stress as his beak chattered and the nightmare slithered its way back through his brain.

Unfortunately, his quarters were sparse in the simple traditions of the Medari warrior codes. There was neither distraction nor comfort in sight, and his mind readily plunged back into the old nightmare.

The Fleet's counselors had taught him breathing exercises as a younger bird, and he focused on them now, allowing the mental image to wash over him. Even as he breathed, he saw through the eyes of a much-younger gunnery officer aboard the long-wrecked carrier *Ethalon*.

The old nightmare was easy to recall, and his therapies said to face it. The fury and pain of watching a world burn seared across his mind as he once again watched the bomber squadrons of *Ethalon* and her sisters sweep over the world the Terrans had named New Hope.

The Terrans had only been the third race that the Council had pronounced the Edict of Excommunication upon—but the Fleet had fulfilled their orders. While it was New Hope, the main world of Alpha

Centauri, that haunted E'tek's nightmares, he'd been present for the destruction of three of the humans' worlds.

He'd been unconscious aboard a search-and-rescue shuttle, pulled from *Ethalon*'s wreckage, while the Grand Fleet had sent their bombers against Terra itself. The Siege of Sol had scarred his soul, leaving him with memories he could not escape, an unspoken fear of the Sacred Council, and a harsh respect for the soldiers of the race he'd helped destroy.

Now he was awake, other memories ran through him and his fingers, missing the delicate down they *should* have been covered with, caressed the tears in his left shoulder-vane. Phase-cannon blasts had skipped shields and armor alike to gut *Ethalon*, and Tam E'tek had almost died in the humans' home system.

Two-thirds of the Grand Fleet, the greatest force the Council had ever mustered, *had* died there. Thirty years later, they were still rebuilding from those losses—a reality kept close to the chest of the Medari's military and religious leaders.

Crossing the room to pick up a drink, he shivered as the cold deck touched his toes and memories flashed through them. He was a soldier. One of the highest-ranking soldiers the Council had now, but still a soldier. It wasn't his place to challenge the Edicts of the Sacred Council.

He had barely picked up the self-warming flask when the communicator on his desk buzzed. He glared at it with the barely concealed rage of a hunting predator and crossed to the desk, taking a long slug of the warm liquor before answering.

"E'tek. What is it?"

"My Lord Great Wing," his chief of staff greeted him. "We may have a situation. A broken phase transmission just came in from one of the old human systems—no identifiers, no authentication codes, nothing. Just one person speaking against a background of weapons fire."

E'tek's shoulder-vanes *hurt* when they snapped to full extension now, but ancient threat-response instincts didn't pay attention to old injuries.

"What did they say?" E'tek asked carefully.

Instead of answering, K'van played the message.

"We're in Centauri," the unknown voice gasped. "Humans mutinied. Old human—"

The message ended with a noise that E'tek was far too familiar with —the sound of a being's life ending in violence.

"Wings up," he said crisply. "I will be there immediately."

~

LISTENING to the transmission again in the brighter lights and more comforting surroundings of his command center, E'tek could not change his initial assessment. The massive amphitheater of the flag carrier *Sedrua* seemed small around him—and the command center was larger than some spacecraft he'd been on.

He scanned the room as he thought. The central point of the command center was a circle of consoles the width of a starfighter, with a massive holotank in the middle of them. He clicked his beak in agitation and settled his gaze on that main display.

"Bring up the strategic map," he ordered.

A starmap appeared in the tank instantly, rotating slowly as it gleamed with blue dots marking the five thousand suns that honored the One God and the Sacred Council of Races.

"Show me the old Terran worlds," he said. Sickly-green lights, the color of an angry Medari's eyes, appeared on the edge of Council space. Forty-three star systems were marked with the color of hostile worlds, even decades after the death of humanity's states.

Even without an order from E'tek, his Mer'ket fleet base was marked with a brighter blue icon that stood out against the map. They were on the edge of the old human zone, a guardian against anything beyond those stars and any resurgence of the humans themselves.

"Mark Alpha Centauri," the Great Wing ordered. The voice had only said "Centauri"—but there was only one Centauri that would matter. One of the green dots grew larger and darker, edging into a vivid green that sent shivers down the back of any Medari.

The star was deep inside the old human zone. Twenty-six days' travel and a day and a half's phase-transmission lag from Mer'ket.

Surrounded on all sides by dead worlds, wiped clean by the fires of the Edict.

E'tek's shoulder-vanes shivered, the noise drawing concerned looks from the command center crew. K'van, on the other claw, knew the Great Wing of old and understood that he didn't have full control of his injured vanes.

"We will investigate," the Great Wing declared. "In force." He turned to K'van and snapped his beak harshly.

"Which of the carrier flocks is prepared for immediate deployment?" he asked.

"A full carrier flock, my lord?" K'van countered. "That seems excessive."

"You have never fought humans, Lesser Wing," E'tek reminded the younger Medari. Few among the Fleet still served who had. Time had seen to that—time and the winnowing of the Fleet the humans themselves had inflicted.

"A full carrier flock is almost certainly a larger boulder than we need, but I would rather drop a larger stone than misjudge and see our foe escape uncrushed," he continued. "Which flocks are ready?"

His Grand Talon had five lesser Talons, each formed of five carrier flocks and several additional cruiser flights. Of the twenty-five carriers, five were always ready for immediate deployment—and K'van already had a listing on the floating screen that orbited E'tek.

The Lesser Wing would argue, but he would obey.

"Connect me to Lesser Wing Kroche," he ordered after reviewing the list. The Kitni officer in question commanded a fast carrier, one of the smaller carriers in E'tek's command.

He might be feeling paranoid, but he still couldn't waste *too* many resources.

Kroche's face appeared on the display orbiting the Great Wing. The Kitni was squat and pale-skinned, the reddish tones of his race almost pink against his black uniform.

"Your command, Lord Great Wing?" Kroche asked immediately.

E'tek had to approve. Kroche had risen higher in the Fleet than most non-Medari officers could even dream of, but he knew his place.

"We have received a transmission from the Centauri System," E'tek told his subordinate. "An unknown speaker warned of a mutiny by human crew—and was killed before they could complete their transmission.

"We do not know what is going on, but the location and the warning suggest dangers I am unwilling to contemplate."

The Kitni bowed his head.

"You wish me to detach a cruiser or three to investigate?" he asked.

"No, Lesser Wing," E'tek replied. "I want you to take your entire carrier flock, with all *twelve* of its cruisers *and* all four of its battleships *and* your carrier and investigate."

There was a moment of silence.

"You believe they have reactivated an old Terran warship," Kroche said. His calm was admirable, but E'tek suspected he heard fear in the Kitni's voice. Kroche, like E'tek, had served in the war.

The Great Wing flickered his vanes in affirmative answer to the question, and he focused a hunting glare on the Lesser Wing.

"I can see no other reason why they would mutiny," he told the Kitni. "The humans who are permitted aboard starships earned their places by being beyond trustworthy…but it has happened before.

"This cannot be tolerated, but…" He raised a featherless hand into the pickup. "You must be cautious. Even a single Terran cruiser, properly commanded, could threaten your command. Step carefully, Lesser Wing. You have fought humans."

"I understand, Great Wing," Kroche confirmed. "I am aware of the range of the Terrans' weapons. If they have active phase cannon…"

"If you have any evidence of active phase cannon, you will destroy them without mercy," E'tek told him. "We will turn a blind eye to the arkship guardians, but warships activated in the old human zone? Those will *not* be tolerated; am I understood?"

"Yes, my lord. When do you wish us to depart?" the Kitni asked calmly.

"Immediately," E'tek told him. "Your flock is ready?"

If it was not, there would be other problems. Ones that one of the highest-ranked Kitni in the Fleet could not afford.

"Of course," Kroche confirmed. "I will draft my plans on the journey and will update you on what we find as soon as I can."

A big fist touched the Lesser Wing's chin in salute, and the image vanished.

E'tek turned his attention back to the holotank, considering the arc of the galaxy. The Sacred Council of Races were the guiding light for fifty-three species and five thousand suns. The potential of a single rogue Terran cruiser shouldn't bother him—the Council was genteelly ignoring the defensive flotillas of the Terran evacuation ships, after all, and there were *fifty* cruisers left guarding the half-dozen arkships that had escaped Sol.

For that matter, the One God knew it had been almost ten years after the Siege of Sol before the last rogue members of the Provisional United Nations Space Force had been hunted down, and they'd caused havoc until then.

There was nothing in the dead zone that had been human space that could challenge the Council...and yet. *Something* itched at his scarred vanes.

Whatever it was, it was out of his hands for twenty-six days.

EIGHT

With two conference rooms in use on two ships, the meeting of Gerard's senior people seemed much sparser than it had before. *Likira*'s space wasn't really designed for this use, but *Excalibur*'s clearly had been. An entire wall of the conference room attached to the bridge turned into a viewscreen, mirroring the table and space on the salvage ship. It didn't *quite* manage to look like a single table across both conference rooms, but everyone could be seen and heard at least.

The air in both rooms was grim and people were quiet, all of them looking at Gerard Arkanis. He stood at one end of the table on *Excalibur* and studied the holographic schematic of the warship shown on both ships.

"So," he said quietly. "Our situation has drastically changed. Yesterday, we thought we were going to have time. Time to find out what was wrong with *Excalibur*. Time to fix her. Time to decide on our next steps."

He shrugged.

"Now we have no time."

Gerard's gaze swept across his gathered officers. Shel was missing now, of course—shot dead as she transmitted to the enemy. Kralnir remained in the infirmary on *Likira*, healing in a tank of his native atmosphere.

Still, he hadn't expected the group to be this quiet. They had come this far with him—surely, they weren't overwhelmed at the first obstacle?

"No one is to blame for what happened," he told them all. "Shel moved quickly and had her fingers in the very software that was supposed to warn us. If Kralnir hadn't collided with her and gone off the air, we might never have known she was moving."

Newell visibly relaxed, and Gerard allowed himself a small smile. The younger man should have known Gerard wasn't going to blame him for this mess. Newell had reacted quickly and with a surprising degree of ready violence.

It had been the *right* response, but it wasn't what Gerard had expected from the former navigator. It seemed he should have asked a few more questions about how Newell had afforded his pilot training.

"The unfortunate simplicity of the matter is this: Shel sent her message forty-eight hours ago. It has reached the Mer'ket Council Fleet base. They have almost certainly dispatched a scouting element—we can hope for only a single cruiser, but they may well send more.

"Regardless of what they send, they will arrive in twenty-five days. *Likira* is unarmed, which means we have two choices: have *Excalibur* ready to fight when they arrive or have *Excalibur* somewhere *else*.

"Anywhere else."

He looked to Vollan, the salvage tech now acting as the battleship's main engineer.

She shook her head and brushed loose blond hair back from her eyes.

"We can't go anywhere," she admitted. "To hide *Excalibur*, Captain Mikos burned almost all of her fuel supplies pushing her into the orbit we're in. We're well inside Six's phase boundary now—close enough to the gas giant that the ship's emergency fuel scoops have kept her reactors running for thirty years.

"But *Excalibur*'s emergency engines take far more reaction mass than running her power plants on standby, and those engines, frankly, might not suffice to push her *out* of the orbit she's in," Vollan admitted.

"We need the gravitics if we're going to go anywhere, Arkanis. She's just too damn big and too damn low."

"Then *Excalibur* needs to be ready to fight," Gerard told her. "Her secondaries were supposedly ready to shoot down our small craft. What about the primary guns?"

Those were the biggest phase cannon ever built by humans, which probably meant they were the most powerful weapons systems in the *galaxy*. But…

"Offline," Vollan said flatly. "I don't know if it's possible to get her online in twenty-five days, boss. There's too many systems we haven't even surveyed, too much small damage to too many places."

"Fuck the small damage," Gerard told her. He looked around at everyone, holding each of the salvage team leaders' gazes for a full second. "Drives and guns, people. We need nothing more and we can settle for nothing less.

"Shields? The armor can take a solid beating on its own," he said grimly. "Sensors? We can relay telemetry from *Likira*'s array. Life support? It's already functioning well enough for the two hundred people we've got aboard.

"Everything can wait except drives and guns," he concluded. "We need to kill whatever comes at us in the first salvo. Otherwise, they call for help and it won't matter what we did—unless we have drives and can get the hell out of here."

The room was silent and everyone's attention shifted to Vollan. She'd been aboard *Likira* almost as long as Gerard had, and she was the most experienced of the human salvage techs. That meant if anyone could say what could be done, it was Alexandra Vollan.

"It's *possible*," she finally said. "I think if we focus our time and effort, we can definitely get the primary cannon online. That alone will consume almost all of the work-hours we've got left—and none of our people have a damn clue what to do with gravitic engines like these.

"The only person we have who could possibly dig into gravitic engines built by engineers who only half-understood what they were doing and were building on a scale no one else dared is Kralnir."

"Dr. Tran?" Gerard asked, turning to the woman sitting at the back of *Likira*'s conference table.

"Kralnir will be up and about within a day or so," Tran said. "It will be another day, *at least*, before he can do any serious physical labor, but he should be able to examine hardware while other people do the lifting.

"His body heals very quickly, but he did take damage that would have killed any of us." Tran shook her head. "I have no files on his species, though. I have records of all of his previous treatments on *Likira*, and it looks like he brought his prior medical records with him when he came aboard, so he clearly knew how little data we'd have."

"That makes sense," Gerard said grimly. "The Blust were the last race the Council pronounced an Edict of Excommunication on, roughly three hundred years ago."

Some of the people in the conference had known that, but from the guilty silence that answered his words, most hadn't. The guiltiest faces had probably believed that Kralnir had potentially betrayed them when he went dark—and now understood how unlikely that was.

"If there is one being on this ship who I *know* believes in and supports the same goals as us, that being is Kralnir," Gerard told them quietly. "If you think humanity is scattered and dying out, look up the Blust in *Likira*'s archives. There isn't much there, but it isn't a fun read."

Gerard had looked up everything he could around the Edicts of Excommunication a long time before. The best guess was that there were around thirty million humans on the arkships that had fled Sol at the end and about fifty million scattered through the refugee camps on the Council worlds. Compared to the thirty *billion* humans there had been before First Contact, that was a terrifying number.

Compared to the estimated *ten* million surviving Blust, it was a miracle. The survivors had eco-formed a midsized planetoid a hundred years after their homeworld had died, with Council assistance and a Council "guardian" force. That planetoid was home to six or seven million Blust, with another three million scattered through ghettos in Council space.

It was a grim portent of the future of Gerard's race—a future he was determined humanity would *not* suffer.

"Vollan, I want you to focus on getting me those primaries," he told the salvage tech. "When Kralnir is up and we bring him over to *Excalibur*, divert some of your people to help him."

He sighed and looked at the holographic schematic.

"Priority has to be the guns. If we can take them down, we can run later. If it looks like we might be able to get the engines online before the Council gets here, we may reassess, but for now, I think we have to assume we're going to have to fight.

"Unfortunately for the Council, we have *Excalibur* to do it with."

Vollan gave him a determined nod.

"She's a bit old and rusty at this point, boss, but we'll get her sharp enough for this."

Despite meeting with everyone virtually, Gerard still ended up taking a shuttle back over to *Likira* for one meeting that he knew could only take place in person.

Entering the infirmary, he saw that Kralnir was up and about in the atmosphere tank. He was sitting on the bed in the tank, wearing his breathing apparatus and adjusting the settings on the mostly repaired piece of equipment.

Gerard picked up a face mask to allow him to breathe inside the tank and knocked on the door.

Kralnir looked up and gestured for him to come in with a tentacle. He was reaching for his heavy cloak as Gerard stepped through the small phase-interface shield that kept the air mix in the tank.

"Don't bother, Kralnir," Gerard said, gesturing for the Blust to wait. "I know what you look like, and after what you've done for us, you have no need to conceal yourself."

He chuckled.

"Though I suppose I won't make you wander around naked, either," he admitted.

Kralnir's translucent skin flickered in several colors as the alien made a gurgling sound Gerard guessed was laughter.

"If you insist, I will forgo the cloak," he conceded, his translated English even smoother now. What moments could be spared by the people with the skills were going into that program out of sheer need.

"The gloves are for another reason, however," he continued, pulling out the garments that covered his tentacles.

"My tendrils can deliver a shock to incapacitate prey," Kralnir told Gerard as he put the gloves on. "There is always some current, and the sensation would be…unpleasant for you."

That hadn't been in the files Gerard had read, but he offered his hand to the other man anyway. Kralnir hesitated, even gloved, but he extended a covered tentacle to shake Gerard's hand after a moment.

"You may have saved us all, Kralnir," Gerard told the man. "Without you going missing and your warning to Newell, Shel might have managed to transmit enough information to doom us—or even done it without us realizing!"

"I did what I must," the Blust replied. "I would see the Council humbled, and I do not much care who breaks them. Your race alone seemed to have a chance to challenge them, with the courage to face them—and the beliefs that would drive you to liberate their conquests."

He shivered his tentacles.

"We had great hopes, but we underestimated the Council. You were defeated."

"Defeated, yes," Gerard admitted. "But not destroyed. Not truly *beaten*—not until we're all dead."

"So others of your kind have said for thirty years, but I did not understand or believe," Kralnir said. "There are many who posture against Council rule, but nothing has ever come of it. But you… With *Excalibur* at your command, you might manage to do something.

"I do not yet believe that you could defeat the entire Council," the Blust said. "But I do not believe your defeat and annihilation are inevitable, either."

"If I thought for a moment we could find a peaceful coexistence with the Council, I might consider it," Gerard said. "But I probably would still attempt to destroy them. War is the path laid before me—I do not need to destroy the *people* of the Council, not even the Medari, but the Council itself must burn."

Kralnir made a gesture with his tentacles that no human could match.

"History is full of war and peace, and the Council has rarely made peace while their enemies still stood," he told Gerard. "Your race has a chance to fight at last, maybe. Or perhaps just you and your allies.

"Either way, I will stand among those allies and fight by your side."

"Today, to be honest, I need you to fix a battleship," Gerard told Kralnir. "Anything else is getting ahead of ourselves."

"That is a beginning," the Blust said with a flash of colors and tendril motions Gerard hoped was a grin. "A prelude to battle. I will fix your battleship, Captain Arkanis—and in trade, you will give my people back their freedom."

BACK ABOARD *EXCALIBUR*, Gerard attempted to use the quiet of the Captain's office to calm his nerves. The space had been designed for that, from what he could tell. By default, the room was sealed from outside noise, with calming lighting and options for calming sounds.

The walls were paneled in woods he'd never seen from trees that were now extinct. Paintings of old ships, from great-masted sailing ships to iron-decked carriers to fusion-rocket cruisers, covered the walls.

On the back wall, normally behind Gerard but the focus of his attention at the moment, was a replica of an eighth-century English longsword. Hand-forged by the best recreationists of the twenty-third century, it bore the words that defined the sword it mimicked.

Whoso pulleth out this sword of this stone and anvil, is rightwise king born.

Excalibur had a complete-enough library of Terran literature—academic and entertainment alike—for Gerard to now know that was the *wrong* inscription for Excalibur. It was the inscription of the sword in the stone, which fit their current state far more accurately than any of the phrases ascribed to the actual king's sword.

Gerard and his people had drawn the sword from the stone of

Alpha Centauri B VI. What happened next... That would define the fate of his people.

And yet.

And yet.

The Captain's safe in the corner was open now. Its old-fashioned mechanical lock had resisted Gerard's software, but the safe itself had failed to withstand a salvager's vibroblade. Secure and protected as the metal box was, it had contained only one item.

That red disk, an oversized case for an almost-microscopic datachip, now rested on the big oak desk. Gerard recognized it—from a story he'd thought was more myth than *Excalibur* herself. Rumors and lies of such disks had killed a dozen people he *knew* of.

Each arkship had been supposed to carry one of these disks. Fate, folly and the war itself had cost humanity all of them. Certainly, none of the arskhips that still made their nomadic way through Council space had one!

So far as Gerard Arkanis knew, the red disk on his desk was the only one of its kind left. A green sphere marked the surface of the disk, the only indicator that it was anything special. The only sign that it contained information the Council and every human leader would kill for.

Myth said the Project Respite disk contained two pieces of information: a phase transmission frequency and encryption protocol that would reach every arkship; and the location of the Respite System.

Respite was a legend. A star system concealed from Council searchers by a quirk of interstellar geography and home to two inhabitable planets. It was holy land and El Dorado alike, the intended final destination of the arkship evacuation.

And Gerard Arkanis was the only person with that knowledge. He stood at the helm of the most powerful warship humanity had ever built, certain that he could stand off at least the first of the Council's attacks.

The arkships had scattered to sail the starry seas alone, each ship a self-sufficient community hiding from the Council and surviving by the skin of their teeth. The frequency on the Respite disk could summon them.

But...Gerard didn't know if they would come. He didn't even know, not for certain, that *Excalibur* would survive to meet them if he summoned them. He needed reinforcements...but Alpha Centauri wasn't the place and now was not yet the time.

He picked up the disk. Unless it was far more secure than he suspected, they could at least copy it.

If everything went according to plan, he would yet fully draw *Excalibur* and summon humanity to his banner. Just yet, though, he did not feel he was humanity's *rightwise king*.

But he would make certain that Project Respite was not lost, no matter what happened to his ship.

CHAPTER

NINE

Drones drifted through space around Alpha Centauri B VI. Gerard wasn't entirely certain he trusted the devices, not after they'd sat in storage for thirty years, but they seemed to be working so far. The robots weren't much, either: just a fusion rocket strapped to a set of passive sensors and a Terran phase transmitter a tenth of the size of any Council transceiver he'd ever seen.

The two-point phase generator could send a message to anywhere inside its range, though it couldn't receive a response unless the person it was talking to *also* had a two-point transmitter. Those transmitters were giving *Excalibur* a reasonably real-time view of the space for roughly a light-minute in any direction of the gas giant.

If everything went according to plan, the Council ships would emerge on a least-time course from Mer'ket and on the far side of the gas giant. The gas giant would be no barrier to *Excalibur*'s phase cannon so long as she had targeting data—but it would completely block the Council Fleet's missiles and particle beams.

Regardless of how well the plan worked, they were out of time.

"Newell, what do you make the time?" he asked.

The young navigator had finally made it over from the salvage ship and was now acting as Gerard's executive officer *and* gunnery officer.

"If they deployed their response immediately on receiving Shel's message, they'd be arriving in the next five minutes," Newell reported. "Rumors I've heard say they keep at least some ships ready for deployment at all times, so they probably deployed within a few hours."

"I heard the same rumors," Gerard said loudly. The entire bridge crew was barely fifteen people. It didn't take much to make sure they all heard him, though the bridge had been designed with acoustics and a sound system to help.

"I don't think we'll see anything for a few minutes—but I think we *will* see something in the next few hours," he concluded. "Take us to battle stations."

Excalibur's computers were smart enough to pick up that command and make sure that everyone in the ship got it, one way or another. New icons flickered up on the main display and the screens surrounding Gerard's command seat.

"Guns are charging," Newell reported. A set of icons on Gerard's screens flicked over to green. "Guns are charged. All primaries and secondaries standing by to fire. *If* they fire."

The guns had passed the basic self-tests, but they hadn't had the time or hands to double-check every single link in their power-supply systems or even in the guns themselves.

"Shields are up," Vollan reported. The senior salvage tech had surrendered her chief engineer hat to Kralnir with surprising grace and cheer when everyone had realized that the Blust knew more than everyone else about everything except the guns—and none of them really knew anything about the guns.

Vollan was now his second, and she was on the bridge because they'd known this moment was coming.

"Current reading on the phase interface is about forty percent power," she continued. "Readiness reports on the emitters haven't improved. We've still only got thirty-four percent of them online, so I'm impressed with her redundancy."

"Everything is redundant here," Gerard replied. "Might just save us yet."

The last of his four human "bridge officers" was silent, and he turned his attention on Beck. The Black woman was running navigation and engines, such as they were.

"Engines are what they've been so far," she admitted. "Kralnir's got teams working through Drive One, but our last attempt to power up brought a dangerous flicker."

She shrugged.

"If it's that or die, we can make a tenth-millicee per second of acceleration," Beck told him. "But Kralnir figures we have about a seventy percent chance of the tidal forces ripping us apart before we clear the phase boundary."

And *that* was why *Excalibur* was still here. Given a full menu of options, Gerard would have taken the battleship somewhere else after Shel's transmission. Everything they'd tested said they had a phase drive.

They just couldn't get far enough from the gas giant to bring the drive up. They had no choice but to fight—and while the battleship couldn't dodge, she could at least shoot.

"Lirrow?" Gerard asked, turning to his last officer as he considered the scanner data on the main display. "Anything?"

"Drone links are holding," the Rowwlan told him. She was using a machine translator now, allowing her to keep up with the human officers' English. "I'm not as comfortable with the communications as I'd like, but the sensors are good. Basic but highly sensitive.

"We've also got *Excalibur*'s own scanners online, but we are clear on all angles. Nothing yet."

"Thanks," Gerard said. He leaned back in the command chair and tried to unobtrusively adjust his leg. He could sit for longer than he could stand, but any unchanging position became painful eventually.

"I do hope the Council is prompt," he told his people. "It would never do for our guests of honor to be late."

That earned him a grim chuckle from the skeleton crew on the bridge, fading into silence as they kept their attention on their consoles. The first sign of the enemy would require rapid and decisive action—and they had no idea when the Council would arrive.

There was only so long they could keep the understrength crew at full readiness. While the ship was ready to fight, Gerard had barely any people supporting Kralnir in trying to get the engines online.

But if the Council's response was slower than he'd feared, they could be trying to *keep* the ship at readiness for a long time—and with less than a twentieth of the battleship's designed crew, that was going to wear them down.

"There," Lirrow suddenly mewled. "Multiple loci phase emergence on the direct route from Mer'ket."

Gerard had the sensors' feed already mirrored to his station, but he waited patiently as his old friend pored through the data they were getting from the drone.

"Numbers and classes?" he asked.

"Uncertain," Lirrow admitted. "All I can say just yet is multiple loci. At least three ships, probably less than ten. I don't *think* I'm seeing anything big—just cruisers, I think."

"At least a half a flight," Gerard said grimly. "Easily a full one with all six cruisers." He shook his head. "I was only expecting three ships," he admitted.

"I have drive signatures now," Lirrow reported. "Six ships, accelerating toward us at three millicee per second."

"How directly?" Gerard asked. "Do they know where *we* are?"

"I *think* they're aiming to make turnover in thirty minutes and slow into a high orbit of the gas giant," she said. "That would fit with their vector. They must have narrowed down the origin of the message that closely."

"ETA?"

"Their max safe velocity is two-seventy millicee," Lirrow pointed out. "It only takes them ninety seconds to accelerate or decelerate from that, so…thirty minutes, pretty much no matter what they do."

He nodded. The six Council ships were a bit over eight light-minutes away. The maximum range of his guns was about nine million kilometers, half a light-minute. With the drones, he could even reasonably *target* an enemy nine million kilometers away.

Eight light-minutes put them just outside the phase boundaries of Alpha Centauri B and Alpha Centauri B VI. They could have cut the sublight distance more closely by leaving the direct route from Mer'ket

—a complicated navigational problem that would only have saved them fifteen minutes.

"Wait," Newell said. "I read them as slowing their accel. Lirrow?"

"They've maxed out their speed at one-thirty-five millicee relative to ACB Six," the sensor operator replied after a moment. "Double those timelines, people."

"I see they're in a hurry," Gerard quipped. *Likira* had a maximum safe velocity under gravitic drive of a hundred and sixty millicee, and she was very definitely civilian.

"They have no idea what they're dealing with here," Newell pointed out. "They're being careful—they want to sort out what's going on, not lose ships."

"So long as they're on that side of the gas giant, I'm afraid we're going to have to disappoint them," Gerard said cheerfully.

Six cruisers was more than he'd hoped for, but even in his worst-case scenarios, *Excalibur*'s armament would suffice to wipe them out.

If the guns worked, which was the problem he foresaw. Council phase transceivers might be bigger than the two-point transmitters mounted on the drones watching the incoming ships, but they were still small enough that every ship built in Council space carried one.

Terran phase transceivers were much larger, but the use of two-point transmitters for short range made up the difference most of the time.

This was not one of those times. If Gerard had been looking at a Terran force, he'd only have needed to take out the command ship to stop them reporting back to Mer'ket. With a Council fleet, any surviving vessel could transmit a warning back to their fleet command.

They'd *probably* be able to leave before a second wave of reinforcements could arrive—but the extra delay of the Council waiting for this force to report back in would buy them days. Days they might end up needing.

"Newell," he said quietly, "lay in the secondary guns as well."

There was no such thing as overkill when the survival of everything they were working toward was at stake. The Council Fleet *could* destroy *Excalibur*. She didn't have escorts or support ships, just *Likira*.

"The secondaries, boss?" Newell replied. "We risk more power issues, the more guns we fire. We'll be fine, most likely, but…it's a risk. And the range is shorter, too."

"There's still a gas giant between us and them at twenty light-seconds," Gerard pointed out. "These are cruisers, not carriers. There are no bombers out there to extend their eyes and weapons range.

"The drone should stay hidden until they're much closer. It's a passive scanner with no engine online. Even if they find it, it isn't evidence. If one of them survives our first salvo, though…*that* will be the call that will bring in an entire fleet.

"We take the immediate risk," he determined aloud. "Lay in the secondaries."

"Yes, sir," Newell replied crisply, bending over his console and gesturing for his people to help. Timers shifted as the new targeting parameters took hold in the system.

The secondary phase cannon had two-thirds of the range and barely a fifth of the energy pulse of the primaries—but there were also four times as many of them.

"They're maneuvering, Arkanis," Lirrow reported. "Sweeping out to get better sight vectors on the gas giant. They want to be sure nothing is hiding behind it."

Gerard nodded grimly.

"Are they going to see us?" he asked.

"We are *very* low," she reminded him. "They'd need to spread wide and still get close to get a visual. But they're aware of the danger."

"They won't see what hit them," Gerard told her. The phase cannon were instantaneous across their range.

Green hexagonal reticules appeared on the main display now, shrinking toward the six red icons of the enemy cruisers as Newell and his people narrowed their firing solution.

"We are in range for the primaries," Newell said calmly. "Range for the secondaries in…twenty seconds. Forward vector remains steady."

Gerard nodded silently, watching the green hexagons close in until they overlapped entirely with their targets—green crosshairs now crossing each icon.

"Range," the other man reported. "Your orders?"

The drone was still hidden—and Gerard trusted the ship's systems and his people if they said they had the shot.

"Fire."

EXCALIBUR SHIVERED around Gerard as dozens of two-point phase transmitters came alive. Capacitors emptied their charge into conduits that his people hadn't dared run full charges through before.

He'd never been present for that many phase anomalies activating simultaneously. Council phase transceivers were ancient, well-shielded and stable technologies.

The anomalies used for the two-point phase transmission were none of those things, and an eerie keening tore into Gerard's ears and mind. It couldn't have lasted for long—maybe a tenth of a second—but it made an astonishing impression.

And then enough power to light a planet for a year sparked across six inches, crossing twenty light-seconds in the blink of an eye as *Excalibur* fired her first broadside in anger.

On the guns that *worked*.

Dozens of red icons flashed across Gerard's screens as system after system failed.

"Shit shit *shit!*" Newell snapped. "Catastrophic failure on primaries five through thirteen!"

"Venting power into space—no, we have flashback," Vollan replied. "We are re-rout—"

Everything stopped. Every screen died. The lights went dark and for a terrifying few seconds, all that could be heard on *Excalibur's* bridge was strained breathing.

Lights came back up after a few seconds, followed by screens as the computers began an emergency reboot.

"Reroute failed," Vollan said softly. Her console lit up and she surveyed the data. "Power cascade through Sector Four, Sector Five and Sector Six power relay hubs. The system is automatically pushing around them and Kralnir is adapting our power systems—hence, lights —but..."

The salvage tech turned warship engineer shook her head.

"Some of the backups are online, but most are dead," she told them. "We don't have enough backups to run power to the guns fed by those routers—which means those guns are as useless as the ones that just overloaded on their own."

Gerard could do the math. Nine primaries overloaded. Four more sectors of power offline meant *another* twelve, at least. Over twenty of his primary cannon were out of commission…and *Excalibur* only had thirty-six main guns.

"Lirrow, please tell me we don't need those guns this instant," he asked, his tone more plaintive than he preferred.

"Not right now, no," she confirmed slowly. "I have a link with the drone, and we have no targets on the board. All six cruisers were destroyed."

"Thank…" Gerard trailed off, unwilling to thank the One God for anything but not having any alternatives come to mind. Shaking his head, he turned back to Vollan.

"Get everyone on those routers," he ordered. "They're equal priority to the engines for you and Kralnir now. There *will* be a second scout force, and I would like to be able to fight *or* run—one or the other, if you please."

"We'll make it happen," Vollan promised.

CHAPTER

TEN

Lesser Wing Kroche—Ansai Kroche of Arm Lotek of the House of Shetalla, but no Kitni expected a non-Kitni to learn more than their face name—was capable of great patience. His people were ambush predators by nature, and his craggy skin was the color of the stones of the desert his family hailed from.

Any Kitni could wait—and to rise to the rank Kroche had in the Council's military, Kroche had waited a great deal—but there also needed to be an understanding of how long he *should* wait.

"Report," he rumbled. The command center of the fast carrier *Kaxis* was filled with members of a dozen races, but all spoke the Medari trade tongue. The realities of the Council Fleet were such, though, that there were no Medari in the center.

Few Kitni, too. The Medari would not subject themselves to the command of another species, but they also would not permit a Wing of a non-Medari race to gather a loyal following of their own people.

His chief of staff was a Loreesh, a trifurcated snake-like alien with prehensile tails for tool use. They slithered up to him and extended a tongue in a disgruntled hiss.

"No report," Shaishess told him. "They are half a day overdue."

Kroche nodded, his face impassive. In other times, twelve hours would have passed without comment. In this case…he'd sent half of his cruisers on ahead, in case something truly dangerous was going on.

They should have arrived less than thirty minutes after leaving the rest of the carrier flock. It had now been fourteen hours since they left, and only silence filled the phase-waves.

He could continue to wait—but he could see no logic that made that the right call.

"Get me Shipmaster Loas K'tai," he ordered.

Shaishess didn't do as good a job of hiding their distaste for the Medari officer as they should have, and Kroche made a chopping gesture with his free hand.

"K'tai is our best cruiser Captain," he snapped. "Obey."

The Loreesh disappeared and a channel opened to Kroche's choice of Shipmaster a few moments later.

"Lord Lesser Wing," K'tai said crisply, the bird's beady green eyes focused somewhere to Kroche's left rather than on his superior.

"Our scouting cruiser flight has gone missing and is now twelve hours overdue," Kroche said flatly. "I assume you realize that, Shipmaster."

"I do," K'tai replied. "What would you have me do?"

"You will take your ship to a point thirteen light-hours from the target gas giant," Kroche ordered. "You will deploy a sensor net and retrieve all possible light from the emergence of our scout flight until their final fate.

"And just in case this is not an *accident*, you will maintain a regular phase-transmission schedule every five minutes," the Lesser Wing concluded. "You will have the power to spare, as you will *not* engage in any combat operations.

"If a threat presents itself, you are to withdraw to the carrier flock."

"You believe a handful of rogue mutineers destroyed six cruisers of the Council Fleet?" K'tai asked.

"I do not know what happened, Shipmaster. That is what you will find out," Kroche rumbled. "This is a simple task, Shipmaster. If it is beyond you, I will find—"

"No, Lord Lesser Wing. I obey. We will report shortly."

~

A HUNTER's patience carried Kroche through the next two hours. Most of the old light showed nothing unusual. The cruiser flight had arrived and progressed as planned…until suddenly they hadn't.

Six cruisers of the Council Fleet, powerful midsize warships rarely matched ton-for-ton, vanished in a single instant of flashing power, and a chill ran down Kroche's spines.

"Recall K'tai," he told Shaishess. "Then call a council of Shipmasters once he has returned."

"I do not understand," the Loreesh admitted, looking at the data. "What *happened*?"

"The Terrans happened," Kroche said grimly. Unlike his Medari superiors, he'd only risen a few ranks since the war. He'd commanded a parasite frigate in the war against the Terrans.

He knew what a phase-cannon strike looked like.

"Ready the Shipmasters," he repeated. "We must plan more carefully for our next moves—and with the understanding of what we fight."

"I obey," Shaishess replied.

Kroche was ignoring them, already bringing up a listing of his resources on the screens next to him. His bridge was much the same as on any carrier—a series of circular decks descending to a massive holotank. Each deck held a dozen stations, but Kroche's station was the largest and best equipped, with the best view of the tank.

His own repeater screens were better for this task, though. His command was a powerful one, one of the largest in the hands of a non-Medari officer, and it should more than suffice for this.

He still had six cruisers, after all, and he'd kept the best officers, if not necessarily the best *ships*. Their main purpose would be screening his battleships, anyway, as the kilometer-long warships with their heavy particle beams were his second-best weapon against Terran phase cannon.

His *best* weapon was *Kaxis*'s brood. As a fast carrier, his flagship didn't carry any of the world-burning bombers. Her brood was thirty parasite frigates—and the three *thousand* drones those parasite frigates commanded.

The frigates were the swiftest ships he had, with far heavier gravitic-engine power-to-weight ratios than anything else he commanded. Their drones were easily expendable, to the point that the laser-armed robots were capable of turning their power cores into hundred-megaton bombs.

The missiles carried by his larger ships were cheaper than the drones, but they lacked the active range and direct control provided by the frigates. And the drones could kill anything if they got the chance to unleash their lasers.

Death by a thousand cuts was still death, after all.

"Shipmaster K'tai has returned," his chief of staff said behind him. "The Shipmasters will be ready for you to address in five minutes."

"Well done, Shaishess," Kroche told his subordinate. "I do not know what these mutineers found...but it will be death of *them* and not of more Council warriors!"

~

SIXTEEN SHIPMASTERS WERE present when Kroche linked in to the conference. Eleven commanded actual warships. Five commanded attack groups of six frigates.

It was in the command of warships that the Medari were most torn when dealing with non-Medari flag officers. They didn't like to be commanded by non-Medari, but they also didn't want to trust that many non-Medari in ship command—especially under command of a non-Medari.

Three of his five frigate-squadron Shipmasters were non-Medari, but seven of the eleven warship commanders were Medari. Nine of the sixteen were of the Council's primary race, the birdlike beings who had first received the grace of the One God.

Kroche did not begrudge the Medari being the One God's chosen first people. He *did* begrudge the way their paranoia occasionally made defending the One God's worshippers harder.

"You have all reviewed the old light Shipmaster K'tai retrieved,"

Kroche said. It wasn't a question. "I don't believe any of you have seen that in person before, but I believe it is covered in our training and tactical-practice scenarios, yes?"

"It is," High Shipmaster Ash L'ret confirmed. *Kaxis*'s commander was the second-most senior officer in the carrier flotilla—which meant she was Medari. The golden-feathered Medar and Kroche had worked together for a decade now.

They did *not* like each other, but they worked together.

"What I do not understand," L'ret continued, "is how. This was not the work of a single hastily repaired Terran cruiser extracted from the debris fields of this system. We are farther from those fields than I anticipated when the call came from Alpha Centauri."

"We face a more-organized opposition than I expected," Kroche told her. "Even scavengers and salvagers are supposed to be barred from these systems. I am aware that rule is often ignored, but it may have permitted an operation to take place here without the Council's awareness.

"The evidence"—he gestured at an image of the deaths of six cruisers and three thousand worshippers of the One God—"suggests we are looking at a large-scale reconstruction effort. While nothing has been visible to our long-range examination yet, I believe we will find a significant facility in low orbit of the gas giant.

"They have clearly been salvaging the fields here for some time and have assembled quite the arsenal of working phase cannon. It seems unlikely that they have done so without assembling at least one mobile warship—a ship they seem to have used for piracy."

Kroche shrugged his massive shoulders.

"Aided by mutineers, clearly," he noted. "One of their attacks was enough of a failure for us to receive a warning. Now we must make certain that the sacrifice of the worshippers of the One God who warned of this is not in vain."

"We are badly outranged in most weapons," K'tai noted, the Medari Shipmaster uncharacteristically quiet. "Records from the war show that—and the fate of High Shipmaster S'doll's flight confirm it.

"They were still twenty light-seconds from the gas giant when they were destroyed. Our best missiles have an active range of *sixteen* light-seconds."

The battleships' heavy particle beams could theoretically reach twenty light-seconds, but they were lightspeed weapons. Their lasers and the cruisers' particle beams were even shorter-ranged than the gravitic-drive missiles.

"We know this enemy's strengths," Kroche agreed. "We know *our* strengths. If we are facing a target that cannot move, we can engage with missiles from beyond even their phase-cannon range. We are far faster than they are and can move into combat range. It is only when the Terrans have room to maneuver that their range becomes an insurmountable obstacle."

He laid his massive fists down on the table and looked each of his officers in the face in turn.

"Our guess of what we face limits their room to maneuver, but we cannot assume we are correct," he concluded. "We must plan to *remove* their freedom of maneuver. We will provide them with a target to force them to commit—and then we will pin them against the gas giant with our frigates and drones.

"Whoever these humans are, I doubt they are sharpened veterans of war against the Council. *We,* on the other side of the dune, have dozens of veterans of the war against humanity aboard our ships.

"We remember this enemy, my Shipmasters. We have faced their greatest might. We will not be intimidated by deserters with salvaged guns. Am I clear?"

CHAPTER

ELEVEN

"Ferrous oxidization," Kralnir told the council of officers. Most of them were now aboard *Excalibur,* but there were still people aboard *Likira.* The salvage ship's fabricators were working overtime, especially now that the guns were a problem.

"Rust?" Newell replied.

"That is what I said, yes," the Blust confirmed.

Their hacked-together translators were surprisingly good…but not perfect.

"What do you mean?" Gerard asked. "Rust in the guns?"

"Exactly," the engineer said, gesturing to Vollan to explain. "Chief Vollan found the source after we found the damage."

"Forty percent of *Excalibur*'s water-reserve tankage was empty when we came aboard," Vollan told everyone. "We assumed that they'd never been filled and didn't think to check for leaks."

She shrugged.

"They were at ninety-four percent when the crew died," she admitted. "Several of the tanks turned out to have improper welds. Not enough to cause major concerns or even serious leakage—but enough to slowly leak out over a couple of decades and raise the humidity levels in several key sections of the ship far beyond the designed parameters."

"Shouldn't the atmospheric controls have stopped that?" Gerard asked.

"Atmospheric control on this ship is all over the place," Vollan told him. "Nowhere is bad enough to risk dangerous levels of anything, but we definitely have entire sections where it's not reliable enough to dehumidify the systems.

"And part of the problem is that the life-support plant return vents for many sections are actually blocked," she noted. "We're pumping sufficient oxygen into the ship to keep everywhere breathable, but we were only pulling air *back* in about two-thirds of the ship.

"So, the remaining third got real humid for a while. Time and circulation eventually handled it—but not before the humidity got up to a hundred percent in sections that weren't supposed to get above *five* percent."

"Key linkages partially or completely oxidized," Kralnir concluded. The Blust flickered his tentacles. He was wearing something closer to a black tunic than his old cloak, covering his torso but leaving his tentacles free to move.

"Few of them were very visibly faulty from the outside, but at full power..."

"Kaboom," Gerard said quietly. "How long to get them online?"

"We would need to trace any failed components, both from oxidization and from the power failure," Kralnir told him. "It depends on our approach."

"What are the options?" Gerard asked.

"Option one, we work cannon by cannon," the Blust told him. "Vollan and I each focus on our areas of expertise in the section. We can probably have a power router online within six hours, and a first gun within twenty-four hours."

"I like twenty-four hours," Gerard said. "What's the downside— and the other option?"

"The downside is the timeline," Kralnir replied. "We might have the first gun in twenty-four hours, but the *last* gun not for ten times that. Maybe longer. We may miss some key problems, or may find repeated problems and save time.

"The other option is to start from power cores and work out, fixing as we go. We focus all hands on each section, fix all power routers first, and get to guns last. One hundred fifty hours to first gun. No more than two hundred hours to last. We would work outward and find problems at the earliest point. We may miss some opportunities for establishing a process for repeated problems."

"But we'll have all the guns sooner," Gerard noted. He could see the argument both ways. On the other hand, the cruisers had only arrived twenty-four hours earlier. The Council wouldn't even be expecting the first message back to Mer'ket for another twelve hours.

"What Kralnir isn't mentioning is that both of his timelines require taking him from the engines," Vollan pointed out. "That will slow down the process there by a lot."

"The engines are…random fish," Kralnir said. "We have not yet learned what is wrong there. The gun damage is clear and easily fixed. It just requires time."

Wildcard, Gerard translated the Blust's metaphor. The engines were a wildcard. He didn't know how long they were going to take to fix.

"I would *really* like engines," he admitted. "If we fix the engines, the guns can take longer to fix because no one will be able to find us."

The red disk in the safe in his office weighed on his soul. He had the ability to raise a banner of hope for all mankind—but he couldn't do that in Alpha Centauri. Not when the Council knew where *Excalibur* was.

"If I could give you a timeline on the engines, I would," Kralnir told him, his tentacles twitching. "I do not know, Captain Arkanis. The usual mistakes are not present. Your people did very good work. Even *I* am not certain why this ship's engines do not work."

"How long to fix the guns if you keep yourself and a support team on the engines?" Gerard asked. "And go with option two? No matter what happens, we should have another twenty-odd days."

"Hundred sixty, hundred seventy hours to first gun," the Blust concluded. "An additional fifty after that to finish them all. But it would take seven days with only sixteen main guns."

"We should have plenty of time," the Captain decided. "That's your approach, Kralnir. Engines remain our priority. I want to get *out* of Centauri—and that means we need to lift this ship out of the gas giant's phase boundary."

The phase boundary was both their curse and their rescue right now. Even if a Council fleet avoided the star's phase boundaries, the gas giant alone had a thirty-light-second phase boundary. The Council couldn't sneak up on them—but they couldn't escape, either.

Not until they had the battleship's main engines online. She'd edged herself *into* this orbit with her fusion rockets, but she didn't have the fuel to get herself *out*—and Gerard's people were too busy *fixing* her to get that fuel.

They needed to leave Centauri.

"Once we can move, our options open up dramatically," Gerard told his people. "We'll fight if we have to, but we have weeks until we're likely to need to. So, we fix the engines."

Kralnir sighed and shivered his tentacles.

"There is one option," he admitted. "One *Likira* makes possible, but it will be neither fast nor easy."

"But it will work?" Gerard asked. "What is it?"

"If we restrict our repairs to using the working fabrication shops on *Excalibur*, *Likira*'s shops can build gravitic-drive nodes," the Blust told him. "It will *not* be fast, but we may be able to provide some basic maneuverability in fifty to sixty hours."

Gerard grimaced. He doubted *Likira* had the ability to fabricate nodes capable of sustaining military power levels. The tech in *Excalibur* might be backward by Council standards, but it would fall somewhere between *Likira*'s civilian engines and a proper warship in power levels.

"What do we lose?" he finally asked.

"I am uncertain," Kralnir admitted. "I will need to do balance calculations, but it is possible that we can install an entire new set of nodes—sufficient, at least, for a sustained half millicee per second and maybe fifty millicee safe velocity—while leaving *Excalibur*'s existing drives intact for future repairs."

"We could mount them on the exterior of the ship," Vollan

suggested. "They'd be vulnerable to incoming fire, but they'd be fast to install."

"This is true," Kralnir said slowly. "We might even be able to provide basic maneuverability faster than I thought. We must do some analysis," he repeated. "And that will be work that takes hands from the guns."

"I *want* phase cannon, Kralnir," Gerard replied. "We *need* gravitic engines. Do what you have to and let me know."

He might regret handing the engineers that kind of blank check— but if it gave the battleship engines, he didn't think he'd regret it very much.

CHAPTER

TWELVE

Gerard should have known his people's luck wasn't going to give them the time they needed. Humanity's luck hadn't been that good in the last fifty years or so—why would it have changed now?

He was sleeping when the alert hit, an alarm in the luxuriously furnished Captain's quarters catapulting him to his feet. It took him a second to remember where he was. The bed was too soft, the floor was carpeted—nothing about the space triggered as *home* for a few seconds.

"Lights," he ordered, wincing as his leg registered its opinion of his abrupt rising. The alarm was still blaring, and he swallowed an angry snarl.

"Computer, receive call, audio only," he snapped. There was a shipsuit by his bed, but the comfort level of the bed had led to a bit of self-indulgent luxuriating. He wasn't dressed and he didn't need his people to see his nakedness.

"Arkanis, it's Lirrow," the Rowwlan officer greeted him the moment the channel opened. "We have multiple phase emergences at the one-light-minute mark—the opposite side from the last force."

Gerard swallowed hard. It had been less than three days! There was no way the Council could have sent a force to check in on their missing ships yet!

"Any idea what we're looking at?" he asked, keeping his voice calm and professional as he began to dress.

"Closer in than last time, so we've got a good look," Lirrow told him, something in her tone telling him she was half-consciously stalling. She mewled a long sigh. "Arkanis, we're looking at a battleship flock. Four ships, one of them at least forty megatons."

The *Terran* definition of *battleship* had required smelting down an asteroid twice *Excalibur*'s final size to provide the raw materials. She was fifty times the size of the Council battleship—a ridiculous level of overkill if the ton-for-ton tech level had been comparable.

Except the tech level wasn't comparable. With the phase cannon, *Excalibur* should have been able to take on a "mere" ten Council battleships...except that theory involved the Terran ship being able to maneuver and having all of her guns.

"Do they see us?" Gerard asked.

"I don't think they're going to have great detail, but yes," his Rowwlan friend said quietly. "They're not going to see much more than power signatures—the same shielding that confused us will work against them—but they know there's something where we are and that something is powered."

"They can't know about the cruiser flight," he murmured, then shook his head. It didn't matter.

"I'll be on the bridge in two minutes," he promised. "Please tell me you took us to battle stations?"

"Of course," she confirmed. "I'm just...not sure what good it's going to do. They'll have transmitted by now. The Council knows we're here."

"That battleship still isn't enough to take us out," Gerard told her. "And if Kralnir's idea works, we're going to be somewhere before anyone else gets here."

But then...he hadn't expected *this* force. He'd misestimated something somewhere. With *Excalibur*'s guns half-disabled and her engines offline...

His people were in danger and Gerard Arkanis wasn't sure he was ready for this yet.

∾

"ANY UPDATES?" Gerard asked as he entered the bridge, limping down the right-hand ramp toward the command chair.

Getting to the bridge in two minutes had required a pace that his leg wasn't truly capable of. He was going to pay for that rush later, but right now he sank into the Captain's seat with an unconcealed sigh of relief.

He tried not to draw attention to his disability, but sometimes he just could not care if his people realized he couldn't actually run or even walk quickly. Today, there were higher priorities.

"They've been deploying what look like sensor drones," Lirrow told him crisply.

More people were filtering into the bridge as they spoke, the battleship waking up again as her enemies once more challenged her.

"Spreading out to get a wider telescope," Gerard guessed. "It's a trick we've used a few times to get details on a salvage field." He shook his head. "Are they going to be able to identify *Excalibur*?"

"That depends on whether they know it exists, boss," Newell replied as he took his own seat. "The Council's largest flag carriers are only a quarter of our mass. I suspect the only reason Terra could even build *Excalibur* was that they were building the arkships at the same time.

"I'm not aware of anything else in Council space that matches her size."

That also explained why Sol's defenders hadn't had any ships of a size somewhere between the five-megaton cruisers and the billion-ton battleship. *Excalibur* was effectively a warship built on an arkship chassis.

"So, once they resolve our size, they know everything we're trying to hide," Gerard concluded. "That's…unfortunate."

He checked the range. The Council battleship and her escorts had moved closer but not much. They were in a trailing orbit forty light-seconds away, well outside the range of the weapons available to either side.

"What are you expecting, my friend?" Gerard murmured, studying the icons on the screen. "You know there's something here...and I doubt you're here by coincidence."

There were no Medari among *Excalibur*'s or *Likira*'s crews now. There were four in the brig, transferred over to the battleship along with another half-dozen prisoners, but they weren't going to help him sort out how a Medari thought.

Both of his ships were badly undercrewed. If he'd had the ten thousand hands *Excalibur* was supposed to, a lot of the repairs would have gone *much* faster.

"I don't suppose we have any details on just *what* a Council battleship has for guns?" he asked aloud.

"Some intelligence files in *Excalibur*'s computers," Newell said. "Particle beams, long-focal gamma ray lasers, gravitic missiles. Best estimate the PUNSF had put their missile and particle beam range at fifteen light-seconds."

"But there is nothing stopping them just lobbing rocks at us," Gerard said grimly. He shook his head and tapped a com channel.

"Kralnir, I don't suppose you have a miracle under your cloak?"

"We are still two hours from completing fabrication of the first wave of nodes," the engineer told him. "That is assuming I remain aboard *Likira* and continue to focus on the task rather than providing support to *Excalibur*'s engineering crew."

"Keep on that, yes," Gerard agreed. "I may have made the wrong call on the guns, Kralnir, but it seemed like the right call at the time."

Their core power network was now guaranteed solid, but it was only feeding sixteen primaries. It *should* be enough.

"If we are prepared to accept risks, I may be able to get the drive online faster...once the nodes have been fabricated," Kralnir said. "I can do nothing for the guns."

"I know. Thank you." Gerard shook his head. "Keep me informed. So far, these buggers are just sitting there."

The channel dropped and *Excalibur*'s Captain leaned back in his seat.

"They're testing us," he said aloud. "And I don't like it."

"Boss?" Newell asked.

"They've set up at double the range of a phase cannon," Gerard pointed out. "They know we engaged the other cruiser flight at standard range. They know the other cruiser flight didn't see us, so they came in on the opposite side to make sure they did.

"They've got to figure we see them, but they're sitting there, outside weapons range, getting the best data they can." He shook his head. "They're testing to see how we engage with a clear threat. Can we maneuver? Can we fire at extended ranges? Do we have escorts to send out?"

"And the answer to all those questions is no," Newell said. "So…if they're testing us, that flock is bait."

Gerard hadn't followed the thought to that, but he nodded grimly.

"Fuck," he swore. "That means there's at least another battleship flock out there…and if someone is using a *battleship* as bait, they have a carrier."

The quiet in the bridge took on an entirely new tone.

"Can we fight a carrier?" Lirrow asked.

"Secondaries and antimissile beams," Gerard replied. "How many are online?"

"We have eighty-seven secondary phase cannon," Newell said instantly. "Lirrow? You've been tracking the antimissile systems."

"We're at forty-three percent capacity for antimissile systems," she told him. "Just over four thousand lasers."

"This ship was built to face carrier fleets," Gerard reminded them all. "Those lasers will handle gravitic missiles and drones from carrier parasites. The secondary phase cannon can hit the frigates that are handling close-range drone and missile-fire support, so long as we can get a solid bead."

He looked at the big tactical display and exhaled.

"How many sensor drones do we have out?" he asked.

"Six," Lirrow told him. "One at each cardinal point of the gas giant."

"Deploy as many as we can," Gerard ordered. "I want a sphere around the entire gas giant at twenty light-seconds. We need real-time or near-real-time targeting data to hit frigates with phase cannon—and by the homeworld they took from us, we are going to kill those frigates."

THIRTEEN

"Missile launch."

Lirrow's report was quiet, landing in the silence of the bridge like a falling anvil.

"Battleship and cruisers have all launched missiles," she continued. "Estimate fifteen hundred inbound. They'll run out of power at fifteen light-seconds and make their final approach on retained velocity."

"We can handle them, yes?" Gerard asked.

"I'd be a lot happier with the two hundred and fifty-six defensive gunners this ship is supposed to have," Lirrow admitted. "Not to mention the ten thousand defensive lasers, the decoy and sensor drones, the electronic warfare suite…"

"Lirrow," Gerard said grimly.

"We can handle them," she confirmed. "We might have to take a few hits on the shield, but it is at least *up*."

Gerard glanced at Kerim Chadwick, the young man holding down Vollan's station. The youth gave him a thumbs-up despite his stressed look.

"What are we at for shields, Chadwick?" he asked.

"Forty-six percent," the dark-skinned tech reported. "It's…fragile. We're not sure how well we'll be able to regenerate the phase shield."

"It'll have to do," Gerard said, watching as the missiles reached their fifteen-light-second powered range and the gravity signatures disappeared. They were still moving at half the speed of light, though, which meant they were still surprisingly visible.

"Lirrow?" he asked.

"Courses are dialed in. Commencing countermissile fire in ten seconds."

As Lirrow had warned, they didn't have the battleship's electronic warfare systems online. Basically, every secondary system had been ignored in the focus on the guns and shields. They *did* have the sensor drones, though, giving her better data on the incoming missiles.

And with their engines burnt out, the incoming missiles couldn't evade the battleship's defenses. Thousands of defensive installations emerged from behind concealed plates in *Excalibur*'s armor, turrets the size of houses aligning on their targets.

For a moment, the lines the computer drew in overwhelmed the main tactical display. Then the system adjusted, laying them in as duller lines behind the tactical icons.

Gerard watched silently as the Council missiles hurtled in. Even one of those missiles would have killed *Likira*. Traveling at half the speed of light, they didn't even need warheads. Their mass and depleted-uranium tips would wreck anything they hit.

Against *Excalibur*'s defenses, even with them barely half-online, those missiles seemed to almost melt away. Hundreds of them died as Lirrow's hands flickered across her screens, allocating lasers and triggering ECM drones. For a moment, he even thought she would get them all.

Then the ship shivered underneath him and red warning icons flashed up on his displays.

"Seven hits," Chadwick reported grimly. "Shields held. We're rebalancing now, but our average power is down to barely thirty percent." The youth shook his head. "We could probably take another round like that...but not two."

"That's what the armor is for, if it comes down to it," Gerard told the engineering tech. "Lirrow, do we have any signs of the rest of our friends?"

"Negative," she told him. "The battleship flock is moving forward, boss. When we didn't dodge… She might think she's got a better chance from closer in."

"Does she?" he asked.

Her cold, purring laugh sent a chill down his spine.

"We have the number on their missiles now," she told him. "If they get into powered range, bigger problem, but if they're sending them in ballistic for more than ten light-seconds, they don't have a chance."

"And what's the powered range on those missiles?" Gerard asked. He thought he remembered, but given the opportunity inherent in it, he wanted to be certain.

"Based off their last salvo, fifteen light-seconds," Lirrow said.

So, they were confident in their ability to survive anything the battleship flock did from farther than twenty-five seconds away.

Gerard's smile was as cold as Lirrow's laugh.

"I'm going to hold you to that ten light-seconds, my friend," he told the Rowwlan. "And they're going to burn."

He turned to Newell.

"We still have no eyes on their support?" he asked. "Are they transmitting?"

"Nothing so far," Newell agreed. "I'm not certain on the phase transmissions, but I'd say they're transmitting at least every four or five minutes. Might be as often as every ninety seconds."

"Full data dump to the flagship, most likely," Gerard agreed. He studied the approaching battleship. "Watch the drones, Harold," he told his first officer. "They're going to try and sneak the carrier in by phasing her at a completely different angle, somewhere they're hoping we don't have covered."

"Battleship is at thirty-two light-seconds and has come to a halt again," Lirrow reported. "The flock has fired. Fifteen hundred twenty-six inbound, same as last time."

Gerard glanced at the numbers.

"Seventeen light-seconds of ballistic. That's more than your ten, Lirrow. Handle it."

"I will," she promised. "They've underestimated how much rust we've knocked off *Excalibur* for you, boss."

"I think they're still guessing what they're facing," he admitted. "They're still testing. Right now…they think they're facing repaired cruisers or some kind of space station assembled from salvage. They don't have a decent visual, not with us this close to the gas giant."

This time, Lirrow's defenses obliterated the salvo. *Excalibur* had been designed to stand off five or six times this much firepower. Even undermanned and half-offline, the battleship could withstand a single battleship flock.

"Their engines are online again," Lirrow reported. "They're keeping their velocity low, only at fifty millicee."

"And no sign of their friends?" Gerard asked.

"Still nothing. We might just be looking at these guys," Newell said.

"We're not," Gerard said grimly. "Lay in the guns. All primaries on the battleship. She might well survive our first salvo—the cruisers definitely will, so let's make sure the big gun goes away.

"Their backup is going to know *exactly* what happened, and we can't get away from them."

He shook his head, watching as the enemy crossed the thirty-light-second line. His sensor data was only four seconds out of date thanks to the drones with their phase transmitters. It would have to be enough.

"Fire at twenty-seven light-seconds," he ordered. "Let's keep some range in reserve. It might be the only chance we've got."

A new countdown appeared in the corner of the screen as the green hexagons once again closed on their targets. Gerard was short a *lot* of guns versus the last fight. There was no chance of a complete sweep now, which meant he needed to focus on making sure the enemy didn't get to fire at a range of their choice.

"Range…now," Newell reported.

Excalibur didn't even shiver this time. These were the guns that had survived full-power shots before, *and* Vollan and Kralnir had checked them over. Sixteen of the main phase cannon fired—and four seconds later, Gerard saw the result.

Seven of their shots had missed. The enemy were maintaining enough evasive maneuvers that he'd expected that. He'd hoped for fewer misses, but it would do. It had to.

Chunks of armor and debris blasted clear of the massive Council warship. *Excalibur's* phase cannon had jumped almost the entirety of the enemy battleship's defenses, and secondary explosions were visible even through drones a million kilometers away.

The cruisers dodged away from their stricken mothership, unsure of what their best course of action was—and *Excalibur's* guns kept recharging.

"Their battleship's drives are still online," Lirrow reported. "She's only got a millicee per second of acceleration, but she is turning to try and open the range. Cruisers have more, but they're holding the range open from her."

"Wise enough, I suppose," Gerard ordered. "Fire on the recharge, Newell."

Two minutes after the first blasts, *Excalibur's* second salvo lashed out. This time, the Council battleship was barely able to maintain any evasive motion...and fourteen hits hammered into her core hull.

The icon vanished on Gerard's main screen. He pulled a visual feed from the drone and nodded in satisfaction as he watched the impact. The big Council ship had just...come apart.

"Cruisers are outside twenty-seven light-seconds and falling back fast," Newell reported. "We should still be able to hit them on the recharge."

"No," Gerard said. "Hold that range in reserve. Let them go. We already know they've told their friends what's going on."

Everyone was trying to lure everyone else into mistakes. What his *enemy* didn't know, however, was that *Excalibur* couldn't be lured into anything with her engines offline. Gerard's ship was staying *right* where she was.

"Kralnir, what's the status on those gravitic-drive nodes?" he asked, hoping for a chance.

"First units are ready to go, last units are in the fabrication cycle," the Blust replied. "Is it safe to send out shuttles?"

"Safer to send out shuttles than to have us stuck here forever," Gerard told him. "Let's go."

FOURTEEN

The phase-transmission update from the cruisers was worse than Kroche had expected. *Aitris*'s Captain had been an old friend, too. Kroche had trusted the Loreesh officer to be careful, and they had been.

And now Noshoisss was dead.

"What am I looking at?" Kroche demanded. "That is not a space station. By the One God's fury, what have the humans done?"

"It is a myth," Shaishess said. "One intelligence no longer includes in their briefing on the sector. You have seen arkships, Lord Lesser Wing. There was a rumor, at the end of the war, that the Terrans had built an arkship-sized warship."

Kroche *had* seen arkships. The Terrans had done a good job of keeping the big evacuation ships away from Council space, but the Council had hunted several down to assess their threat level.

The ships were impressive. Built from the smelted metals of multiple asteroids, they were ten or more kilometers long and massed a billion tons. They were also completely immobile sublight, built beyond the phase boundaries and moved by phase drive only.

The Council had assessed their threat as negligible. Any arkship that drew too much attention to itself was forced to pledge conversion to the One God, but that was only right. It was by the One God's mercy that they continued—and the fact that while the ships themselves were harmless, each was still guarded by phase cannon–equipped cruisers.

The arkship convoys weren't worth the price of destroying them.

But a warship that size…

"It couldn't have been built here, and even the Terrans would have expected a warship to move," he noted. "Their fusion engines would never have sufficed. Only gravitic drives could move that kind of behemoth."

"That might explain why it isn't moving, Lord Lesser Wing," Shaishess suggested. "And why they risked so much to take it. If they could repair her sublight engines, then she would represent a singular threat to the Council."

"She is only one ship, however large," Kroche replied. "And we fight in the light of the One God. Nonetheless." The big Kitni rose to his feet, studying the data from the cruisers. "We have spent enough blood and time *assessing* this enemy.

"If they cannot maneuver, they cannot escape—but we also cannot lure them into a trap. There is a time for patience and cleverness, my warriors.

"That time has passed. *Kaxis* and her flock will phase into the enemy system and maintain a range of thirty-five light-seconds from the gas giant. We will use frigates and long-range missile bombardment to disable the ship.

"Then we will capture her and tear down her technology for the glory of the Council and the One God. The Terrans may have failed to make her move, but I believe the Council Fleet *can*."

Kroche raised his hand, the retractable claw on his wrist snapping out in an age-old gesture.

"We will defeat these mutineers and claim their prize for the One True God," he told them all. "Phase when all are ready."

FIFTEEN

"First node installation is complete," Kralnir reported. "Everything appears good, but there are twenty-nine more to go."

"Any resource or assistance you need, let me know," Gerard replied. "Right now, we're a rat at the bottom of a hole, and we can't even dig deeper. I want to be somewhere else."

"We have as many people aboard the shuttles as will be useful," the Blust engineer replied. "More hands will serve no purpose and may be needed elsewhere."

"I know," Gerard said. "Thank you."

"We are vulnerable out here, my Captain," Kralnir reminded him. "Remember that most of all."

That was the biggest problem now. The cruisers had vanished, but Gerard was waiting for the real attack to arrive. He expected to come under fire sooner rather than later, and he had no idea how he was going to protect the engineers and shuttles working across *Excalibur's* hull.

But their only real chance of escaping all of this was to get the sublight drives online and clear Alpha Centauri B VI's phase boundary. *Excalibur* was at the bottom of a gravity well. Sooner or later, the Council would drop enough rocks to overwhelm their defenses.

"Captain, we have contacts," Lirrow reported sharply.

"Understood. Report," he ordered.

"It's not good," she replied. "I mark ten contacts. Multiple battle-ships...and one seventy-megatonner."

"It could be worse," Gerard told her. "Seventy megatons is a *small* carrier, after all. Range?"

"Coming in at ninety degrees from the ecliptic," she reported. "They were generous with the phase boundary as well. I make the range just over two light-minutes."

"And the cruisers that left are almost certainly over there," Gerard guess. "No games left. Beck, how much maneuverability do we have?"

"Hasn't changed," she told him. "Until we get the new nodes hooked up, we can pull half a millicee for a few seconds. Anything more might break the ship."

"What about maneuvering?" he asked. "Can we rotate the ship?"

"We don't have enough fuel to move her, but we can rotate her, yeah," the black navigator confirmed. "What are you thinking?"

"Keep *Excalibur* between any incoming fire and the current work crews," Gerard ordered. "Whatever it takes. We can take the hits on the shield, even the armor. Those repair shuttles installing the nodes can't."

"I'll coordinate with Kralnir," Beck promised. "We'll keep them as safe as we can."

"Frigate deployment," Lirrow said loudly. "No bombers detected, but I have thirty frigates on the screens." She paused. "I estimate that'll be three thousand parasite drones, but I have no read on them."

"You won't for a while," Gerard replied. "*Excalibur*'s files say they'll keep the drones aboard until the edge of phase-cannon range. After that, any of the frigates can control upward of a thousand drones apiece, so it's a multiply redundant command net."

He considered the screen.

"Given what we've shown them, I'm guessing they'll deploy the drones at twenty-eight light-seconds," he said. "Of course, I don't think the main guns have the track to *hit* the little bastards at full range."

"We can try?" Newell asked.

"No. We let them close and we open up with the secondaries at twenty," Gerard decided. "My guess is that we have a decent chance of wiping out the frigates at that range—and that the drones are a *lot* less dangerous without close command."

AI could only do so much, after all.

"Frigates are inbound at ten millicee per second," Lirrow reported. "I knew they were fast, but damn."

It didn't take long for the frigates to reach their maximum safe velocity, and Gerard watched the distance evaporate at a third of the speed of light.

"I have parasite drone deployment," Lirrow said. "Twenty-eight-point-two light-seconds." She exhaled a long sigh. "Can't validate numbers; there's just too many of the damn things. Three thousand looks about right."

"We're going to have some trouble aiming through them, even with our sensor drones," Gerard noted. "But we'll do what we can. Newell?"

"Their evasive maneuvers are going to be a pain. Our data feed is not *quite* real-time, and when their velocity is shifting by several millicee every second in evasive maneuvers, well… It's not easy, boss."

"The good news is that I don't think anyone over there has any more experience in frigate-versus-phase-cannon combat than we do," Gerard said drily. "Do your best."

"*They* have doctrine and training," Newell pointed out. "*I* have a hundred guns I had never seen one of before a month ago. But I have them outranged…and they're almost *in* range."

"Fire at will," *Excalibur*'s Captain ordered.

The bridge was silent for several seconds, and then the lead frigates crossed the twenty-light-second mark.

"Firing," Newell said calmly.

Again, *Excalibur* didn't even vibrate. If the capacitor-charge icons on Gerard's consoles hadn't suddenly emptied, he might not have been sure her guns had fired—until frigates started vanishing off his screen.

"Multiple hits, multiple hits," Newell said. "Guns on recharge. Estimate…twenty-two targets destroyed."

"Frigates have increased their evasive maneuvers and are breaking off," Lirrow reported. "Enemy drones continuing on. I guess twenty light-seconds' lag is better than sixty?"

"They'll follow them in," Gerard guessed. "They're just trying to block our sensors…I think."

"They do realize our sensors are now *behind* them, right?" Lirrow asked.

"No," he realized. "They don't. I think they either never realized our drones were out there, or everyone has forgotten."

Separating the frigates and parasite drones would shield the frigates from sensors mounted on the battleship, but it actually made the frigates *easier* to target via the phase-transmitter sensor probes *Excalibur* had deployed.

"Come to papa," Newell crooned. "Come on…and *got you.*"

Excalibur's guns flashed again—and this time, the Council drones weren't in position to confuse anything. Over a hundred guns fired at eighteen frigates. The parasite warships weren't big enough to take even one hit from the secondary guns.

"Targets destroyed, frigates are clear," Newell reported. "Their drones are still on course…can they still engage us?"

"Yes," Gerard said grimly. "They've got to be less effective without close control, but…

"They're too small for reliable targeting with the phase cannon," Newell warned. "If they can operate without the frigates… Each of those things has a laser *and* a hundred-megaton warhead."

"Do your best," Gerard ordered. "Let's not underestimate anything."

"Main fleet is moving," Lirrow reported. "I have more drones launching from the carrier—backup units, I guess? Hard to read numbers again, but I'd say at least a thousand."

"I…" Gerard considered. "*I* would cover the capital ships with them and try and close to weapons range," he guessed. "They're out of games, so I'm guessing they're going to try and push through our fire until they can return it."

Looking at the level of firepower heading his way, he knew they could probably manage it. They'd only get three salvos from the primaries and maybe two from the secondaries before the enemy reached their own range.

Without the ability to evade, they couldn't even try to keep the range open.

"Kralnir reports half of the nodes are in place and I'm rotating the ship to keep him covered," Beck said quietly. "Maybe…thirty minutes?"

"We don't have thirty minutes," Gerard admitted. "So, we stand and take it."

"Drones are inside laser range," Lirrow noted. "We are engaging with lasers…and they are firing back."

"Shields are holding," Chadwick reported. "Losing…a quarter-percent per second and we're keeping them balanced. This…might not last."

"Neither will they," the Rowwlan said grimly. "They are charging forward. They may be in suicide mode."

"They would be if I was in command," Gerard admitted. "Do what you can."

The Council missiles had come in at higher velocities, but they hadn't still been evading. The incoming drones *were*, running through preprogrammed evasion routines that Gerard's people had no chance to recognize.

The space between *Excalibur* and the enemy was full of coherent light, and he kept an eye on the shield-strength figure. *Somehow*, Vollan's people were keeping the shields balanced, but it couldn't last forever—and it wouldn't stand up to the parasite drones' suicide charges.

"All hands, brace for impact," he ordered.

Dozens of the drones—possibly more—plunged through everything and dove into Excalibur's armored flanks. Explosions rippled across her surface, and Gerard felt his ship shake around him as new red icons flashed up on his displays.

"We just lost two primaries and half a dozen secondaries," Newell reported grimly. "I *think* they've just been knocked around, but there's no way to tell. The main fleet will be in range in ten minutes."

"Arkanis, it's Kralnir." The Blust engineer had a direct line to Gerard's command channel at this point. His mission was as important as anything else.

"Give me good news," Gerard asked. He was on the edge of begging.

"We're down to the last three nodes and everything *looks* right," the Blust told him. "That's the good news."

Gerard blinked.

"What happened?"

"We lost two nodes to the incoming fire. We should have extras on *Likira* now. I am taking two shuttles back to retrieve them." The Blust paused. "Cover us, if you can."

"Enemies are firing missiles," Lirrow said softly. "Numbers non-assessable at this range. Minimum four thousand."

"You don't have long, Kralnir," Gerard warned.

"I will be quick."

IMMENSE AS *EXCALIBUR* was by any rational measure, there were forces even she could not shrug aside. Lirrow's team had come up to speed far faster than Gerard had any reason to hope, but the massed missile launchers of six cruisers, three battleships, and a carrier were beyond what they could deal with.

Dozens of missiles hammered into the battleship, and Gerard *felt* the ship lurch under the impacts.

"Shields are down," Chadwick reported grimly. "We're cycling emitters and the armor has mostly held, but we have multiple sections open to space."

"Hostiles are not slowing," Lirrow said. "They will enter main gun range in one minute."

Gerard's attention riveted to another set of icons. There were work shuttles on every side of *Excalibur* now, with teams working on the last of the original installations and now Kralnir working on replacing the two nodes taken out by the drones.

They'd been lucky in the missile salvo. They'd taken hits, but both the shuttles and the nodes had gone unscathed.

"Beck, is there any way we can cover the shuttles better?" he asked.

"We could only cover Kralnir by uncovering the others," she admitted. "And…they're all scheduled to finish at the same time."

"We're covering them as best as we can," Lirrow told him. "I can't stop us taking hits, but I *can* control where we're hit."

"Do we fire at extreme range, boss?" Newell asked. "It looks like they're coming *into* range, but I can't guarantee kills on anything except the cruisers."

Gerard closed his eyes as he desperately tried to math out the scenario. They could guarantee kills on the cruisers, but each cruiser only had a third of the launchers of any of the capital ships.

"Target the cruisers, two at a time," he finally ordered, hoping it was the right call. "Open fire at…"

A moment of indecision hit, indecision that would haunt him for a *long* time.

"They're firing!" Lirrow snapped.

"Return fire," Gerard snapped. "Maximum rate, hit them with everything we've got as fast as we can. Kill the cruisers first, get those launchers out of the fight!"

Seven heavy phase cannon per cruiser should be enough for guaranteed kills. Despite everything, Gerard knew he could batter the hell out of the people coming at him. He just wasn't sure he could do it fast *enough*.

Even ballistic missiles were a threat in the volume the Council carrier flock was hurling his way. The only "good" news was that it took ninety seconds to reload those launchers, almost as long as it took to cycle his primary cannon.

The deaths of the two closest cruisers had made an impression, he noted. The formation was adjusting now—he was losing accurate imagery on his targets, and he grimaced as he recognized that this opponent *had* fought phase cannon before.

There were enough veterans of the war that they had to meet one eventually. He'd hoped there wasn't one here—but now, as it came down to the final push, it was clear that there was at least one.

"We've got it," Kralnir snapped. "Last node is booting. You'll have maneuvering in sixty seconds, Captain Arkanis."

Gerard looked at the cascade of incoming fire. *Any* significant acceleration would render the ballistic salvos meaningless and turn the tide of the battle…except that the incoming fire was going to land in forty-five seconds.

"Arkanis—*Likira!*"

"And you'll still have your ship," the Blust said calmly as Gerard's attention snapped to the screen and the icon of the salvage ship. "I'm afraid I didn't leave *Likira* when I was supposed to, my friend, and there isn't anyone else left on this ship but robots."

They'd need every hand they could get. The only people on *Likira* had been the fabrication teams, and Gerard suddenly *knew* that Kralnir had sent those away on the shuttles. The salvage ship had been in a lower orbit, well protected from the enemy by the big battleship—but she had five millicee per second of acceleration and *Excalibur* had none.

The salvage ship swept out in front. She was a smaller vessel by an order of magnitude, but Kralnir knew the missiles weren't accelerating anymore and where they were coming from, and he threw the salvage ship at them.

Likira's meteor defense system wasn't designed to stop missiles. Her armor and phase shielding were light. Her anti-meteor lasers were toys. Gerard wouldn't have expected her to survive a single missile.

Somehow, she swept away over two thousand, clearing a path through the salvo that could have doomed *Excalibur*.

Her death throes vaporized more. Gerard would never be sure how many missiles made it past Kralnir's sacrificial charge, but *none* of them made it past Lirrow…and then *Excalibur* shivered beneath him.

"Secondary gravitic drive online," Hillary Beck said quietly. "I can't guarantee how *much* accel we've got, but we are moving."

"Take us around Six, away from the Council ships," Gerard ordered. "Newell, sustained fire on that carrier. We've pissed them off and I'm betting they'll come after us with everything they've got."

CHAPTER

SIXTEEN

Kroche leaned back in his chair and grunted in anger as he watched the Terran ship start moving. The sacrifice play of the other ship had gutted his last chance at a ballistic kill, and another pair of his cruisers died as he watched.

"Full reverse, all ships," he ordered sharply. "Get us of out that thing's range."

"My lord?" Shaishess replied.

"*Obey*," Kroche snapped.

Only when the fleet was hurtling backward from the enemy, their sudden reversal leaving most of a phase-cannon salvo to impact empty space, did he relax and look at his serpentine chief of staff.

"What is their acceleration?" he asked calmly.

"We're reading two point three millicee per second," Shaishess reported. "They cannot outrun us."

"They *can* put a gas giant between them and us for the next thirty minutes," Kroche pointed out. "They *can* extend the time period where we are in range of the fury of those long-range phase cannon and we are not in range of our weapons. So long as they can maneuver, we cannot hit them with ballistic missiles."

He shook his jowls in an emphatic *no*.

113

"This battle cannot be won, Shaishess. We have spent blood and time we could not afford, and I will spend no more of the lives of the worshippers of the One God without *purpose*.

"Patience, my brothers," he said more loudly. "We did not know our enemy and we have laid our mark on them. We will shadow them until they leave this system, and we will call the greater fleets of the Council.

"They will be hunted like prey across all the stars by the true worshippers of the One God, and while they may evade us today, they will not escape His fury. Patience," he repeated.

It was easier for him than many of his crew, he knew, but he also knew he was correct. They *might* be able to cripple or destroy the Terran ship, but he would lose most of his fleet.

"This is not mercy, my enemy," he murmured, quietly enough that no one could hear him. "Nor is it victory. I deny us both a final victory today—and I have reinforcements to gather from five thousand suns.

"You have nothing. No one to gather and nowhere to hide."

Kroche would be patient today, but he had faith in E'tek. This strange human ship's liberty would be short-lived.

CHAPTER

SEVENTEEN

"We scared them off!"

Newell's joyful shout echoed through the bridge. Gerard let the cheers that followed wash over him, even as he watched the position of the enemy ships.

They were going to follow *Excalibur* and try to identify her phase destination. That was fine. Gerard could already see ways to avoid that.

"You seem unimpressed," Lirrow half-whispered. She'd stepped onto the command dais and *also* wasn't joining in the celebration.

"We're moving but we're slow," he told her. "Now they've broken off, they won't bother following us. The call about who we are and what *Excalibur* is will soon spread. They will gather a hunting fleet and none of these stars will be safe."

"I know," she told him. "And I'm afraid of what comes next, Gerard. We've lost friends…but we *live*."

"Then why are *you* unimpressed?" he asked in turn.

She bared her fangs.

"Victory yanked from our teeth at the final moment is never a good taste," she said. "*You*, however, must sell this to the crew *as* a victory. We now have gravity drives. We have a phase drive. We will have

115

enough time to repair the ship…but I do not know what the plan is now, Gerard Arkanis.

"The Council burns worlds and breaks races, and the galaxy turns. Nothing changes. Nothing ever has. One ship, however mighty, cannot change this."

"Then why are you here?" he asked. "You are as much a part of our victory as anyone else."

"I am a fatalist," Lirrow told him. "But that does not mean I am without hope. And I look at you and I believe you have a plan. That you have an answer. You've held it like a protected kitten till now…but this is the last barricade, Arkanis. Everyone here has stood with you, but soon they will begin to wonder.

"If you have a plan, you must share it. People need hope."

Gerard nodded and bowed his head slightly to her.

"I agree. Thank you." He considered for a moment, then held out a hand to his friend. "Help me stand? I don't think I should sit for this—and I think needing someone else is going to make a handy point."

The black-furred Rowwlan chuckled but helped him stand, positioning his arm on her shoulder to keep him upright despite his knee.

"Look to me," Gerard ordered loudly. "Ship, project me to everyone."

The bridge crew turned their attention on him, and he felt the light of several pickups focus on him as he leaned on his friend.

"My friends, my family," he told them. "We are victorious. The Council Fleet has refused to press on to the last, and we are on our way to safety. We will enter phase in twenty minutes, carrying this ship to at least temporary safety.

"We have faced an entire carrier flock of the Council Fleet, and we have not only survived but we have done everything we needed to," he continued. "That *is* a victory, even if I think they will claim otherwise.

"But well-begun is only half-done!" He gestured with his free hand. "You know me. You know I can only walk short distances. I cannot stand to give a speech on my own—but with Lirrow's help, I can stand for you.

"*We* cannot stand against the Council alone. Even with *Excalibur* as our blade, we cannot defy *five thousand suns*."

The bridge was quiet. He suspected the whole ship was silent.

"But we are victorious today, *and that is a beginning!*"

That brought back the cheers and he grinned with his people—and slid his free hand into his jacket and removed a copy of the Project Respite disk.

He'd made three. The original was in the Captain's safe. One was in a safe in Engineering, a mystery box that his officers knew to open if something happened to him. The last had been aboard *Likira,* in a similar safe.

"But to fight on, we cannot stand alone." He held the disk in his fingers as he studied his people. "The humans among you know the legend of *Excalibur* and the sword in the stone. You know what was written upon that blade: *Whoso pulleth out this sword of this stone and anvil, is rightwise king born.*

"We have pulled this sword from the stone of Alpha Centauri. We must be a banner for all humanity—and for all others who would stand against the Council. Will you follow me in that course? As your Captain—your leader, your marshal?"

Your King went unspoken. That was a challenge for a later day, but he suspected they all heard the words regardless.

The cheer seemed to shake the entire ship, and Gerard Arkanis raised the Project Respite disk.

"Among the gifts *Excalibur*'s crew left us is this," he told them. "The only intact Project Respite disk I know of. We have access to a phase channel that will reach every arkship, every remaining Terran warship.

"We have a symbol to call them to—and once they are gathered, we have a secret haven to take them to. A place where we can rebuild and find other allies, other weapons, that can be turned against the Medari Sacred Council."

If nothing else, he suspected that the other arkships could be converted into battleships to rival *Excalibur.*

"We are the symbol," he told them. "We will send the word for them to gather with us at the only place humanity could ever gather: Earth. Our message will be very simple:

"*Excalibur is risen. The time is now. Gather home.*"

FIRE, STEEL & PETROLEUM
A DIESELPUNK SHORT STORY

FIRE, STEEL &
PETROLEUM

A DIESELPUNK SHORT STORY

The big twin-cylinder motorbike was done. Afageon knew it just looking at where he'd propped the vehicle up when it had guttered to a stop.

The smell of iron and petroleum flickered through the air—and so did the drifting smell of smoke from the village behind him. There was no blood or flesh in that smoke.

So far.

One of the big trucks rolled back down the gravel road, and a grizzled old woman—the mayor, Afageon thought—jumped down.

He hadn't had time to collect names. Things had moved too quickly. Even *he* was feeling it, and he could see it in the woman's eyes.

"There's still plenty of fuel in the trucks," she told him loudly, following his gaze to the fallen bike.

"It's the wrong purity," Afageon replied. She knew that too. She hadn't lived under the guardianship of Knights like Afageon for this long without knowing that. "Engine would seize up before we made it a league."

He pulled the stubby carbine from the saddle holster and ejected the magazine. Only six rounds left. Afageon had fired off the rest before he'd even reached the village. He reseated the magazine.

"I don't suppose your people have any four-seven ammo?" he asked.

"Not a rifle in town would fire that, Sir Knight," the mayor told him. "And…well, we haven't had a gunsmith in a bit. We're mostly out of huntin' rounds at that. We've half a dozen shotguns, maybe two dozen shells for all of them."

The Knight nodded heavily.

"Get me the best shotgun and half the shells, ma'am," he told her. "Then you get your people up on those trucks and you drive north.

"You drive until you hit the Keep at Chatham, or till you run out of fuel. If you run out of fuel, you walk. If anyone falls, you carry 'em. You get me, ma'am?"

"I'll get you the shottie," she promised. "But…surely you'll ride with us, Sir Knight?"

"Trucks can't outrun raiders on bikes, even raider bikes," Afageon told her. "No, ma'am, I will remain and hold the road."

There was a long silence. Somewhere in the village, a fuel tank exploded.

"They'll come for you."

Afageon checked his sword and the carbine and smiled at her.

"I am a Knight of Cadrellion," he told her. "By fire and steel and petroleum, they shall not pass."

THE RAIDERS GAVE him a tenth of a day by his watch, time Afageon spent digging up the road with his folding shovel. They'd go around it easily enough, but it would slow them down. It gave him time.

It let him shoot the leader before they ever saw him. The man, clad in a mismatched collection of leather and scrap metal, seemed to freeze in position before sliding sideways off *his* bike—a rusted twin-cylinder machine that had probably once belonged to a Knight like Afageon.

He racked the slide on the carbine and fired into the bike's gas tank. It wouldn't explode, but even raiders knew to watch for sparks and fuel and fire.

Engines screamed in the moonlit night as a dozen motorbikes

careened away from their leader's body. A third of Afageon's precious four-seven bullets cracked into the bike of the first raider to turn around.

A miss. Even a Knight couldn't land every shot, not in the dark like this.

His bike could do him one last service. He flicked the lever that brought up its powerful arc light, highlighting the gang on the gravel road as he stepped forward and bellowed the words every raider within a hundred leagues of here had to know and fear.

"I am a Knight of Cadrellion! By fire and steel and petroleum, these lands are protected. Turn back or die!"

A hail of gunfire answered, bullets smashing into the dirt around the bike Afageon was already walking away from.

He didn't miss with his fourth bullet, a second raider falling from their bike. The others swiftly dismounted, taking cover behind their vehicles from a shooter they couldn't detect in the dark.

The borrowed shotgun was heavy on his shoulder, his sword a familiar weight at his side. This dozen was only the scouting party. Even if he scared them off, there would be five times as many in town.

All he could ever do here was buy time.

"Cadrellion will burn!" one of the raiders shouted back. "And her raggedy knights with h—"

Five bullets down, but another hail of fire swept through Afageon's position and he hadn't moved fast enough this time. His tabard and hauberk were reinforced, but they were intended to protect him from a fall, not bullets.

He stifled a scream of pain as fire burned through his arm and shoulder. He tried to lift his carbine properly to take another shout and bit down more pain.

One-handed it was. Even a Knight of Cadrellion was going to have problems hitting like that.

It was dark again, a final raider bullet finally having put out his bike's light—and the raiders' bikes didn't have the batteries to have light with the engines off. The moon gave enough light for him and the raiders to continue their dance, but it could only end one way now.

Nine of them. One of him.

His last four-seven went wide, his one-handed firing stance unable to support the carbine enough, and he discarded the heavy weapon and hugged the ground under the raiders' response.

They seemed far more casual with ammunition than most. He'd noticed that before, though. This group was well-equipped. Either a captured gunsmith or *something* meant they weren't worried about their bullets.

Afageon pulled himself to the pile of dirt where he'd dug up the road. That gave him a rest for the shotgun as he unslung it. With only one usable hand, he wasn't going to be able to reload the double-barreled gun, but that was what it came down to.

"I smell blood," one of the raiders shouted. "Yer bleeding out, knight. Come on out and we'll make it quick. Make us find you…and we won't."

He didn't have a clear shot at the speaker. He could line the shotgun up on a couple of the laughing companions, but… The buck-shot would spread handily, but it wouldn't do much against even raider leathers at any range. He needed them to get closer.

"Why don't you come and find out the *steel* part of the oath means, chucklehead?" Afageon shouted back.

That got him more laughter—and more bullets, several definitely landing in the shallow pile of dirt in front of them.

But the raiders were now moving toward him, moonlight glinting off rusted scrap metal in their armor and he judged it as carefully as he could.

"Come out, come out, mister knight," the apparent new leader chortled. "I though you were a hero, not a mou—"

With even a moment's hindsight, Afageon knew firing both barrels at the man had been a waste. The raider went down like a sack of wet potatoes, but now Afageon was out of bullets. He couldn't even break open the shotgun with his left arm hanging uselessly at his side.

He shifted to reach his sword. He'd already given a good account of himself and bought the villagers time. Surrender wouldn't even buy him a quick death at this point, which meant there was only one way for a Knight of Cadrellion to go down.

The remaining raiders were spreading out in silence now. They'd guessed where he was, and they were done taunting. They knew their work, even if he'd made it as hard for them as he could, and they guessed he had cover of some kind.

The moonlight would betray him if they got the right angle. He was out of time and swallowed hard against a spike of fear.

A Knight of Cadrellion was *expected* to fear. They were *expected* to recognize their risks and enemies.

And they were expected to do what was necessary regardless.

By fire and steel and petroleum, this land is guarded!

His sword was in his hand and his time was up—and then one of the raiders stopped.

"Listen!" she hissed. "*Engines.*"

Afageon heard them a moment later—the distinctive sound of perfectly tuned big twin-cylinder motorcycles. At least a dozen of them.

"Fall back on the town," the woman snapped. "We were to catch villagers, not fight a flying wing of Knights!"

The others fell back quickly toward their bikes, but the woman remained for a moment, clearly looking roughly where Afageon was lying hidden.

"Not bad, Sir Knight," she whispered, barely loud enough for him to hear her. "Might kill you another night. You might kill me then, too. Today…today you get lucky."

She strode back to her bike and was gone in a blink of an eye, the only remaining sound and presence that of Afageon's sibling-Knights riding to the rescue—as the Knights of Cadrellion were sworn to do.

By fire and steel and petroleum!

BALEFIRE
A DARK FANTASY NOVELLA

BALEFIRE

A DARK FANTASY NOVELLA

Alsan remembered the balefire. He wasn't supposed to, but images of blue-white fire wiping away his world still haunted his dreams more often than he preferred.

The Church of the Intercessor would probably have preferred he *didn't* remember, but the gaunt-looking knight felt it was better this way. It was his task to decide whether to condemn a village to balefire to drive back the forces of the Abyss or to attempt to save it.

Only the Intercessor Themself had spared his life when a demon had infested his childhood home. His village had vanished in the destructive magic of the Inquisition's balefire—and if anyone was to condemn another village to that fate, Alsan felt that it should be someone who had lived through it.

It wasn't like the balefire was the only horror that haunted his sleep or waking thoughts, and many of those images were in his head as he rode up to the blockade across the road. A dozen local militia blocked the roughly cleared path, all of them wearing red bandanas to mark that they had been drafted by the Intercessor for this duty.

"Where is the Wardpriest?" he asked the woman wearing the high-est-quality armor. If she *wasn't* in charge, he'd eat his own armor—and it wasn't like militia bothered with insignia.

"Dey over there," the militiawoman replied, gesturing toward a tent in the middle of the road a few dozen yards farther up. "Watching the stone."

"Thank you," Alsan said with a bow of his head.

"You the paladin?" she asked.

"By the Intercessor's grace," he confirmed.

"Can you save them?" she said. "I've a cousin who married into Redgarton."

"I don't know yet," Alsan admitted. "That's why I have to talk to the Wardpriest."

The local nodded grimly. She clearly didn't *like* his answer, but there was understanding there. It was the best Alsan could hope for.

He rode past the militia. His skin tingled under his armor as he approached the tent, and he'd have known the runestone anchoring the ward was under the cloth even without the warning from the militia.

"Wardpriest," he called out as he dismounted. "The Intercessor sends aid."

He waited for dem to respond, checking over his armor and gear. Riding, he only wore the breastplate and greaves of his armor harness, but the vambraces and gauntlets and helmet were on his horse.

"Sir Paladin," the priest finally greeted him as dey stepped out of the tent. Dey looked haggard, deir traditional gray robe askew and stained with dirt. "Your arrival is welcome. I fear for the people of this town."

"That is always our duty," Alsan replied. He tugged on one buckle, making sure the weight of his gear was evenly distributed on his horse, then gave the animal a reassuring pat.

"It is *also* our duty to fear for everyone around them," he continued. "The ward is solid?"

"Four roads into the village," the Wardpriest confirmed. "One of us on each road, two more in the farmlands to fill out the circle. We... cannot guarantee that none of the infected escaped."

"We never can," Alsan admitted. "You should be able to tell if the *demon* escaped, however."

"*Something* is inside the barrier," dey said. "The ward strains."

"Good. And the balefires?"

There was a long silence and they both looked at the tent. The rune-stone anchoring the ward had another purpose. The Wardpriest had very little power of deir own—dey were neither Sealed nor Sanctified, neither protected from Abyssal influence nor able to wield the Intercessor's power—but the runestones were made by Mages working in the city guilds.

And if those Mages were anything like the priests of the Intercessor sent to deal with demons, they wept over their work every day.

"They are ready," the Wardpriest told him. "Is that..." Dey swallowed. "Is that your order?"

"Not yet," Alsan replied gently. "But I have to know if we are ready to unleash them."

He studied the invisible barrier rippling out from the runestone in its tent. Unlike the Wardpriest, Alsan *was* both Sealed and Sanctified. Abyssal influence would wash off him like water off a duck, and he could wield the Intercessor's Grace to heal others.

He could also feel the ward, a spherical barrier some two leagues across. That it was truly spherical had proven critical on one hunt of his, when an Akacha demon had tried to dig under the ward.

The Akacha were creatures of fear and knowledge, in some ways the most dangerous of the infiltrators the Abyss sent into the world.

"What do we know?" he finally asked the Wardpriest.

"The town healer encountered a strange illness five days ago," dey told him. "Within a day, she had ten victims. She sent a runner to the abbey for a Priest-Mendicant. The abbess sent three—and the senior of them sent up a red flare within half a day of arriving."

Alsan nodded, hiding the pain that sentence gave him. The Intercessor's priests carried a series of small colored rockets, designed to send messages at a distance without requiring anyone to approach.

Given the infectious nature of the Abyss, it was a necessary tool—but the Priest-Mendicant would have known that a red flare would lead to exactly this situation. If Alsan hadn't been within a few days' ride, the Abbess might have been forced to make the call to balefire the village herself.

Without one of the Intercessor's Sealed and Sanctified holy

warriors, all the local priesthood could do was destroy the village and wipe out its people. The balefire *would* kill the demon—but it would also kill everyone and everything else inside the ward.

"What do you know about the illness?" he asked.

"I spoke with the senior Mendicant through the ward a day ago," dey said quietly. "Manifests as dehydration initially, then the skin cracks into open sores that start weeping pus.

"Only three had died then—but there are at least fifty infected in Redgarton."

"How big *is* the town?" Alsan asked.

"Including the farms we've caught in the ward, about a hundred and forty souls," dey said.

"All right." Alsan turned to study the ward again. "Fifty infected a day ago, you said?"

The Wardpriest nodded.

"If only three have died, we're still likely only looking at one demon," Alsan noted. The Abyss's infiltrators would attempt to open a path for other demons, but it was a slow process that consumed human souls.

There were *other* ways into the world—or there would be far fewer demons all told—but that was the threat.

"What do we do, Sir Paladin?" the Wardpriest asked.

He sighed. "What is your name?" he asked dem.

"Korian, sir."

"Korian," Alsan addressed dem. "We have a chance. If I can find and kill the demon swiftly enough, we can save everyone still living."

He turned back to his horse and considered the animal. She whinnied cheerfully at him, and he patted her mane. If he brought the mare into the ward, she would suffer the same fate as everything else if he failed. She'd earned better than that.

"Help me with my horse, Korian," he instructed the Wardpriest. "I need to decide what equipment I'm taking in with me."

"You're going into the ward?" Korian asked. Dey sounded surprised, despite Alsan having just said he was going to hunt the demon.

"It is the only way," Alsan confirmed. He studied the sky. The sun was at its peak. "Give me until dawn, Wardpriest Korian."

Dey helped him unbuckle his horse's saddle and lower it to the ground, silent as dey considered his words.

"And then what?" Korian finally asked.

Alsan smiled grimly as he laid out his tools. He'd stick with the light harness, just the breastplate and greaves. A silver-edged longsword. Three daggers—one steel, one gold, one rock salt. Only the steel was good for more than one blow, but steel did little to demons.

A silver amulet of the Intercessor's five-pointed star went around his neck, and a set of metal vials went on hooks on his sword belt. If he knew more about what he was facing, there were more esoteric tools in his saddlebags, but they were for very specific types of demons.

Most of whom wouldn't be spreading a plague. The plague limited it to, oh, only about six kinds. All of them awful.

"If I have not returned by dawn," he told Korian as he tightened his belt, "you will send my horse and remaining gear to the monastic fortress at Seven Peaks, where my name will be recorded in the halls of the knights who came before me."

"Sir?"

"Because if I have not returned by dawn, I am dead, and you will balefire Redgarton," Alsan told the Wardpriest calmly.

REDGARTON WASN'T much of a village. That was for the best, in Alsan's opinion. He stood in the road, still a good distance away, surveying the place that hid his enemy.

The two-league circle of the ward likely encompassed at least twenty farms, potentially more. There were no separate farmhouses in a place like this. The farmers' homes were huddled together for protection against the night and wildlife.

A protection that doomed them when the Abyss broke through. Tucked in together, the forty or so houses he could see offered no real way to quarantine the sick or demon-infested. Towns like this would have their secrets, yes, but their populations lived in each other's pockets just as much as any city dweller.

Four larger buildings were placed around the perimeter, each serving triple purpose as homes, businesses, and the bases for the town's watchtowers. If Redgarton was like most villages Alsan had visited, those buildings were the tavern, the general store, the blacksmith, and the Church of the Nine.

Neither of the two outer buildings he could see clearly had the iconography of the Church of the Nine, which meant the church was likely across town. The sick would be there. That was where the healer would have taken them at first—and where the Priests-Mendicant of the Intercessor would have set up when they arrived to help.

He checked the sun again. It was descending from its peak, but he still had most of the afternoon left. His entire task was a race against the time limit he'd set himself, but that was the nature of his duty.

If he didn't succeed, he would die with Redgarton. Whatever divine magic had preserved him from balefire as a babe was insufficient to protect him as an adult. Enough children survived balefire to provide about a quarter of the Intercessor's paladins...and enough of those paladins had called balefire on themselves for Alsan to know those paladins had no greater protection against the Intercessor's final defense than the demons they hunted.

He checked his harness again. Four blades and a thin layer of articulated steel seemed like a frail shield against the power of the Abyss, but he'd walked this path before. This would not be Alsan's first demon.

He was determined that it would not be his last—and that it would not take the village of Redgarton with it. To do *that*, he needed to look at the sick.

The Paladin of the Intercessor said a silent prayer and started walking again.

∼

THERE WAS a clear area in front of the church that Alsan presumed acted as the town square. In normal times, there would be markets and festivals and celebrations there.

Instead, the square was deathly still. A dozen middle-aged men milled around the edges, swinging between confused uncertainty and angry glares at the closed doors of the church.

An older woman sat on the steps in front of those doors, freely returning the glares of her fellows. She wore the traditional blue robes of a healer, with the hand-carved wooden flower of a priestess of the Mother hanging around her neck.

All of the locals' attention turned to Alsan as he approached the church. There was no question as to what and who he was—they couldn't *not* know that the town was warded, and only one type of person was allowed through a ward.

Only one type of person wore steel plate armor inlaid with the pentacle of the Intercessor. Alsan didn't need to introduce himself. His short-cut hair and gleaming armor answered most questions before they were even spoken aloud.

The healer rose to her feet as he approached.

"The Priests-Mendicant have sealed the Church," she told him. "We are trying to prevent the plague from spreading."

"It will spread regardless, I suspect," Alsan said quietly. "Abyssal infection does not play by the normal rules, Sister. I must see the sick."

She studied him and grunted. "What good does it do any of us? Let them rest, Sir Paladin."

"I wield the Intercessor's Grace, Sister," he reminded her. "I can help them. And even if I cannot, by seeing them I may perhaps help the rest of this town. There is always a chance."

The square was still, and he was sure the other villagers could hear him.

"I will not burn a town that can be saved, Sister," he continued. "Let me through."

Neither of them had any illusions about his ability to push the old woman aside. He was as unfooled by her apparent frailty as she was by his gaunt face and lanky frame. If Alsan needed to move the healer aside, he *would*.

But that was not the way of the Intercessor's holy warriors. Nor was it *Alsan's* way.

"It is not my place to bar a paladin of one of the Nine," she finally conceded. "Do what you must and what you can, Brother knight."

"That is both duty and oath, Sister," Alsan assured her.

She stood aside as he strode up the steps, and he could *feel* her anger and fear.

And her guilt. *She* was the one who'd called the Priests-Mendicants, after all. If Korian and deir fellows unleashed their balefires, some would argue that the healer had doomed the town.

Alsan himself would blame the *demon*, but he could understand why the Sister would feel guilty. He had yet to forgive himself for the time he'd arrived too late and had been left with no choice but to unleash balefire.

He was in Redgarton to make certain he never had to give that order again. That thought carried him up the steps and into the church, where the sickly-sweet smell of rotting flesh hit him like a brick to the face.

Carefully built windows brought natural light into the main sanctuary with the shutters open. The lower windows had been closed to seal everything inside, but the others provided enough light for the three Priests working in the space.

They'd discarded their formal robes, likely days earlier, and were clad in a gray tunic and hose familiar to any priest of the Nine. Without the robes, there was no way for Alsan to pick out the senior of the three healers, so he carefully closed the doors behind him and waited for them to notice him.

It didn't take long. The door was only supposed to open to admit the ill, so a stranger was unexpected—and like the villagers, the priests knew that only one type of stranger would enter the village now.

"Sir Paladin?" the leader said as dey finished with deir patient and crossed to Alsan. "I had feared none of your order were close enough to intercede."

"The Intercessor finds ways to bring us where we are needed," Alsan said calmly.

The priest was an older individual, with short-cropped hair and a swirling tattoo around deir eyes that marked their status as one of the dem.

"So They do," the healer agreed. "I am Mket, Priest-Mendicant of the Intercessor. These are Podrei and Bara."

Dey indicated deir companions.

"How bad has it got?" Alsan asked.

"Eleven have died but we still have seventy in here," Mket said grimly. "Our chance to save the town may already be past."

"Perhaps," the paladin agreed. "But I am not giving up yet. If I have not returned by dawn, the Wardpriests will do their duty. I have my own tasks, however, and we must act on the presumption that we can save them all."

"With the infection this widespread, won't we lose many of these souls anyway?" Podrei asked. The dark-haired woman was on her way to another patient with a pitcher of water as she asked, but it was clear both junior priests were listening.

"An Abyssal infection doesn't follow the normal rules," Alsan reminded them. "If we can destroy the source demon, the infection itself will die. Then their sores will heal over time.

"You may still lose some," he conceded. "But most will live if we can find the source."

"Of course," Mket agreed. "Do you need to examine them?"

"Yes," Alsan said. "It is possible I may be able to do something you cannot."

He could tell that none of the three were Sanctified. While their treatments and skills were not *entirely* mundane, most of the power in their working came from others who prepared salves and unguents for them.

"Grace may be the only chance for some of them," Mket agreed. "Come, Sir Paladin."

"My name is Alsan," he told dem quietly. "We will fight this horror together, Dem Mket. Show me the worst of them."

Mket nodded and gestured for Alsan to follow. Dey led the way toward one of the better-lit portions of the church. Where the darker portions held newer patients on rough pallets, the first few patients were in folding cots that had likely been kept in the church's basement.

One of the purposes of a Church of the Nine was to act as an emergency hospice like this, after all.

Their destination was in the center of the sunlight, just in front of the shrine of the Creator.

"Bratax. The town smith," Mket said, gesturing to the man. The size of the man would have suggested that to Alsan even without the descriptor—as would have the silver hammer the smith wore on a thong around his neck.

Bratax's clothes had been cut away to expose his flesh to the sun and to make applying salves easier. That made his state all too clear to Alsan's eyes as he looked over the man.

The smith's skin looked like a salt plain where water had swept over and evaporated. Ridges of skin had pulled apart, leaving long bloody cracks on the man's flesh. Someone had clearly attempt to stitch up the worst of the cracks, but the stitches had already failed.

Several different poultices and salves had been applied, but to Alsan's eyes it was clear that the Priests-Mendicant had already given up hope for this one.

"We were about to give him the last drink," Mket said quietly. "It might save his soul from the demon if we send him to the Keeper early."

"It might," Alsan agreed, studying the man. There wasn't a lot of space around Bratax, just enough to squeeze past the other victims. The paladin was immune to Abyssal and most normal infections as well, which meant he had to mentally salute the courage of the Priests-Mendicant.

None of the three were Sealed. They were as vulnerable to the demonic infection killing their patients as their patients were.

"I may be able to save him," he told Mket. "There are risks, but Grace may work where medicine has failed."

"I have seen Sanctified healers work," Mket told him. "Do what you can, Sir Alsan."

Alsan nodded and gestured the healers to make space. Kneeling next to Bratax, he removed the leather gloves that would support the gauntlets he'd left behind—and this was *why* he'd left the gauntlets behind.

He'd been a paladin for over fifty seasons and had lost count of the number of times he'd served as a channel for the Intercessor's Grace. It required skin-to-skin contact, and it worked better if he'd known the person when they were hale.

Still, he knew enough of what skin *should* look like to know he could heal Bratax's wounds. If Grace was sufficient in the face of the Abyss...which was always the question.

Only balefire could guarantee the destruction of the Abyss's influence, but Grace would spare the innocent.

Alsan stretched his hands and laid open palms on the smith's flesh. The skin was hot enough to the touch to hurt the knight's fingers, but he brushed aside the slight pain with a flicker of Grace.

He could feel the infection now. He had distantly felt it from the moment he'd entered the church, but now he was touching one of the victims, and it surged against his senses like a wild beast.

The village smith was *full* of Abyssal energy. It was twisting the man's insides in ways that weren't even visible on surface, the lesions on his organs as vicious as the cracks on his skin.

Alsan took in all of that knowledge, the sinking ill feeling of touching the stuff of the Abyss, and then called the full power of the Intercessor's Grace to him. The heat faded as a cool rush of energy, like a wash of gentle rain, ran down his arms and into his patient. The cool energy of the Grace drove back the sick heat of the Abyss, and for a few moments, Alsan believed his Grace was enough.

Then Bratax's eyes snapped open, a spray of yellow pus flying away from the motion, and he lunged to his feet. The cracks on his skin were suddenly wider now, and the slow ooze of pus became a river of fluid as the dying man smashed Alsan aside and charged at Podrei.

Grace still connected the two men, and Alsan managed to keep his balance. He threw Mket to the ground himself as he leapt over one of the sickbeds and collided with Bratax's charging form.

The infected blacksmith hit the ground with the paladin on his back...and was still.

Several of the more-aware infected were now screaming as Alsan quickly checked Bratax's pulse. Sighing, he rose and looked at the two Priests-Mendicant around him.

"The infection fought back," he told them softly, projecting to carry past the screams. That was an odd skill that a paladin required far too often. "I know what I'm hunting now."

"Then get out of here," Mket snapped. "You're scaring the rest of the patients—and if all you're going to do is kill them faster, we have gentler ways to do it!"

"I didn't kill him," Alsan objected—but he let the priest herd him out of the church.

"It's a Brazu, Dem Mket," he told the priest as they reached the door. "The worst of the plague demons. All you can do is make them comfortable while I find it."

Mket nodded grimly.

"You've already warned we're counting toward the final dawn, Sir Alsan," he noted. "Anyone we can keep alive until dawn will be saved one way or another. Like you, we will do what we must."

"I need to know how a Brazu came through," the paladin replied. "The town leaders, where are they?"

"You just killed the smith," Mket pointed out. "The Church was run by a priest of the Father, but he is one of the dead. The tavernkeeper and shopkeep will be trying to keep the villagers calm. They likely understand how bad the situation has become.

"Ask and the villagers will lead you. Now leave us to our patients!"

With a silent nod, Alsan left the church.

THE INTERCESSOR'S knight didn't make it far. There had been a dozen or so men and the healer scattered around the village square when Alsan had gone inside.

Now, at least thirty men, women and dem filled the square—and the healer who'd been guarding the church doors had disappeared. Twilight was falling across Redgarton, but its fading light glinted off pitchforks and hunting spears as the small but very real mob glared at Alsan.

He spread his hands to show that he hadn't drawn a weapon and stepped down into the square.

"I am Sir Alsan, a Sealed and Sanctified Paladin of the Intercessor," he told them. "I need to speak to the town leaders: your tavernkeeper and storekeeper."

The two business owners and the smith would be the only people in town who would handle real currency on a regular basis. Everyone else would mostly trade in credit at the tavern and the general store, settling accounts at the end of the harvest when the tithe and tax collectors came through.

The crowd shifted, a whispered conversation going on that Alsan couldn't hear.

"So, what, you can torture them like you did those?" someone finally yelled, a pitchfork gesturing toward the church behind Alsan. "We know what paladins do. They lie and they scheme and they burn towns to the ground!"

"We won't have it!" another villager shouted. "Begone. Leave!"

Alsan kept his hands spread and kept his face calm. There was an undercurrent to the crowd he didn't like. It wasn't just fear. There was something *else* there and it worried him.

"There is a demon in your town," he told them. "One born of violence and betrayal. I need to know about every suicide in the last season."

"No one's answering your questions," the first speaker, a big red-haired man holding one of the few real weapons in the crowd—a cross-hafted and narrow-headed stabbing pike, a man-killer instead of a hunting spear.

"Begone, murderer," the redhead shouted.

"I cannot," he told them. "No one can leave the ward until the demon is destroyed...one way or another."

That was something a paladin had drilled into them long before they ever went after their first demon. A Sealed individual could cross *into* a ward, the same gift that protected them from Abyssal power allowing them to cross that line of divine might...but *no one* could come out of one.

Only by lowering the entire ward could anyone leave, and the Intercessor's knights knew, more than anyone, that they could not risk the escape of a demon.

"Leave or be driven out!" a broad-shouldered woman with a metal torch in her hands. "We're done with you and the lies of your church. The Intercessor will save us!"

"It is through my hands and yours that the Inter—"

Alsan didn't see the bow until after the leather-clad hunter at the back of the mob had loosed his arrow. With Grace in his veins, he could have done *something*—but he hadn't actually expected the crowd to attack him.

The arrow flashed out of the night and into Alsan's chest, almost perfectly centered above his heart. Against tempered steel, the broad hunting arrowhead simply shattered, but the impact drove him back a pace with a shocked breath.

That breath acted as a signal and suddenly the crowd was upon him, spears and pitchforks lashing out at the knight with fear-driven strength. A spearpoint scored along his armor before he could move, but that was the last blow to fully land before Alsan started moving.

He left his blades sheathed. These people were *not* his enemy. He let a pitchfork's tines slide along the surface of his armor, trusting the steel and the angle to protect him as he grabbed the next hunting spear that came stabbing his way.

He regretted leaving his gauntlets and vambraces behind now, but he ignored the splinters of the rough wood as he pulled the spear forward, unbalancing its wielder and then snapping the shaft just behind the spearhead.

The broken spear and its owner fell to the ground as Alsan dodged backward, barely avoiding a woodcutter's heavy axe coming toward his neck. He stepped into area cleared by the axe-wielder's swing, dodging several more spears and pitchforks that now caught only empty air.

Alsan hammered a shoulder into the woodcutter's torso, taking deir breath away as he grabbed the haft of the axe. Dey stumbled backward, tripping over deir own feet and falling to the ground as the knight stepped forward with deir axe.

A pitchfork lost its points to a carefully measured swing, and then the haft hammered into the stomach of a spearwoman trying to bring a boar-hunting spear to bear.

Grace flowed through his veins now, healing overextension injuries even as he inflicted them on himself. Alsan was stronger and faster than the people attacking him, but the key advantage of a paladin was that he could push his body well beyond human limits—and heal the damage that inflicted even as he tore his muscles and tendons.

He heard the second arrow before he saw it, dropping the axe as he sidestepped and grabbed the projectile out of the air. Spinning, he snapped the flexible arrow shaft into the throat of a second woodcutter before the man could swing his axe.

The woodcutter stumbled backward, gasping for breath as Alsan dropped the arrow and dodged the speaking redhead's war-spear.

The man not only had a real weapon, he knew what he was doing with it. A series of carefully restrained strikes drove Alsan back toward the rest of the mob—but the knight could tell that the crowd was now more scared of him than of whatever had driven them to this.

The moment wavered in the balance, and Alsan took the chance. He let the war-spear hit him, the heavily tempered steel gouging an ugly scratch across the left side of his breastplate—and he grabbed the weapon before the villager could pull it back.

A swift yank sent the redhead to the ground and left the spear in Alsan's hands. He spun it in the air, slamming the butt into the stomach of the woman coming at him with the metal torch. She folded like a puppet with her strings cut, and the knight fell to one knee to catch the torch before it could light anything on fire.

"*Enough!*" he bellowed, Grace filling his voice with volume and power.

"Enough," he repeated more softly as the whole square paused. "I don't want to hurt anyone, but if you do not *end this*, I will have to draw steel."

The mob hesitated. Hesitation become a pause—and then, finally, a halt as the villagers pulled away.

The torch thankfully had a spike for planting in the ground, allowing Alsan to put the bulky light source aside without risking the fire he'd grabbed it to prevent. Holding the war-spear in his right hand still, he offered his free hand to help the redheaded villager back to his feet.

"I need to know the answer to my question still," he told them all as the crowd wavered around him. "Did anyone commit suicide in the last season?"

He swept his gaze, the steely flint look of a paladin on duty, across the crowd.

"No one," the woman he'd taken the torch from told him. "Not a one of us had even passed in the last season, not before this plague came. It was looking to be a good harvest—we hoped to even make it through the winter without losing a soul."

And then the Abyss had reached its tendrils into their village. And yet...

"Are you certain?" Alsan asked gently. "There is a Brazu in your town, a demon of plague and ichor...and one that does not infiltrate on its own. They are born of death and violence, of suicides or the murder of children.

"*Something happened here,*" he told them all. "I will not condemn an entire village for the actions of a handful, but this beast did not crawl from the Abyss on its own."

The big woman who'd tried to hit him with the torch spat on the ground.

"I run the shop here, paladin," she told him. "My partner, dey was the closest thing we had to a constable afore this plague took dem. Worst we ever dealt with was the odd drunk traveler at Hestan's tavern."

Her chin indicated the redheaded man who'd wielded the war-spear.

"There's no violence here. No suicides. I don't know what your answer is, knight, but I fear you may be wrong."

Alsan wished he was, but he'd only seen two Brazu before in his life, and the books were clear on their sources.

"Not a one?" he pressed. "No suicides? No accidents that might have been? No..."

"Not one death in over a season, Sir Knight," she snapped.

But Alsan's gaze wasn't on her. It was on Hestan as the tavern-keeper tried to get out of the way of the discussion between him and the shopkeeper.

"That's not true, is it, tavernkeeper Hestan?" Alsan asked, stepping toward the man with the spear still in his hand. "Or you wouldn't be trying to hide your face from me and your friends, would you?

"Will you speak truth—or will you doom this town to the balefires?"

Hestan froze, panic and fear and anger warring on his face before his gaze fell to the spear in Alsan's hand and then rose to the silvered sword on the paladin's back.

"Can you kill it?" he whispered. "But even if you do…you'll burn us all anyway."

"I am here to spare this town from balefire, Hestan," Alsan told the tavernkeeper gently. "If I can destroy the demon, the plague will die with it and your people will be free. I will not burn a town that can be saved—not least because if this town burns, *I* burn with it!"

He held Hestan's gaze until the man fell to his knees.

"I swear to you, it was not my idea," Hestan finally said. "My wife…Eladra. She is dead now, taken by the plague. But…she was barren. Even the healer couldn't help us. There was no way she could bear a child, and that was destroying her."

Alsan nodded without judgment. It was not his place to pass judgment over mortals at all, in fact. His duty was to guard them from the Abyss and to destroy demons. Mortal crimes were for mortal judges—and even mortal judges would know there was *far* more to the motives than that.

The tavern, after all, could only pass to a child of Hestan's body.

"What did she do, Hestan?" he asked gently, when the tavernkeeper fell into silence.

The silence continued until the shopkeeper stepped up beside Alsan.

"What did Eladra do, Hestan?" she asked harshly. There was guilt in her voice, too. Alsan could hear it—potentially even the realization that she'd contributed to the social pressure that had driven a horror.

"There was a woman. Liada," Hestan said, his voice broken and halting. "She was the apprentice of an irregular traveling tinker. Young, healthy. She looked quite a bit like Eladra, and they struck up a friendship.

"And when the tinker left, everyone thought Liada left with him… Even me, for a few days."

Alsan ground his growing anger under the iron boot of his will. He needed to know the whole story, however evil it was, to know what had come to pass here.

"Then Eladra told me what she'd done," Hestan told them. "She'd kidnapped Liada… Not sure what happened to the tinker, but she may have even killed him. I don't know—I didn't know, I swear!"

"And she wanted you to sire a child on this poor girl," the woman standing next to Alsan said flatly. "A child of your blood, that could inherit the tavern as an orphan could not."

"What could I do?" Hestan whimpered.

"Not rape an innocent girl because your wife demanded it," Alsan said flatly. The tavernkeeper turned desperate eyes on the knight, and Alsan shook his head. "This is not mine to judge," he said, repeating his earlier thought aloud. "I *must* know what happened."

"We realized she was pregnant ten days ago," the tavernkeeper whispered. "So did she. Eladra wanted to celebrate and…I don't know…I think she thought Liada would also be happy? Or some such?

"But Liada found a knife and killed herself."

The town square was silent, a dozen of Hestan's neighbors staring at him as he confessed his sin. The other woman, at least, seemed to recognize that the *town* had as much a part in Eladra's madness as anything else, and her eyes were dark as Alsan met her gaze over Hestan's body.

"We didn't know what to do with the body…and then Eladra fell ill…and I started having nightmares and couldn't go in there… I don't know what happened to the body," he whimpered.

"I can guess," Alsan said, letting the gravel of his anger fill his tones.

He turned to the woman at his left. "Shopkeeper."

"My name is Ista," she said quietly. "I did not know. We should have, somehow. I…I know I was blunt to her about the risks of her barrenness. I…Hestan's family…we…"

She swallowed hard and no more words came for a moment.

"That is between you and the Nine now," Alsan told her heavily.

"But you are the last of this village's leaders. Hestan's fate is in your hands."

"I…" Ista glared at the man kneeling on the dirt. "I do not feel that I can judge him. Otan, Lok. Bind him and take him to the smithy. There is a cell there that should hold him."

Two of the villagers obeyed Ista's words. Hestan didn't resist, allowing them to lead him away.

"A Priest-Justicar of the Father can be summoned once this is over," Alsan said. "That is a decision you can make."

"Agreed." Ista looked after the departing man. "Eladra was my friend, Sir Alsan. I would never have dreamed…and yet…" She shook her head. "And yet I know how much her inability to bear Hestan a child ate at her. I know *she* knew his family wanted him to put her aside. I know *I* warned her that the tavern would be lost to his kin if he did not have a child of his body.

"I know she was afraid."

"It is in our moments of weakness that evil consumes us," Alsan told her. "And it is in the evil of our hearts that the Abyss finds its gateways."

Some claimed the evil in human hearts *was* the Abyss. Alsan knew better. The…*things* that came from the Abyss were not necessarily worse than human evil—but they were definitely *different*.

"What do we do now, Sir Knight?"

"I need some supplies," he told her.

"I run the shop here," Ista reminded him, her tone heavy with grief and guilt. "What do you need?"

With a sharp gesture, Alsan broke the spearhead and guard off Hestan's spear. He checked the heft of the staff that left him and nodded calmly.

"A staff"—he lifted the spear haft—"and salt. All of the salt you have, Ista."

"I can manage that," she told him. "Anything else?"

"All of the prayers you can muster," Alsan told her. "A Brazu is among the worst demons to enter the world—for it to be here, Liada cursed you all with her dying breaths."

It wouldn't take much. There were no special words or languages to summon the attention of the Abyss and its denizens. Only *intent* mattered—intent and souls.

"She *knew* what she was doing, I fear…but I do not blame her."

"Do we all deserve to die for not knowing how far we pushed her?" Ista murmured.

"No," Alsan told her. "You are not innocent, but I will not permit your town to die for the petty evils of Eladra's family and supposed friends. But I also cannot blame the final victim for reaching to the last weapon available to her."

He grounded his new quarterstaff and looked over at the tavern in the distance.

"Salt, Ista," he reminded her. "Ground or rough, whatever you have. If you have any large chunks, they would be best."

EVEN IN THE most organized of stores—and no village store was what a city merchant would call *organized*, in Alsan's experience—gathering those kinds of supplies took time.

Darkness had well and truly fallen across Redgarton as the paladin tied a bag of salt to the broken tip of his ex-spear quarterstaff. The jagged edge of the staff worked perfectly for his plan, more than a regular staff would have.

Now he stood in front of Hestan's tavern, studying the darkened building in the flickering light of torches the villagers had set up, and considered his options.

He sighed.

"Afraid, paladin?" Dem Mket asked, the Priest-Mendicant appearing unexpectedly out of the night. "That seems uncharacteristic. What do you need?"

"Fear is a tool, Dem," Alsan told the healer absently. He began to adjust his harness, removing the baldric holding his sword to his back. "Like the silver on this sword."

He offered the scabbarded blade to the priest.

"Brazu are immune to silver," he observed. "Take this and hold on to it for me. It will only get in the way."

"Fear is a weapon," Mket replied—but he took the sword. "One the Abyss wields with a delicate skill."

It was fear, in the end, that had driven Eladra to her madness. Fear of losing her husband. Fear of losing their business. Fear of the anger of her family and Hestan's alike. But fear was a many-faceted thing.

"Fear is a weapon we can turn against them," Alsan said. "It sharpens the senses, focuses the mind. No paladin can live without fear. Only in understanding and commanding my fear can I wield Grace and stand against the Abyss."

"The dawn awaits, Sir Knight," Mket observed after a moment. "And with it, the balefire of your brethren."

"Indeed. Look to the people of this town, Dem Mket," Alsan told the priest. "Keep the sick alive while I finish what has been begun. If I destroy the demon, they still look to you and your fellows for salvation."

"We will care for them; you have my word," Mket replied. "And you will destroy this beast?"

"That is my oath," Alsan said calmly. He hefted the stick with its bag of salt and smiled grimly. "You look to the town, Dem. I will look to the demon."

Mket fell away, stepping back to join the rough line of villagers at the edge of the light.

They were watching Alsan. A mere few hours before, those same locals had tried to injure or kill him. Now, he could draw the link of that mob back to Hestan's words, the tavernkeeper desperate to hide his own sins at any price.

The man's confession might now save a hundred souls from the Abyss. That thought finally pushed Alsan into motion, walking forward toward the double doors at the entrance of the building.

The doors swung open smoothly. Whatever the tavernkeeper's flaws, he'd taken good care of his business. There were no lights inside, but Alsan had expected that.

"Intercessor guide me," he whispered, summoning Grace and channeling it into the five-pointed star he wore around his neck. The silver amulet lit up brilliantly, a tiny sun that filled the tavern's main room with sharp light and stark shadows.

With his staff in hand, Alsan moved inside and let the doors swing shut behind him. He was alone in the taproom, looking around at sturdy tables and a simple bar. There were still barrels of ale behind the bar—but most of the kegs would be in a cold cellar to keep them cool.

A tavernkeeper would brew their own beer, but whatever supply of barley and hops they put together at each harvest had to last a full year. They would keep it in a basement, probably with at least three cats to protect it from vermin.

The cats would be long gone, and someone should have noticed that. Cats *hated* the feeling of the Abyss—and unlike dogs, they did not trust their humans enough to overcome that distaste. A dog would stick with its owner and merely become distressed if an Abyssal creature was nearby.

Redgarton almost certainly had *no* cats at this point.

Alsan was allergic to the furry little hunters and generally preferred to observe them at a distance—but he had to admit that they made for an excellent early-warning system. It was a shame that was often dismissed as superstition.

He sighed. The tavern's cats would have been the first to go, since the cold cellar was the most likely place for Hestan and his wife to have hidden their kidnap victim. It would be solidly built, with thick layers of earth to muffle sounds, and no one except the pair of them would ever go in.

He *hated* going underground, but that was his duty.

Holding the amulet out in front of him, he crossed the tavern to the smaller door that led to the owners' quarters.

The door was locked, but while the lock was solid, the door was not. A swift two-handed blow from his staff detached the lock from the old wood of the door, allowing Alsan into Hestan's home.

There wasn't much back there. A few bedrooms and a small sitting area separate from the taproom. There was only one kitchen in the building—why have your own kitchen when you're making food every night for a third of the village—which added some space to the apartment.

Everything in the room was much what Alsan expected. It was the solid but plain furniture of a rural village's "upper class," the men, women and dem who provided key services to their fellows and stood between them and the nobles and churches they paid taxes and tithes to.

The loss of the tavern and its home would have shattered Hestan's family's prestige and limited wealth. They would have pressed *hard* for him to find a new wife. It might seem poor to a child of the cities, but this was wealth and power in a town like Redgarton, and his brothers and sisters would have done much to protect it.

There was a second locked door off to his right. The position was right for it to access the cellar, and it would be strange for the tavern-keeper to have locked the bedrooms in his house.

This lock was an addition, not built into the door. It was still heavy and well-made, but it detached from the wall easily enough under Alsan's Grace-fueled strength. Nothing about it screamed *dungeon* or *prison*, but others would have come into Hestan and Eladra's home.

They couldn't have been too obvious about their prisoner.

Throwing the door open and allowing the amulet to light up the stairwell, Alsan saw the last layer of the kidnappers' security. The new door built at what he assumed was the bottom of the stairs was heavier than either of the old ones—and this one had chains across it, sealed with several heavy locks.

If Liada had been a tinker, the locks that imprisoned her could easily have been her own stock-in-trade. Few towns had anyone capable of making good locks, and they were one of the common trade goods of itinerant peddlers like the victim had apparently been.

Most tinkers would know how to both repair and pick locks, a skill set that made them both necessary and eyed with suspicion by the very people who *bought* their locks.

These were solid enough to withstand even Alsan's Grace-fueled strength, but, like the tinker the tavernkeepers had kidnapped, *he* knew how to pick locks.

Something about the smell of the stairwell, though, told him it wasn't going to be necessary. The Brazu was content to remain in the cellar and infect the town by proxies, but it would not permit itself to be trapped.

Alsan could *smell* the Abyssal infection now. Not just the one on the other side of the door, but closer. He poked at the chains with his staff and was unsurprised when they calmly disintegrated, leaving the door completely unsealed and easily pushed open with the same staff.

"I've been waiting for you," a scratchy voice said from inside the cellar. The distortion could easily have been a minor cold, and the voice was a soft feminine contralto that might have intrigued him in other circumstances.

"I know," he told the Brazu as he stepped fully into the space, letting his Grace fill the room with light. "But you have to know there is no escape here. Destroy me and the balefire will take this town…and you."

He couldn't see the creature. There was a soft-looking mattress tucked against the side of the cellar, away from the beer kegs and brewing equipment, but it was empty except for the spray of blood across the fabric and the wall.

Liada had not taken her own life particularly cleanly. That, too, fit the pattern. She couldn't have done the ritual more perfectly if she'd known exactly what she was doing.

In Alsan's experience, that was more common than people thought. There wasn't *that* much information out around the ways to reach the Abyss, but there sadly didn't need to be. Human instincts at the edge of desperation were good enough to summon the worst of the Abyss's creatures.

"That's what you have to think, isn't it?" the demon asked in Liada's voice. "But I have a secret for you, paladin. Your Wardpriests? They don't *want* to destroy the town. They won't look that closely when *you* tell them all is good and they are to stand down.

"They certainly won't look closely enough to realize that I'm wearing your skin."

Alsan stepped sideways, Grace flowing through his limbs as he twisted out of the way of the blow, and deflected the creature with the staff.

The Brazu hit the ground and skittered away in the brilliant glow of his amulet. Then it rose to face him, bringing a smile to Liada's face that sent a shiver down the knight's spine.

Liada had been dead for ten days and her body showed it. The corpse was mostly naked and he could *see* the maggot hanging onto her upper lip for dear life. Her arms were covered in crusted blood, marking where the tinker had sliced her wrists to summon the demon.

There were other scratches across her belly, where Liada had likely clawed at her own skin to do *something* about the rape babe growing inside her. She'd found another way, and now her dead body was merely a vessel for a much more awful thing.

And it showed. None of her limbs were angled correctly, and her skin had been peeled back from her fingers to create deadly fused spikes of bone. The Brazu had warped a gorgeous young woman's body into a horror—but it had kept her face intact enough that the smile could almost still be pretty.

"I really don't think it's going to end that way," Alsan told the monster. "I swore an oath, after all."

"Does your oath give you strength and speed beyond mortal men, Sir Knight?" the Brazu asked. "The Abyss fills the bones of this toy. You cannot kill me. You cannot even *hurt* me! You will die here, little knight, and I wi—"

Alsan was done listening. He spun the staff in his hands and lunged. Grace *did* give him strength and speed beyond mortal men, and the bag of salt slammed into the corpse's mouth.

Then the jagged end of the staff tore the bag open, spilling salt everywhere. It was across the demon's mouth and torso, spilling down its hands as Alsan pulled the staff away, spreading salt through the air as the bag trailed behind his weapon.

The Brazu screeched, pawing at the salt with one hand—but lunged at Alsan with the other. The bone spikes were infused with Abyssal power, grinding along the tempered steel of the knight's armor and nearly reaching his skin despite his harness.

Alsan spun, catching the demon with the staff and pinning it to the ground for a moment. The salt *hurt* the Brazu, but so long as it was in Liada's body, it was still protected from most tricks that he could pull.

He let it fling him backward, twisting in the air to land on his feet as he dug into his belt for one of the metal vials he'd brought with him. Concealing it in his left hand, he charged back at the demon.

The salt was a distraction, enough of one for him to sweep the staff behind the creature's leg and send it crashing down. The bone claws drove into his armor as the Brazu fell, though, and he *felt* it crack along the line where Hestan had gouged through the steel with his spear.

His armor broke, and his skin *burned* as the Brazu's fused fingers stabbed into his flesh—but in the same moment, he popped the lid off the vial of cinnamon and dumped the entire contents into the creature's screaming mouth.

It flung him away a moment later, and he focused Grace on the burning wound. He was a paladin because he was Sealed, immune to Abyssal corruption…but the active poison of a Brazu-inflicted wound was a very different problem.

The wrecked armor impeded his movements, but he managed to pull away the broken part of the plate and toss it aside. Grace flowed from his hands in a cooling rush, washing away the poison and closing the wound.

Then a sickening crunch drew his attention, and the light from his amulet turned with his head to focus on the body.

The cinnamon had done its work. Liada's body was purified by salt and burned by cinnamon, the combination of those reagents and even the presence of Alsan's Grace rendering the corpse useless to the Brazu.

Her body had fallen to the ground, collapsed against the kegs of ale, but it *writhed* now. Alsan could *see* the fluid of the Brazu's control retract toward the womb.

It was not, after all, Liada that had become the Brazu's true flesh. Her unborn child had not yet had a soul, but the sacrifice of the mother's soul combined with the fetus's potentia had opened a portal that allowed the Brazu to use what existed of the babe as an anchor.

Now the pregnant belly of the corpse bulged as the Brazu pulled its essence back to itself…bulged and then *burst*. Trails of ichor mixed with blood and gore lunged out of Liada's stomach, taking the shape of tentacles that *pulled* the unformed grotesquery that had been her child out into the world.

The ichor took form as the Brazu abandoned the body it had worn as armor. It appeared more of a creature of the sea than a human now, with tentacles reaching out toward Alsan as the paladin once again rose to his feet.

"Now we see each other plain," he whispered. "In the Intercessor's name, I abjure thee. Return to the Abyss of thy own will and I will not destroy thee."

No one in the Church of the Nine was entirely clear about what happened to a demon destroyed in the world. Did its essence return to the Abyss, to try again? Or was it destroyed forever?

Alsan certainly didn't know—but he figured giving the creature a chance to leave could never hurt!

The Brazu laughed, a sickeningly wet, multilayered sound as it formed mouths in its fluid surfaces to respond to him. Laughter was its only response—until it flung a tentacle of ooze at his head.

He blocked it with his staff, but the demon had been expecting that. The fluid extension wrapped around the wooden haft of the broken spear and *yanked* it out of Alsan's grip with astonishing strength for a creature made of ooze around a tiny corpse.

The staff went flying, and Alsan leapt backward as three more limbs lashed through where he'd been standing. One had been very clearly aimed at where his armor was missing, the chunk of flesh he'd already suffused with Grace once.

Alsan could only channel so much of the Intercessor's Grace at a time, and he could rapidly feel his limit approaching. More tentacles lashed across the room, the Brazu seeming to grow as it pushed him back.

Each limb contained a portion of the demon's essence and was a vulnerability, but the demon was *fast*. Even faster than Alsan, and he felt his armor *crack* as a blow finally landed.

He fell backward, absorbing as much of the impact as he could. His armor was definitely the worse for wear—but armor was easier to replace than paladins, let alone entire villages. He leaned into the next few blows, letting them slide along his armor and further crack the breastplate.

The creature's strength was *incredible*—but it seemed to have no idea what it was doing with it. Its attacks had little subtlety now that it had been torn from the body it had used for armor.

And then Alsan realized exactly what the Brazu's plan was. Each attack had cracked his breastplate a little more, and now several of the tentacles latched on to his armor and pulled. With a tearing sound that hurt as much as any of the blows had, the demon ripped Alsan's armor apart.

Pieces of metal went flying, and a heavier pseudopod snapped out directly at the paladin's heart. He suffused his limbs with Grace and pulled out his next trick—a fist-sized chunk of rock salt, the largest Ista had kept in stock.

He barely got the chunk of salt in the path of the tentacle in time, and his hand *burned* as the ooze wrapped around the rock.

Then the salt was gone from Alsan's hand—as was the tentacle, the Brazu yanking its limb back as it realized what he'd done. Unfortunately for the creature, the chunk of rock salt was already half-melted into the acidic ooze of the creature's strike.

Salt was as much of the world as anything could be, the element of earth forged and purified by water. To a creature of the Abyss, it was utterly toxic. Even cinnamon, a deadly toxin to the creatures on its own, was at its most effective paired with salt.

The ooze of the Brazu's outer shell was drying out, desiccating as Alsan watched, but he knew that wasn't enough. He'd poisoned the thing, but it was as capable of recovering from poisons of the world as he was of recovering from poisons of the Abyss.

He lunged forward, dodging a feeble-but-still-deadly attempt to strike with a remaining tentacle—and the rock-salt dagger he'd concealed at the small of his back came with him.

Even as the demon attempted to embrace him in a deadly wrap of acidic tentacles, he plunged the fragile blade into the core of the creature—the tiny bag of flesh born of rape and petty human evil.

Rock salt made for a terrible blade, and the dagger broke apart as it pierced the Brazu's fluid exterior. Enough of it remained intact for his strike to finish, embedding a chunk of pure earth in the central anchor of the demon.

A dozen mouths opened in the Brazu's surface to scream…and then were suddenly, utterly silent. The creature collapsed in on itself, the ooze drying to dust as Alsan watched.

Only Grace had sustained him this far, and he stumbled away from the dead demon and its days-dead summoner. His wrecked armor cut against him through the doublet he wore underneath, and he winced as he undid concealed clasps, allowing the remains of the breastplate to fall to the ground.

He only made it to the stairs back up to the tavern before the last of Grace fled him and exhaustion pulled him into unconsciousness.

ALSAN AWOKE to someone laying a cold cloth over his forehead. He grabbed their wrist and held them in a firm grip as he opened his eyes to find Ista, the shopkeeper, standing over him.

"Peace, Sir Knight," she told him. "We found you in the tavern, unconscious and unarmored. What happened?"

"Apologies, lady," he said, releasing her. "The demon is destroyed. I need to speak to the Wardpriests."

"No one dared to enter the cellar," Ista told him. "There was…the most foul of smells."

"Let no one enter the *building*," he instructed. "When we have lowered the ward, we will balefire the structure to destroy the remnants of the Abyss."

He was on a cot, presumably in the shopkeeper's home, and he swung his feet off.

"I need to go," he told her. "The Wardpriests will not wait long past dawn."

He'd never met a Wardpriest yet that would balefire a town without hesitation—and he thought that was a *good* thing. He'd ordered dawn. In his experience, that would mean half an hourglass or more after a white thread could be distinguished from a black one.

But it would not be *much* longer than that. No one became a Wardpriest without knowing their duty.

"One of the Priests-Mendicant set off to speak to them," Ista said. "Dey believed dey could buy you time to recover."

"Perhaps," Alsan admitted. "My clothes and armor, Ista?"

Someone—presumably the shopkeeper—had stripped away the

acid-ruined remnants of his doublet. From the way her eyes lingered, she may have enjoyed the process more than was necessary.

"Your doublet was wrecked," she replied. "Here. This was my husband's. Before the demon's plague took him."

He'd have guessed that the moment he accepted the garment. It was clearly the tunic of a village constable, padded and reinforced with hardened leather. It wasn't the breastplate of a knight, but it would serve for any need Alsan would have today.

She helped him put it on and passed him the greaves he'd been wearing.

"Not much left of your armor, but it seems wiser to wear it than not, Sir Knight," she instructed.

"I must catch up with Dem Mket if I can," Alsan told her. "Thank you for your help, Ista. Your townspeople are lucky to have you."

She smiled sadly. The tightness around her eyes spoke to the revelations of the night and her knowledge of her own part in Eladra's fall.

"They were luckier to have the usual eight to speak for them," she said quietly. "Now there is only me and Sarl, the healer."

"The Abyss only takes, it never gives," he murmured. "But the Church of the Nine is a creature of this world. The Intercessor will see to what needs to be done."

There would be no tithes called for from Redgarton this turning of the seasons. Monks of the Creator would join hands with the people of the village to rebuild the tavern once the balefires had taken it. The priests of the Nine knew the costs of an Abyssal attack—and the Intercessor defended against the Abyss in more ways than one.

"Go," she urged him. "All of that only matters if your Wardpriests don't destroy us all!"

He nodded. He had faith in the humanity of Wardpriest Korian and deir compatriots. Given any seemingly legitimate reason, they would hesitate—but he also had faith in their *duty*. On any word except Alsan's, their hesitation would only give him time.

Until Alsan returned to the edge of the ward, Redgarton was still condemned by the already-rising sun.

～

DAWN WAS WELL past by the time Alsan reached the edge of the ward. Standing on the same road where he'd met Korian the day before, he could feel the oppressive power of the magic quarantining Redgarton.

Even Alsan, the only person whose command could lower the barrier, couldn't pass through it while it was up. No power known to the Church of the Nine could. Once contained inside a ward, nothing could escape.

But a prisoner could stand on the edge of the ward and carry on a conversation with someone outside it. He could see Korian's tent as he stepped up to the edge of the shield, shivering against its power.

A militiawoman was standing outside the Wardpriest's tent and shouted something into the structure as she saw Alsan approach.

The Wardpriest took longer to emerge than he'd expected. Dey had likely been communing with the other Wardpriests—almost certainly arguing over how long to wait before unleashing the balefires.

"Sir Alsan," Korian greeted him with clear relief. "Is it done?"

"It is done," Alsan confirmed. "There was a Brazu in the town and it has been destroyed."

The Wardpriest seemed to sag around deir bones.

"Thank the Intercessor," dey said. "Shall we lower the ward?"

Alsan started to agree, then paused.

"A Priest-Mendicant was supposed to let you know what had happened," he said slowly. "Did any of the Wardpriests hear from dem?"

"Yes, a letter was delivered by a thrown rock to the north wardstone," Korian confirmed. "Signed by Dem Mket?"

Alsan nodded slowly. That fit a pattern that was taking shape in his mind, and he didn't like it. He didn't like it all.

"That was the one," he confirmed. "Dey hoped to buy a few hours for me to awaken from the injuries I had taken. Grace will only sustain one so far."

He didn't have much Grace in him even now. He'd drawn far more on the Intercessor's gift than he preferred to do in a single day, but this was what it was *for*.

"I haven't had a chance to examine the infected yet," he told Korian slowly. "I am lifting the order for the final dawn, but I am not releasing the ward yet."

The Wardpriest looked confused.

"How long do we wait for you?" dey asked. "We cannot hold the barrier forever. Eventually, it must be lifted or balefired."

Alsan grimaced.

"If you haven't heard from me by tomorrow, send for another paladin," he ordered. "Because something will have gone very strange, at the last. I will speak with you each day until I can allow you to lift the ward."

"Of course, Sir Alsan," Korian agreed. "We are yours to command until the town is freed."

"I honor and appreciate your service and your duty, Wardpriest Korian," Alsan told the younger dem. "Yours is never a pleasant task, but I must be certain all remnants of the Abyss are either purged or contained for easy destruction."

The bodies of the dead, for example, would need to be carried into the tavern—by Alsan himself, unless he miraculously found an unknown Sealed in the village. The corruption should be quiescent now, but that didn't mean it was *safe*.

"Is there any way we can assist you, Sir Alsan?" Korian asked.

Alsan felt at his neck, where the hilt of his sword should have been, and grimaced again.

"I need to borrow a sword."

THE WEAPON Korian acquired for Alsan was a militia sidearm, a leaf-bladed short sword of inferior steel. With neither the length nor the silver edge of Alsan's usual longsword, it was still better than nothing —and Alsan's sword hadn't been with the rest of his gear when he'd woken in Ista's house.

The league-long walk back to town was eerily quiet. There were birds inside the ward, he was sure of it, but they were silent this morning. Even the animal life of Redgarton knew something was still wrong.

"We are free, then?"

Alsan hadn't seen Mket approach. The Priest-Mendicant emerged from a stand of trees near the road as if dey'd been waiting for the paladin.

Dey probably had been.

"The balefire will not fall," Alsan confirmed softly.

Mket still had Alsan's sword, he noted, the long blade worn across the healer's body in a way entirely at odds with the pale blue robes of deir order.

"I have ordered the ward sustained until I have examined the infected," he continued. "I must confirm that all Abyssal influence has been cleaned from this place before we risk lowering the barrier."

"Of course, of course," Mket replied easily. "With the Brazu destroyed, we should be able to treat the victims, even without Grace. Whatever assistance we can give you, Sir Alsan, it is yours for the asking."

Alsan smiled thinly. "Then perhaps you can answer a question for me."

Both of them stood in the road in the unnatural stillness. Despite deir calm words, Mket was blocking Alsan's way into Redgarton and still had the paladin's sword.

"Of course!"

"How long has Dem Mket been dead?"

The question hung in the stillness for several long seconds. Then Mket—or the creature wearing deir body, at least—chuckled bitterly.

"Three days," dey admitted. "Dey was very good at hiding deir illness, until dey stumbled out back and vomited out deir soul. Such a pure and tasty thing, the soul of a dedicated priest like dem.

"The other two have been too busy to realize anything was wrong. I'd hoped I'd fooled you, too, but I suspected when I didn't feel the ward go down."

"Akacha," Alsan said quietly, drawing the short sword. "I've met no other that could conceal their aura so tightly—or sustain a corpse so well. I felt your essence in the mob."

"That was going to happen anyway," the demon told him—and

then drew Alsan's own sword. "Your order has burned too many towns to ash to be trusted by anyone. Funny, that, isn't it?

"The people of this town trusted Hestan and Eladra—a rapist and a murderer!—more than they trusted you. Only the tiniest of nudges sent them into a rage."

"If they'd killed me, you'd have burned with everyone else," Alsan noted.

The Akacha laughed, a shrill, trilling giggle that sounded *wrong* coming from the kindly older dem whose body it wore.

"You forget, my knightly friend, that your Seal is bound to your soul, not your flesh," it told him. "Once you are dead—*however* you die —your body is mine to do with as I wish. I would have sacrificed my foolish cousin for my freedom, but preserving it could have been...*useful.*"

"And now?"

Alsan was opening the distance, considering his options. He was unarmored, and the Akacha had a reach advantage on him if it ever drew the sword. He doubted he could get close enough to land a strike even with the sword undrawn—there was a *reason* it was willing to carry on this conversation.

"Now I'm mostly considering how to kill you while doing the least visible damage," the demon admitted. "I could make it very quick and painless if you like. Just...a touch and your heart stops."

"I will not permit a creature of the Abyss to walk free," Alsan replied. "If you want my body, demon, come and take it."

"That was the plan," the demon told him with a shrug. It didn't draw the sword. The sword was just suddenly in its hand, and it studied it with a wry grin.

"So many of my kindred would be unable to even touch this weapon, you know," he conceded. "It's a fine toy. I can *sense* the death in it. The dozens of my cousins you have slain."

The blade pointed at Alsan.

"This is not revenge," the Akacha observed. "I have little attach-ment to them. But it lends an interesting weight to how we came here."

"I've killed Akacha before," Alsan murmured, keeping his sword between himself and his enemy. "You die the same as anything else."

"So do paladins."

The demon finally moved. It was no longer in front of Alsan—it was behind him, the longsword stabbing forward in a measured strike that should have removed his left kidney.

Except that Alsan *had* fought Akacha before and was expecting the maneuver. He dove forward the moment it moved, rolling around the sword and coming back to his feet with one of his metal vials in his hand.

"Catch," he said, flinging the closed vial at the demon.

It did, grabbing the vial out of the air and giggling again as it tossed it aside.

"And what was that supposed to do?" it asked.

It had given Alsan time to open a different vial. Grace ran through him as he drank its contents, sustaining his body against a poison that *should* have killed him—and, since it didn't, functioned as super-charged adrenaline.

Between Grace and the poison, he had the speed to duck away from another perfectly measured stab as the Akacha teleported again. Then another. And another.

The demon wasn't faster than Alsan was while riding Grace and Fire. But it didn't need to step through intervening space. It wasn't even moving its feet. It had assumed an appropriate stance when it drew the sword, and it just moved itself around to attack him.

And that was his opportunity.

The Akacha appeared in front of him, the longsword lunging toward his vitals again…and this time, he let it strike. He twisted with it, letting the blade slice through skin and muscle without striking anything *utterly* vital—but taking the injury to allow him to close with the demon.

The short sword slashed across the Akacha's throat, slicing over an inch deep into the creature's stolen flesh and sending blood spraying across the dirt road before the demon flashed away.

Alsan focused Grace through his side, healing the wound in a blink…and realized that was all he had. It was taking all of his remaining Grace to sustain himself in the face of the Fire he'd drunk.

The Akacha could tell, too. It stood a dozen feet away and giggled at him again. The gaping wound in its throat sprayed more blood as it made the noise, the creature clearly utterly unconcerned with the injury.

"You die, Sir Paladin," it told him—and flashed over to him again.

Steel couldn't harm an Akacha, but Alsan knew that. It was all he had for the moment, and he struck at the creature's stolen arm as it stabbed at him again. He couldn't hurt the *demon* with steel, but he could sever tendons in its stolen body.

The silvered blade scored along his side, leaving a thankfully minor flesh wound Alsan could no longer heal—but the blade kept going as the tendons allowing the Akacha to control Mket's hand parted beneath Alsan's borrowed short sword.

He grabbed the crippled arm as he let his own blade fall, pulling the demon toward him and making sure its fingers only touched the hardened leather of his borrowed constable's jacket.

The Akacha was sufficiently thrown by the betrayal of its stolen body that it fell into him before it could heal itself, stolen blood covering them both and concealing Alsan's movements.

He rolled with the demon, locking his legs around the creature to pin it in place. Then he gasped for breath as they flashed through a suddenly airless void. Heat and cold alike assailed him in that moment as he was brought *with* the teleporting Akacha.

Neither of them had been expecting that—but Alsan, at least, had been planning on having the monster grappled.

His last weapon was the gold-bladed dagger, and he sank it deep into the base of Dem Mket's throat, praying he'd remembered where the Akacha would store its essence.

The spasm that followed snapped the soft metal blade in two and flung Alsan aside. He *felt* his leg snap as he hit the gravel road...but only silence answered his momentary gasp of agony.

A moment passed. Then another. Slowly, the paladin levered himself up on his unbroken leg and looked back at the demon. A finger's breadth or so of gold still protruded from the throat of its stolen body, just below where he'd sliced it open with the sword.

The body was contorted, the demon having broken several of its bones to escape Alsan's grapple, but it was still. There was more of a sense of the Abyss to it now, as the Akacha died, than there had been when the demon had controlled it.

The paladin painfully dragged himself over to the body and opened his last vial. A mix of gold dust, rock salt and cinnamon poured into the gaping hole he'd carved in Priest-Mendicant Mket's throat.

There was a faint sizzling sound, unlike anything natural, and the sense of the Abyss began to fade.

"I'm sorry, Dem Mket," Alsan told the body. "But I think you understand."

The Priest-Mendicant had sworn a very similar oath to the paladin, after all. The world would stand and the Abyss would be denied.

The Intercessor's priesthood would pay *any* price to keep the world safe…but a broken leg and a dead priest were a far cheaper bill than an entire village given to the balefire!

BLUE LANCER
A SUPERHERO SHORT

CHAPTER
ONE

Even in this modern age of Sentinel Corps, Licensed Heroes and Registered Talents, most people expected to be able to go to the bank without getting interrupted by a teleporting psycho wearing a black mask with gold dollar signs for eyes.

Today, the people in the barely suburban branch favored by Joshua Hammond hadn't been so lucky. The masked figure appeared in the middle of the room with a thundercrack.

"It's your unlucky day, folks!" he snapped. "Everybody down on the floor or you start losing body parts!"

A security guard rushed past Joshua with a sidearm drawn. Good reflexes, decent training…suicidal reaction. Dollar Signs disappeared as the gun went off, and appeared next to the guard, his hand swinging in a gentle slap at the back of the guard's head.

Unfortunately for the guard, that slap resulted in the back third of his head vanishing and appearing several feet away. The human brain doesn't function in two pieces, and down the security guard went.

"Now, now, that's just silly!" the teleporter exclaimed. "You're going to all sit down, nice and well-behaved, until our fair city's latest Sentinel Corps subsidiary shows up and starts listening to me.

"You *do* trust Lake City's Special Talent Squad to save you from little old Cashout, don't you?"

Joshua managed to swallow an audible groan. He'd *suspected*—there couldn't be *that* many psychotic teleporters, after all—but masks were a dime a dozen when Talents played, and the dollar signs were new.

Cashout suddenly appeared behind the cashiers' registers, looming over the poor tellers.

"Please, *please* tell me one of you chuckleheads was smart enough to hit the panic button," he said brightly, then paused. "Ooh! Bright flashing lights! Awesome!

"Now empty the cash drawers in a bag, please. Let's keep this nice and simple. I'm not here for the cash, but it's just *so* handy."

A number of the sudden hostages were trying to sneak toward the door while Cashout was distracted. Joshua knew better, but he tried anyway. If half a dozen of them tried to get out, Cashout wasn't going to mark Joshua as being any more important than the rest.

He wasn't surprised, however, when the masked Talent appeared in the middle of the door. A foot flashed out of nowhere and kicked the lead runaway to the ground.

"Uh-uh, people. We're playing the hostage game, so anyone who tries to run dies."

It was somehow worse that Cashout didn't sound any less cheerful while informing people he was going to kill them.

"I can see you…and I can catch you before you make it far," he continued. "Ooh! Sirens!"

The psycho was having *far* too much fun, but Joshua heard it as well. Police cruisers came screaming around the corner to block the roads—and Cashout was suddenly outside, in front of the bank.

"Hello, Lake City's finest!" he shouted. "Any of you who get within a hundred feet of the door die. And just so we know where we stand, for every cop who gets in that zone I have to kill, I kill a hostage, too."

"What do you want?" one of the cops replied through a loud-hailer.

"I want you to get in touch with everyone's favorite Blue Man Group reject," Cashout told them. "You get the Blue Lancer down here and I promise I'm only going to kill *his* painted-up ass.

"But if I see *one* costume out there that ain't the Lancer, I kill a hostage. If even *one* of Sentinel Corps super-cops steps past that hundred-foot line, I kill five.

"There's thirty or so folks in there. I can hand you a *lot* of bits before I run out of innocents. We clear?"

Joshua managed not to groan. The irony wasn't lost on him at all—there were two components to the Blue Lancer. The man who built the high-tech armor the Unregistered Talent vigilante used, and the man who wore it.

Unfortunately for his sanity and for Cashout's demands…both of those men were arguably Joshua Hammond.

NEVER IN JOSHUA'S life had minutes ticked by quite so slowly. He didn't have any gadgets or tech on him. There was a *super-suit* in the trunk of his car, a set of blue-enameled powered armor that, among other things, included a jammer that screwed with Cashout's teleports.

The first time they'd fought, he'd barely managed to hold Cashout off while the cops evacuated the area. After that, his other half had taken over for one of the blackout workshop periods Joshua had slowly grown used to, and built the jammer.

The other two times they'd fought hadn't worked out for the teleporting robber at all, even if he *did* have superstrength without his teleportation.

Without the suit, however, Joshua was "merely" a genius-level electronics engineer with a part-time job playing substitute for Lake City Electric. When the guys who had the full-time jobs took vacations or got sick, Joshua went to work.

It wasn't the most stable of work, but it paid the bills and covered the cost of the garage full of gear his other half had insisted on over the years.

It wasn't, however, a line of work that left Joshua looking or feeling very able to take on Cashout without the armor. Martial arts were *much* more useful with exoskeletal muscles and kinetic beams.

He was trying to work out how to sneak out the back of the bank when the phone on one of the tellers' desks rang.

Cashout was there instantly, looming over the terrified young man, with his deadly hand hanging in the air.

"Well?" he said sharply. "Answer it, boy. We're all just *panting* to hear who's calling!"

The teller picked up the phone. He didn't even manage to say anything before whoever was on the other end gave him instructions and he looked helplessly at the Talented criminal looming over him.

"It's for you," he told Cashout.

"Put it on speaker," the masked man ordered. "Let everyone hear this."

The teller hit a button and laid the receiver down.

"This is Cashout," the criminal snapped. "Whaddya want?"

"This is Innocent, of the LCPD Special Talent Squad," a firm female voice replied. "We want you to come out with your hands and surrender peacefully. I can't say I'm *expecting* that, but it would go easier for everyone."

Cashout laughed.

"You're fast and strong, babe," he told the super-cop. "But I'm not afraid of any Sentinel Corps rent-a-cop. I see your masks and outfits outside, people start dying. Bring me the Lancer, or there's going to be a lot of blood on the streets—and on your lily-white gloves."

Innocent was the current Licensed Hero face of the Special Talent Squad, a curvaceous and super-strong young woman in a white hood and tight-fitting bodysuit. Sentinel Corps was made up of hyper-capitalist, power-hungry scum, in Joshua's opinion, but they sure knew how to brand a superhero.

"The Blue Lancer isn't a Licensed Hero," Innocent replied. "He's a vigilante. A criminal, barely better than you."

Now *that* hurt. Joshua had saved a lot of lives over the last few years. He might have left a few criminals in body casts along the way, but he wasn't the one who'd decided to pick on civilians.

"Then I'd suggest getting this all over the news, babe," Cashout said with a leer in his voice. "Because if the Lancer hasn't shown up in ten minutes, I'm going to kill a hostage. And one every hour after that until his painted ass is grass.

"Am I clear?"

He hammered down on the hang-up button before Innocent could reply.

Joshua swallowed hard. It was *impossible* for the Blue Lancer to show up. Even if he had a backup who could fit in the suit—which he didn't; he'd never trusted anyone enough to tell them about his other identity—the only key to his trunk was in his pocket.

In ten minutes, people were going to start dying. Even if that wasn't going to be his fault...one of them was, sooner or later, going to be *him*.

That didn't leave a lot of good options, did it?

"Aww, shucks."

Cashout didn't sound particularly disappointed at all as he turned to face the collection of hostages.

"It seems there's no hero to save the day today! The Sentinels are following orders like good little cops and the Blue Lancer is MIA!"

Joshua took a quick look around him at the rest of the hostages. Bank tellers. Old women. Teenagers. One baby in a *stroller*.

"Sorry to say, but the ten minutes is up, which means one of you is gonna have to die." Cashout sounded disgustingly pleased with the situation...until Joshua stood up.

"Sit your ass down, kid," he barked. "You don't get to volunteer as tribute in this gig! *I* pick the corpse, and I can think of much better choices for proper effect."

Even with the mask, Joshua could tell that the psycho was looking over the set of teenage girls.

"I might," he told Cashout. "Given that I *am* the Blue Lancer."

Cashout was struck dumb in surprise. That was better than Joshua had hoped for, though he knew better than to try and make a run for it.

"That's bullshit," someone said behind him, and Joshua swallowed a sigh as he realized what that someone was going to do. "*I'm* the Blue Lancer."

"No, I am!"

At least three people were standing. One was probably the most intimidating massive black man that Joshua had met in his life. Another was one of the teenage girls.

As another middle-aged man rose to his feet, Cashout cleared his voice loudly.

"The problem with your little Spartacus gig, you idiots, is that I'm perfectly willing to kill you all."

"Which is why the rest of you should *sit the fuck down*," Joshua snapped harshly. He was in combat stance now, moving sideways as he circled, drawing Cashout's attention away from the hostages.

"We've fought three times, haven't we?" he asked the psycho. "Once, you gave me a run for my money. Last two times, I kicked your ass. You're not much if somebody's jamming your one trick, are you?"

Cashout's attention was now *entirely* on Joshua.

"And what are you without the suit, I wonder?" he asked aloud. "Billionaire playboy philanthropist?"

"Nope. I'm just a dude with a black belt and a garage full of funky toys," Joshua replied. He'd managed to move far enough that the front windows were behind him, at least. Another couple of meters and he might be able to make a run for the garage.

Cashout didn't give him those meters.

There wasn't even a blur. One moment, Cashout was standing two meters away from him, mocking him. The next, the masked Talent was right in front of him and punching him in the chest.

Joshua went flying. He smashed *into* the window behind him with enough force that he went through it and then went skidding across the ground.

"Yeah, you're *definitely* our Blue Man reject," the Talent told him as he walked out of the bank. "Let nobody say I don't keep my word. You showed up, I kill you, everybody else lives."

"I can get my suit if you want a fa—"

Joshua went flying again as another blow slammed into his chest. He had enough time to question how he was still alive before he hit *something* and everything went black.

CHAPTER

TWO

Cobalt woke up.

The first thing he registered was that he *wasn't* in the workshop where he normally woke up. Cobalt was well aware of the nature of his existence, and his access to Joshua Hammond's memories was spotty at best.

He normally relied on the combination of those spotty memories and the recording systems in the battle suit to tell him just what Joshua had got up to lately. Cobalt didn't really approve of Joshua's use of his tech to white-knight around the city…but he shared a body with the idiot, which meant that if he wanted to live, he needed to make sure Joshua lived.

That plan didn't seem to be going particularly well. Cobalt *hurt*. Unless he was severely mistaken, Joshua had managed to get himself thrown into the roof of a car. A Toyota of some kind, good tech.

He could feel the electronics, wires, motors and everything around him. He was embedded *in* the car.

"Hey, blue boy!"

A garishly masked figure was walking out of a bank, and Cobalt managed to pull together enough of Joshua's memories to realize just how screwed he was. His other half was a lot tougher than he thought he was, and Cobalt shared that resistance to injury, but without the battle suit, there was no way that they could take on Cashout.

"Are we having fun yet?" Cashout mocked him, and Cobalt processed the situation at a speed no human could match.

The battle suit was one hundred and sixty-two meters away. If Joshua couldn't make it, Cobalt couldn't. His access to Joshua's muscle memory was somehow even worse than his access to his other half's regular memories. Joshua was a black belt in two martial arts.

Cobalt's total lifetime experience, discounting his fragmentary access to Joshua's memories, was under six months. He knew science and technology…that was it.

He knew the tech around him. A Toyota wasn't a weapon, wasn't a battle suit…but it had potential.

Cashout was taking his time crossing the parking lot, but Cobalt's math said he had under ten seconds before the teleporter reached him.

He couldn't do anything with the resources around him in ten seconds.

Not if he used his *hands,* anyway.

And Cobalt knew damn well that he was one of the most powerful minds in the city.

HE'D NEVER DONE anything like it before, but that hadn't stopped him from doing anything else in his limited lifespan. Cobalt spent four of his precious seconds mentally establishing the diagrams of what he needed to do.

The car shell was aluminium and plastic. A single layer wouldn't work for armor, so he'd need to double up. The engine was too bulky; it would need to be completely rebuilt. That was fine, though, since he'd need most of its components to build the servomotors.

Not much gas. Thirty liters wouldn't take what he was doing very far…but it was what he had.

It would be enough.

Four seconds mapped what he needed to do. It took seven to *do* it, but fortunately, Cashout froze several meters away as Cobalt set to work.

It looked like the teleporter had never seen someone transform a Toyota into a battlemech before. He clearly needed to watch more Michael Bay movies.

Eleven seconds.

In eleven seconds, Cobalt had bent his will upon the reality and the machinery around him and made them what *he* wanted.

There were limits, unfortunately. Turning a Toyota into a ten-foot-high fighting machine was one thing. He could do that.

The only things in the Toyota's components he could turn into *weapons*, however, were the spark plugs. His new electrified fist was the size of the folded-over car door it had started as, and he still didn't have Joshua's martial arts skill.

Cashout flickered aside in a defensive teleport as the blue fist slammed into the pavement, lightning crackling out from the spark plugs he'd spaced equidistantly around the new hand.

"Now, *this* is new," the teleporter said gleefully. "Killing you unarmored was going to be just fine, but you building armor out of a random *car*? Oh, this is way too cool."

He grinned.

"Ripping that off you piece by piece is going to be *great*."

Cobalt swore and swung at the teleporter again. Cashout wasn't there when his fist landed. The new suit was fast enough, but *Cobalt* couldn't adapt for Cashout's movements.

This, he supposed, was why he had Joshua.

While he was realizing that, however, Cashout demonstrated that he *did* have the martial arts knowledge Cobalt lacked. He'd built a bipedal war machine…and the teleporter hammered into the legs with his entire body.

Cobalt's latest project fell over.

It took him a few seconds to regain his composure, during which Cashout teleported away with several of the outer plates.

That was bad. There was only so much armor plating Cobalt had been able to assemble out of the chassis of a Toyota. Fortunately, the teleporter was distracted, and Cobalt managed to slam the electrified fist into him.

Cashout went flying and Cobalt lumbered back to his feet, shaking his head inside the miniature mecha. He charged after the other man, only for Cashout to disappear as he teleported around behind him.

Cobalt managed not to overbalance and even withstood the teleporter slamming into his back. He reached behind him with his non-electrified hand and grabbed the other Talent. He tried to throw him, but Cashout teleported out of his grip before he finished the motion.

Running away wasn't an option. Cobalt figured the suit might be able to make forty kilometers an hour, and Cashout could demonstrably move faster than that. He didn't have a way out of this fight—and he had *no* idea how to switch control of their body back to Joshua.

Normally, he went and *slept* to surrender control. That wasn't going to work with a super-powered bank robber coming right at him.

Unable to dodge or intercept Cashout's attack, Cobalt touched the electrified fist to his own torso armor. Electricity arced over his body as the teleporter hit him.

The mecha fell backward and Cobalt knew he wasn't going to be able to catch himself.

Thankfully, Cashout went flying, electricity visibly sparking off him as the shock rippled through his body. The teleporter hit the ground himself, rolling in partial unconsciousness.

Cobalt levered himself back to his feet and lumbered after Cashout. He slammed the electric fist down, only for Cashout to roll out of the way.

Then, without even rising, the other Talent grabbed the electrified gauntlet and teleported.

Sparks scattered away from the masked thief as he emerged, but he tossed the spark plug–equipped glove away and grinned as smoke rose off him.

"So, what's your plan now, hey, blue boy?" he demanded.

There was a flash of white and Cashout went flying as a woman in a white body suit collided bodily with him.

"I don't know what *his* plan is," Innocent told him. "But *my* plan is to punch you into unconsciousness and put you in a cell."

"I can still kill the damn hostages, you bi—"

Cobalt didn't have the electrified fist, but he had an invulnerable and super-strong distraction. He slammed into Cashout with the full mass of his crude mecha, intentionally crashing to the ground with the rogue Talent underneath.

The suit ground across the surface. Unlike his other half, Cobalt didn't care if he crushed the rogue Talent to death. At a minimum, he'd shattered a bunch of the other man's bones.

Unfortunately, the grinding turned into an uncontrolled slide that slammed the entire oversized battle suit into the wall of the bank—and it seemed Cobalt hadn't done a good enough job of adapting the shock absorbers and safety restraints.

Blackness took him.

CHAPTER

THREE

Someone was breaking through the armor.

That mental alert woke Joshua up. When you spend a significant chunk of your life inside a specially built combat suit, your armor *is* your life.

Opening his eyes, he heard another chunk of armor get torn off and realized he wasn't in anything even remotely resembling his Blue Lancer suit. Whatever the hell he *was* inside was a lot bigger than that and a lot cruder.

And it was facedown on the ground and—he managed to interpret the screen in front of him—embedded partially in a building. Cobalt had clearly built *whatever* this was with the same iconography and controls as the main suit.

How long had he been out? He only had the vaguest sensation of time while Cobalt was in control, but it only felt like minutes.

Someone—someone *spectacularly* strong—ripped another chunk of armor off the back of the weird mech-suit, and cold air whistled into the cocoon holding Joshua. He didn't have any time left to sort out what the hell Cobalt had done.

All he could do was hope that this big suit responded to the same controls as the usual suit. He moved…and the suit moved with him.

He heard a feminine voice shout in surprise behind him, and he used the sensor panel to locate the unknown. Years of martial arts practice helped him move around her, an aikido move to avoid an opponent, and he looked down at his potential attacker with at least fifty centimeters of bonus height.

Even through the suit visor, he managed to meet Innocent's eyes. They were very pretty eyes, he noted in the back of his head. Not the bright blue or green of grand romance arcs, nothing you could drown in, per se, but a warm brown color that suggested a thoughtful compassion to the woman behind him.

The woman who'd just been trying to rescue him from what looked like a wrecked suit, he realized.

What the *hell* had Cobalt done?"

At that point, he located Cashout. It looked like the teleporter was still alive, but from the way he was lying, he'd definitely broken a few limbs, and whoever had cuffed him up and attached a power nullifier to the back of his skull had *not* been gentle.

"Are you okay?" Innocent demanded, her voice far warmer and gentler than it had been when she'd been arguing with Cashout earlier.

"I'm fine," he said without thinking, then shook his head. The *last* thing he needed was for a Sentinel Corps Rent-a-Hero to have samples of his voice!

He dodged around Innocent again and took off as fast as the suit would take him.

Either surprised or unwilling to chase him, Innocent let him go.

THE MECH-SUIT MADE it *maybe* four blocks before it ran out of power. Far enough for Joshua to ditch it out of sight of anyone looking for him and dodge into an alleyway. He knew the area around his bank relatively well, so he found his way away from the battle armor with ease.

Cobalt had somehow built an entirely new suit with Cashout attacking him. Joshua didn't think he'd been underestimating his other half before, but it was pretty clear he needed to reassess the super-intelligent genius who made his armor.

Despite that, though, the suit was *wrecked*, and it wasn't just that Innocent had been tearing plating off to try to rescue him. Multiple chunks of the front were missing, with the distinctive clean cuts of Cashout's teleports. One of the gauntlets was missing and the other was badly dented.

Cobalt had won, but the suit was definitely a write-off. Joshua didn't feel bad about leaving it behind at all. He still needed to get back to the bank and recover his *actual* suit.

Without being seen, hopefully. It was bad enough that there was going to be video footage of his admitting to being the Blue Lancer to Cashout. He could spin that if he had to—enough people had been lying to protect the other hostages, he could cover himself with that blanket.

But that wouldn't work if they IDed him and got to his car's trunk before he did.

With Cashout in chains, the bank was now crawling with Lake City SWAT. Hanging out above the building, providing oversight, was the Hawk, the blue-armored flying Talent who worked as Innocent's partner.

Like Innocent, the Hawk was a Sentinel Corps Rent-a-Hero, a member of LCPD Special Talent Squad. They often seemed to serve as Innocent's delivery mechanism. The white-clad Talent was super-strong and nearly invulnerable, but she couldn't fly under her own power.

The Hawk could. Presumably, they had other powers as well, but nothing that had shown up to Joshua's research.

Despite the hovering Hawk and swarming cops, however, the parking lot was mostly empty, and Joshua had parked at the far end. Keeping a careful eye on the law enforcement activity, he got to his car and popped the trunk.

If he just drove off, that would attract attention. However, there was nothing to his car to suggest the usual contents of its trunk at all. Still watching the Hawk, the most likely person to see what he was doing, Joshua leaned in and tapped the icon on the folded suit in the trunk.

A preprogrammed routine unfolded the suit out of the car and opened it up like a weird hollow mannequin. With a sigh of relief, he stepped into the suit and let it close around him.

He'd be elsewhere when the police swept the parking lot and would come back for his car later. There was enough shopping outside the cordon that that shouldn't be too questionable.

And so long as the Blue Lancer suit was somewhere—*anywhere*—else he was safe. At least until they pulled the video footage, anyway.

Joshua would cross that bridge when he came to it.

A QUESTION OF FAITH

A CASTLE FEDERATION NOVELLA

CHAPTER

ONE

Aballava System, Castle Federation
June 5, 2706 Earth Standard Meridian Date/Time

Fleet Admiral Darius Moonblood was *old*. He could feel it in his bones most days, even in his nanomatrix-laced left leg and his completely artificial right leg. Almost a hundred and twenty years old, even twenty-eighth century medicine could only do so much and he was well past due to retire.

Today, though, that argument hadn't won yet and he stood on the observation deck of the Castle Federation Space Navy's battle station Aballava Defense Seventeen and watched the latest addition to his command slowly decelerate into her parking orbit above the gas giant.

The star system he stood in was one of the quieter systems available in the seventeen-system Castle Federation. Aballava was a daughter colony of Castle, a mere half-billion or so people. There was no way this system could have supported the fleet resting in orbit of the gas giant Llandudno.

Vagabond was the newest arrival, the ship he was here to see, but she brought his Counter-Clockward Fleet up to six Alcubierre-Stetson drive battleships. Each battleship represented a full twentieth of the gross system product of a moderately well-off system.

Which meant that his fleet had a price tag equal to roughly *half* of the annual income of the entire star system.

"Admiral Moonblood," a polite voice interrupted his thoughts. "Captain Michaud sends her regards and invites you to join her for dinner aboard *Vagabond* this evening if that fits with your schedule."

Moonblood quirked his lips in a slight smile.

"And would you, Commander Itzel Barre, have let *Vagabond* arrive without having made sure I was available to dine with her Captain?" he asked.

Senior Fleet Commander Itzel Barre was his operations officer, a tall and dark-skinned woman who took careful responsibility for everything her Admiral got up to.

Once he'd convinced her not to *babysit* him, she'd become very useful. He was old, not broken.

"Of course not," Barre confirmed cheerfully. "I've been in communication with Captain Michaud's XO for the last week, since they left Castle."

Quantum-entanglement communications and the immense q-com switchboards in major capitals had brought the galaxy closer together. If only that had resulted in the peace and commonality so many had expected.

He sighed. His neural implant was advising him that he'd just received a briefing update from the Senate, probably the geopolitical update he'd been waiting for.

"Arrange a shuttle, Commander," he told Barre. "Assuming you haven't already. *We* will join Captain Michaud for dinner."

"Of course, Admiral. Anything special I should arrange for?"

"I *want* to see a demonstration of her lances," Darius admitted. "But since they're still so classified I believe we're trying to pretend the stars themselves don't know the beams exist, that isn't happening."

He shook his head with that same small smile.

"No, Commander Barre. I believe we will be fine with whatever Captain Michaud puts together."

∼

*V*AGABOND LOOKED ALMOST stubby in comparison to the rest of Darius's ships. An immense, rough arrowhead, she was thicker at both the front and the back than the *Crown*-class battleships that filled out his fleet; she was also a hundred meters shorter.

There were reasons for that. Both ship classes had spinal mass drivers running the full length of the ship. The kilometer-long *Crown* had three of them as the battleship's main guns, using mass and gravity manipulation to fling a hundred-kilogram projectile across space at a third of the speed of light.

Vagabond had a single mass driver that managed the same velocity by dint of being sixty percent larger than any of a *Crown*'s guns, but it was entirely a secondary weapon compared to her real weapons.

The positron lances weren't overly noticeable from the outside of the ship, the weaponry mostly concealed beneath the smooth layers of her neutronium-laced armor, but they were *far* more dangerous. A mass driver used the age-old method of flinging a high-speed chunk of metal into somebody.

The newly developed positron lances took the antimatter output of a zero-point-energy cell, normally used for fuel for engines or reactors…and focused it into a coherent beam of positrons with a range of easily hundreds of thousands of kilometers.

The guns might be "merely" rated as two hundred kilotons per second versus the hundred-plus megatons of the kinetic impact of the mass driver rounds…but Darius was grimly aware of all of the ways the lightspeed weapon was superior.

He wanted a fleet of *Vagabonds*. Instead, he had one. Starships were far too expensive to be produced in vast quantities. If the handful of *Vagabond*-class ships being built proved their worth, the fleet would be refitted. But even that would take time…time the old man wasn't convinced his nation would get.

"She's pretty, at least," Barre said beside him.

"Just *pretty*, Commander?" he asked.

"I'd probably stab a friend in the back to command her," she said with a chuckle. "I mean, not a really *good* friend…but an okayish one? Stars know, Admiral…*antimatter guns*?"

"Someone was far too clever when they came up with that," he agreed, his implant keeping a careful mental eye on the shuttle as it swooped around to the battleship's shuttle bay. "I hope it's enough for what's coming."

Barre snorted.

"Last intel suggests that the Imperium hasn't even realized we've *experimented* with positron lances, let alone that they're working on them."

"Look at the reports from Condor," Darius said quietly. "The Commonwealth tested something similar to our positron lances against the defenses there. I don't think anyone was supposed to see it, but one of our agents got the data out."

"Condor was a pirate base. The Commonwealth did everyone a favor clearing it out," Barre replied.

"They had reason to be there, yes," he agreed. "But there always seems to be a reason for the Commonwealth to invade, doesn't there? And each system they annex brings them closer to us and the systems we've promised to protect."

"The Senate won't pick a fight with the Terran Commonwealth," his right hand woman told him. "Would they?"

Darius grimaced.

"Every one of our trade treaties for the last two centuries has included a promise that the Castle Federation would defend our part-ners in the face of attack," he noted. "Most of the multisystem powers do that—it helps encourage everyone to keep the peace, and it's an easy giveaway that gets us better terms and we never expect to have to honor beyond fighting pirates."

He ran a hand over his right thigh, the sensors in the plastic and metal not *quite* responding the same way as if he touched his left leg. He'd lost it in a fight against excessively clever pirates a long time before.

Even ten years later, his particular reaction to regen had been iden-tified and they might have been able to regrow his leg…but nobody was going to remove a perfectly functional prosthesis for *might*.

His companion was quiet. She'd known him long enough to know that if he was drawing his own attention to the prosthetic, he was being melancholy.

"We won't pick a fight with the Commonwealth, but I'm not sure nearly as many people pick fights with Terra as their propaganda would have us believe."

"But sir...it's the Terran Commonwealth," she replied. "Not the bogeyman."

Darius chuckled as their shuttle slid aboard *Vagabond*, automated shutters sliding closed behind them.

"I may be an old war horse jumping at shadows," he admitted, "but the Commonwealth not being a bogeyman, Commander Barre, is starting to feel like an opinion contrary to the facts."

He rose with the ease of decades of practice as the shuttle slowed to a halt.

"Come on. Let's see what Captain Michaud has prepared to feed us."

CHAPTER

TWO

Violetta Michaud was almost as tall as Darius himself with platinum-blonde hair to his pure white. She also put on an amazing table and Darius was impressed with the food as her stewards delivered and cleared away plates in rapid succession.

When the last dessert plates were cleared, wine was poured and the stewards retreated. Only the four senior officers remained, and Michaud hesitated for a moment before nudging her XO.

"The Senate, the Navy, the Castle," he reeled off in practiced tones after realizing that, Senior Fleet Commander or not, he was the most junior officer left at the table. "I give you the Federation!"

"The Federation!" the other three officers replied, and Darius sipped his wine.

It was as good as the rest of the meal, and he studied Michaud and her XO carefully as they sipped their own wine. Senior Fleet Commander Easton Adema was a broad-shouldered man, probably only *young* to eyes like Darius's. He kept his focus on the wine—but Michaud returned his gaze calmly.

"I have a verbal briefing from Joint Command," she finally told him. "Including the note from Fleet Admiral Carson to me that you are, in fact, *senior* to every officer in the Joint Command."

"And some day, they'll haul me off a flag deck and give me a desk job like that," Darius replied with a chuckle. "Until then, I stand on our most threatened frontier. What does Bob have to say?"

He used Fleet Admiral Robert Carson's nickname with an intentional edge. Michaud took it in stride—but Adema had to swallow quickly to keep his wine under control.

"The Chief of Naval Operations," Michaud replied calmly, "wanted to let you know that we *believe* the Imperial detachment at Mossflower has been reinforced. Admiral von Santiago is believed to be up to eight battleships now."

"That should have been in my formal briefing," Darius pointed out. "Which says she has *six* battleships."

"Carson didn't tell me why this was going verbally," the Captain admitted. "Only that it wasn't reliable data that he wanted you to have anyway. 'To keep his eyes on the prize,' I believe were his words."

"He wants me watching Coraline, not Terra," Darius agreed. "He *knows* I'm not as readily distracted as some think, but he worries." The old Admiral shrugged and grinned. "He doesn't need to," he told the other three officers. "I can watch two ways at once."

"If von Santiago has been reinforced to eight ships, that leaves us outnumbered and outgunned if she moves, doesn't it?" Adema asked.

"Not with *Vagabond*," Darius replied. "If the positron lances work as advertised, she has no idea what she'd be walking into. However, she wouldn't move, anyway. Aballava and Caerleon have significant fixed defenses. Von Santiago would want at least twelve battleships before she'd move against either—or absolute certainty that she knew where *we* were and that we didn't know she'd deployed."

"It's a shell game," Barre added. She knew the strategy. "We have three systems at risk on this front: Aballava, Caerleon and Celliwig. All three are daughter colonies from Castle—we're on the Counter-Clockward frontier of the Federation and we're too damn close to the Imperium.

"But Aballava and Caerleon are both fortified sufficiently to stand off half a dozen battleships on their own. Caerleon is ten light-years from Celliwig, five from Aballava. Aballava is six from Celliwig, which means that we're three days from either here, but it's five days between Caerleon and Celliwig."

"So, we sit in the middle with the assumption that we likely deploy to Celliwig," Michaud concluded.

"Exactly," Darius agreed. "We're only six days' travel from Castle, so its not like we're isolated out here. But luring us away from the defenses and jumping on us with half again our tonnage is von Santiago's dream.

"It's about the only way the Imperium is going to open up our Counter-Clockward flank short of picking up their entire fleet and coming right at us," he concluded. "They've got fifty-eight battleships to our fifty-four. I'll take those odds, given that I know we've got two *Vagabond*-class ships and have reequipped the fleet with antimatter-warhead missiles."

"That was the other thing Carson wanted me to warn you about," Michaud said after a moment to process. "Like the reinforcements at Mossflower, it's not certain yet…but he thinks there's weight to the reports that the Imperium is deploying their own antimatter missiles."

Darius leaned back in his chair with a long exhalation.

"What I'm hearing, Captain, is that our CNO is having a pissing match with JD-Int and making his own decisions about what is and isn't valid intelligence," he noted.

"I can't speak to the Joint Department of Intelligence, sir," Michaud said carefully. "Or to Admiral Carson's relationship with them. Only the messages I was asked to pass along."

"I know," he conceded with a throwaway gesture. "The Federation has only fought pirates for a long time, Captain. We're not exactly the most *efficient* of military machines. Shit like this happens." He grimaced. "It's why I don't have Carson's job. He can handle Senatorial politics. I can't."

It wasn't even that Robert Carson played the political game and Darius didn't—nobody became a Fleet Admiral in a peacetime navy without playing politics. Carson just enjoyed it more than Darius did—and Darius trusted the other man to have Castle's best interests at heart.

Which left the navy with an energetic politician in charge at home and a capable old war horse on the critical frontier. They both figured it was a win for everyone.

"Anything else my old friend decided to hand me, Captain?" Darius asked.

"Just those two bits, sir," she noted. "I'd prefer not to get caught up in *Admiralty* politics, sir."

"Don't count on that for long," he warned her. "And I doubt you managed command of our newest and shiniest battleship by not playing politics, either."

Darius grinned at the moment of displeasure that crossed Michaud's face. He'd got her in one. She *played* disinterested in politics, but she wouldn't have her command without getting involved.

That meant she was one of Carson's protégés. Darius could do worse.

"Dinner has been a pleasure, Captain, but I need to get back aboard Seventeen," he told her. "I'm old and I need my sleep. Experience says the q-com will have delivered a small legion of snakes into my inbox by morning.

"I'll let you know which ones I'm sharing with you once I've seen them."

"Of course, Admiral. I appreciate you taking the time to join us," Michaud replied.

"There are just over twenty-five thousand officers and crew aboard the battleships of my fleet, Captain," he pointed out. "I can't know them all, but it is my business to know as many of them as I can—and my Captains, Captain Michaud, are the hands through which I control enough firepower to devastate worlds.

"I *must* know those hands. So, here we are."

He was halfway through turning to leave when the Priority-Alpha-One alert hit his implant like an angry lightning bolt.

CHAPTER

THREE

Getting a secured pod aboard *Vagabond* to link into the q-com network was easy enough. Captain Michaud's office was only a few steps from the woman's dining room, and she readily placed it at his disposal.

That, Darius had expected. He *hadn't* expected to find himself facing an equal number of Senators and Admirals when he answered the call. The three uniformed officers represented the core of the Castle Federation's High Command—and including him, the call now held eighty percent of the Fleet Admirals in the entire Federation.

The three Senators, equal members of the Federation's thirteen-person executive, were linked in from a different location. All three Admirals were in one place and all three Senators were in one *other* place...and even managing to get those six people into *two* rooms was an achievement.

Darius's intended demand of Robert Carson died unspoken on his lips as he absorbed the situation, falling back on clipped recognition of everyone.

"Carson, Laurent, Bhattacharya," he greeted the three Admirals. He knew all of them. The Senators were less known to him, but his neural implant connected the faces to the histories and memories he *did* have of the three women.

"Senator Pan, Senator Christensen, Senator Falk," he continued. "I'll admit, I'm only used to meeting Senators one at a time. What's going on?"

"You're familiar with the Boudicca System," Senator Falk said immediately. The dark-haired woman was the current Senator for Castle itself, the first-among-equals of the Federation's executive branch.

"A long-standing trade partner of ours," Darius replied instantly. "Current trade volume around two trillion annually, twenty-five light-years from Castle and sixteen from Aballava."

"And, like most of our trade partners, operating under a promise of protection from the Federation in the face of major threats," Falk completed. "They have activated that part of their trade agreement with us."

"And the Counter-Clockward Fleet is the closest major military formation, of course," Darius agreed. "Have they briefed us on what kind of threat they're facing? I'd prefer to deploy the *correct* level of force."

"It's not clear," Carson cut in. "The only solid data we have is that someone ambushed and destroyed *Defiant* while she was patrolling the outer system. She was an older vessel but still an A-S battleship."

"So, they're running panicked," Darius said crisply, considering the situation. "Are we showing the flag or seriously attempting to handle the problem?"

Falk closed her eyes for several long seconds, then focused her gaze on him. Everyone else on the call waited to let her field that question.

"I appreciate your frankness, Admiral," she finally said. "And to be equally frank, were the situation different, I would leave the force levels entirely to you and Admiral Carson."

That didn't sound like someone who was going to let him decide his own force levels. Darius leaned back in his chair and studied the images of the people around him. Those images *looked* present, but they weren't even projected holograms. For a call at this level of security when he was away from his secured base, the entire meeting was inside his head.

They were seeing him behind Michaud's desk, the visuals pulled from the battleship's computers. Given that everyone else was in their usual secured facilities, they probably had a hologram of him.

"What is the situation, then, Senator Falk?" he asked.

She gestured to Pan. The pale Senator for Aballava smiled thinly.

"The most important part is that Boudicca has a similar agreement with the Coraline Imperium," Pan told him. "Intelligence has confirmed they've sent the same request to the Imperium."

"Which is risky as hell, since we think that the Imperium is the most likely culprit," Carson cut in. "Boudicca is being used as bait. Von Santiago wants to lure a portion of your fleet out and ambush it."

"Potentially," Pan said coldly.

Darius got the unspoken message there. Fleet Admiral Carson was, once again, going off on a tangent civilian intelligence didn't support. Quite probably, even JD-Int didn't agree.

Of course, everyone tolerated Carson's flights because he was right at least as often as he was wrong.

"Von Santiago has a larger fleet than I do," Darius pointed out. "Head-on, I think the Counter-Clockward Fleet is a match for hers, but these kinds of games are dangerous."

"Regardless of how much the Imperium is involved in these attacks, we have every reason to believe that von Santiago will sortie to Boudicca with a significant portion of her fleet," Pan said. "Imperial policy would be to overawe the locals with force—but the Coraline Imperium is far from immune to opportunism."

And a battleship fleet in orbit of a planet without battleships of its own just *screamed* opportunity to Darius.

"If we send nothing, the Imperium will likely deal with Boudicca's problem…and then annex the system," Pan concluded. "They'll have invited the viper to their own home. To counter that, we need to show the flag in force. In *enough* force, Admiral, to make certain that von Santiago does not act against our friends in Boudicca."

"That will take my entire fleet," Darius told them. "Von Santiago is doing the same calculation. She *probably* doesn't think we'll take the system by force if she lets us, but I don't see any scenario where she won't send at least six battleships."

"Agreed," Falk told him. "And those are your orders, Admiral Moonblood. You are to take the *entire* Counter-Clockward Fleet to the Boudicca System. You are to intimidate Admiral von Santiago into refraining from any extreme actions, and you are to find and deal with whoever is threatening the system—be they Imperial or otherwise."

"And if they're Commonwealth?" Darius asked softly. "If it's not the Imperium, there aren't many others likely to challenge us here."

There wasn't *anyone*. There were only a handful of single- or multi-system powers in the region who'd even dream of it—the Renaissance Trade Factor and the Star Kingdom of Phoenix came to mind—but they were closer to allies than enemies.

It was just the Imperium...and the nine-hundred-pound gorilla looking for its next banana.

Falk sighed loudly.

"There are no grounds to believe the Terran Commonwealth is poking at a minor system on the edge of nowhere with enough force to kill a battleship," the Senator pointed out. "Let's not jump at ghosts, people."

She was clearly including Darius's fear of Terran involvement in with Carson's certainty of Coraline involvement.

"Given the age and maintenance status intelligence tells me that *Defiant* suffered from, it is entirely possible that she suffered a catastrophic failure," Falk continued. "Our worst-case scenario is local pirates with a flotilla of sublight gunships or *maybe* an old battlewagon.

"But the Boudicca System is a point of tension and contest between us and the Imperium. Coraline will act, which means *we* must act. Sending your entire fleet appears the best way to protect our ally and avoid a potential war."

She shook her head.

"Do you think you can manage to get us through this mess without a war, Admiral?"

Darius smile grimly.

"Senator Falk, so far as I am concerned, avoiding a war is my *job*," he pointed out. "The decision to start a war generally rests with you and the Senate, not Admirals.

"What are my rules of engagement if I find the 'pirates' and they are agents of a hostile power?"

"Our promise to Boudicca is that we would protect them," Falk told him. "You will do so. I would prefer *not* to end up in a war with anyone over that star system, Admiral, but the Castle Federation does not break its promises.

"Am I clear?"

Darius inhaled and nodded.

A blank check, then. Because *that* was always a good sign.

CHAPTER

FOUR

Sixteen light years was eight days' flight at the maximum acceleration Darius's Alcubierre-Stetson drive battleships could manage. If someone had destroyed the Boudicca System's only major warship, there was a significant chance the system would already be screwed by the time he arrived.

The only *good* sign was that Darius was certain von Santiago was still in her anchorage in the Beschel System. That put her just over twenty-two light-years from their likely shared destination, which bought him a bit over a day of leeway.

That wasn't enough in his mind, and he walked back into the dining room with a plan already taking shape in his mind. Barre, Michaud and Adema had clearly been waiting for him to finish his call, the three of them sitting in silence around the room as he returned.

"We're deploying," he said flatly. "Captain Michaud, congratulations; *Vagabond* is now my flagship. I need the flag deck online ASAP.

"Barre, I need my staff and my travel gear aboard *Vagabond* as soon as you can arrange it," he continued, turning his attention to his operations officer. "Once you have the wheels turning on that, I need *every* Captain in a virtual conference in one hour.

203

"If there's anything stopping them from warping space immediately, they need to bring it to that meeting," Darius concluded. "I'll brief everyone in that meeting, but assume that we need to be underway in three hours or less."

Barre turned to Adema instantly.

"Commander Adema, can I borrow an office?" she asked. "I imagine the flag deck offices aren't fully on—"

"We shipped out directly from our testing," Michaud cut the Senior Fleet Commander off. "The systems were suspended, but I just issued the activation commands. Everything should still be in place and ready for you and the Admiral's people to set up without preparation."

Adema was silent for a thoughtful moment, probably reviewing Michaud's messages and his own files on the flag deck.

"It might have been egotistical," the XO admitted, "but we kept the furniture and everything in place. *Vagabond* is, after all, the most advanced warship in the Counter-Clockward Fleet. We hoped to be made your flagship, though admittedly I expected less *urgent* timing."

"Well done," Darius told them. "In that case, I'll pull directions to the Admiral's office from the ship's network. Captain Michaud—you just arrived. I *know* you're going to have supplies you need restocked before we move. Have a list for Barre by that meeting.

"Any questions, people?"

Everyone in the room was already multitasking with neural-implant coms while they listened to him.

"Then let's get moving. I'll brief you in an hour."

DARIUS SPENT most of the hour assembling a briefing packet that was fired into everyone's neural implants the moment the meeting began. It took a few seconds for the fleshy part of his subordinates' minds to pick up and process the new "memories," but it was still faster than spending thirty minutes explaining it all.

"Questions?" he asked as the virtual images of his Captains refocused on him. Even Michaud was on her bridge. The conference table he sat at the head of was entirely fictional, with most of the Captains who appeared to be sitting at it actually on their bridges.

"What's our expected threat level?" Captain Dusko Jamison, commanding officer of *Croatia* asked. "We're deploying the entire fleet?"

"Our worst-case scenario at the moment is that this is a Coraline ambush, the opening move of the war we've been building towards for the last twenty years," Darius replied. "In that case, we can assume a threat specifically calibrated to wiping us out. That's von Santiago's fleet plus a couple of extra battleships.

"I'm *expecting* von Santiago with six to eight battleships," he continued. "My worst case is ten."

His *true* worst case wasn't something he could share with his subordinates. The Admiral had to watch the sprawling and expanding imperium based on humanity's homeworld and regard them as a threat. His subordinates needed to focus on more immediate threats.

"*Someone* jumped and destroyed an A-S battleship without leaving enough behind for long-distance scans to resolve her attacker," Darius pointed out. "That means modern stealth and ECM."

"They've got to know *what* happened, at least," Michaud argued.

"Everything we've got from Boudicca is in the packet I sent you all," he said. "Their best guess is that between one and three vessels of indeterminate size and energy signature ambushed *Defiant* at close range and engaged her with heavy mass-driver fire. Nothing unusual, not even antimatter warheads."

Just cee-fractional slugs with impact energy measured in the dozens to hundreds of megatons.

"Even the energy signatures of the impact should give us more than that," Barre said. "I'm looking at the data and it's frustratingly limited. Shouldn't they have live q-com data?"

"Boudicca doesn't have their own q-com switchboard," Darius reminded them. "They purchased entangled blocks from us and from Coraline, but they don't trust either of us enough to run *military telemetry* through our hardware, whatever promises we've made."

Quantum entanglement was inherently a two-point communication system. That meant that, for example, *Vagabond* carried several hundred thousand entangled particles whose other half lived on a station in Castle orbit.

Any change to the particles on *Vagabond* was reflected at the switchboard station. There, routing codes would tell the system control who to send the data to and would then relay the change to the particles entangled with the intended recipient. The largest delay was the fiberoptic cabling in the switchboard station, providing an instantaneous communication link across any distance people could transport the particle blocks over.

But the people in control of the switchboard station could access your data. They weren't supposed to—the Federation switchboards weren't allowed to access civilian coms without a warrant—but they could. And very few nations provided legal protection to foreign powers renting their communications equipment.

"So, because Boudicca doesn't trust us, they don't have the data that could actually let us help them," Barre concluded aloud. "Messy. Do we have a plan, sir?"

Darius smiled thinly. His operations officer was calling out the obvious problems and softballing him the questions he needed to answer for everyone. They were a well-oiled machine at this point, and he was going to miss her when the promotion he'd already recommended went through.

Rumor said there were some *very* odd things going on in JD-Tech's weapons R&D programs. If he had his way, *Captain* Barre was going to be at the heart of an entirely new generation of warfare—but that was the future.

"Our mission is threefold," he told them all. "First, we are showing the flag in serious force. We are going to reassure Boudicca and our other trade-partner protectorates that we mean our damn promises. We will protect them in the face of external threats and will do so without annexing them as unwilling true protectorates."

The Federation already had three of those: a daughter colony, a religious colony with minimal spaceborne industrialization, and a star system that was one wrong word from *another* civil war. All three would hopefully eventually become full members.

But *hopefully* and *eventually* were risky words.

"Secondly, we show the *Coraline Imperium* the same thing," he continued. "Whether this is an Imperial ploy or not, von Santiago will be present with a major fleet. We'll discourage her from opportunism and remind the Imperium that we both agreed to protect systems like Boudicca.

"It's our one common ground with the Imperator, people. We want to use it to avoid a war if we can," he told them.

"Of course, our *official* mission doesn't include either of those priorities," he told them, his thin smile not even twitching. "Officially, we are being deployed to secure the sovereignty and security of a trusted friend and trade partner against a clear and present threat.

"That is the third part of our mission but, sadly, in many ways the least important." Darius shook his head. "Our most likely scenario is either local sublight warships or a rogue battleship."

There weren't supposed to be any of the latter, and pirates with A-S ships were a recurring nightmare for any government. An Alcubierre-Stetson warp drive required multiple Class One Mass Manipulators, boson-manipulating systems capable of creating black holes from nothing *and* preventing those black holes from eating the solar system around them.

A Class One Mass Manipulator required years to grow its exotic-matter coils. They were probably the single most expensive technology known to humanity—and an A-S drive required a minimum of four of them. The drive was forty percent of the price tag of a warship and almost ninety percent of the price tag of a civilian freighter.

Most star systems that couldn't build Class Ones couldn't afford to buy someone else's. The corporations that fielded A-S freighters were immense entities, but even they would blink at the price tag of a private warship.

"Wouldn't the locals know if their battleship had been jumped by local ships?" Jamison asked.

"I would assume so, but they don't have enough data," Darius pointed out. "Boudicca has asteroid belts and clusters that are relatively easy to hide in with a bit of work, and our hostiles have already demonstrated modern image-baffling systems.

"Boudicca doesn't *have* those systems, so I'm still leaning towards a third-party actor," he concluded. "That might be Coraline. It might be someone else—though I couldn't see, for example, the Trade Factor trying to pull a stunt like this. It could well be the 'mighty Black Syndicate!'"

That got a chuckle from his officers. The "Black Syndicate" was often the opposing force in their training simulations, an entirely fictitious crime syndicate with the resources to deploy battleship squadrons against the Federation.

They couldn't run *all* of their simulations with the Coraline Imperium as the enemy, after all, and Darius felt like the only person who regarded the Commonwealth as a threat most days.

"It doesn't matter who they are," he concluded. "Our orders are clear: we *will* secure the Boudicca System against any and all threats."

There was a long pause, then Jamison coughed delicately.

"To be clear, sir, that includes the potential of starting a war with the Coraline Imperium," he pointed out.

"It does," Darius agreed crisply. "And that is explicitly covered under my orders."

From the expressions on his Captains' faces, everyone *else* registered the problem with being handed a blank check.

CHAPTER

FIVE

"You have no idea how glad we are to hear that you are coming, Fleet Admiral," the woman on the other end of the link told Darius. The data flowing along with her visual told him that she was Princess Admiral Alexa Burgundy, the heir apparent to the Boudicca System and one of their seniormost military officers.

She was at least fifty. There was just a point, somewhere around a hundred, where *everybody* started looking like children.

"The Federation does not break its promises, Your Highness," Darius told her. Not lightly or without reason, anyway. "My current ETA is just over four days. You'll forgive me if I keep the magnitude of my force to myself for the moment in case there are leaks along the way of our communications channel."

Stars knew there was no way Burgundy was alone, whatever she was presenting on the call. Darius was comfortable with the security on his coms *until* they reached the Boudicca System, but he could be polite and suggest there could be problems anywhere along the way.

"I hope your force is significant, then," she told him. "A guardship squadron will reach *Defiant*'s position today, but without the A-S drive, reaching the outer asteroid belts is a time-consuming endeavor."

The reports told Darius that *Defiant* had been over a light-day out

209

from Iceni, Boudicca's inhabited planet. Getting sublight guardships that far in four days was impressive. They would only be capable of the same hundred and twenty gravities as his battleships at most and had far more limited fuel, after all.

"I am comfortable in the ability of my force to engage any threat to your system," Darius told her mildly. "Do you have any more data on just *what* kind of threat we're looking at?"

"The scans suggest a minimum of two vessels, but unless the guardships can retrieve datacores from *Defiant*'s wreckage, we're unlikely to learn much more."

"I'll need the complete telemetry from your guardship sweep," Darius said. "Even the damage pattern can help my people decipher what we're looking at, Your Highness. A sublight guardship has a far different weapons fit than a battleship."

Even the largest guardship was unlikely to have more than a hundred-and-fifty-meter mass driver. The physical dimensions of the smaller sublight ships didn't allow for them. Without antimatter missiles or a positron lance, they would have had to badly surprise *Defiant* to be a threat.

Which, again, brought Darius back to battleships. Which meant Coraline or Terra, really.

"We should be able to arrange that," she allowed. "We are currently relaying a q-com link from the squadron via Castle. I'll have the CO forward you the information as well."

He smiled thinly. It was a near-certainty that Burgundy had either had or was planning to have the same conversation with Admiral von Santiago. It was even possible that her father, King Wessex III, was having that conversation with the Imperial officer *right now*.

"I would appreciate it, Your Highness," he said. "The better we work together, the more likely we are to be able to find the people who killed *Defiant* and avenge her." He paused. "Why guardships, though? Wouldn't there have been civilian vessels closer to the wreck able to retrieve survivors?"

"A few, but none were willing to take the risk for the rewards we could offer," Burgundy said levelly. "Without knowing our enemy, my father and I were hesitant to send unarmed ships into a battle zone.

The civilians might have been able to save some lives that have now been lost…but we could also have simply managed to get more people killed.

"The life-support craft and safety bunkers aboard *Defiant* are rated for thirty days without central power or life support," she concluded. "Anyone who survived the initial attack should still be alive."

Darius nodded. She wasn't wrong but he suspected at least one captain had named a price they'd go out for…and *he'd* have paid it, no matter how egregious. The Burgundies owed their people that.

"We'll see what your guardships discover," he told her. "We can certainly drop out of warped space and study the wreckage ourselves, if that would be helpful."

"Absolutely not," Burgundy snapped. "Once we have finished sweeping for survivors, *Defiant* becomes a war grave under Boudiccan law. Further prodding of the dead is disrespectful and unnecessary."

"I see," Darius allowed. He doubted Burgundy knew what he saw —but the theory that this was a local faction had just cut to zero. Burgundy didn't *know* who'd killed the battleship but she suspected… and the suspicion *terrified* her.

"I look forward to your arrival at Iceni, Admiral," the Princess told him. "Once you have arrived, my father and I would be delighted to host you and one of your senior officers for dinner. I presume you wouldn't want to remove more than one officer from your ships, given the unknown threat."

"You presume correctly," he agreed. A dinner sounded like a solid opportunity to try and sort out the Burgundies' thoughts on what was going on. He knew they hadn't told the Castle Federation everything, but it sounded like there was more going on under the surface.

"I would be delighted to join you and your father for dinner when we arrive," he told her. "I look forward to seeing the sensor data on *Defiant*. Is there anything we can provide prior to our arrival?"

"What assistance can be provided without a physical presence has already been offered by your government," she demurred. "We'll speak more in person, Admiral. Four days, you said?"

"Four days, one hour and thirty-two minutes," he told her, pulling the data from his implant. His fleet would be making turnover in that hour and thirty-two minutes, reversing the one light-year per day per day acceleration that flung them across the stars.

"Hopefully, we'll all be here to greet you," Burgundy said grimly. "The lack of activity from *Defiant*'s killers is worrying me, Admiral."

"You have a significant sublight defense fleet, Admiral," he reminded her. "I'm certain you will be fine."

He had to say it, after all, even if he didn't believe it. Boudicca was going to be fine, after all—at least until he and von Santiago arrived.

Whoever was playing this game wouldn't want to damage their bait, after all.

"THAT WAS *NOT* SUBLIGHT GUNSHIPS."

Fleet Commander Rhianna Diamond was Darius's logistics officer, the black woman in charge of making sure that every one of his six battlewagons was fully equipped and prepared for any task the Admiral put before them.

Most relevantly in the staff meeting reviewing the data from the guardships surveying *Defiant*, she was the person in his staff with the most engineering experience.

Darius had made the same assessment of the damage pattern they could see on the shattered battleship, but he made a go-ahead gesture to the logistics officer. There were few opportunities for the fleet's logistic officer to shine in front of her colleagues. He *needed* to give her this one.

"Explain, please," Captain Michaud asked. "I see a wrecked battleship and fifteen hundred dead. I'm not sure what's ruling out gunships."

The gunships had still been sweeping for survivors and escape pods when Darius had called the meeting, but he doubted they were going to find enough survivors to change Michaud's math. Six hundred and eighteen people had been pulled from the wreck—all too junior or in the wrong roles to have had access to the ship's sensors.

Defiant had been overstrength for her crew, a normal consequence of a generally undertrained and underequipped single-system military.

The Boudicca fleet's data said that she'd had twenty-one hundred and seven souls aboard.

"You haven't seen a wrecked battleship before, Captain," Darius pointed out softly. "I have. So has Commander Diamond. Rhianna?"

"The impact points are the key," the logistics officer told them all. "Look here and here." Chunks of the wreck highlighted. "Those are *single-impact* fractures of the neutronium matrix. Usually, if the neutronium lattice breaks, it's from multiple impacts."

The "neutronium" in the ship's armor wasn't really *true* neutronium, but it was so compressed that it made no real difference. It was also expensive enough and hard enough to make that even battleships had only so much to armor themselves with. A single thin layer of the near-impenetrable material coated a modern battleship—and made up multiple megatons of the ship's mass, thin as the layer was—but it was suspended in a shock-absorbing matrix and reinforced with simpler armors.

"To overwhelm the armor and break it with a gunship's three-hundred-meter mass driver takes multiple hits in a small area," Diamond continued. "You overwhelm the support matrix and force a crack in the neutronium layer, then shatter it with the final hit. It's a question of probabilities and sustained fire—usually, you're looking at twenty or more hits inside a hundred square meters."

She gestured at the highlighted chunks.

"The armor broke here to a single high-power hit," she repeated. "A battleship's main guns will do that one time in ten. No guardship mass driver is going to do it."

Darius had drawn the same conclusion. Now he watched it dawn on a group of officers—Barre, Michaud, and the other half-dozen members of his flag staff—who'd never seen real capital-ship-on-capital-ship action.

The Federation had fought roughly fourteen of those in the last century—a time period that roughly coincided with Darius's own career. He'd served in or commanded eleven of those actions. Diamond had been in the engineering teams cleaning up after the last one.

"Those ratios are included in our engagement parameters," Barre noted. "I never thought about them in the sense of the damage left afterwards, though."

"We need to," Darius replied. "Sometimes, what happened is almost as important as what we need to do about it. This mess"—he indicated the ship—"is worse than you're thinking, too."

He had everyone's attention now and he smiled thinly as he highlighted more impact points.

"These four points are potential single-impact fractures as well," he told them. "Hard to say, as the ship broke apart in these locations, but look at the angles."

Michaud saw it first, the Captain swallowing audible as it sank in.

"That's at least three different attack vectors," she noted.

"With battleship guns," he agreed. "The Boudiccans' data already suggested that *Defiant* was jumped by multiple enemy vessels, but we all assumed that meant multiple gunships. My assessment is that she was attacked by at *least* three battleships.

"Given that we can only really confirm three *attack vectors*, three ships is probably lowballing it, too," he continued. "It's possible that three ships came in from three different angles with minimal mutual support. It's more likely that they had support."

"Six battleships, sir?" Barre asked. "*Defiant* wasn't worth that."

"She was if you needed her to die and die hard without telling anyone who hit her," Darius told his people. "*Defiant* was the bait. The Boudicca System is the trap. What I don't know is *whose* trap or what the mechanism of the trap is."

"It has to be the Imperium, doesn't it?" Michaud asked. "There's no one else out here with six battleships."

"Both the Renaissance Trade Factor and the Star Kingdom of Phoenix field fleets of approximately twenty A-S battleships," Darius pointed out. "We and the Imperium are both hovering around fifty. The Terran Commonwealth, on the other hand, fields a fleet of approximately six *hundred*.

"There are also a number of single-star nations in the region that have fleets of between three and five battlewagons. An alliance of several of them could also assemble a six-ship fleet."

Darius shook his head.

"The likelihood of most of these scenarios is low," he conceded before any of his staff pointed it out. "Most likely, we *are* looking at a Coraline Imperium operation. Which raises a distinct problem, people."

"We know von Santiago's battleships were still at their anchorage when *Defiant* was attacked," Barre interjected. "Intelligence has now verified her strength at eight capital ships, all modern battleships.

"So, if this *is* an Imperial operation, we are likely looking at *fourteen* battleships." His smile thinned to a pale white line. "I believe that we can face those odds, with the aid of *Vagabond*'s weaponry and the traditions and skill of our officers and crew.

"But we need to realize that those are the odds we face and prepare ourselves for them. It may be necessary for us to abandon the Boudicca System to the enemy—but if we do so, people, we will do so officially at war with the Coraline Imperium!"

CHAPTER

SIX

Boudicca System
June 14, 2706 Earth Standard Meridian Date/Time

Looking at the Boudicca System, Darius could see at a glance what it had to offer its trade partners. Trade between the stars wasn't easy, but the nature of A-S ships—immense and expensive—meant that most things that were traded were both expensive and available in large quantities.

The sheer amount of radiation boiling off the systems' two immense asteroid belts provided a clue. Radioactive fissionables could be found in any star system, but readily available and easily refined radioactives allowed for an excess that could be exported for less than many systems could extract and refine their own resources for.

The planet probably also had the usual half-dozen refined products that their neighbors thought they made best and bought in bulk, but the asteroid belts gave them a reliable fallback.

They also meant that someone could actually be hiding an entire battle squadron in the system without anyone being any wiser. The presence of *two* asteroid belts radioactive enough to hide starships left an icy chill crawling up Darius Moonblood's neck as he sat at the center of *Vagabond*'s flag deck.

"All ships have completed emergence, Cherenkov flares are dissipating," Barre reported. "We have both direct and q-com links with all units."

"Good," Darius said distractedly, studying the star system chart and checking the astrographic map in his neural implant. "ETA to Iceni orbit?"

"Six hours, unless we have a reason to push?" the operations officer asked.

There was nothing, theoretically, stopping *Vagabond* or the rest of the ships in the Counter-Clockward Fleet accelerating at hundreds or even thousands of gravities. Her engines and inertial compensators played a terrifying precise game with Newton and Einstein, however, which had distinct plateaus in its *efficiency*.

At the first of those plateaus, a properly built ship could accelerate for months on relatively limited fuel. That only gave them a "mere" thirty to forty gravities. The second plateau, known by the imaginative label of "Tier Two Acceleration," allowed a modern warship to achieve a hundred and twenty gravities.

Tier Three acceleration allowed around four hundred gravities but would empty the battleships' fuel tanks in hours instead of weeks. A fourth tier was being studied but would empty a warship's fuel tanks in *seconds*.

The theoretically secret antimatter missiles tucked away in Darius's magazines had Tier Three engines. His ships could push to the same thrust if they needed to—but he wasn't *that* certain he could refill his antimatter and hydrogen fuel supplies there.

"My math says that von Santiago will arrive between six and eight hours from now," Darius told Barre. "I would prefer to be in orbit already when she does so, but beyond that, no. There's no need for a rush."

Boudicca couldn't stand off his fleet or von Santiago's, but the fortress and guardships could easily tilt the thin line of balance between their fleets. In orbit of Iceni, all of those weapons were available to back Darius up if von Santiago did something stupid.

Hopefully, that would be enough to keep everything aboveboard—but that was assuming there wasn't a hidden Imperial squadron in the asteroid belts.

"We can do that," Barre confirmed. "Anything else I should set up?"

"I'm supposed to meet the King and Crown Princess for dinner on arrival," Darius replied. "Get in touch with the locals and get that organized."

His gaze rested on the closest approach of the asteroid belt to Iceni. Four light-minutes was *probably* a safe distance if someone was hiding there, but the warning signs on his displays still made him uncomfortable.

Defiant had been ambushed by at least three modern battleships, and those ships hadn't been seen since. Somewhere in this star system, *someone* was watching him. Waiting. Deciding on their next move... and he wasn't even certain who they were.

"YOU'LL BE MEETING with King Wessex III and Crown Princess Alexa Burgundy, as you expected," Barre told Darius as the two of them made their way through *Vagabond*'s corridors toward the shuttle bay.

Both of them had shed the single-piece shipsuit that mimicked slacks and a collared shirt in favor of their dress uniforms. Those were black slacks with a white dress shirt and black jacket, with both the slacks and jacket piped in gold to mark their service as the Castle Federation Space Navy instead of the Castle Federation Marine Corps.

"Just the two of them?" Darius asked. "They invited us both. I was expecting a larger affair."

"The diplomatic files suggest that the Princess acts as Minister of Defense as well as the third-ranked officer of their Fleet," the ops officer told him. "They haven't sent us a guest list, but nothing in my communications suggested that the dinner was going to include anyone else."

"I wonder if they were hoping to include von Santiago and get us to play nice," Darius murmured. It's what *he* would have done if the two local heavyweights had both sent real fleets to his system. "On the other hand, she's late."

Her earliest arrival time would have been just as his ships entered Iceni orbit half an hour before. He had expected her to arrive exactly as early as she could without *obviously* having known something was coming.

Instead, it looked like she'd left the Imperium over an hour later than he'd left Aballava. With the extra travel time, she'd be there… shortly. But not soon enough to join anyone for dinner.

"Works to our advantage either way, sir," Barre told him. "I would have expected the Imperium to have factored that into their plans when they set this up."

"Never underestimate luring your enemy into a false sense of security," Darius warned. "Michaud and the others will be keeping the ships at Status One. They'll be at battle stations before we're off the ground, let alone in orbit."

"Let's hope it doesn't come to that. It would be *nice* for this all to have been a misunderstanding, not the opening shots of a war."

"I'm not sure luring us away from Aballava's defenses would be worth trashing the Imperium's reputation with the potential neutrals," Darius replied. "I just can't see any reason why the Commonwealth would play these games."

"Even if they are as actively expansionist as you think, sir, we're still a long way from the nearest Commonwealth system," his ops officer countered as they reached the shuttle bay. "You're jumping at shadows."

"I know," he conceded. He linked his neural implant in to the battleship's scanners, projecting an image of the space above Iceni in front of him. There was no hologram and no one else could see the virtual display as he looked at the floating daggers of his fleet.

A dozen fortresses and thirty guardships orbited Iceni, a powerful defense force by most standards. Against the six arrowheads of his battleships, they looked like toys. Even the fortresses were limited to six-hundred-meter mass drivers. If it came to a fight, his older battle-ships could take them all on their own.

But still, those fortresses were the real barrier there. They were the only thing the Boudiccans had right now that could threaten a battle-ship, so they became the focus of his attention as he brought up their stats on the virtual display.

Long practice allowed him to cross the hangar deck to the shuttle without being distracted by the display only he could see. One of the stations was larger than he'd thought, he realized. There was an eight-hundred-meter-wide platform in geostationary orbit above the capital, with three of the largest mass drivers he'd ever seen on anything other than a battleship.

His attention to the crown jewel of Iceni's defenses meant he saw the moment its secondary weapons opened fire on their own capital.

CHAPTER

SEVEN

Even if Darius had been on the flag deck and expecting it, he couldn't have changed what happened. The command lag between running the fleet from a virtual system projected by his implant and being in the physical command center wasn't *that* long, after all.

There was no time. Even if his ships' defensive lasers had been online, they were optimized to stop mass-driver fire coming *at* his battleships—and their efficiency in that role already left much to be desired.

A dozen slugs fired from the station before someone managed to regain control, plummeting into the atmosphere like the fists of an angry god. They took just over twenty seconds to travel from the station in its forty-thousand-kilometer-high geostationary orbit to the capital city that station was supposed to protect, and no power in the galaxy could have stopped them.

Each of the slugs hit with the force of a fifty-kiloton nuclear bomb, crashing their way across Iceni's capital city with boots of fire and death.

"What the hell is happening?" Barre demanded, realizing her boss had stopped in his tracks and bringing up her own display. Her shocked silence after the question told Darius she'd seen the answer for herself—and his orders to check in with the locals died unspoken as the battle platform that had just murdered its capital city exploded.

It didn't die alone, either, and Darius swore aloud as the reports trickled in. *Every* battle station in Iceni orbit had just exploded in the actinic blasts of matter-antimatter reactions.

"We need to get back to the flag deck," he ordered. "Barre, get the fleet to battle stations and get every tactical analyst we've got on working out what in *Starless Void* just happened."

"Someone fucked Iceni," Barre told him. "And us. Stars guard us. There are twenty million people in that city and fifty thousand on those battle platforms."

"Get everyone moving!" he barked, linking his implant com to Michaud as he turned back to the flag deck.

"Captain, you saw this?"

"I'm not sure what the hell I just saw," *Vagabond*'s Captain admitted. "And I'm *supposed* to know when it happens this close to me. Our defenses are online, I'm scanning for threats, but..."

"There *will* be a follow-up," Darius said grimly. "It's a question of what kind. Get your coms people on raising the Boudiccan Fleet's guardships. They're the last thing this system has in orbit, and they're going to be panicking.

"The last thing we can afford is for them to panic at *us*."

"We didn't do this," Michaud snapped. She paused. "Right?"

"*I* didn't order it," he told her. "I'm reasonably sure no one else did. We control the situation, Captain, and that means we keep the locals from shooting at us while we work out the best way to help them."

"*Vagabond* has twenty-two shuttles that are capable of search and rescue and a six-hundred-Marine strike battalion," she reeled off crisply. "I can't speak to the rest of the fleet, but I can put those boots on the ground for rescue efforts in under sixty seconds."

That contingent was standard. Darius had over a hundred shuttles and thirty-six hundred Marines ready to go. It was overkill for most situations that required Marines and underkill for any situation that would require more than a few hundred.

For this, however, those thirty-six hundred pairs of hands—hands clad with radiation-impervious power armor—could save lives. Potentially hundreds of thousands of lives.

"Thank you, Captain," he told her. "I needed that reminder."

He flipped from the channel with Michaud to a channel with the Majors who commanded those battalions.

"Marines, I assume you are following the unfolding disaster around us," he said crisply as he finally walked back onto his flag deck. His people were already filling the central display with updates on the status of Iceni City.

"Well, I *was* sleeping, but someone blew up a city and suddenly I was magically in power armor and halfway into a shuttle," Major Dimitri O'Neill replied dryly. The Marine commanded *England*'s Marine contingent and he was the senior Marine officer in the Counter-Clockward Fleet.

He'd also served under Darius for almost twenty years in one unit or another, and had a better idea than most of what he could get away with.

"That's where you need to be," Darius replied. "How long to drop, people?"

The responses were nonverbal, transferred along the datalink, and he was surprised by the results. Three-quarters of his Marines were already in armor, and half of the armored Marines were in shuttles.

None of his battalions were going to need more than another sixty seconds to drop.

"Drop simultaneously in seventy seconds," he ordered, giving them the extra few seconds. "There are millions of people in the blast zones alone, tens of millions in the shrapnel zones. We'll attempt to make contact with rescue authorities from here, but the local government is *gone*.

"Coordinating the disaster response across Iceni City may well fall on you. Can you handle that?"

He was *expecting* the wolf-howl that answered, and it still hurt his mental "ear."

"I'll take that as a yes," he concluded. "Get going, people. I look to you to save the innocents tangled up in this mess."

"We're Castle's damned Marines, sir," O'Neill told him. "We'll save everyone we can."

The channel dropped and Darius shook his head sadly as he closed the channel and took his seat.

"Barre?" he said softly.

"I'm here, sir," his ops officer replied. "Fleet is at battle stations and all scanners are sweeping the area. There is *nothing* to suggest that the battle stations were fired upon."

"No," Darius confirmed. "That was antimatter containment failure, Commander. I've seen it before. Someone got bombs—potentially quite small ones—into the most critical and secured portions of those stations.

"The Boudicca System was betrayed and I'm not convinced they're even the target."

He was searching the scan displays for what he knew had to be there.

"What's the radius of our q-probe net?" he asked softly. The q-com-equipped sensor probes were the closest thing he had to FTL scanners. By getting the robotic spacecraft out into space, they gave him real-time eyes wherever they were.

"We've established a net at one light-minute, sir," Barre told him. "We didn't want to expend the drones for more."

"I want a net out to ten light-minutes," he ordered. "I want a maximum thirty-light-second delay for anything that happens in that radius."

"Understand, we're on it," the woman replied. "What are we looking for, sir?"

"The only other invitee to this party I know of," Darius told her. "Admiral Trinh Hoa von Santiago."

The Coraline Imperium.

~

"ALCUBIERRE EMERGENCES!"

Darius had been waiting for the report. Now he waited patiently for the expanding network of sensor probes and his tactical teams to tell him just what he was looking at.

"We've got eight emergence signatures," Barre reported as the data flowed to her console and implant. "Engines are online; we're looking at about eleven million tons apiece. Resolving volume as they close, but that sounds like neutronium-armor battleships to me."

"And me," Darius confirmed. "And the right number of ships to be Admiral von Santiago."

"What do we do, sir?" Barre asked.

"What we have to," he said calmly. "Formation Delta-Zulu-Nine on their approach vector. Maintain battle stations and get me an ETA for their arrival."

"Understood."

DZ-9 *appeared* straightforward enough, but its true purpose was to conceal *Vagabond* from the Imperium. For the opening salvos, at least, the rest of the Counter-Clockward Fleet would cover the new battleship from the enemy.

Even as Barre was passing his orders, Darius was running the timeline of von Santiago's arrival. Something didn't add up.

"Barre, take a look at this once the orders are passed," he told her quietly, tossing what he was looking at onto the main display. It was timing. It was *all* timing.

She blinked away the coms and studied it.

"They would have arrived just in time to see us launch the Marines," Barre noted. "Gives them quite the *casus belli*, sir. Whoever set this mess up for them did a damn good job."

"Indeed," Darius murmured, considering the situation. "I need the q-probe net adjusted as so," he continued, sending her new layout. "Standard battle focus on the Imperials—but let's keep our eyes on the asteroid belts. As we move out to intercept von Santiago, we become more vulnerable to an A-S ambush."

"I don't think anyone is foolish enough to thread the needle like that, sir," she replied.

Taking a warp-space bubble within about ten light-minutes of a star or a couple of light-minutes of a planet or gas giant was dangerous. Activating one in that gravity shadow was effectively impossible, but you *could* take a ship into the shadow under the Alcubierre-Stetson drive.

It required a careful balance of power, gravity and navigation. Meeting the *perfect* requirements to do so without wrecking your ship was possible, but incredibly difficult—hence "threading the needle."

"An in-system jump like that would be preprogrammed," he noted. "You wouldn't be jumping into the shadow of Iceni, just pushing the edge of Boudicca's grav well. It would be safe enough."

"Short-range jumps take days to get calculated. It wouldn't be worth it," she argued.

"Except they hit *Defiant* days ago and haven't done anything since," Darius countered. "That fleet has had days to program their jump. And if they're coordinating with von Santiago, they knew where she'd come in from."

"Even if they didn't," Barre admitted, "there was no reason to do anything fancy. Sir…what do we *do*?"

"Von Santiago's sensor data is going to be pretty damning," he told her. "She arrives at a planet that's clearly been bombarded, with the fortresses wrecked and the capital burning—and then sees us drop Marines."

He shook his head.

"What's the local fleet doing? Is anyone sufficiently in charge that I need to be talking to them?"

"They're in full SAR mode," Barre told him. "I don't think we're getting a guardship out of Iceni orbit, even in the face of an active threat."

He felt as much as saw her grimace.

"At this point, they'd probably surrender to the Imperium for the two hundred shuttles on board von Santiago's fleet."

"Any coms from von Santiago yet?" he asked, feeling *Vagabond* shiver beneath him as the battleship began to move. All six of his ships were accelerating now, moving away from the planet to protect it from its potential conquerors.

In the long run, the truth would probably come out about what had happened there. By any rational standard, though, von Santiago would be justified in finding out that truth *through* the wreckage of his fleet.

Where *he*, on the other hand, had every justifiable reason to think the whole mess stank of a setup. He *couldn't* let von Santiago's fleet approach Iceni.

"Nothing yet," Barre reported. "She came out six light-minutes away and is burning in at a hundred and twenty gees."

"We'll match that shortly, which puts us two and half hours or so from weapons range," Darius noted.

"Far less for missiles and positron lances, sir," she pointed out.

"I know," he conceded. "But…let's hold off on those unless *they* use them, shall we?"

"Admiral? Surely, an alpha strike before they expect us to engage is an advantage we can't give up?"

"It also commits us to a battle before they can act," Darius said softly, his thoughts running away with him. "If we fire first, if we assume they are the enemy, the war forever rides on us."

"Sir, who else could it *be*?" Barre demanded.

"I don't know, Commander. Not with certainty. But it comes to one simple question of faith."

"Sir?" Barre repeated, a tired-sounding echo. She shared his own Stellar Spiritualist beliefs, a path that didn't lend itself to much faith in any active divinity…only in the strength of humanity, seemingly alone in the universe.

"Would the Coraline Imperium, expansionist as it is, murder this many people they promised to protect?" Darius asked softly. "Do I believe they have fallen that far? Or do I have faith in their humanity— in their *honor*—and believe they meant the promises they made?"

He gestured at the star map in front of them.

"Because if the Coraline Imperium *isn't* responsible for this, Admiral von Santiago thinks *we* are—unless she, in her own terms, faces that same question of faith in *our* honor."

"We would never bombard a neutral capital!" Barre snapped.

"I know. So tell me, Senior Fleet Commander Itzel Barre…you have faith that *we* didn't do this. That our officers would defy those orders. Why would you expect the officers of the Imperium to do any different?"

She was silent for a long time as the velocity and range numbers on the displays continued to change.

"I don't know them," she finally asked. "And they are threatening my fleet, my comrades. To assume they are innocent…"

"Requires faith," Darius said softly. "And it requires a new question, as well. If I *know* that we didn't do this and I have faith that the Imperium would not sink so low…who would?"

He sighed.

"Unfortunately, I can far too easily see what our mysterious player *wants*."

"I don't, sir," Barre snapped. "This still looks like an Imperial plot to take Boudicca and ambush our fleet to me."

"Look at the screen, Commander, and realize that we are hours away from turning the cold war between us and the Imperium hot," he told her gently. "Unless you and I and Admiral von Santiago can find the faith to find a different way, the two most powerful nations in this sector of space are about to expend that power fighting each other.

"If you were an outsider, someone planning a war to bring this region under your control, what could you desire more?"

She was silent again.

"If this wasn't the Imperium, why isn't von Santiago contacting us?" she asked softly.

"Because according to her sensor data, my Marines are currently assaulting Iceni City," he told her. "Given time, she'll realize her error. But I don't know if she'll realize it in time."

"What do we do, sir?"

Darius looked at the red icons of the incoming fleet and sighed.

"Move the q-probes closer to the asteroid belt," he ordered. "Do it quietly. I'm not sure how close we need to get to see a fleet hidden in those rocks, not with that much radiation in play."

None of the asteroids were putting off a *lot* of radiation, but the aggregate effect of billions of tons of slowly decaying material over millions of years left a lot of confusion in the belt.

"There are eight battleships bearing down on us, sir," she pointed out calmly. "Our missiles have a range of over *fourteen* million kilometers against them. Even *Vagabond*'s positron lances can rip them up at three or four light-seconds. Add ten percent of cee to our main guns, and we and the Imperium have a range of about two light-seconds there. We're giving up a massive advantage if we hold to mass-driver range."

"I know," Darius conceded. "But I think, Commander, that we need to have faith. And we need to make our mysterious third party *dance.*"

Barre studied the screen for a few more seconds, then turned to look at him.

"You may have faith, sir, but if I may make a suggestion?" she asked.

"Carefully, but certainly."

"Make contact with von Santiago," she told him. "We've got two hours before we're in *any* kind of weapons range—and we're blowing through mass-driver range in *seconds*, if it comes to that. If we've got a third party in play, we can't radio her without attention.

"But there's an Imperial embassy on Castle with a q-com to *their* switchboard. I wouldn't want to bounce tactical coms through that many relays, but you can at least talk to the woman and tell her that *we* didn't blow up Iceni.

"Let's put the question of faith to the test before the only failure state is fire and death!"

CHAPTER

EIGHT

"The situation in the Boudicca System is—"

"Far too complicated for us to play diplomatic games, ambassador," Darius snapped, cutting off the man in the insignia-less black uniform in his head. Ambassador Reto von Argent was a classic member of the Imperium's Elector class. There were strong expectations of military and civil service that came along with the "von" in the middle of the man's name, and Reto von Argent had met them all.

"Insufficient data is making it back to *either* of our home systems for a final decision to be made. Only the people here and now have enough information to decide the fate of a star system that could change everything."

The Federation had strict policies over how much intervention the Senate would take in an active engagement. By making contact with the home system, Darius was putting his entire plan—all of his decisions and actions—at risk of being countermanded.

Only tradition was protecting him now—tradition and the fact that his potential delusion was the only chance to avoid a war.

"I cannot provide you with a q-com link to a military officer in an operational zone, Admiral," von Argent finally said. "Your request is beyond unreasonable. I'm surprised your government even put you in contact with me."

"They didn't," Darius told the other man. "I'm linked to you thanks to a personal favor. I am risking everything, Ambassador, in a grand gamble. On faith."

"Then I really don't think I can help you," the ambassador replied, but his tone had shifted. The tragic hero, sacrificing everything for the greater good…that was an image with *weight* in Imperial culture.

"My faith is in your Imperator's honor, Ambassador von Argent. If *you* share that faith, you have to realize that the best chance for peace is for von Santiago and me to speak directly and avoid a conflict.

"Or do you *know* that your Imperium has set us all on a course for war?" he asked gently.

Von Argent had clearly been about to disconnect but he stopped now, leaning back in his chair and studying Darius Moonblood's image.

"We have fought your Federation before," he said quietly. Like Darius, von Argent had served in at least one of those battles. "We know your blood, your iron."

"You've fought *me*, Ambassador," Darius pointed out. "Trust *my* honor, if nothing else. I have faith in the honor of Coraline. I don't believe your people killed tens of millions that they were sworn to protect. Do you for *one void-cursed second* believe we did?"

"The conversation you suggest could easily be read as treason by all three of us," von Argent told him, his voice still soft and quiet.

"Von Santiago doesn't have to take my call," Darius replied. "You're the ambassador. Desperate grasps for peace are your job."

He smiled.

"And I am very old. If my career, my freedom—even my life are the price my Federation demands for a desperate attempt at peace, so be it. I have given my life to the Federation. Why should I stop now?"

Von Argent was silent for a good minute.

"How long until you're in weapons range, Admiral?" he asked.

"You know I can't answer that question," Darius replied.

"No time, then, to ask others or get permission," the ambassador concluded. "What's the Montrose quote, Admiral? Your people have always been fond of it."

"'He either fears his fate too much, / Or his deserts are small, / That puts it not unto the touch, / To gain or lose it all,'" Darius quoted. "You'll connect me?"

"I might well still hang for this, Darius Moonblood. But I *know* Jacob von Coral—and you are right. I have faith in his honor.

"I will connect you to Admiral von Santiago.

THE CONNECTION TOOK LESS time than Darius was expecting. Despite von Argent's recognition of the time constraints, he'd still expected the ambassador to run the effort by *someone*.

Instead, he found himself looking at the rotating seal of the Coraline Imperial Navy battleship *Resolution* while the computers connected them.

A moment later, a stunning pale-skinned woman with raven-black hair appeared in front of him. Like his own image, it was separated from her surroundings to conceal the flag deck she was sitting on, but he recognized her from file footage.

"Ambassador, this is not the time for..." She trailed off as she processed his image. His uniform was probably the most immediate thing she recognized, but Darius doubted that Admiral von Santiago didn't know who he was.

"This is the only time for talking, Admiral von Santiago," Darius told her. "Before one or both of us makes a mistake that cannot be undone and sets our nations on a course that we cannot retreat from without bloodshed."

"This is a diplomatic override channel," von Santiago snapped. "What the *fuck* are you doing on it? This is treason!"

"It's treason if I'm wrong, maybe," Darius replied. "But then, if I'm wrong, I have misjudged your Imperator, your nation and you—and blasting your fleet to debris would be my moral duty.

"So, I must ask, Admiral von Santiago. Is the wreckage behind me an Imperial covert operation?"

She stared at him.

"I arrive in this system to a bombed ally and Federation troops landing in the wreckage, and you have the *gall*, the audacity, to ask if *I* am responsible for *your* atrocities?" she snarled. "You will pay for the blood you have shed, Moonblood. I will burn you down and *dance* in your ashes."

If von Santiago was lying, she was one of the better actors he'd ever met. With the diplomatic override channel, Darius was getting a level of emotional sideband that would *never* be shared with a potential enemy—and as he realized that, he consciously activated it on his side.

Because if she *wasn't* his enemy, he needed to make her see that. The fact that the channel was still open suggested there was a chance.

"I didn't do this, von Santiago," he said, his words soft and urgent. "Someone hijacked and sabotaged the Boudiccans' orbital defenses. I'm here for the same reason you are: to investigate the destruction of *Defiant* and honor our promises to protect this system.

"My people are convinced *you* did this, that all of this is a false-flag operation to justify you attacking us. Since they know *we* didn't do it, they only see one player."

"I only see one enemy on my screens, one man who burned a city and lies to cover—"

The neural implant recorded *everything*. There was no line between Darius's organic memory and his molecular circuitry chips that augmented it. Pulling everything he'd seen while the platforms fired on Iceni from his memories was the work of moments—the moments he was using to convince von Santiago he wasn't a villain.

A military channel wouldn't have let him dump that recording through it. But this was still a *diplomatic* channel, and von Santiago's voice cut off as she processed what he'd sent.

It wasn't just what he'd seen and heard. It was what he'd *felt*. A recording could be faked, even the emotional channels…but she was in a channel with those same emotional sidebands talking to him at that moment.

Either she would believe him or she wouldn't. He had nothing else he could provide, not without more time.

"My god in heaven," she finally whispered. "This was not us,

Admiral Moonblood. But if I accept that it was not *you*, I am left with more questions than answers…and still with a shattered city that cries out for vengeance.

"I want to believe you, Admiral Moonblood," she told him. "But there is no one else. These lies are…"

"You know I'm not lying," he said. "Someone *else* did this. Someone who destroyed *Defiant*. Someone who *wants* a war between the Imperium and the Federation. I believe that your people didn't do this. I know mine didn't.

"Someone else is here."

"We need to prove that."

"I know. I have a plan."

CHAPTER

NINE

At the speeds the two fleets were closing, it would take over twenty minutes to cross missile range and less than a minute to cross mass-driver range.

While Darius wished for a missile that could survive the multi-million-gravity of a capital-ship mass drive for long enough to be fired from his main guns, right now they were secondary to the calculation at play. Not a single missile dotted the display as the two fleets, fourteen battleships in total, lunged toward each other.

"Have I mentioned this is an *incredibly* stupid idea, sir?" Barre said calmly, watching the range numbers tick down.

"You have," Darius confirmed, his tone equally calm.

"Then may I reiterate that this is the most Voids-told awful, potentially insane plan I have ever heard *anyone* come up with?"

"We have the positron lances. They don't," he pointed out. "Are the targeting parameters laid in?"

"They are. I may have received an unexpected lesson in old Czech, German and Lakota profanity along the way," Barre replied. "I don't think your Captains are impressed with your plan either."

Darius smirked.

"I did not live to be the Federation's oldest and most respected

239

admiral to be intimidated by Captains a third of my age, Commander Barre," he told her. "But I *am* the Federation's oldest and most respected Admiral, so they will obey my orders."

"*Eloquently*, but yes."

"Good." The range was now just over a million kilometers and shrinking at over twenty thousand kilometers a second. "Get me the Captains on a channel. Fleet orders."

She nodded to him a moment later.

"Captains, you have most of your orders already," Darius told them. "We flip once we pass the Imperials and begin emergency deceleration at Tier Three thrust levels to sustain weapons range for as long as possible."

"Best case, sir, we're going to spread out to hell and gone over a couple hundred thousand kilometers," Captain Jamison pointed out.

"Stay inside the range of *Vagabond*'s lances," Darius ordered. Ten seconds left. "I know you all think this plan is mad, but I assure you of this: Captain Michaud is ready to *correct* affairs if they go off script."

Five seconds. Only silence answered him on the channel.

"To the right war, Captains. Stars guide our way."

Range.

EVEN WITH THE powerful mass manipulators playing games with the mass of the projectiles and the gravity around them, a thousand-meter mass driver accelerating a projectile up to a hundred thousand kilometers a second was a loud and obvious event.

Vagabond vibrated around Darius as her solitary spinal gun opened up. New icons flashed across the big holodisplay on the flag deck and his own virtual displays. None of those icons were *certain*, not with an inactive projectile, but they could at least estimate impact time.

Lasers flared across the screen, thin white lines drawn in by computers to represent invisible beams. Some slugs were knocked aside. Others were going to hit their targets, and Darius winced as *Vagabond*'s armored hull rang like a bell.

"Eleven-degree deflection hit, no damage, we're venting deck seven gray-water tanks," a voice said in his mind from the ship's tactical network.

Both his fleet and von Santiago's were spewing gases and volatiles now, the gouts of superheated steam that could mark critical damage.

"*Denmark* is dark. *Poland* is dark."

Barre's litany of names was a grim reminder. Each name was marked by a grayed out icon on the screen and gouts of further volatiles.

He didn't know the *names* of the ships on von Santiago's side suffering the same fate, but three of the Imperial battleships were out of the fight as the two fleets slid past each other at just over a hundred thousand kilometers' separation. Secondary mass drivers were in play now, and several more impacts shook *Vagabond*.

"No damage, no damage," the engineering officer on the tactical net announced. "Venting atmosphere from nine decks."

"*England* is dark," Barre announced, then exhaled a sigh a moment later. "Out of range. We're accelerating to reclose the engagement. Von Santiago is down three as well. We made a righteous mess of things, sir."

Darius nodded silently, his attention riveted somewhere else. The battle had been a show. Had the right people been watching?

"Did we learn anything?" he asked.

"Yeah. You know that assumption that the Imperium doesn't have positron lances?" his ops officer asked. "*Resolution* might be a flying egg instead of a proper arrowhead, but she's only got one main gun. Just like *Vagabond*."

Egg was a rather dismissive description of the elongated ovoid that was the Imperium's standard ship design, but the point stood. If *Resolution* only had one mass driver, she'd traded the mass for *something*.

But, like *Vagabond*, she hadn't fired those guns. The entire engagement had been "fought" with old-style weapons.

"We've got them!"

Darius's gaze and mental attention snapped to the speaker, a junior tactical analyst in Barre's department who *probably* shouldn't have shouted so loud.

"I have twelve battleships moving in the asteroid belt," the analyst reported. "Q-probes have confirmed power up of Class One mass manipulators, A-S jump imminent."

"They're not running," Darius said aloud.

"Every sensor in this system that can see what happens next is focused on Iceni," Barre replied. "If we and von Santiago die, they get their war."

"They'd have to wipe out a lot of civilian shipping to be sure, but there are no other A-S ships in the system and the only q-coms left are aboard our vessels," Darius agreed. "If they do this right, *both* of us would think the other side had reinforcements."

"Estimate jump in ten seconds," the analyst reported. "The asteroids are screwing up vectors, but they're *definitely* coming in-system toward us and the Imperials."

"What do we do?" Barre asked softly.

"Order all ships to load missiles and set Imperial IFFs as friendly in our systems," Fleet Admiral Darius Moonblood ordered, his voice level and calm. "If our real enemy is so kind as to show themselves, let's teach them why you don't *fuck* with our protectorates!"

DARIUS DIDN'T EVEN KNOW for sure who the strangers were. He could *guess*—the list of people with a reason to send a dozen battleships to try to start a war between the Imperium and the Federation was short. The list of people at least theoretically *able* to was longer...but the overlap was very, very small.

At least in his head, it consisted of one name: the Terran Commonwealth. The wonderfully democratic, egalitarian and *aggressively expansionist* nation at the heart of human space. The people absolutely convinced it was their righteous duty to bring all of humanity into one unified state.

No matter how many had to die to create their ideal world.

"Bandits have entered warped space, estimated emergence...now."

Barre had it perfectly. So, it appeared, did their presumably Terran opponents. With twelve ships against eight, they'd had enough overwhelming firepower to split their forces. Seven ships appeared a quarter-million kilometers away from von Santiago's five "survivors." Five appeared a similar distance from Darius's fleet.

There was no call to surrender. No attempt to negotiate. Mass drivers fired the moment they emerged…and Darius didn't even need to give an order.

"All ships engaging," Barre reported. "Missiles launching." She paused. "System requires validation for positron-lance deployment."

"Verified."

The single word hung in the flag deck like the Sword of Damocles —and then *Vagabond*'s true main battery fired in anger at last.

Each of *Vagabond*'s four broadsides was equipped with six quarter-megaton-per-second positron lances. Twenty-four beams of pure anti-matter flashed across space at the speed of light, and the closest unknown battleship died.

And Darius's people didn't let up. Even as the three "survivors" of the clash with the Imperials unleashed their missiles on the fleet attacking them, the ships that had gone dark brought their systems back online.

The Terrans had been watching from light-minutes away, unable to move q-probes close enough for certainty without giving away the game. When a dozen-plus ships had vented atmosphere and volatile gases, it had created enough confusion to cover the fact that the ships shutting down their engines hadn't been disabled or destroyed.

There hadn't been a single real hit in the entire "battle" against von Santiago's fleet, and the six ships that had supposedly died now came back online with a vengeance, flinging mass-driver and missile fire into the teeth of their new enemies.

"Imperial missiles look equivalent to ours," Barre reported as giga-ton-range explosions pocked the force attacking von Santiago. "*Resolution*'s positron lances are lighter, if that makes anyone feel better."

"Not really," Darius murmured, watching as von Santiago's flag-ship lunged at two Terran battleships, absorbing direct hits from their main guns to line up her positron lances and obliterate both ships.

Vagabond was doing equally deadly work. The two positron-lance-equipped ships were worth more than the rest of the combined fleets.

As Darius watched them cut through the Terrans, he was grimly certain he was watching a revolution in action.

The missiles were helping…but the lances were carrying the day.

"Enemy missile launch!" Barre snapped. "Remaining enemy ships are launching AM-drive missiles; I have over sixty new contacts."

"Lasers?" Darius asked calmly.

"Already tracking," she reported as a *third* battleship died under *Vagabond*'s guns. "Last bandits are turning to run. Your orders, sir?"

In a perfect world, he'd disable those ships. Interrogate their crews, learn why they were there and confirm the Commonwealth's aggression.

It wasn't a perfect world. He needed to make certain Boudicca was safe…and there was one way to very definitively do that.

"Order to the Fleet and inform von Santiago," he said coldly, watching the Terran ships run.

"No one escapes."

CHAPTER

TEN

Boudicca System
June 16, 2706 Earth Standard Meridian Date/Time

"Coraline Imperial Fifth Fleet, arriving!"

Those were not words Darius had ever expected to hear aboard one of his ships—let alone aboard one of the Federation's most advanced, most classified ships. Even *he* had actually asked permission before inviting Admiral von Santiago aboard *Vagabond*.

He'd got it, and now the raven-haired woman with the slightly aslant eyes stopped at the end of the shuttle ramp to salute the honor guard.

Those guards weren't Marines. The Navy Military Police did a passable job, but Darius suspected von Santiago could tell the difference.

Of course, *her* Marines had joined his on the surface hours before. Between their two fleets, they'd put over ten thousand power-armored troops on the surface. The search-and-rescue teams Iceni's shattered government had mustered might have had five thousand suits of equivalent hazmat gear.

Those Marines were saving lives, and Darius was grateful the Imperials were down there. It couldn't hurt that his people were working alongside their Coraline equivalents to save lives instead of fighting each other.

"Welcome aboard *Vagabond*, Admiral von Santiago," Captain Michaud greeted her new guest with a crisp salute. "We're not quite in the shape we'd want to be to be receiving guests, but I hope you'll forgive us."

Vagabond might have been the deadliest ship in the fray, but her enemies had registered that. Even the neutronium-laced armor of a modern battleship failed in the face of antimatter explosions. They were *functionally* intact, but they'd paid for their victory.

"*Resolution* is in worse shape," the Coraline Admiral admitted. "Our enemies might not have had positron lances of their own, but they adjusted their threat parameters for them quickly enough."

Darius stepped forward and bowed slightly.

"You'll forgive us if I don't tell you how many ships like *Vagabond* we have," he said drily. "Welcome aboard, Admiral. It's a pleasure to meet you face to face at last."

"Instead of glaring at each other across twenty light-years of space and wondering which of us would get the attack order first?" she asked. "I think that question, at least, might be laid to rest for a while."

"That's at a higher level than even mine," Darius replied, offering his hand. "But I look forward to the thought, it's true."

She smirked and he had to remind a portion of his hindbrain that he was sixty years her senior *and* still, arguably, her enemy.

"I understand we have a call scheduled with Ambassador von Argent," she replied. "I hope that may give you some assurance."

"I can hope," Darius agreed. "But I am very old, Admiral von Santiago, and I did not get that way by false hope."

"And yet you trusted me to help you fake a battle to lure out a potentially nonexistent enemy?" she murmured. "I'm not sure I'd share your fortitude without hope, Admiral."

"I lay little weight on hope, Admiral," Darius conceded, gesturing for her to walk with him. "I lay *everything* on faith. Faith in the honor of the Imperium. Faith in my people. Faith, Admiral von Santiago, in everything I had read on you."

He saw her shiver at the thought.

"I did not think that kind of faith in humanity was a Stellar Spiritualist teaching," she noted.

"The stars are far-off, uncaring things," Darius observed. "They watch, but it is only humanity who can act. Only humanity who can have faith—and in the end, the only thing we can have faith in is each other."

"You sound more like an atheist than a Spiritualist, Admiral."

"I do not believe that we require guidance," he told her. "I do believe that we are judged and held to a higher standard by the stars who watch us. I have faith in *that*, Admiral von Santiago. The question was whether I could have faith in *you*."

"Please, Admiral Moonblood," she replied. "We have risked treason and failure together to answer your question of faith. Please call me Trinh."

They shared a smile.

"Then I must insist you call me Darius."

Barre and Michaud joined them in the small conference room, Darius's operations officer leading her Imperial counterpart in with them.

A few seconds after they took their seat, *Resolution*'s Captain linked in virtually, a holographic image of the man filling the empty seat next to Barre. Lord Captain Khayyam Kariuki had the rare trait of being even darker-skinned than Darius's operations officer.

"Ambassador von Argent asked to speak to us all," von Santiago told him. "Von Coral and I were already supposed to be here."

Darius concealed his surprise at the name and took a second look at the operations officer. The dark-haired woman sitting across from Barre was *not* who he'd been expecting. The last report had said that von Santiago's operations officer had been a man.

Captain Samantha von Coral was the Imperator's cousin. Technically, she was on the list of potential replacements if he died—though the Electors did tend to pick from the previous Imperator's adult children if available.

Before he could say anything more, the link from Castle came live and the holographic image of the Coraline Imperium's Ambassador appeared standing at the end of the table.

Von Argent looked *exhausted*…but also like the cat that ate the canary. A moment later, Senator Falk's image joined him from yet another location. The two politicians were standing, facing the seated officers.

"Senator," Darius greeted her. "I wasn't expecting you to join us on this call."

"Once I found out that von Argent was reaching out to von Santiago and she was supposed to be on your ship, I added myself to the discussion," she told him. "Much of what we have to tell will remain classified on the part of both of our nations.

"You and von Santiago would have been briefed regardless, but your staffs will also need to be read in, and I believe your Captains deserve to know what their sacrifice and courage purchased."

The Battle of Boudicca had been a massacre in the end, but most of the ships had been damaged and three battleships had been completely lost.

"I serve the Senate and the Federation, Senator."

"Far beyond any rational request on our part, yes," Falk agreed brightly. "At the end of this conversation, Ambassador von Argent will be meeting an aircar to bring him to the Senatorial Chambers. There, he and I will present the document we've been working on since your victory."

That was less than eight hours earlier. They'd worked *fast*.

"The Senate will approve it. Jacob von Coral has already indicated his approval. While we intend to keep it secret for the immediate future, by this time tomorrow, the Castle Federation and the Coraline Imperium will have concluded a draft treaty of mutual nonaggression and defense."

Darius was glad he was already sitting. He might have fallen in sheer shock.

"The presence of what appears to have been an entire Commonwealth battle fleet in territory both of us regard as under our protection is intolerable," von Argent told them. "Examination of the ships and interrogation of the survivors will give us more answers, but my Imperator feels that we cannot wait for certainty.

"The risk is too great. We must act *now*, to agree to stand together against this threat. He has suggested that both of our nations begin to send envoys to the various small nations around us. A larger alliance is needed here—neither of our fleets can stand off the Commonwealth.

"Not alone. Not together."

"But if we bring in the Trade Factor, the Star Kingdom, and the other single-system nations around here with fleets, we might be able to change that," Falk told them. "Both of us intend to begin a crash rearmament program to update our ships with positron lances.

"*Officially*, those programs are targeted at each other. Our alliance will likely become an open secret quickly enough, but the longer we can keep Terra in the dark, the safer we all are."

"I almost wish I was wrong," Darius admitted, considering the industrial and military might of the Commonwealth. "Stars as my witness, I wish I was wrong."

"So do I, Admiral Moonblood, but you were correct to suspect a third party at Boudicca—and there is no one else. If the Commonwealth comes for our stars, we will be ready. Will you, Admiral Moonblood? Admiral von Santiago?"

"My life is the Imperator's," von Santiago noted. "I will stand against any enemy. I'll admit, though, that it's reassuring to not be watching our closest neighbor."

Darius nodded, bowing slightly to Falk's image.

"I serve the Senate and the Federation," he echoed his earlier words. "If the Commonwealth comes, they will have a rude awakening."

～

The Commonwealth began their invasion by assaulting the Star Kingdom of Phoenix on August 3, 2708.

Thanks to the secret treaties forged in the two years prior to that invasion, the Alliance of Free Stars was ready for them and Admirals von Santiago and Moonblood led a relief fleet that prevented Phoenix from falling to the Commonwealth.

Admiral Darius Moonblood did not survive the victory at Phoenix, but he left an entire region of space with a hope for freedom.

PULSAR RACE

A STARSHIP'S MAGE UNIVERSE
NOVELLA

CHAPTER
ONE

It wasn't much of an apartment. A fifty-sixth floor one-bedroom unit in Serendipity City, the capital of the Xanth System on the planet Anthony, it had solid bones and would probably have been more homey if Mage-Captain (Retired) Ivan Halloway had done anything to personalize the space.

The hawk-nosed Mage ignored the mess and looked out the window over his home city. He'd been back for two months and had yet to decide if he was going to stay in his apartment. His pension, boosted by his promotion to Mage-Captain on retirement, would pay for a larger place, possibly even a house on the outskirts.

But Serendipity was the capital of a MidWorld star system of the Protectorate of the Mage-King of Mars. It wasn't a cheap place to live, so keeping more of his money in his own account sounded good to him.

Mostly, though, he knew he was being indecisive. Serendipity spread out around him, his hundred-story apartment building one of six in a pentagonal cluster—and one of maybe sixty around the down-town core.

Ivan started at the chime from his console. He wasn't expecting any calls today, though there were a number of old friends he'd connected with since his retirement. He took a glance at his reflection in the window and then snorted at his own vanity.

He was still the same tall and dark man who had drawn female gazes throughout his teen years and his twenty-five-year career in the Royal Martian Navy. His hair was starting to grow out—another thing he was feeling indecisive on—but it showed no gray.

Whoever was calling probably wasn't going to care that he was wearing a sleeveless vest instead of a suit or uniform. Ivan tapped on the computer he wore on his left wrist, sighing as he mistyped and started playing the recorded message he had saved—something *else* he hadn't decided on.

"Mage-Captain Ivan Holloway, this is Sarah Tapiti at the Xanth Royal Reserve Station," a female voice greeted him, mispronouncing both his first name—*EYE-vahn*, not *YEH-vahn*—and his last name.

"We wanted to talk to you about your reserve status. I have a copy of your muster-out forms, and it appears that you did not fill out the section requesting active or inactive reserve status. By default, that puts you in full reti—"

Ivan cut off the recording. He didn't want to be reserve Navy. He could see the signs—there was a civil war coming and he wanted *no* part of it. Hell, there had very nearly *been* a civil war near Xanth, between the Sherwood and Míngliàng Systems, right before he'd chosen retirement at the end of his fifth five-year commission.

There were so many things a Mage could do with their power and the money that power brought. Ivan felt no need to die for the Mage-King instead of living for himself.

He *finally* managed to accept the incoming call, stepping back into his living room and directing the video to the wallscreen above his never-used fireplace.

"Hey, Ivan," the man on the screen greeted him.

"Karl," Ivan responded. Karl Charpentier was one of his oldest friends. They'd gone through school here in Serendipity together until Ivan had been pulled into the Mage tracks. They'd stayed friends after that, even through both of their careers.

"I see you still haven't finished unpacking," Charpentier said with a chuckle. "Our city isn't going to eat you, you know."

Ivan shared the chuckle.

"It's not Serendipity I'm scared of," he told his friend. "Just habit, I suppose. You can always be reassigned at the drop of a hat in the Navy."

"Civilian shipping is *so* much more consistent," Charpentier replied. "You should consider it."

"I have three different messages from the Guild in my inbox telling me the same thing," Ivan said. The Mage Guild's main job in the twenty-fifth century was matching Jump Mages looking for employment with jump-ships looking for Mages.

Among the many things the Navy had trained him for, Ivan was a fully qualified Jump Mage with the silver polymer runes inlaid into his hands that allowed him to interact with a starship's jump matrix.

"Plus at least eight other messages asking me to come in for assorted interviews," he continued. "Everyone seems to find the concept of a fortysomething retired Mage problematic."

"There's not that many like you around," Charpentier told him. "You're a rare and valuable commodity and everybody wants you to work for them."

"Including you?" Ivan asked. "What do you need, Karl?"

His old friend was silent for a few moments, pulling long sandy hair back with both hands in a long-familiar nervous gesture. Holding his hair back, he swallowed and bowed his head slightly.

"You know I'm divorced, right?" Karl asked. "I think we talked about that."

"Messy disaster, you got the ship and Lyle, and she got everything else?" Ivan vaguely remembered the conversation. They hadn't been drinking that heavily, but neither of them could drink like they had when they were nineteen, either.

"Yeah," Charpentier confirmed. "Penny wasn't responsible for everything that went wrong after that, but she started all of it." He sighed. "I guess I can't blame her for getting bored sitting at home taking care of Lyle while I fucked off around the Protectorate, but I still hate her a bit for leaving Lyle."

Lyle was, if Ivan remembered correctly, Karl's eleven-year old son. Ivan wasn't clear on what Lyle's living situation was, but he doubted the boy was living on *Restoya*, Charpentier's owner-operated jump-courier.

"I know what jump-courier rates look like, Karl," the ex-Navy Mage pointed out. "I can't imagine you're hurting just because your wife took the bank account and the house."

The channel was silent again and Charpentier looked like Ivan had punched him in the gut.

"I fucked up," the courier captain finally whispered. "Divorce, midlife crisis, worry about the kid…I can give a billion excuses, but it's all on me. I fucked it up but good and the crew quit."

"All of them?" Ivan asked. He wasn't sure how many people a civilian jump-courier would have aboard, but the Navy ones he was familiar with ran a crew of twenty—six of them Mages.

"All of them," Charpentier confirmed. "*Restoya* is a well-built ship with good robots and computers. I can *fly* her on my own, but maintaining her on my own is a life-eating job and…well…without Mages, I'm fucked."

Only a Mage could cast the spell that would jump a starship a light-year away. Karl Charpentier was *not* a Mage, which meant he'd hired them. If he was having problems hiring new Mages…

"You got yourself blacklisted?" Ivan asked.

"Five Mages walked out on the same day," his old friend told him. "Doesn't matter if I'm officially blacklisted. No Mage will jump for me."

That was…fair enough.

"What did you *do*?" Ivan demanded.

"What do you *think*?" Charpentier replied. "I took sympathy as something more and made a pass I shouldn't. Took no for an answer, but apparently I'd been enough of a general shithead through the divorce…" He sighed. "Look, Ivan, I don't blame them one bit. But I'm in a hole. A deep hole."

Charpentier swallowed hard and met Ivan's gaze.

"I put myself here and I probably made it worse along the way," he said grimly. "Doing my damnedest to keep Lyle in the style and schools Penny got him used to. Holding it all together, paying for it all somehow, but…

"I need your help, Ivan, or I'm going to lose *Restoya*," he finally said in a rush. "I'm deep in debt, and if I don't come up with four mil in the next thirty days, I default. I default on *Restoya*, I have nothing."

"Four million," Ivan repeated. "Martian dollars, I'm assuming."

"Exactly."

That was more than Ivan had made in total in twenty-five years in the Navy. How the hell had Charpentier even ended up that deep in debt?

"How much of it have you got?" Ivan asked with a sigh. He didn't want to get involved—he'd been considering never leaving the planet again—but he and Charpentier went back a long way.

"Nothing," Charpentier admitted. "I'm tapped out, Ivan. I'm..." He sighed. "The bank has given me almost a year of leeway; that's why the hole is that big. I've borrowed from places I shouldn't to keep things floating, but I need to make a forty percent payment on the main loan to get back into good standing, and nobody is going to lend me that. Not when my income is all over the place."

"Even if I jump for you, you need half a dozen Mages to run at your usual speed," Ivan told his friend gently. "We can't make four million in a month, even if we pay nothing except docking fees and fuel."

"I have a plan," Charpentier told him. "*Restoya* is way faster and more maneuverable sublight than most people think. It shaved a few hours off each end of the critical deliveries and made me a pile of money—Penny's got that money now, but the ship is still a racer."

"You can't win an intersystem race with one Mage—and even *this* star system doesn't have that many sublight races," Ivan said slowly. Xanth had more than most, both legitimate and...otherwise. Some were straight acceleration courses, but most were based around some degree of navigation and obstacles.

All of the legal ones were safe. Some of the others weren't.

"I know exactly how many sublight races Xanth has, yeah," Charpentier agreed. "I've run in most of them over the last year—and won most of them, too. I was hoping to get a partnership or something, but...buzzbugs. Nothing."

"So you end up here, thirty days from a payment you have zero dollars toward," Ivan concluded. "How do I help?"

"You will help?"

"I've known you for thirty-six years, Karl Charpentier," Ivan snapped. "I'm not leaving you or your son to swing."

If the bank took *Restoya*, that would clear most of Charpentier's legal debts and he could sign on as a captain or pilot for a larger shipping firm. He'd *hate* that, but he'd survive—but from the sounds of it, Ivan's old friend had debts that wouldn't be cleared with the seizure.

"How much shit are you still in if the banks take your ship?" the Mage asked.

Charpentier hesitated.

"I'm not helping you if you don't tell me everything," Ivan told him.

"I've borrowed over a million from la Cosa Nostra," Charpentier admitted. "I didn't *know* who was behind the loan sharks I went to, I swear! Not until a gentleman showed up and told me they now owned all of my debt."

"Fuck." Ivan stared at the image of his old friend as a familiar shiver went through him. The *last* thing Ivan wanted was to get involved with the interstellar iteration of the Sicilian and American Mafias. He'd spent twenty-five years quietly dodging any posting that he expected to involve shooting. He didn't want to tangle with one of the largest criminal organizations in the Protectorate.

"But I have a plan and it answers everything," his friend insisted. "Have you heard of the Black Pulsar Race?"

"The illegal race run *by* la Cosa Nostra through whichever pulsar they think the RMN isn't watching this week?" Ivan asked drily. "Yes, I'd heard of it. The Navy *really* doesn't like it. A few too many people tend to die on that run."

"I have an invitation," Charpentier told him. "I won enough of the illegal races in Xanth to earn that. Prize is over six mil, Ivan. I pay off my note and my debt to the mob, and then hand you a draft for a million dollars."

"But you need a Mage to get you to the Pulsar," Ivan concluded with a sigh. A million dollars was a lot of money, but did he even *need* it? His pension would cover the apartment, and even *he* wasn't sure what to do with his time.

It would, he supposed, make it unnecessary for him to sign up for the reserves for the extra money—and if he never signed up for the reserves, they couldn't recall him when the war with the UnArcana Worlds inevitably started.

"We have to get to the starting point, jump to the race course, and then jump to the finish point when the course is done," Charpentier laid out. "I have the coordinates for where we meet everyone."

"The Navy would pay you for those," Ivan said. He was sure la Cosa Nostra had a plan for if those coordinates leaked, but the Navy would still pay for them.

"Not six million, they wouldn't," his friend replied. "What they'd want would be the endpoint coordinates, where la Cosa Nostra and the other criminals hang out and the rich and dumb bet on which of us dies. We don't get that until we finish the course.

"I'm not sure of the exact details, but I only have one set of coordinates and a date."

Ivan wanted to say no, to back out, to run and leave his friend to his own devices…but he'd already said he wouldn't leave Charpentier and the kid to swing.

He should have asked what his old friend's solution *was* before he'd said that.

"I won't…" He sighed. "Look, I'm retired, and I was never a good soldier, but I can jump for you. Just this one, then I'm out."

"That's all I need, Ivan," Charpentier promised. "This should be safe enough. I *know Restoya* can do it."

"Karl…I've seen the Navy's records on the Black Pulsar Race," Ivan said. "A quarter of the competitors don't come back. *A quarter*. Just… keep that in mind, okay?"

CHAPTER

TWO

"Welcome to the Mage Guild of the Xanth System; how may I help you?"

Ivan couldn't help but smile at the perky cheerfulness of the young man behind the desk. Serendipity City's office of the Mage's Guild was an entirely normal-looking twelfth story suite in one of the central office towers. The reception area was carpeted in dark blue carpet that matched the comfortable-looking furniture and went well with the sparkling white walls and reception desk.

"I need to do a Ship's Mage registration," he told the youth. "And I'd like to talk to whoever is running registration, if that's possible.

"I could help you with the registration here if there's nothing complicated," the young man replied. "But if you want to speak to Miz Kush, I'm afraid she's out for a late lunch. She should be back in the next twenty minutes or so, if it's important?"

Ivan considered it for all of ten seconds, long enough for the youth behind the desk to start looking awkward, before smiling and shaking his head. His curiosity over what the Mage Guild was telling people about Charpentier wasn't that important.

"No, if you and I can go through the registration together, that will be fine," he said. "Identification number is CT-5385, *Restoya*. I'll be

261

taking a temporary position as senior Ship's Mage under Captain Charpentier."

"Of course, of course," the young man replied. "If you want to take a seat, please, sir Mage? My name is Simion Dumitrescu and I'll be delighted to help you."

An unseen command opened a concealed cupboard in the gleaming white desk that disgorged a blue-upholstered rolling chair. Ivan took the seat calmly—he was keeping up enough of the physical exercise program the RMN had trained into him that he could keep standing for a while but he was still closer to fifty than forty.

"I see *Restoya* here, yes," Dumitrescu told him. "Um. That's odd."

"What's odd, Mr. Dumitrescu?" Ivan asked.

"Just the history of the ship, sir Mage," the youth replied. "All five of her Mages resigned on the same day fourteen months ago. Odd situation, no explanation given—but we do have a flag on the file to warn potential Mages about that."

"I'm already aware of it," Ivan said. "Captain Charpentier was quite honest about the problems his ship had had."

"Yes, of course," Dumitrescu said slowly. "I also have a note on here to warn potential Mages that *Restoya* is subject to a Notice of Potential Seizure by a syndicate of local banks. Both first and second mortgages have applied for the Notice. If you take a position as her Mage, you will be obligated to return her to this system by the date specified."

The youth blinked.

"I haven't seen this before," he admitted.

"If I don't, what happens?" Ivan asked. "I haven't heard of that myself either."

"If you don't cooperate with the Notice, you'll lose your good standing status with the Guild and be regarded as liable for Captain Charpentier's mortgages in the case that the ship cannot be seized," the youth read off.

"Apologies, sir Mage, this is from the file and the Notice itself; I'm not—"

"I understand, Mr. Dumitrescu," Ivan told the young man. "That's definitely something I needed to know, and I will keep in mind. Any other flags on the file I should be aware of?"

"There is one more flag around Captain Charpentier's general credit rating. The Guild keeps an eye on Captains' fiscal standings, and Charpentier is currently rated double F in our files. We wouldn't lend him money."

Or work for him, Ivan guessed. The Guild valued transparency on both sides of the deals it tracked and mediated. That wasn't great for a Captain in trouble, but as the Mage signing on, he appreciated it.

"I'm aware of Captain Charpentier's situation," Ivan said. "Do you need me to mark a waiver or something confirming that I've heard the lecture?"

"I have to confirm I warned you about all flags on the account, but that's all," the Guild receptionist told him. "I'm not sure I'd take the job, if I was a Mage."

"I owe Charpentier and I'm trying to avoid boredom in retirement," Ivan replied.

"I have your record here, I see," Dumitrescu said. "Thank you for your service, Mage-Captain!"

"Just...*Mage* is fine," Ivan said, shifting awkwardly. Tradition said that any retiring officer was promoted one grade to boost their pension. He'd *actually* retired as a Mage-Commander. He'd never even held the courtesy "Captain" title, though he knew other Mage-Commanders who'd been made Captain of their own destroyers.

"All right, everything is loaded in and checked off," the secretary said. He slid a tablet across the white desk. "If you can sign and thumbprint the pad, Mage-Captain, you will be on the records as Captain Charpentier's Mage. Everything official and documented."

Ivan wasn't entirely familiar with the document he was signing, so he took a few seconds to read it. It was just a summary of what they'd discussed and a recognition that as Ship's Mage, he had legal responsibilities to both the ship and the Protectorate.

Those responsibilities paled in comparison to those he'd had as a Mage for the Royal Martian Navy, though. He signed the tablet.

"I've never been a civilian Jump Mage before," he told Dumitrescu. "It's going to be an experience."

"Good luck, Mage-Captain," the youth replied. "From all the flags on the file, it sounds like you might need it."

"I appreciate it, Mr. Dumitrescu," Ivan said. "Luck is something I find is never in sufficient supply!"

~

To his surprise, Ivan was intercepted in the main lobby by a tall Asian woman waving him down.

"Mage-Captain Halloway?" she asked. She managed to get the first syllable right, which was more than the Navy Reserve office had managed. "I just got an update from my office, but you are Ivan Halloway, right?"

She got his first name wrong, and Ivan sighed as he stepped out of the rush of traffic toward the woman. The ground floor of the office tower was a boutique mall of some kind, and it was busy this afternoon.

"I am," he conceded. "I'm not sure we know each other?"

"I'm Jade Kush, one of the Guild administrators for Xanth," she told him. "You just activated a Ship's Mage contract, yes?"

"I did," Ivan agreed, eyeing the attractive woman—probably at least a decade younger than him—carefully. "I even listened to and acknowledged all of the warning flags."

"I got that too," Kush agreed. "Umm." She hesitated, looking around the lobby mall as if to see whether anyone was listening.

"Look, that ship...*Restoya*. Something weird is going on there," she told him.

"My understanding is that Captain Charpentier had a midlife crisis and pissed off his crew," Ivan replied. "That's weird, I suppose, but not uncommon enough to worry about."

"I've seen that three times in the last year alone, Mage-Captain Halloway," Kush warned. "Most Captains are smarter than that, but there's always a few idiots. We encourage Mages to get out of those situations where it's possible...and we can always make it possible."

"Karl won't be taking anything out on me," Ivan said. "I know the situation and I know him."

"That's fair, that's fair," Kush said swiftly. "But I wanted to warn you."

"I think you just did," Ivan replied, starting to feel a bit frustrated.

"Not about what's officially in the files," the woman said. "We did initially attempt to source new Mages for Captain Charpentier; it's our job, after all. We eventually stopped."

"Why?" That was not something Charpentier had mentioned.

"Because we had four separate candidates go from *eager* to *I'm out* in twenty-four hours, all of them before they even met the Captain," Kush whispered. "I have no proof, Mage-Captain, but I think someone might have threatened them."

Ivan nodded slowly. He *really* wished he'd learned all of this before he'd agreed. He didn't have it in him to back out now, but he was starting to get more and more uncomfortable with each conversation he had around his old friend's ship.

"Thank you, Ms. Kush," he said. "I appreciate the warning, but I've already signed and Captain Charpentier is an old friend. We'll make it work, no matter what."

"Fair enough," she said cheerfully, her voice louder now. "Good luck with your new ship, Mage Halloway. Let me know how it goes."

"I will, Ms. Kush."

He walked away from her, waiting until he was out of the lobby and presumably out of her sight before shaking his head with a sigh.

Just what the hell had Karl Charpentier dug his way into?

Ivan needed to make another stop, it seemed. A stop he'd hoped to *never* make.

CHAPTER

THREE

T he sign outside the office said it belonged to "Maple Leaf Investment Services" and had a logo of a purple three-part leaf Ivan wasn't familiar with. Even inside the office, there was nothing unusual except, perhaps, for a lack of the busily wandering staff most offices had.

"I can't tell you much, Halloway," the woman behind the desk told him with a shake of her head. Jessie Theodore had been the intelligence officer on the first cruiser he'd served on. They'd stayed in touch after that, even after the raven-haired woman had transferred to the Martian Interstellar Security Service.

"Firstly, I don't *have* much on la Cosa Nostra in Xanth," she warned him. "That's more in the MIS's bailiwick."

The Martian Investigation Service and the Martian Interstellar Security Service were one letter off on their initials—and most people who knew both figured that was intentional on the MISS's part.

"No one in the MIS owes me favors," Ivan told her with a smile. "And I need to know how deep I've got myself."

Theodore shrugged.

"You still have most of your clearances," she conceded. "Need to know is iffy in this case, but we don't really lock down civilian orga-

267

nized crime data the same way as we would, say, somebody's covert ops."

Ivan spread his hands in a shrug as he leaned back in his chair. Nothing in the MISS office was particularly high-quality. There was an active attempt to make the whole place as plain and uncomfortable as possible, probably to keep people from asking too many questions.

"I don't know or care about anyone's covert ops," he admitted. "I care about whether la Cosa Nostra is going to put a bullet in me for jumping Karl Charpentier's ship."

"I'll have to do some digging," Theodore told him. "And I don't owe you *that* many favors, Ivan. Buy me dinner?"

He chuckled.

"Is that remotely appropriate?" he asked her. He was reasonably sure she didn't mean it in a romantic sense, though he could be wrong.

"Favors for favors," she said. "If something I turn up manages to actually be classified in a way I can't share, dinner won't buy that. But most of what I can do for you is poke into theoretically public records with tools you don't have. Reasonably appropriate, so long as I do it in my off hours."

"I can do dinner, but my time is pretty crunched," Ivan said thoughtfully. "I need to be aboard *Restoya* by morning, and I've still got a pile of errands to run through."

"I'm booked tonight as it is," Theodore said. "Consider it a rain check. You're coming back, or are you on *Restoya* for good?"

"Even if I'm on *Restoya* for good, Karl's kid is at a boarding school here," Ivan said. "We'll be back."

He hadn't told her about the race. He wasn't sure he wanted to admit to *anyone* just what Karl Charpentier was planning.

"I'll email you then," she told him. "And you can get me a *nice* dinner when you're next in town."

"It's a deal," Ivan promised.

She smirked.

"Yes, it is," she agreed. "I look forward to it. I'll send you what I find. Now get out of my office before someone starts thinking you've blown our cover."

"Jessie...I'm not sure anyone who actually cares *doesn't* know where your office is," Ivan said.

"You know that, and I know that, and even my boss knows that," Theodore said. "But there are appearances to keep up! We are spies, after all!"

~

ONE OF THE advantages of living in a planetary capital was the ready availability of both taxis and public transit. Ivan had moved back home months earlier and still hadn't acquired a vehicle of his own yet.

It was mid-autumn in Serendipity, though, and the weather was perfect for him to walk home. The Maple Leaf office was only two kilometers from his home, and the store he wanted to stop in at was on the route.

He could call a taxi, but it felt lazy and he was still getting used to *having* ready access to outside. If he was going to ship out on *Restoya*, he wasn't entirely sure when he'd get to be outside again, either.

He was most of the way to the store and enjoying a gentle breeze when a low-slung dark red groundcar pulled to a stop next to him. There was nothing around for the vehicle to be stopping for, and Ivan unconsciously stepped away and summoned a small amount of his magic. Sparks glittered around his concealed fist as a large woman in a pitch-black suit stepped out of the car.

Something in the way she moved told him she was armed, but she only bowed slightly to him.

"My employer would like to speak with you, Mage-Captain Halloway."

"Do I know your employer, miss..."

"No," she said calmly. "He would like to speak with you anyway."

Ivan looked around him, trying not to feel panicked. There was no one close enough to intervene if the woman got violent. He could take her down, but he needed more of a reason than a rude invitation.

"I must decline your kind invita—"

"Get in the car, Mage Halloway," the stranger cut him off, flicking back her suit jacket to reveal the matte-black shape of a weapon of some kind. Hopefully, it was a stungun with the taser SmartDarts that, theoretically, wouldn't kill him.

"And if I refuse?"

"We go on our way and the next invitation is significantly less polite," she told him. "You will meet with my employer, Mage Halloway."

She'd dropped the military rank after the first time, Ivan noted absently, but she was at least getting his last name right.

"Fine," he said grumpily. "Where are we going?"

"Get in the car," she instructed.

Sighing, Ivan obeyed. It turned out to be a more spacious vehicle than he'd guessed from the outside, with two sets of benches facing each other rather than forward. The door closed behind him, and the threatening woman entered the front of the vehicle to join the driver.

Ivan was not alone in the car. He didn't recognize the heavyset man sitting across from him—but he *did* recognize the golden medallion the stranger wore at his throat. Ivan wore the same medallion: the marker of a member in good standing of the Mage's Guild, a recognized wielder of the Gift.

Where Ivan's simply had the three letters *RMN* to note that he'd been trained as a Navy Mage, the stranger's medallion had the three stars of a Jump Mage and the paired swords of a Guild-trained Enforcer, a Combat Mage.

"Jester, take us for a drive," the stranger ordered. "Loop our friend's apartment block a couple of times; that should give us plenty of time for our conversation."

There was no response from the front of the car, but a privacy barrier slid up, leaving Ivan alone with the other Mage.

"In answer to the question you asked my lovely associate, we aren't going anywhere," the stranger told him. "You may call me Aquila, Mage Halloway. May I call you Ivan?"

"I prefer to keep that to my friends," Ivan said, trying not to quail *too* visibly under the hard gaze of his new companion. The stranger had got it right, though, which was better than most.

"What is all of this about?" he asked.

"You've taken a new Ship's Mage position, Mage Halloway," Aquila said. "One aboard a ship of some interest to me: *Restoya*."

"If the ship is of interest to you, you should talk to her Captain," Ivan replied. "I'm just helping out a friend."

"Oh, I know, I know." Aquila made a throwaway gesture, one that drew Ivan's gaze to his long, delicate fingers—fingers that had the distinctive small burn scars that came from using fire magic.

A *lot* of fire magic.

"And…representatives of mine have spoken to Captain Charpentier. He has proven unwilling to negotiate, and quite frankly, Mage Halloway, I have run out of patience with him."

Aquila's tone was ice and Ivan found himself physically trying to move farther away from the man on the other side of the car.

That brought a thin smile to the big man's lips that chilled Ivan even more.

"I had arranged one fall for Captain Charpentier, but with your assistance, he has found what may well be a way out of my trap," Aquila said. "So. I find myself required to assemble a new trap, which I find irritating, but one that will put *Restoya* in my hands with no one the wiser."

"As Ship's Mage, I am expected to defend the ship," Ivan managed to squeak out. Aquila regarded him curiously, like an owl studying a mouse that had just tried a particularly *dumb* trick.

"You could certainly make the task of my team significantly easier, yes," he noted. "And I have the greatest of admiration for the officers of His Majesty's Royal Martian Navy. It would upset me to order your death, Mage Halloway."

He said it so calmly, so matter-of-factly, that it took Ivan half a second to process what had just been said.

"I have an alternative that will serve both of our needs," the crime lord told him. "We will pay you, of course," he added with a vague wave of those strangely delicate fingers.

"Charpentier is already paying me," Ivan replied.

"Charpentier is offering you a portion of a prize he hasn't won," Aquila pointed out. "A prize he will not win."

Ivan wasn't even sure how Aquila knew that part—or if it was just a lucky guess. Or an educated one, he supposed.

"We will pay you ten thousand now and one hundred thousand once my team has taken possession of *Restoya*," Aquila continued. "Martian dollars by credit chit. There will be appropriate invoices and tax deductions filed. Everything will appear completely aboveboard."

And if Ivan refused, the only question was whether he died on Anthony or in deep space aboard *Restoya* somewhere. He *wanted* to protect his friend, but he knew where his limits lay…and Ivan Halloway knew he had no physical courage.

"I can just walk away," he whispered.

"That is no longer acceptable," Aquila snapped. "This is my offer, Mage Halloway: my people will insert a ship into the Pulsar Race. Once they contact you, you will disable Captain Charpentier and hold his ship on course until they board.

"You will be safely dropped off anywhere you wish, so long as you never speak of what happened. One hundred and ten thousand dollars and your life, Mage Halloway."

Ivan swallowed. He couldn't see a way out of this.

"Two conditions," he finally managed to force out against his fear.

"Conditions, Mage Halloway?"

"Yes," Ivan said, quailing under Aquila's eyes. "Charpentier's debts are cleared. All of them. You take his ship, but he owes no one anything. I get the feeling you can do that."

"It is certainly possible," Aquila admitted, his sharp gaze still burning into Ivan. "And your second?"

"Karl lives," Ivan stated firmly. "I'll help you steal his ship, but my friend doesn't get hurt."

Even if he was left with nothing but the clothes on his back, Karl Charpentier was a brilliant pilot, engineer and starship commander. His skills and history were known—he could find new work that paid well enough to keep his son taken care of.

The car was very silent as Aquila continued to study Ivan, his gaze burning into the ex-navy man's eyes.

"Very well," the crime boss conceded. "I will clear Charpentier's debts once *Restoya* is seized. He will suffer no injuries he does not bring upon himself. Sufficient, Mage Halloway?"

Ivan didn't get the impression he was going to get much more out of Aquila, so he nodded meekly.

"Jester, bring us around to our friend's building," Aquila ordered. "Singer, give him the money once he's on his way.

"We're done here."

CHAPTER

FOUR

Xanth was a solidly prosperous MidWorld System, which meant that the inhabited planet had six midsize orbital stations. Other systems had larger or more complicated stations, but Xanth had gone for single-ring spoke-and-wheel designs. Ships docked at a center spire that remained motionless, and then people took transit pods out to the rotating rings with their half-gravity of centripetal pseudogravity.

Charpentier was waiting for Ivan when he got off the shuttle, the sandy-haired man looking utterly at home in the microgravity of the docking bay.

"That's all you're bringing?" he asked as he saw the small bag Ivan was carrying with him.

"I'm not staying on your ship long-term, Karl," Ivan replied, shaking his head at his friend. He had no idea how he was going to tell Charpentier that there was no way he was keeping the ship. Either way, though, he'd never planned on staying aboard *Restoya* for long.

"And I guess the Navy taught you to pack light," Charpentier conceded. "Come on; I want to get to one of the observation decks. I want you to *see* my baby before we fly on her!"

Ivan chuckled.

"And here I thought I was going to have to ask," he told his friend. "I'll see the simulacrum, but it's not quite the same."

While the one-hundredth-scale silver model at the heart of any jump-ship *was* the starship in several critically important senses, it was also only one color and didn't give you any sense of scale.

"I've already made a reservation for lunch. Come on."

Ivan followed his friend through the busy station, dodging around people who were clearly much less used to microgravity. There *was* a path where the ground was inlaid with gravity runes, but it was roped off and only available to members of assorted clubs.

If Ivan was planning on becoming a pilot long-term, he'd get that membership, but his plan was still to return to Serendipity. He was surprised, though, that *Charpentier* didn't have one.

"You don't have a Captains' Club membership or something?" he asked his friend as they reached the edge of the receiving bay.

"I did," Charpentier said. "Wasn't essential, though, so I let it lapse. Every expense I can cut helps pay for Lyle's school. So far, so good."

"Isn't school paid for by the Xanth government?" Ivan asked. They'd certainly gone to a system-run school.

"Penny wanted him in a good school, so he ended up at Pleathers," Charpentier said. "That's where his friends are, his soccer team is…I can't pull him out and send him to a regular school after he's been there for five years."

Ivan whistled silently.

Pleathers Academy was probably not the *most* expensive or prestigious school on the planet, but it was definitely up there. Unless he misremembered, the current system governor had graduated from Pleathers.

It was *that* kind of school. No wonder Charpentier was falling deeper into debt every day he couldn't get his ship flying properly.

"When this is over, I'd appreciate it if you could jump me to Sherwood or somewhere," the captain told him. "I think I can probably hire Mages in most systems. I just have a reputation here."

"One you earned," Ivan pointed out. It definitely hadn't helped that Aquila, whoever Aquila actually *was*, appeared to have been harassing every Mage who'd thought about working for Charpentier.

"One I earned," Charpentier agreed grimly. "I don't pretend I didn't fuck up, Ivan. I might think my entire crew walking out was a bit excessive, but I did try to kiss my senior Ship's Mage."

Ivan shook his head.

"My friend, if everyone walked out after that, you'd been digging for a bit," he pointed out. "Midlife crisis doesn't buy you *that* much patience."

They traveled in silence for a minute after that before Charpentier sighed.

"You're right, of course," he conceded "In…just about every detail. *Fuck.* I didn't think I was being that bad at the time, but I think I was being a whiny, demanding shit from the moment Penny sent me the divorce papers to the moment the crew walked out.

"No *wonder* Sonia was only sympathetic at best."

"Learn. Improve. Apologize. Don't do it again," Ivan told his friend. "You've got to stop digging sooner or later and you've got to make it right."

"I know," Charpentier agreed. "Got a few requests for references along the way. I've given them where asked—and good ones, too. They earned those."

"So you're probably not *completely* hopeless. But you've got some ground to make up, too."

"That I do," Ivan's friend agreed. "I know that. For now, though, we're here."

THE OBSERVATION-DECK RESTAURANT wasn't the nicest of its kind Ivan had ever seen, but it was better than he was expecting Charpentier to bring him to, given the man's money trouble. It had the selling point and major feature, however, of magical gravity. Runes were inlaid into the carpet throughout the space, allowing the patrons to set their feet on the ground and walk around in a standard one gravity.

"Reservation for Charpentier," Ivan's host told the young man at the front.

"Ah, yes, table with the view of *Restoya*, correct?" the youth replied.

"Yes, please."

"Of course, Captain Charpentier. Follow me, please?"

Ivan and Charpentier crossed the runic carpet to their table, Ivan nudging at the silver polymer in the fabric with his toe as they went. Gravity runes required regular maintenance by trained Mages. They were omnipresent on Royal Martian Navy warships, since no RMN warship shipped out without at least four Mages aboard—four *Jump* Mages, specifically, since there was usually at least one Combat Mage in the Marine contingent as well.

They were less common on civilian ships and stations. Ivan wasn't even sure what the cost-per-square-meter to maintain something like this was, but he doubted it was cheap—and a casual glance at the menu confirmed that.

It wasn't a particularly *nice* restaurant, but it had gravity and it had a view to the outside, and that meant it was pricey.

"Look, there," Charpentier said, drawing Ivan's gaze away from the tablet the waiter had left them and up to the window above them. "There she is."

Ivan knew the dimensions of the station he was sitting in by heart —he knew the dimensions of most standard space stations in the Protectorate, plus RMN warships, plus the most common civilian designs—which allowed him to sense the scale of the ship easily.

Restoya was about a hundred meters long and roughly twenty on a side, looking like nothing so much as a detached skyscraper with rockets strapped to the bottom. Unlike most proper cargo ships, she didn't have any attachments for the standard ten-by-ten-by-one-hundred-meter cargo containers.

From what Ivan remembered, she had about the same cargo capacity as two of those containers, but it was internal instead of modular. The ship probably massed a hundred thousand tons fully fueled and could carry another twenty thousand tons of cargo on top of that.

Not carrying cargo would increase her total delta-*v* if Charpentier had her fully fueled. She was big for a racer, but she had the overpowered engines of her type.

The design suggested she was intended to maintain thrust at all times, using one gravity of acceleration to keep her crew's feet on the ground.

"Do you have any other crew for her?" Ivan asked.

"Not at the moment," Charpentier admitted. "There's a few techs on the station I pay on an hourly basis to help keep her fitted and maintained, but there wasn't much point in hiring permanent crew when I didn't have Mages.

"She's automated enough that I can fly her on my own. I can definitely *race* her on my own; I just can't get out to this race without you."

Ivan nodded, taking in the lines of the ship. No weapons, not even defensive missile turrets. The engines were powerful, but the limitation on any ship was the crew's ability to handle acceleration.

With their powerful gravity runes, any military ship could outrun *Restoya*—as could any other civilian ship with the same magic built into their hull.

Karl Charpentier's ship was solidly built and capable, but Ivan wasn't even entirely sure how his friend had managed to win the local in-system races...let alone why Aquila was so fascinated with the jump-courier.

LUNCH WAS SURPRISINGLY DECENT, the menu's simple selections proving to be of high quality—if not necessarily of a quality Ivan would normally have matched to the prices. He was tempted to argue with Charpentier over the bill, but he knew he'd lose and he let it go.

This time, anyway, even if it made him feel guilty over everything going on.

As they reached the docking tube that connected to *Restoya*, Charpentier went on ahead to deal with access codes and release paperwork. While Ivan was waiting, floating patiently against a wall with the ease of a man who rather *enjoyed* silent contemplation, Theodore finally messaged him.

I don't know what you're into, Ivan, but if you can get out, you should. All of the mortgages on that ship have been bought up, secured by a series of numbered companies. So has the rest of Charpentier's debt.

The companies are pretty well locked down in a mire of legalese. I can't dig far enough to find out the true owners without stepping over the line of what I can appropriately do with work resources, but I'd guess you're looking at just one player.

Someone owns everything Charpentier owes and the whole thing has mob fingerprints all over it.

Get out if you can. If you can't…be careful.

You owe me dinner. A much nicer dinner than you were planning. Poking at mob companies draws attention and that's the last thing I'm supposed to do here.

Jessie

Ivan shook his head and swallowed a curse. The last thing he had wanted to do was get Theodore in trouble. He knew her well enough to know that she'd probably pushed further than *was* appropriate, both for work resources and potentially for her own safety.

And he couldn't get out now. He'd promised Charpentier and he'd made a deal with Aquila. He wanted to run, to hide, to tell Charpentier that he'd changed his mind and they were both safer this way.

"Everything's cleared," Charpentier told him, the starship captain pulling himself to a halt next to Ivan. "What's going on? You look like someone walked across your grave."

Ivan forced a smile.

"Probably just about that," he told his friend. "I think I might have just agreed to a date with an old friend when we get back, and I have no idea how to even *do* dates anymore."

"Ha! Well, my friend, you are talking to the completely wrong divorced middle-aged man for help with *that*," Charpentier replied with fake cheer. "I learned my lesson and have been focusing on my kid."

"Where is Lyle, anyway?" Ivan asked, shifting the subject.

"Pleathers has them on campus ten months of the year," Charpentier replied. "He spends the occasional weekend at his grandmother's, like I said, but he's mostly at school. Semester isn't up for another six weeks. Hopefully, by then I'll have everything sorted out enough that I can spend a few weeks with him."

"We'll make it happen, one way or another," Ivan promised. Guilt wormed at him as he said it, though. How was he going to do that? Pay for the kid's tuition out of Aquila's blood money?

He'd find a way. Everyone was supposed to live through this, and from what Ivan could tell, Charpentier would be better off if his ship and his debt all went away.

Or so Ivan would keep telling himself, anyway.

"Come on," Charpentier said, shaking aside the vagaries of the moment. "I've done a lot with *Restoya* over the years. I think you'll be impressed, even coming from the Navy!"

CHAPTER

FIVE

Despite knowing that *Restoya* wasn't a military ship and almost certainly didn't have magical gravity, Ivan still stumbled in the air a bit as he passed over the diving line between space station and spaceship.

"You all right?" Charpentier asked.

"Yeah, yeah, I'm fine," Ivan replied. "I was expecting gravity for some reason."

"We did some tricks to optimize it—only having runes every two decks and none in the cargo layers," his friend told him. "Sonia tied them off when she left, made sure they were safe without charging—which, of course, means they don't create gravity right now."

"The ship is built for thrust, though, right?" Ivan asked.

"She is," Charpentier confirmed. He gestured around the utilitarian space they were in. "These are the engineering decks. Two five-meter decks at the base of the ship, containing engines, the fusion reactor, et cetera, et cetera. There's a ten-meter 'deck' above here that holds our fuel, then two ten-meter decks of storage space."

"Simulacrum chamber is at the center of the ship?" Ivan asked. It always was, so it sounded like it was in the middle of the cargo container.

"Yep," Charpentier said. "At the center of the ship, we have three three-meter working and living decks wrapped around the chamber itself. That has the workshops for the Mages, the support infrastructure for managing cargo, and the quarters for the Mage contingent.

"Four more cargo decks above that to get us to our twenty-thousand-cubic-meter storage capacity, and then three three-meter decks that cover the rest of the crew spaces." The Captain smiled in quiet pride. "It's a standard fast packet courier, designed more to carry data than cargo, but we've got the space for high-value goods and the speed to leave everything else in the dust.

"I upgraded the engines a while back, too. They're still fusion, not the antimatter the Navy uses, but they're rated for twenty-five gees at full load. Thirty if we're running without cargo."

"What's the point?" Ivan asked, considering the ship as Charpentier led him toward what looked like an elevator. "Even with civilian magical gravity, that only gives you, what, ten gravities?"

"Ten gravities fully compensated," his friend corrected. "Most people can reasonably operate in up to three gravities—not for extended periods, but it can be done. So, thirteen is all anyone would expect from us. *Restoya* has a few other tricks I'll introduce you to as we go, but suffice to say…"

Karl Charpentier grinned.

"No one in the races I took part in was expecting a courier to pull sixteen gees," he told Ivan. "That's the best we can pull without renewing the gravity runes, but *with* the runes, we should be able to pull thirty."

"Thirty," Ivan repeated. The number didn't quite process. *Thirty gravities* of acceleration? The Navy used the most efficient magical gravity-rune matrices known and kept them well charged. That let them easily handle fifteen gravities without blinking.

The Navy never pushed past the acceleration their runes could handle, though. He'd read the studies that said that the lost crew efficiency was almost never worth it.

"I guess that makes sense for a courier," he slowly allowed.

"Everybody in the courier business has six Mages aboard if they possibly can," Charpentier told him. "Which means that if I'm competing with a peer, we're jumping at the same rate. Being able to cut six hours off the beginning and end of the trip isn't much, but it's an advantage I had over those peers."

"And how much thrust are we going to need for this Black Pulsar Race?" Ivan asked. He could recharge the runes, though getting all of the runes on even a small ship would take him hours.

"All of it, if we can get it," his friend said. "We're not just racing other ships. We're racing a pulsar and its radiation beams. Timing is *everything*, and the extra acceleration gives us a window nobody else will have."

"All right," Ivan said. "Show me these tricks of yours, Karl. I want to know what I'm getting into before I start working magic on this ship."

THE CHAIR WAS unlike anything Ivan had ever seen in a simulacrum chamber before. On a Royal Martian Navy ship, the bridge and the simulacrum chamber were the same space, buried at the armored center of the warship.

The Captain's seat was directly behind the simulacrum, set up to allow the Mage commanding the starship to reach the silver model without rising. That was the only thing this chair had in common with the bridge of an RMN warship.

Most civilian ships had mobile platforms positioned near the simulacrum that swung to keep the Mage's feet aligned with thrust or maneuvers. They existed to give a Mage an anchor in zero gravity as they hung on to the model that couldn't move from its spot at the center of the ship.

Like those platforms, the chair was suspended in a mobile structure that would move it to keep the Mage aligned with the ship's thrust.

Unlike Navy Captain's seats or civilian support platforms, the chair on *Restoya* had restraints built into it, safety bars that would close down to hold the Mage in place. The viscous material upholstering both the chair and those safety bars gave oddly under Ivan's hands as he poked at it. Strangest of all were the syringes positioned near the neck rest, automated injectors that would need to be adjusted to the Mage's height and size.

"All right, Karl, what the *hell* is this torture device?" he finally asked.

"It's an acceleration chair, the best you can build," Charpentier told him. "I helped design it myself, and we're at least two years ahead of anything being manufactured just yet."

He tapped the safety bars hanging above it.

"The safety bars will expand to provide full body pressure," he noted. "The layer over the face is, obviously, transparent. The chair will adjust to keep your hands on the simulacrum, though my understanding is that you wouldn't be able to jump while we were under thrust anyway."

"Not thirty gees of it, no," Ivan agreed, studying the device. "Full body pressure to keep blood and organs where they should be, resisting blackout and other side effects. Okay. Ow. The injectors?"

"There are a number of different medications that can be used to resist the effects of acceleration," Charpentier said. "They range from hemoglobin supports to add an additional level of positive pressure to your veins to straight-up stimulants."

"And that's a cocktail of all of them, I would guess?" Ivan asked, tapping the injectors.

"Yes," his friend agreed. "It's…not safe, before you ask, but it's not going to kill you except in major doses. Without it, the chair alone can keep us functional and alive up to ten gravities."

"But to make full use of the engines and squeeze out that extra six gees…"

"We juice up and burn like crazy," Charpentier confirmed. "Most I've ever run it for was an hour. Add in magical gravity and we run all the way up to thirty."

"You're insane," Ivan said conversationally. He was supposed to turn the ship over to Aquila's men…and now he was wondering whether Aquila's people could even *catch* the courier ship.

On the other hand, he now finally understood just what value Karl

Charpentier's ship held for the crime lord—*Restoya* herself was a prize beyond measure with these systems, but the ability to duplicate the chair he was looking at was just as valuable.

What Protectorate crime lord, after all, would turn down ships that could outrun the Royal Martian Navy?

CHAPTER

SIX

I t only took Ivan seven hours to refresh the gravity runes on *Restoya*. Charpentier had been telling the truth when he said that they'd been designed to minimize the work and that his Senior Ship's Mage had shut them down neatly.

Very neatly. Ivan was impressed both with the work and the care shown by the woman. She might have been kicking Charpentier to the curb and taking the crew with her, but she'd cared enough to do the work well. It wasn't just that she'd shut down the gravity runes safely but that she'd done so in a way that was easy for Ivan to undo.

The easiest ways to disable the runes would have made his life *much* harder. Sonia Harcourt had erred on the side of making *her* job harder to make the job of whoever was reactivating the runes easier.

Charpentier had burned a few bridges, Ivan was sure, but the work he saw in front of him suggested that the foundations might be there if the man apologized appropriately.

That wasn't *his* problem, though. He'd continue to remind Charpentier that he was an idiot but fixing the mess Charpentier had created was up to Charpentier.

He went through the matrix attached to each set of working decks and made sure everything was online and charged. The matrices weren't what he was expecting, either, which made sense. *Restoya* very clearly had military-grade gravity runes, fully capable of neutralizing fifteen gravities of thrust or providing one gravity of *down* while in dock.

The latter was finally present when Ivan walked onto the starship's bridge and looked around himself with a grin.

If he hadn't already suspected that using the ship as a racer had always been at least a *bit* in Charpentier's mind, the bridge would have screamed it at him. There was a standard set of support consoles for the crew they didn't currently have, but the pilot's station and the Captain's station were combined into an elevated position that was basically a cockpit on the very front of the ship.

Charpentier's chair descended out of that cockpit, rotating to level with the deck as the Captain waved to his new Ship's Mage.

"How are we doing, Ivan?" he asked.

"We have gravity, as you can tell," Ivan told him. "Your jump matrix looks clean. Sonia did a damn fine job of shutting everything down. We're good to go."

"Amazing," Charpentier said. "I just finished getting the last of the fuel sorted. We don't need much in terms of supplies for two of us for a couple of weeks, though I laid on extra just in case."

Ivan didn't ask where his friend was getting the money for the prep for this run. He really didn't want to know—hydrogen was cheap enough, but tens of thousands of tons of compressed hydrogen added up *fast*.

"So, where are we going?" he asked. "And when?"

Part of him wondered if he should send whatever Charpentier *did* know about the Pulsar Race to Theodore. It couldn't hurt, and having the MISS owing his friend a favor might help him out after he lost his ship.

"We've got a ways to go, almost twelve light-years," Charpentier told him. "That's six days to be safe, right?"

Ivan smiled. Charpentier was used to civilian Mages, who operated on Guild rules. They could only jump every eight hours and every twelve was preferred.

"I trained in the Navy, Karl," he replied. "I can do that in four without straining myself. Three if we really need to rush."

The Navy only recruited Mages of a certain minimum power and trained them hard. Ivan was trained for a standard rate of a jump every eight hours—and easily capable of jumping every six for three days.

"Let's...hold that in reserve for now," Charpentier said slowly. "Four days would be handy, though. That would give me a chance to head down to the planet and visit Lyle before we get going."

Ivan's heart twisted but he kept his smile up. If everything went according to what little of the plan he knew, Charpentier was supposed to be unharmed. That was the deal he'd made with Aquila, after all.

And yet...and yet.

"That strikes me as a damned good idea, Karl," Ivan told his friend. "This race kills people; we both know that. That's why it's illegal and why they're offering millions in prize money."

"I know," Charpentier agreed. "All right. Can I get you to watch *Restoya* while I grab a shuttle to the surface? Allowing six days, we would have had to get going tomorrow. If you can cut that, I can take a day and be back the following morning."

"That gives us plenty of time," Ivan assured him. "Go. Lyle's more important than most of this bullshit."

He suspected that even the divorce hadn't seen Charpentier spending as much time with his kid as Lyle would like. He could call his friend out on that, but that, too, was Charpentier's problem to fix.

ALONE ON *RESTOYA*'S bridge that evening, Ivan drank from a glass of wine and watched the stars out the viewscreen. Part of him wanted to call Aquila and tell the crime lord to come take the ship. That would be easier for everyone in many ways...but he didn't actually have a way to get in touch.

And he suspected that Aquila wanted *Restoya* to disappear, wrecked in the Black Pulsar Race like so many ships before her. No one would ever question that, once it was known what Charpentier had been doing.

There was a problem with that idea, but Ivan was trying very hard not to confront it. He was afraid. He could admit that to himself as he sat alone under the stars. It was very much in Aquila's power to kill him and Charpentier.

Either he did what the crime lord wanted, or they both died. He'd made the best deal he could and it should keep them all safe.

But still…

He'd entered Jessie Theodore's contact information on his wrist-comp before he even realized what he was doing.

"JT, what's up?" she answered, somewhat blearily. "Wait, Ivan?"

"Yeah, I have some possibly work-relevant info for you, Jessie, but it can't have come from me," he told her. "Hence, personal line, I guess."

"You sound unsure of yourself," Theodore answered. "What's going on?"

"It's all tied up with that mess of Karl's," Ivan said. "Um." He hesitated.

"Are you okay, Ivan?" she asked.

"No," he told her. "But that's my problem. Would your bosses be able to do anything with the start point and time of the Black Pulsar Race?"

The call was silent.

"Maybe," Theodore conceded. "You got that from your friend, did you?"

"It can't have come from either of us," he insisted. "We're already high on somebody's shit list."

"Believe me, Ivan, I can bury my sources," the former military intelligence officer said. "Might be better to transfer the data in person. You have time for that dinner?"

Ivan chuckled. It was a weak thing, undermined by his fear, but she got it out of him regardless.

"Not unless you're on orbital four," he told her. "I'm attaching it under encryption. Jessie…he needs the race purse. I don't know if that matters to your bosses, but…"

"I get it," she said. "We'll cover our tracks; don't worry. Are you okay?" she repeated.

"I…" Ivan trailed off. Somehow, he suspected Jessie Theodore wouldn't be nearly as insistent on dinner if she knew he was selling Charpentier out to Aquila. *He* knew he was a coward. He didn't think she'd realized that yet.

"It's my problem, not anyone else's," he finally told her. "We can talk when I get back."

"If you're jumping Charpentier into a mob race, you know your odds of getting back aren't great, right?" she asked.

"I know," he conceded. "But everyone around me seems to have a plan. I think we'll be fine."

Ivan had his own plan, too. He just didn't *like* it.

"I'm warning you now, Ivan, we've had the start coordinates before," Theodore said. "It won't break open the local scum. The *end* coordinates, that's where they have the big party. Get me *those* before everyone leaves and, well…"

"I doubt the party lasts long enough for me to jump a courier here and for the Navy to get back there," he told her. "This is what I've got."

"It's not worthless," she said. "I'll obfuscate and put it in the hands of the right people."

She was silent for a few seconds.

"These are dangerous people you're playing with, Ivan," she reminded him. "Be careful."

"Always," he promised. "I'll be fine, Jessie."

The question was how much he'd sacrifice to stay that way.

CHAPTER

SEVEN

"Are you ready?"

Karl Charpentier's words hung in the silence of *Restoya*'s simulacrum chamber as Ivan studied the calculations on the screen below him. A screen to his right, attached to the acceleration chair, showed Charpentier's face in the cockpit of the bridge.

Eleven jumps had brought them to the middle of nowhere, a little under two light-years away from one of the nastier-looking astronomical formations Ivan had ever seen. Even the starting point, a full light-year way from the *binary pulsar* they were about to race through, was going to be unsafe.

"How long after everyone arrives does the race start?" Ivan asked.

"Twelve hours is the plan," Charpentier told him. "We're about that early, so it'll be a full day for us."

"A full day hanging out next to a binary pulsar," Ivan replied. "Sounds like fun."

"Where's your sense of adventure, my friend?" Charpentier said. "Radiation should only be sweeping this direction every seventy-five hours or so, according to the charts."

"Nobody gets this close to *one* pulsar, let alone two," Ivan said. "What the hell have you got us into?"

"I knew it was through the binary," his friend admitted. "I assumed you did. There aren't that many pulsars in the Protectorate, let alone near Xanth."

"Every so often, I feel like I should have asked a lot more questions before I promised to help you," Ivan said. He was understating it by a lot, too. He never should have promised to help Charpentier. His friend would have been better off if he hadn't, even.

There was no backing out now, though.

"I'm ready," he finally told Charpentier. "Coordinates are confirmed. Any complications they told you about?"

"We should be jumping in about a light-second clear of everyone, and we'll maneuver to rendezvous from there," the pilot said. "And then we wait for them to send us the jump coordinates and the position of the first beacon."

Ivan nodded slowly.

"How many beacons?"

"Sixteen. The last gives us new jump coordinates for the exit position. They're supposedly set up to require about an hour to navigate between each beacon."

"Sixteen hours," Ivan replied. "And how long do you plan on taking?"

"Well, you said it would take you six hours to rest before jumping, so that gives me a minimum, doesn't it?" Charpentier asked. "Shall we, my friend?"

"All right."

Ivan reached out for the simulacrum. The silver model was almost semiliquid, though it was nowhere near hot enough to actually be molten. The whirling lines of the rune matrix that expanded his magic converged there from all over the ship, all of it meeting at the simulacrum itself.

Those lines, the seventy-six characters and fourteen connectors of Martian Runic, covered the surface of the silver model of the starship as well. There were only two spots on the simulacrum that weren't covered in runes.

Ivan's palms, inlaid with their own silver runes, settled into those gaps with the ease of long practice and intense training.

He studied the numbers one last time, looking at the screens surrounding him with a view of the empty space around *Restoya*, and then unleashed his power into the simulacrum.

The world vanished…and then reappeared as a wave of crushing exhaustion hammered into him.

"Jump complete," he reported.

"Checking coordinates," Charpentier told him. "Exactly on target; I'm scanning for…well, that was easy."

New icons appeared on Ivan's screen. Every surface of the simulacrum chamber was covered in high-resolution screens, creating the illusion that he was floating in deep space. It allowed him to understand the space around him better than anyone else aboard the ship.

Even struggling against the weariness of the jump, he followed Charpentier's highlight. A motley-looking collection of ships was already gathered at the *exact* coordinates they'd been given.

Four were siblings to each other, armed civilian ships. At a quarter-million tons or so, the jump-corvettes were toys compared to Martian warships—but they dwarfed the racers and their weapons would be perfectly capable of obliterating any of the racers that did something dumb.

"That looks like a starting line to me," Ivan said. "Anybody going to shoot at us?"

"That would be against their own interests," Charpentier pointed out. "The race organizers need the underworld to trust them. At the beginning and the end, under the eyes of everybody, we're safe."

"And in the middle?" Ivan asked.

"A quarter of the racers disappear," his friend said grimly. "I'm pretty sure no one cares if the pulsar gets them or the other competitors do!"

CHAPTER

EIGHT

estoya slid into the starting zone next to the rest of the racers as Ivan entered the mess to pour himself a cup of coffee. One wall of the combined kitchen and dining area was a full screen, and a few commands on his wrist-comp set it to a view of their competition.

Coffee came first as Ivan eyed the other ships, though he paid more attention to what he was doing as he actually put together a meal for the two of them. The supplies were about as plain and cheap as he'd expected, but they were plentiful enough.

They had almost twenty-four hours until the race itself, so he busied himself making pierogies from scratch. It was a complicated process that fully engaged his attention, enough so that he missed Charpentier joining him in the mess until the other man grabbed a cup of coffee and leaned against the prep counter, staring balefully at the starting lineup.

"I hate this part," the racer said quietly.

"The waiting?" Ivan asked.

"That's part of it, but also looking at the other racers," Charpentier told him. "No one is running the Black Pulsar Race because they *want* to. Everyone here is desperate and, well…"

He sighed and gestured at the screen.

"*Restoya* is big for this work," he admitted. "There are two other couriers out there, but we've got ten thousand tons on the bigger one. Acceleration, fuel capacity…all of that factors into the victory, so often the smaller ships have an edge."

"But?" Ivan asked after a moment of silence.

"Nobody builds a race in space that is a straight-line acceleration course," his friend explained. "They're multi-point courses, usually cutting around planets or asteroids. The closer you can cut the path, the better off you are. But that has its own risks, and smaller ships are vulnerable—and that's when we're *not* racing through pulsars."

Charpentier drank more of his coffee as they both stood. The only sound for several minutes was Ivan's knife as he cut the shells for his pierogies.

"So, the smaller ships are higher-risk?" he finally asked.

"Yeah." Charpentier stepped up to the wall and tapped one of the ships. "This guy has no business here at all. That's a five-thousand-ton speeder. She's a glorified shuttle I didn't think anyone *could* put a jump matrix in…and I watched an almost-identical ship crash and burn cutting too close to a gas giant three months ago. And that race was *legal.*"

Even some of the races back in Xanth had been illegal, Ivan knew. The legal ones were supposed to have all of the measures in place to make sure everyone was safe…but they could only do so much when ships were flinging themselves around at ten to fifteen gravities.

"We knew this race lost ships," Ivan reminded Charpentier. "That's part of why I still think this was a terrible idea."

He had a long list of other reasons, too, but he couldn't tell the other man most of them.

"I know." The courier captain studied the competition again, then waved vaguely at them. "Nothing out there will break twenty gees," he noted. "Acceleration isn't everything, but it's the single biggest factor in the game. We can out-burn them all, though we'll want to choose when we pull that out of our hat carefully."

"I think that one's on you, Karl," Ivan told him. "As I understand it, we get the jump coordinates at the last beacon? Between the beginning and the end, I believe I nap."

Charpentier chuckled.

"Basically," he agreed. He was pacing the length of the wallscreen now, looking at each ship in turn. "I saw someone try to do one of the in-system races with a Mage cooperative once," he said. "They'd get the beacon coordinates and microjump. I think they must have had ten Mages aboard to make it work."

"That seems doable," Ivan said as he started to carefully lower the pierogies into boiling water. "Not exactly easy on the Mages—micro-jumps are a *bitch*—but doable. Did they win?"

"No," Charpentier admitted. "Four of the beacons were too close to the planet for them to safely use the teleport spell, and it turned out they hadn't put particularly good engines on the ship they were using. Some of us managed to make up the time in the gas giant's atmosphere and cut ahead of them. They came third in the end."

He grinned.

"*I* won."

"Remind me again why you're this desperate for cash?" Ivan asked drily. "If you kept winning races…"

"There aren't that many races," Charpentier admitted. "Maybe six legal and four illegal a year. If I won *every* one of them, I'd pull a total purse of maybe two million. But fuel isn't cheap, and the acceleration drugs aren't cheap, so each race sets me back fifty to hundred grand.

"I made two million in prizes but spent most of a million to compete. If I had a year before the bank needed their money, maybe— but if I came second in even one race, the margin got thinner," he said quietly. "And, well, I *started* in the hole."

Hence the massive payment the man needed to make. Ivan nodded his understanding, watching his pierogies carefully as much to be sure his friend couldn't see his face as to make sure they didn't overcook.

If he followed the chain correctly, Charpentier had borrowed from the mob to fund the races he needed to win to pay off his mortgage debts…and it sounded like he'd discovered it wasn't going to be enough *after* he'd started doing that.

The hole was entirely of Charpentier's own making. That didn't make it any less of a terrible place to be. Ivan truly wished he had another way to help him out of it than the plan he'd made.

CHAPTER

NINE

"All racers, this is the Race Master," a noticeably accented voice said over the radio. There was no video attached to the transmission, though Ivan's console in the simulacrum chamber chirped receipt of a data package.

"You should all have now received the coordinates of your jump emergence and of the first beacon," the Race Master told them. "They're basically the same, just enough difference that no one should be emerging in the same place as the beacon."

The man on the radio chuckled and a shiver ran down Ivan's spine.

"If someone does that, everybody loses," he noted. "Of course, the poor bastard who tries to coexist with a beacon loses most."

Ivan felt *Restoya* tremble around him as Charpentier brought the courier ship's engines online. He was busy pulling the coordinates into his own jump calculation program and running the numbers. Many Mages used a program they'd coded themselves, but he used the standard RMN system.

He'd spent twenty-five years jumping with the Navy's code, after all. He knew it like his own skin.

"We have eyes and a rescue ship on the first three beacons," the

303

Race Master continued. "Same on the last two. In between, well." The shrug was almost audible. "You knew what you signed up for.

"I remind you, as most of you start to finish up your jump calcs, that jumping early is a disqualifier," he said. "Not least because I won't be transmitting your decryption keys for the beacons until I give the order to jump."

Ivan was done. The numbers were on his screen and he burned them into his brain as he took a deep breath and touched the strangely viscous material of his acceleration seat. He wasn't sure when Charpentier was going to bring the engines to full, but he wasn't going to be leaving the chair for the next sixteen hours.

Fortunately, his shipsuit had plumbing connections and he had both coffee and sandwiches readily to hand. He wouldn't be able to eat while they were under thirty gravities, but he should be good for anything else.

"We ready?" Charpentier's image on the bridge link screen asked.

"I am," Ivan replied. "You?"

"Yeah. This is going to be nuts," Charpentier warned. "I'm opening at sixteen gees. If they pay attention, they already know *Restoya* can do that. I'm betting at least the two big boys can match us, one way or another. We won't be alone, but I want to get well away from the pack before I open all the way up."

"How far back can someone fall and still make any money?" Ivan asked, realizing he probably should have checked in before.

"Fifth, but that's not relevant to us," Charpentier told him. "Even second and I lose the ship, Ivan. It's first or we're fucked."

Ivan swallowed his instinctive response. Thanks to Charpentier's choices and failures, they were already fucked. It was only a question of whether the deal Ivan had cut was going to unfuck them *enough*.

"The count begins," the Race Master announced. "Decryption key transmission will commence in thirty seconds."

There was a carefully measured silence.

"You will jump thirty seconds from *now*."

Ivan nodded, as much to himself as to Charpentier, and focused his attention and energy. He was only vaguely aware when his console chirped that they were receiving a second data packet.

"Five. Four. Three. Two. One.

"Jump."

Ivan stepped across the depths of space and took *Restoya* with him.

TWENTY-TWO SHIPS APPEARED with them on the other side, and Ivan closed his eyes in exhaustion. A moment later, he felt the slight shift as the engines opened up. The switch from one gravity of magical "down" to one gravity of subjective thrust wasn't subtle, even if the end result was theoretically the same.

He forced himself to open his eyes again and take a drink from the coffee bulb next to him. Every ship was accelerating toward the first beacon, but it was a "mere" hundred and ten thousand kilometers from their position.

The first choice every racer had to make was whether they would accelerate the full distance or slow down as they reached the beacon. It was a gamble, one they'd have to repeat with each beacon.

They had to ping it from within ten thousand kilometers to get the next beacon's coordinates. If they were at zero relative to the beacon, they could immediately accelerate exactly toward the next beacon. If they were moving at high speed, they'd need to adjust their course—which could easily require them to counter their entire existing velocity.

But if the next beacon was on or close to a straight line past the first, it would give them an advantage over the ships that slowed.

"We'll hit zero velocity ten thousand kilometers short of the beacon in twenty-seven minutes," Charpentier told him. "One of the other couriers is pulling seventeen gees. We'll see whether he flips."

"Who do you think will get there first?" Ivan asked.

"Mister shuttle racer," the pilot replied. "He's piling on fifteen gees, putting him near the top of the pack, but straight-line acceleration is all that toy has. He'll burn straight for the first one and hope that he gets lucky.

"I could be wrong, of course, but I'm hoping *someone* gets there first," he continued. "The course the first guy sets informs everyone else's choices. We still need to ping the beacon from within ten thousand klicks, but if we have an idea of which beacon he's headed to…"

"What if they're giving everyone different beacons?" Ivan asked. The thought made a terrifying amount of sense to him. It would confuse the racers trying to take advantage of someone else's course—and it would let Aquila lead *Restoya* off out of sight of everyone else for the ambush Ivan knew was coming.

"They might. It would be against the rules for a legal race, but this *isn't* a legal race," Charpentier admitted. "Would be quite the trick, too. I guess we'll find out in fifteen minutes or so."

Ivan nodded and finally let his attention shift from the other ships and the beacon to the *real* problem. The two pulsars were spectacular, rapidly rotating neutron stars orbiting each other at a distance of a single light-minute.

Even as Ivan looked at them, the screens around him darkened to protect his eyes from the flash as one of the poles swung close enough toward them for the radiation beam to be visible.

He didn't need to see the data from the beacon to know that the Black Pulsar Race was going to take them right between the two spinning blades of astronomical death.

THE OTHER COURIER SHIP, the largest racer after *Restoya* herself, made turnover slightly ahead of them. Charpentier followed suit, as did most of the other ships pulling fifteen gees or above.

As the pilot had predicted, the tiny five-thousand-ton racing shuttle blazed past them toward the beacon. Of the ships still burning directly for the beacon, it was the fastest and Ivan had to swallow a sense of foreboding as he watched the racer leap ahead.

Charpentier had been worrying about that ship and it was rubbing off. They were taking risks, cutting things short. Ivan *knew* he was going to have to watch at least one ship die today. There was no way around it—not in a contest that had *never* had every racer finish alive.

"I hope the rescue ship has him locked in," Ivan muttered.

"That will only help him for a couple of hours, assuming everything goes on schedule," Charpentier replied. "And in any case...do *you* see a rescue ship?"

That sent a chill down Ivan's spine, and he looked at the screens again. Not just the visual around him, which was enough to pick out the cluster of high-acceleration racers who were choosing to decelerate toward the beacon, but the long-range radar and passive scanners.

The Race Master had *said* there was a rescue ship, but there was nothing out there. No one was watching them at all.

"They lied?" he asked. "That seems an odd thing to lie about."

"It is," Charpentier said grimly. "Even in a race like this, I wouldn't expect them to lie about that."

The channel was silent.

"Our racer will hit the beacon in five minutes," the pilot continued. "I guess we all see what's going on then."

"Two beacons after that before we bring the engines to full?" Ivan asked.

"Exactly. By then, we'll start to see the clusters of who is going to make it and who is going to fall behind," Charpentier told him. "That's when we break everyone's rules."

"I may take a nap after we see what this guy does," the Mage admitted. He was exhausted. The jump spell was the single most draining spell he knew. It wasn't necessarily *complicated*, but even that was mostly because it was so ritualized and standardized that he could do it in his sleep.

It just took everything he had out of him.

"Good plan," his friend replied. "If they're following standard race layouts, that won't be long, but it'll give you at least an hour."

"I thought you said we'd be an hour between beacons," Ivan asked.

Charpentier chuckled.

"The beacons are set up to be one hour apart for a ship doing a zero-zero course at ten gravities...on *average*," he specified. "I get close to zero—no course is ever straight-line, like I said—but I have never run *any* course at ten gees, my friend."

Ivan grimaced.

"Once we go to thirty, how long will we be *at* thirty?" he asked.

He saw Charpentier's grin widen and he knew the answer.

"The rest of the way, Ivan," the pilot told him. "We burn hard and we burn until it's over."

Deal or no deal, Ivan had to wonder if Aquila's people were ready for that—and deal or no deal, he was definitely going to hope that they weren't!

~

"THERE HE GOES," Charpentier murmured.

The pilot in the racer shuttle reached the ten-thousand-kilometer bubble around the beacon first. Not by much, five other ships were making the same gamble, but by enough that he was also the first to change course.

The beacon wouldn't acknowledge any transmission from more than ten thousand kilometers away. The right transmission from inside that bubble, using the keys they'd each been given, would send an encrypted package back.

The racers then decrypted that package for the coordinates of the next beacon. This early on, Ivan figured the beacon was probably the three hundred and fifty thousand kilometers of "one hour's flight at ten gravities" away. If he'd been in his old destroyer, they could probably find it.

Even in this mess. The pulsars' radiation beams weren't making too much hash of the region yet, but Ivan could tell that *Restoya*'s sensors were having trouble. The courier ship was upgraded in many ways, but her sensors clearly weren't one of them.

They could still pick out the ship fifteen thousand kilometers ahead of them. The racer didn't have that much of an edge yet.

"I make it a seventeen-degree course shift," Ivan noted. "He won his gamble."

"Indeed. I'm adjusting our course and flipping us," the pilot replied. "We'll pick up velocity as we head toward the beacon, though we can't make up what he's got on us unless we increase the acceleration."

"And?"

"Not yet," Charpentier said with a smile. "The next three or four beacons are going to be quiet," he told Ivan. "Probably at least two hours before things get exciting."

"How are you defining *exciting*?" Ivan asked. "I mean, my read says I could sleep until the last beacon."

"That's true enough, I suppose," his friend admitted. "Assuming you can sleep through the maneuvers and fifteen subjective gees when things get crazy. I'm expecting at least one attempt to play chicken before we're done."

"I'm going to take that nap," Ivan replied, yawning against his fatigue. "Wake me up before things get crazy, will you?"

So far, he hadn't seen any sign that any of the racers were Aquila's planned boarding team. That meant there was someone else out there —potentially the supposed rescue ship, in fact—who was going to intercept them at some point.

And Ivan, much as he hated himself for it, was going to hand them his old friend's ship.

He'd need to be awake for that.

CHAPTER

TEN

It was a struggle for Ivan to wake up, even as a chirpy happy alarm chimed at him from somewhere. Even once he was mostly awake, it took him half a minute of wondering what the *hell* he was sleeping in before his mind caught up with where he was.

The acceleration chair was supremely adjustable and surprisingly comfortable. He'd managed to stay awake as long as he'd meant to—and the moment he'd lowered it into a sleeping position, he'd been out.

Years of military service had given him the ability to sleep wherever he wanted and wake up easily. The sleep had been deeper than he'd been used to, though, and waking up wasn't normally this hard for him.

It was amazing what a few months outside the Navy could do to his instant wake-up.

Ivan blinked away the last of the sleepiness from his eyes and silenced the alarms.

"Good, you're awake," Charpentier told him. "It's been three hours. We're on beacon six and this is a fucking hell zone. Take a look, Ivan."

Ivan did.

Whoever had put together the beacons for the Black Pulsar Race clearly hadn't heard about the "an hour for a ship making ten gees" rule. Each of the beacons had been almost a million kilometers apart and *Restoya* was now twenty light-seconds closer to the two pulsars. The zigzagging course was clear and terrifying, as they were now well into the zone where the beams swept on their regular cycle.

"Please tell me you have those cycles programmed in," Ivan said aloud.

"You better believe it," Charpentier agreed. "I had the full astro files on the system plugged in, and I've been validating the actual sweeps against them as we move. My course is clear and I'm triple-checking every time I switch the drives."

"Good to hear," Ivan said faintly. His attention turned to the ships that were still with them. It was a smaller collection than he'd expected. Some of the ships making fourteen-plus gees had clearly gambled wrong on when they'd need to turn.

Four of them were still with *Restoya*. Close enough to be seen. The racer shuttle was still out in the lead, the ship's slightly lower acceleration clearly offset by a damned fine pilot.

Between the racer and *Restoya* was the second-biggest racer, a heavily overengined courier ship whose crew was probably taking multiple subjective gees as they ran at the same sixteen gees as *Restoya* herself.

Ivan and Charpentier were in third, with two midsized ships trailing a few thousand kilometers behind them. The entire lead cluster was in a sphere maybe fifteen thousand kilometers across.

"Are you expecting things to get messy soon?" Ivan asked.

"Not sure, but the hair on the back of my neck is standing up," Charpentier said. "Something isn't right here. Smells like my back is being measured for a knife."

Ivan managed not to twitch uncomfortably.

"What are you expecting?" he asked instead.

"I'm not sure, but I think it's— *What the?*"

Ivan didn't see what had happened. One moment, the lead five ships were continuing on in a rough cluster, all heading toward beacon seven.

The next, there were only four. The racing shuttle with the unexpectedly skilled pilot was just...*gone.*

"Going evasive!" Charpentier snapped. "Ivan, if you can cover us at all, now is the time!"

Restoya jerked sideways at twenty gees, barely in time to avoid the racing shuttle's fate. This time, Ivan *did* see what was going on. Even in the midst of the chaotic storm of the twin pulsars, a laser beam stood out.

"Someone is *shooting* at us," he barked. "Our new first-place dude has some kind of laser. Your sensors *suck*; I can't even resolve the power level."

He grunted as another five-subjective-gravity burst smashed him into the acceleration chair.

This time, the shot hadn't been aimed at them. One of the racers behind them disintegrated as the beam took them head-on. Suddenly, there were only three racers in the lead bubble—and given how much trouble Ivan was having seeing the rest of the racers, he suspected no one else knew anything was going on.

"How do they have weapons?" Charpentier demanded as he twisted the ship through another set of evasive maneuvers. "It's the *one damned rule.* No one is supposed to have any weapons."

"I can't stop a laser beam, Karl!" was Ivan's only response. "Keep us from getting hit!"

There was nothing he could do, not with a jump matrix. All *Restoya*'s runes could do was augment his jump spell. If he'd been aboard a proper warship with a true all-purpose amplifier, the racer-turned-pirate would already be dead.

Not that Ivan had ever actually turned an amplifier on a ship with living crew. He'd actively avoided any posting that had even the slightest chance of combat—he *knew* his weaknesses.

Acceleration crushed him again and he activated the acceleration chair's full functions. The injectors held off for the moment, but the safety bars expanded, wrapping him in a full cocoon of pressurized gel.

"Thanks, was going to tell you to do that," Charpentier said grimly.

"I don't know what the range on that laser is, but it's just us and them now."

Three ships had died in under a minute and *Restoya* was on her own in between two pulsars.

"What do we do?" Ivan asked.

"You're the navy officer; why are you asking *me*?" his friend snapped. "All I can do is dodge around the bastard and prep for full thrust. What kind of range *is* he likely to have?"

"It looks like a standard RFLAM turret," Ivan replied, surprising himself as the answer popped into his head. "Probably concealed to prevent the Race Master detecting it, but it's a standard half-gigawatt beam with six cycling chambers. He can fire once a second forever, and the focal point will adjust out to about four light-seconds, but in *this* environment, he can only really target us at about half a million klicks."

A Rapid-Fire Laser Anti-Missile system was the key missile defense of any warship worth its salt—and while the five-hundred-megawatt system was common on smaller Navy ships, it was also available for civilian use.

A lot of freighters and courier ships that expected to travel the Fringe or other less-secure areas would have two or three of the turrets. Against an unarmed civilian ship like *Restoya*, though, the beams were just as effective as a real battle laser.

"Check the injectors," Charpentier ordered. "We're juicing up as soon as you're ready. I was about to pull this anyway; I just wasn't expecting to be *shot at*."

Another set of beams flashed through where they might have been, and Ivan said a prayer of thanks to any deity that happened to be listening. If their enemy had brought two of the turrets in, they'd already be dead.

As it was, they were dodging one laser at a time and Karl Charpentier appeared to actually be up to that task. Ivan had known his friend was a good pilot, but in that moment, dancing through the storm of radiation between two pulsars and being chased by an enemy with a lightspeed weapon, he realized that he'd been wrong.

Karl Charpentier was an *amazing* pilot.

"Injectors are lined up and clear," Ivan reported. This was going to suck. There were two of them, covered in plastic casings and aiming tubes now pressed against the base of his neck. The needles did *not* look small.

"Let's make this…"

Silence.

"Karl?" Ivan asked—and then looked at the screen. They still weren't alone, but it wasn't the same ship. The RFLAM-armed racer was gone, expanding clouds of radiation marking where multiple nuclear warheads had converged on the pirate.

"Who is *she*?" Charpentier demanded, staring at the ship now emerging from the cloud of the pulsar's storm.

"Armored corvette, probably heavily shielded," Ivan said absently. "Not a custom job, but perfect for this environment. Multiple launchers, probably fusion missiles, based off our racer friend, and a couple of real battle lasers."

"What's her accel? I do not want to be hanging around this place!" Charpentier snapped.

Ivan didn't say anything. There was a pinging icon on his wrist-comp that told him everything he needed to know—as if he hadn't already guessed.

That was Aquila's ship and his people were here for their prize.

"She's got your maneuver cone, Karl," Ivan said quietly as he disconnected the injectors.

"What are you doing, Ivan?" his friend demanded.

Ivan looked through the camera, remembering the calculations he'd made earlier and making sure that nothing had moved significantly since he'd prepped the bridge during Karl's visit with his son.

"I'm sorry, Karl; it was this or they killed us both," Ivan told him—and then used a burst of magic to pull the pin on the gas grenade taped to the bottom of Karl Charpentier's acceleration seat.

His friend had enough time to give him one utterly betrayed look before the expensive knockout gas took effect.

CHAPTER

ELEVEN

Ivan was waiting at the dock when the mob team arrived. The first people aboard were clad in heavy exosuits, two-meter-tall suits of ceramic and metal that weren't supposed to be available to civilians.

Somehow, he doubted that had given Aquila's people any particular difficulty. The two-hundred-thousand-ton heavily armored corvette hooked up to *Restoya* wasn't supposed to be available to civilians, either, and would have been a lot harder to acquire.

"Mage Halloway?" a female voice emerged from the lead suit of armor. "The ship is under control?"

"It is," Ivan confirmed. "I've moved Captain Charpentier off the bridge. Your pilot can take control whenever you wish."

"Where is Charpentier?" she asked.

"On a stretcher just past here," Ivan told her. "He and I are to be delivered back to the Xanth System. That was the deal."

"I am aware of your deal with Maestro Aquila," the woman said grimly. "Bravo team, secure Engineering; Charlie Team, the bridge."

Six more troopers in form-concealing fatigues and safety helmets swarmed past Ivan. They split into groups of three, heading toward their destinations with the confidence of people who had schematics projected in their helmets.

"Il Maestro sends his regards, Mage Halloway," the woman continued. "Lead us to Charpentier and you will receive your payment."

A chill ran down Ivan's spine. The deal was that Charpentier wasn't going to be hurt, but the two exosuits were both carrying ugly-looking weapons. They weren't the heavy penetrator rifles the Martian Marines carried, designed to take down other exosuits, but they were still big, nasty guns designed for augmented muscles.

"All right," he said. He led the way back toward the bay he'd stored his friend in.

Ivan wasn't expecting Charpentier to *forgive* him for this, but he'd done everything he could. All he had left was to hope that Aquila's people respected the deal the mob boss had made.

The door slid open and Ivan shivered at the sight of his friend. Karl Charpentier looked calm, laid out on the gurney. He'd wake up in an hour or so if no one did anything, and he was otherwise unharmed. Ivan had spent a good chunk of his "advance" acquiring the military-grade knockout gas grenade.

"Confirm the ID," the woman ordered the other exosuit. The armored figure advanced, slinging the big gun as they pulled out a medkit and took a blood sample.

The sample slid into the kit and silence filled the room for several seconds.

"Confirmed," the man replied. "It's definitely Charpentier."

"Good. Kill him."

"What?" Ivan demanded. "That wasn't the deal."

"Maestro Aquila promised you that Karl Charpentier would suffer no injury but that which he brought upon himself," the woman told him. "He earned his death mark long ago by his own actions. Nothing has changed."

The soldier unslung his shotgun and was moving across the room. Everything seemed to move in slow motion as Ivan faced the death of his oldest friend because of his actions.

Ivan knew he was a coward. He'd known that since he was a teenager, and every action he'd made in his entire life, in his entire military career, had been made with that in mind. To make certain that his flaws never compromised his work, never hurt anyone else.

And he'd failed. His fear, his concession to Aquila's threats, was going to kill his friend.

The exosuited soldier was laying his shotgun against Charpentier's head, making sure he wouldn't miss. There was no time. No chance to reflect. Only a moment.

Not to decide.

To act.

Ivan barely knew he'd cast the spell. Three blades of force slashed across the room, separating the shotgun from the gangster's hand…the gangster's arm from his shoulder…and the gangster's head from his torso.

Exosuit armor was *far* from enough against a fully trained Navy Mage. The woman in charge of the team barely had time to open her mouth before Ivan turned, a blast of superheated plasma erupting from his hand and burning clean through her chest.

Armor clattered to the floor, pieces of humans still inside it, and Ivan froze. He'd never killed anyone in his life, and now two people were dead from his magic—but his friend, the man he'd tried to keep safe, was alive.

There was still a ship attached to *Restoya*. There were still six boarders on the courier.

Mage-Captain (ret.) Ivan Halloway straightened.

He'd *made a deal*. If Maestro Aquila had broken that deal, his people were going to learn why everyone feared the Royal Martian Navy.

IVAN WENT TO ENGINEERING FIRST. The boarders had come through the airlock attached to the midship decks around the simulacrum chamber, so the bridge and the Engineering section were equidistant.

He was confident that Charpentier's security systems would frustrate both sets of boarders for a while, but the team in Engineering would be able to cripple or destroy the ship without access to the computers and controls.

The bridge team would need to get into the computers to cause any harm at all. The engineering team had direct access to the fusion reactor and the fusion rockets. Either of those would suffice to obliterate the entire ship if mishandled—and disabling either would render *Restoya* almost useless in any case.

Ivan had learned many skills in his years in the Navy, many of which he'd barely used. He was almost as battle trained as a Combat Mage, but this was the first time he'd used those skills in earnest.

He'd never been trained in *stealth* and so he simply walked into the main engineering deck, looking around for the boarding team. They were clustered around a set of consoles he recognized as the main control center for the drones *Restoya* currently had in lieu of an engineering crew.

"Wait, you're not supposed to be here," one of them snapped on seeing him. "What the hell?"

"He's supposed to be *dead*," another snapped, diving for the weapons the boarders had left lying on top of the consoles.

Ivan almost appreciated the confirmation. Once he'd known Aquila had planned to murder Charpentier, he'd figured his own life was likely forfeit. The whole point of taking *Restoya* during the race was to create secrecy.

The mob boss was never going to rely on Ivan's remaining silent. He'd known that all along, really.

For now, though, he let the boarders reach their weapons. He didn't have it in him to kill unarmed men, even in the weird fugue state he was currently operating in. The moment they raised their weapons toward him, fire flashed from his fingers. Half-meter-long bursts of superheated air hammered into all three men at once, flinging them backward across the consoles.

A gun discharged in the silence, a burst of fléchettes slamming into the ceiling harmlessly.

And then a voice spoke, one from someone who *wasn't* in the space.

"What the hell is going on? Bravo team, respond. Alpha, respond."

Only silence echoed.

"*Dawnbreaker*, Contingency O, Contingency O!" the voice snapped.

Whatever orders followed from that were lost as the speaker cut to a channel that wasn't playing live in the engineering spaces. Somehow, though, Ivan suspected he was running out of time. He needed to make sure that the remaining team didn't escape.

Unfortunately for them, he was a *Jump Mage*. He wasn't refreshed enough to jump the entire ship. Teleporting the sixty meters between the engineering spaces and the bridge, though?

That he could do.

He appeared in the door leading from the transit pod to the rest of the ship and found himself facing the three troopers of the boarding team running in his direction. All of them were armed and all of them were looking at him.

It wasn't enough to save them. Force blades flashed and gunfire blazed in *Restoya*'s bridge. The boarders went down...but Ivan had chosen his emergence point badly. A spread of shotgun fléchettes hammered into his shoulder, sending him reeling back.

He wasn't wearing armor. His shipsuit could withstand some impacts—it was designed to act as an emergency spacesuit, after all—but it was also exactly what the fléchette darts were intended to defeat.

Pain tore through Ivan and he swore as he tried to move his right arm. That was *not* happening. He couldn't tell how badly injured he was, but his arm wasn't obeying his commands and the pain was getting worse by the second.

He didn't have time. Focusing again, he somehow managed to conjure enough magic to cast the jump spell one last time. This time, he brought someone *to* him, yanking the gurney carrying Charpentier to the bridge.

Ivan could feel blood dripping down his torso inside his suit as he stumbled to the gurney. It had a full medical kit on the lower shelf, which would probably be his salvation, but first he picked up an injector he hadn't been able to keep himself from preparing and pressed it to Charpentier's neck.

It hissed. For a moment, nothing happened—and then the stimulant hit and the pilot's eyes snapped wide open.

"What the *fuck*?" he snarled as he struggled against the bonds.

"Wait," Ivan told him, his voice sounding hoarse even to himself as he sliced the bonds open with magic. "I fucked up, Karl," he whispered. "Ship is clear...but *their* ship is still locked on and... and..."

He realized he was now sitting on the floor next to the gurney.

"I'm a bit done," he told his friend. "I'm sorry."

"You're fucking insane, is what you are," Charpentier told him—but the medkit was apparently open now. The knife in his friend's hand didn't even give Ivan pause, even in the half-moment he thought the pilot was going to kill him before it cut away the shipsuit.

"That's a mess and this is a terrible fucking idea," the other man continued as he sprayed plastiskin over the wound. "I'm trapping fléchettes in there and we'll have to deal with that later, but right now, you need to stop bleeding to death."

"Still...corvette," Ivan warned. The bleeding appeared to have stopped, but everything still hurt.

"I know," Charpentier agreed. He was wobbly himself. "Can you stand? Lean on me. We don't have time."

"They'll send more people."

"They haven't yet, not according to the airlock camera." Charpentier helped Ivan into an acceleration couch. "And we'll talk about just what the *hell* you thought you were doing later, but right now, yeah. Corvette."

"What are you going to do?" Ivan asked. He felt the injectors settle onto his neck, and swallowed hard as the acceleration seat closed in around him.

"First rule of spaceflight, Ivan," Charpentier said as the injectors hissed. "*Every engine is an equally powerful weapon.*"

CHAPTER
TWELVE

The injectors stabbed home at the base of Ivan's neck, and the safety bars expanded to lock him into a full cocoon of gel packs again. The drugs hit him like liquid fire, burning through his body in a blaze of heat that left him gasping—but when the fire passed, his shoulder didn't hurt anymore, either.

He didn't know what the drug cocktail did, but it apparently included some effective painkillers. Ivan could *feel* the steel darts in his shoulder still, especially with the measured pressure of the acceleration couch, but it didn't hurt.

His attention was back to being sharp again. There were stimulants in the mix too. He was going to have to get the recipe from Charpentier later, just in case. This wasn't something he wanted blasted into his veins without full knowledge again.

Right now, he was able to focus on the screen in front of his eyes in time to watch *Restoya*'s engines flare as Charpentier yanked the racer away from the pirate ship. Docking connectors tore with a force that reverberated through the entire courier, and then the two ships spun apart in space.

The pirate ship's crew were probably still trying to raise their boarding team when the massive fusion rockets that propelled Karl

Charpentier's ship lined up with their hull and went to full power. Engines that could fling a hundred-thousand-ton courier ship around at three hundred meters per second squared could melt steel at hundreds of meters.

The corvette was only *seventeen* meters away.

Armor, hull plating, weapons, sensors…it all melted under the heat and force of *Restoya*'s engines. What was flung away from their ship wasn't a starship anymore. It was a mangled pile of wreckage.

A pile of wreckage that exploded moments later as the containment systems on its own fusion reactor failed.

"The pulsars will eat the debris," Charpentier said grimly. "Whoever is waiting for them to come home is going to be waiting a long damn time."

Ivan felt sick. He'd just killed eight people. His friend had probably just killed another thirty or more. What the *hell* were they doing?

A fléchette ground into his shoulder blade under the pressure of the acceleration couch, and he realized that there was a limit to the painkillers in the drug cocktail in his bloodstream.

"You okay?" Charpentier asked.

"There are still steel darts in me," Ivan pointed out.

"Magic them out," his friend said coldly. "Right now, I'm trying to adjust my course back to the race. The course that got fucked when *you* knocked me out so these people could board my ship."

"I know," Ivan said. He focused on the feeling in his shoulder. He didn't have nearly enough medical training to make a decent Mage doctor, but thanks to the painkillers, he could locate the darts with a surprising degree of accuracy.

Especially the one digging into his shoulder blade. He exhaled, *knowing* the problem with what he was about to do, then teleported it out.

"Fuck fuck fuck *fuck*," he swore. There was no need to put pressure on the wound, thankfully. The acceleration couch did that already.

"What?" Charpentier demanded.

"To get a three-millimeter dart out of my shoulder, I just took a couple cubic centimeters of flesh with it," Ivan admitted. "I don't know what painkillers are in this cocktail, but they're not enough for *that*."

There was silence on the intercom for a moment.

"Good. Care to explain *why* you fucked me?" Charpentier asked.

"You know Aquila, I assume?" Ivan asked. The pain was fading. He'd managed to get all but one of the darts. The last one was going to be a problem later, but he wasn't getting it out now. It was at least not stabbing into his bones.

"Il Maestro Aquila," the courier captain replied. "Vaguely. I know he's a mob boss. Some of the guys I borrowed from work for him."

"He tried to buy *Restoya* from you?" Ivan suggested.

"Not that I'm aware of," Charpentier said. "But a few offers came down that could have been him, I suppose. I wasn't selling. This ship is almost as important to me as Lyle."

"He wanted the ship," Ivan explained. "He bought all your debts, Karl. He was going to take it when you missed your payment, but then you found a Mage and had the invite to the Black Pulsar Race.

"He gave me a choice: turn you over or die." He swallowed. "I..." There weren't words. There was no way to confess his cowardice.

"I made him promise to clear your debts and spare you," Ivan said in a small voice. "It was all I could do. Or he was going to kill us both."

"And that's supposed to be enough?" Charpentier growled.

"No," Ivan agreed. "It was the best I could do. Then, of course, they decided that even that deal wasn't worth keeping."

His friend was silent.

"The boarders were going to kill you, Karl," Ivan said. "I could live with selling your ship out from underneath you to save us both, but I wasn't going to sacrifice you to save myself."

"At which point you, what, killed them all?" Charpentier said dryly.

"Yes," Ivan confessed, feeling sick. "I was trained as a Navy Mage, Karl. I'd never used that training, but I can fight with magic. They never even saw it coming."

"So, what now?" the pilot asked after several more seconds of silence.

"I'm not even sure how you got an invite to this race," Ivan admitted. "Not if Aquila sponsors it."

"La Cosa Nostra is only one of the sponsors, and I don't think

Aquila even runs la Cosa Nostra in Xanth," Charpentier replied. "He's probably higher up than I thought, but he's not in charge. If we finish the race, we should still get paid."

"Then we finish the race," Ivan told him. "You can keep the damn prize money, Karl. I owe you this, no matter what. And…I need to think about things when this is over."

"About what, how you apparently like to sell out friends?"

"I'm a coward, Karl," Ivan said. "I know that, I plan for it, I work with it. If you'd asked me what I'd do with a gun to a friend's head and a gun to mine, I'd have told you I would have let you die."

"You didn't." There wasn't forgiveness in Charpentier's voice, but it wasn't as cold as it had started.

"I might have misjudged…myself," Ivan told his friend. "Whatever happens in the rest of this, Karl, you won't face it alone. I owe you that. I've got your back, till the end of the road."

"You're right," the pilot said slowly. "You owe me that. As for the rest…fuck, I don't know, Ivan. You sold me out…but you saved my life, too. I need to think about this."

"Unless something's changed, you think best when flying," Ivan pointed out. "We've got a few hours of that ahead of us."

"And neither of us is going anywhere," Charpentier said. "That's two people who tried to kill me in this race, and what I can see suggests we're still in the lead. Somehow.

"I have no intention of letting anyone catch up to us! Thirty gees till the end."

Ivan groaned.

"You'll forgive me for not sympathizing with your pain as much as I might have yesterday," the pilot said with an unforced chuckle.

THIRTEEN

They didn't see another ship for the remaining twelve hours of the race. Astonishing displays of astronomical stellar power, radiation beams that could cut a ship in half like a toy, beacons that had somehow placed themselves in the middle of the deadly storm…but not a single ship.

"So, the sixteen-hour estimate was bullshit, I see," Ivan noted. "I make that beacon twenty."

"So do I," Charpentier agreed, the pilot starting to sound exhausted. He'd been flying for hours upon hours—and while a lot of it was straightforward, a lot of it hadn't been.

There wasn't much in terms of debris out there, but the radiation beams and gravity waves that made that the case were hard to maneuver around.

"Hold on one moment," the pilot said. "We are at one hundred KPS relative to the beacon and within the bubble, transmitting…"

Charpentier exhaled, a long deep sigh.

"Receiving," he told Ivan. "That looks like jump coordinates to me, Ivan. I'm cutting the engines to fifteen gees. Are you going to be able to walk?"

"Walk? Yes," Ivan said. "Use my right shoulder? No." He sighed against the gel of the acceleration couch. "I've also probably bled all over the couch."

"There are *bodies* on my bridge, Ivan, and the couch put pressure on the wound," Charpentier replied. "Believe me, wiping down the acceleration couches isn't high on my concerns."

"Also bodies in Engineering and near the main airlock," Ivan told him. "We…probably will want to deal with those before we get back to Xanth."

"I have no interest in dealing with murder charges, so yes," the pilot agreed. "For now, you should be able to unlock the couch and get down to the simulacrum chamber. This place is gorgeous and terrifying and apparently full of people who want to kill me.

"I look forward to never seeing it again."

Ivan chuckled as he hit the release on the acceleration couch. Drug injectors—they'd fired once an hour for the last twelve hours—withdrew from his neck. The upper layers of the cocoon folded back into the safety bars and then folded back to the side.

He could *feel* the crusted scabs on his shoulder from both the original wound and the new one he'd created removing the darts. The plastiskin was mostly holding, but he winced as he moved.

He was no doctor, but he suspected it was going to take careful medical attention to save his arm. Medical attention he wasn't going to get on a mob ship—not that he'd trust, anyway.

"I'm on my way down," he told Charpentier. "Soon, we'll be clear of this mess."

BLOOD LOSS and having been motionless for twelve hours left Ivan dizzier and slower than he'd expected, which meant it took him five minutes to reach the simulacrum chamber instead of one.

To his surprise, Charpentier didn't say anything when he finally brought the intercom video online.

"It'll take me a minute or two to calculate the jump still," Ivan told the other man.

"I know," Charpentier told him. "I'm watching the scanners for the rest of the racers."

"And?" Ivan asked, bringing up his calculation program and plugging in the coordinates. Looked like they were exactly one light-year away. Apparently, whoever was watching and betting on the race was only really going to see the end.

No one would ever really know what happened to the ships that hadn't made it all the way. Even the ones that Ivan and Charpentier had seen destroyed…who could they tell? They'd been in the middle of the illegal race themselves, after all.

"I'm getting pings back near beacon seventeen, but nothing solid yet," the pilot replied. "I think we're several hours ahead of everyone else. That's what thirty gees buys us."

"I can't imagine you're surprised," Ivan said. He glanced at the sensor data himself. He needed to factor a lot of information into the jump. Current velocity relative to the pulsars, the gravity effects of the two massive stars, even the cycle of their radiation beams.

All of that went into getting them out of there, and it was slowing down his calculations.

"No. None of the ships in this race ever had a chance so long as nobody killed or kidnapped us."

Charpentier's voice was dry and Ivan grimaced. Something blinked across the sensors as he did so, a momentary blip of something that shouldn't have been there.

It didn't factor into his calculations, but it was weird.

"Karl, did you see the safety ship that's supposed to be watching the end of the race?" he asked.

"No," the other man admitted. "That's weird, though I guess they might not keep their promises at an illegal race."

"They might not," Ivan agreed slowly. "Calculations are done, but if I may make a suggestion?"

"Can I trust it?"

Ivan grimaced again.

"I think so?" he told the other man. "If we can get our money and get the hell out ASAP, I think that might be the best plan."

"At least one major sponsor of this event is trying to kill me," Charpentier replied. "I agree completely. Money and gone. I suspect they're used to it. Are we ready?"

Ivan double-checked the calculations and nodded.

"We're ready," he announced. "Jumping...*now*."

The world shifted around them, taking them away from the binary pulsars where Ivan had betrayed a friend, saved a friend, won the race...and was reasonably certain he'd had a momentary glimpse of the familiar pyramid profile of a Royal Martian Navy destroyer.

A ship that should have had *no* way to find anyone in the mess of the pulsar's radiation storm.

THE JUMP COMPLETED and Ivan staggered against the fatigue that swept over him. Carefully, ever so carefully, he lifted his right arm away from the simulacrum and let it rest at his side.

"Six hours," he told Charpentier over the intercom. "In six hours, we get the hell out of here. Think we can get the money by then?"

"I bloody well hope so," the pilot replied. "Hang on."

New icons flickered across Ivan's screen. There were *dozens* of ships out there. None of them were big. Most were yachts, the private jump-craft of the wealthy and race-crazy of a dozen star systems. The kind of people who'd show up to an illegal race to bet on the outcome.

"Race Master, this is *Restoya*," Karl Charpentier announced. "We are transmitting all beacon keys; we have completed the race."

"*Restoya*, this is the Race Master," the same noticeably accented voice greeted them. "Beacon keys received and validated. Congratulations. You're the first to make it out...well under the expected minimum time. I do believe that's a new record."

"She's a fast ship, Race Master," Charpentier replied. He paused. "What happens now?"

"I'm transmitting you holding coordinates," the Race Master said. "Proceed to those coordinates and stand by. There will be a celebratory gala once all the ships have returned."

"What happens if not everybody returns?" the pilot asked.

The Race Master chuckled, the sound chilling.

"We'll be having the gala in ten hours, then," he replied. "That's always something we have to account for."

"Understood. Moving to the coordinates as instructed," Charpentier replied. Engines hummed around Ivan, a relaxing sound compared to the vibrating roar of the ship running at thirty gravities.

There was a pause, with the channel still open, and then the inevitable question got asked.

"When do I get my money?"

"At the gala, Captain Charpentier," the Race Master replied. "We need to show off our winner, after all."

Damn. Ivan had really been hoping.

CHAPTER

FOURTEEN

Ivan had seen three of the racers wrecked by a fourth—and that fourth vaporized by a mob warship more concerned with capturing *Restoya* intact than anything else. He expected to see eighteen ships appear at the finish line under the eyes of the gathered rich gamblers.

Only sixteen made it, trickling in over the following ten hours in clumps of three to four.

He spent most of those ten hours resting and patching up his shoulder. Charpentier mostly left him alone, the two of them staying apart to dwell on their own thoughts as they considered the issues before and behind them.

Fortunately, the sickbay aboard *Restoya* was as automated and designed for single-person use as most of her other systems. Ivan had his arm and shoulder in a carefully designed sling and cast that gave him enough mobility with his forearm to hold on to a simulacrum while immobilizing his shoulder.

The design had, in fact, already been in the sickbay's computers. He was far from the first Jump Mage to need to teleport a starship after being shot.

"Ivan, it's time to go." Charpentier finally appeared in the sickbay while Ivan was considering painkiller selections.

"Do we know where the gala is taking place?" Ivan asked.

"On *Stardust Dreamy*," the pilot told him. "It's a luxury liner most of the time, but it's apparently owned by the Cloud Mountain. *Not* la Cosa Nostra, I checked."

Ivan caught the edge of his friend's familiar smirk and returned the smile.

"Think I can beg off from having been shot?" he asked.

"They don't know that, and we can't tell them," Charpentier pointed out. "Besides, we need an escape route if everything goes sideways."

"Define *escape route*," Ivan asked.

"You can teleport, right?" his friend said. "Can you teleport us both to the ship?"

"Yes," Ivan said slowly. "Better than I can teleport you to me from a distance, at least." He sighed. "All right, all right, I'll come with. I wasn't expecting a fancy gala."

"I figured you wouldn't, so I made sure I had a tux in your size," Charpentier said with a grin. "It won't be perfect—I picked it up with Lyle and, well, it didn't account for a cast—but it'll serve."

"What kind of going-to-shit are we planning for now?" Ivan asked as his friend produced a pair of suit bags from behind the door. He stripped down and started dressing, using magic to float the clothes around so as not to ask Charpentier for help.

"After what you said, I'm still half-expecting Aquila to pull something," the pilot admitted. "He might even find some way to refuse the payment when I try to pay off the debt, too. It's going to be a mess."

"The legal debt is at least run through banks, right?" Ivan asked. "He owns it, but it's in a structure with regulations and rules. He's got to take the money."

"True, true," Charpentier agreed. Even with Ivan using magic, he was dressed first. The pilot's black-and-white tux was perfectly sized to him. He looked like he was *born* for this kind of party.

Ivan took a moment to adjust his with magic as he carefully slid his arm into the right sleeve. Even that couldn't get it to the perfection of a good tailor given the time to do it right, but it looked better than he'd been afraid of.

He checked his wrist-comp, setting up a program that would constantly update the numbers for a teleport back to the simulacrum chamber of the courier ship.

"*Something* is going to go down," Ivan finally said. He didn't want to tell Charpentier he thought he'd seen a Navy ship. Even if he *had*, the Navy only had a handful of people capable of tracking jumps.

They wouldn't waste one on this mess, would they?

"So we'll be ready to go. I think we get the money first, before we're expected to mingle," Charpentier told him. "Are you good?"

"I'd be better if we were back on Anthony, having beers and watching your kid," Ivan replied. "For now, I'm as good as I'm going to get."

"Then let's give these rich bastards their money's worth."

Restoya had her own shuttle, but apparently Charpentier had negotiated a pickup. The shuttles from *Stardust Dreamy* were very obviously the support craft of a luxury liner. The one that delivered Ivan and Charpentier to their destination had magical gravity and an automated wet bar.

Both of them took a drink from the bar, but Ivan didn't touch his. He realized as they were leaving the shuttle that Charpentier hadn't either.

There'd been no discussion about that, but both of them were clearly on the same page. This probably wasn't a trap, per se, but they weren't out of the woods yet.

"This way, please; this way, please," a woman in an even tighter-than-usual shipsuit with strategically placed transparent patches greeted them as they exited the shuttle. "Captain Charpentier, Mage Holloway?"

She got the name wrong. Ivan didn't bother to correct her, just falling in behind as she led the way.

"It's always a pleasure to meet the winners of a race like this," she told him. "That must have been such a rush."

"Parts of it always are," Charpentier told her. "Parts are just…math. Spaceflight is a lot of math."

The woman smiled flirtatiously and continued a conversation with the pilot that Ivan judged she was *far* less interested in than she was pretending to be.

That didn't matter. She delivered them to a room that was clearly a waiting area and settled them into comfortable chairs.

"I'll bring you drinks," she told them. "Any preferences?"

"Vodka and water," Ivan told her. He was tempted to tell her to hold the vodka, for that matter. He didn't trust *anything* aboard a ship owned by the descendants of the Chinese crime families.

"Whiskey on the rocks," Charpentier said.

The hostess bowed, the transparent patches showing a not-quite-indecent amount of skin, and slipped away.

"I think that woman might be as much of a trap as the rest of the ship," the pilot murmured. "She's *good*."

"If you were a paying client, her time is probably on the rate sheet," Ivan replied. "And I wouldn't bet on her getting more than a tenth of what you paid, either."

"I know," Charpentier agreed. "I'm sorry I dragged you into this."

"I'm sorry I caved when they threatened me," Ivan told him.

"I know," Charpentier repeated. "You came through. Let's get out of this and then we'll talk for real, okay?"

"Okay."

Another hostess appeared at that moment, leading a man and woman into the room. The man wore a similar tux to Ivan and Charpentier, and the woman was clad in a stunning floor-length red ballgown.

The woman stepped over to Charpentier and offered her hand.

"Captain Charpentier, I'm Captain Akane Yamada," she told him. "This is my husband, George. We are apparently second…which makes me wonder what happened to the ships ahead of us other than yours."

"We didn't happen to them," Charpentier said. "More than that…I think is probably best left to speculation."

Yamada raised a perfectly groomed dark eyebrow at his words but let that rest as two more pairs of racers were brought in.

Drinks arrived a few moments later, accompanied by the fifth-place racer—on her own. Like Ivan and half the people in the room, she wore the gold medallion of a Mage.

Apparently, it was the Captain and the Ship's Mage who were expected to receive their prizes. In the last woman's case, she was obviously both.

"Water," she snapped when her hostess offered drinks. She surveyed the room coldly, clearly assessing each of the teams that had come in ahead of her.

Ivan didn't touch his drink. He noted that Charpentier took several of the ice cubes out of his, popping them in his mouth and slowly eating them instead of drinking the whiskey.

"Pilots and Ships' Mages," a now-familiar accented voice greeted them. Ivan looked up to see a small dark-skinned man of clear Chinese extraction standing at one end of the room. "Welcome aboard *Stardust Dreamy*. I am your Race Master and tonight's master of ceremonies, so I will run you through the plan."

Ivan laid his drink aside and focused on the man.

"The last of our guests and the lesser racers are coming aboard now," the Race Master told them. "Once the important people are in the main hall, the ceremony will begin. You will each be called on stage, in order, where I will present you with an envelope containing a coded credit chip with your winnings.

"You are welcome to validate the amount, though I ask that you wait until you have *left* the stage to do so," the man, probably a senior Cloud Mountain member, told them. "The gala will continue for some hours, and we ask that you stay and socialize for at least the first hour. These people won and lost great deals of money on your journey over the last few days, and they want to put faces to names.

"Our portion of those bets pays for your prizes, so we like to keep them happy. Once the hour is up, any of the hosts or hostesses can arrange a shuttle back to your ship for you."

"What about security?" the fifth-place racer demanded.

"Cloud Mountain guarantees the safety of everyone aboard *Stardust Dreamy*," the Race Master told her. "You may not see your guardians, but you are under our protection for the entire gala. No one will harm you. You have my word, bound by the Oaths of Ninety-Nine Blades."

That was actually worth something, Ivan judged. He could be wrong, of course.

A gong sounded.

"That is the warning that my part in the festivities begins," the Race Master told them. "I look forward to awarding you all your well-earned prizes."

The Cloud Mountain boss walked out through the door he'd come in through, and the racers looked at each other.

"Could have given us the damn chips now," the Mage racer grumbled. "Would help my trust issues, that's for sure."

"It's all ceremony and games from here," Yamada replied. "Be patient, Captain. We will all be paid. Cloud Mountain is good for it, even if their partners decided to pull out now."

CHAPTER

FIFTEEN

Even knowing that they were aboard a top-tier luxury liner did not prepare Ivan for the reality of *Stardust Dreamy*'s Great Hall. Summoned out onto the stage with Charpentier, he inhaled sharply as he took in the view.

The Hall was on top of the ship, a long, transparent observation dome with magical gravity. The roof was a bubble a hundred meters long and thirty wide. *Restoya* could have fit inside the Great Hall with ease—and was relatively easily *seen* through the roof. *Stardust Dreamy* had been positioned so that the crowd could look up and see the neatly arranged line of the surviving seventeen racers.

"Dear patrons, sponsors and organizers, I give you the winners of the Twenty-Four-Fifty-Eight Black Pulsar Race, the crew of *Restoya*," the Race Master announced. "The top prize this year is seven million, two hundred thousand Martian dollars."

A small red envelope appeared in the Race Master's hand, and he offered it to Charpentier.

"Spend it well, my friends," he told them as the pilot took the envelope. "May I suggest booking on *Stardust Dreamy*? We'd be delighted to have you back!"

That got a chuckle from the crowd. Charpentier bowed stiffly and then led the way off the stage into the crowd.

"So far, so…"

Aquila materialized out of the crowd, several people scattering out of his way as the broad-shouldered Mage and la Cosa Nostra Maestro walked calmly but steadily toward Ivan and Charpentier.

Behind them, the Yamadas collected their own red envelope to further applause, but Ivan's attention was riveted on the mob boss and the two tuxedoed bodyguards accompanying him.

"Congratulations, Captain Charpentier, Mage Halloway," Aquila told them, offering his hand. "You weren't who I expected to win, of course, but all of this is a gamble, isn't it?"

"So I'm told," Ivan murmured. "You win some, you lose some."

"And sometimes, the deck is even more rigged than you think," the mob boss said, his voice still perfectly calm. "Winning can have unexpected consequences."

"That may be, but I find keeping my promises covers me against many problems, don't you?" Ivan asked the crime lord, his tone equally level even while part of him wanted to hide behind Charpentier and cower. "Broken promises cause *so* many complications."

"You're not as clever as you think you are, Mage Halloway," Aquila told him.

"That's Mage-*Captain* Halloway," Ivan corrected the mob boss. "Something you should, perhaps, remember before you come at me or my friends again. What use is His Majesty's Protectorate, after all, if those of us who served it don't protect people?"

There was a long silence as Ivan held Aquila's gaze and then, to his surprise, the mob boss nodded and inclined his head.

"Perhaps," he allowed. "I suggest you make certain your friend pays his debts."

"He will," Ivan said genially. "And if you'll excuse us, I believe some others wish to speak to the winner of the Black Pulsar Race."

"You're braver than I thought," Aquila said with a surprising chuckle, then swept away with his bodyguards.

There were, in fact, several people hovering at a distance who wanted to speak to the winners. They had only a few seconds of peace before the crowd descended on them, but Charpentier put his hand on Ivan's shoulder.

"If for nothing else, my friend, I might just forgive you for that conversation alone," he murmured.

"You're welcome," Ivan replied.

"Captain!" An elegantly dressed man with a decorative sword stepped forward. "What a pleasure to see someone beat out all expectations like that. Two hours under par! How did you do it?"

"That's a secret," Charpentier told the stranger. Ivan couldn't help but notice that no one was giving names. That made sense—and made Aquila's use of their names a not-so-subtle power play all on its own.

"Surely you can give us a hint?" the man asked.

A fifth round of applause swept through the Great Hall.

"That's the last prize," Ivan said. "What happens now?"

"Why, we wine and dine the victors," the sword-wearer told them. "You were one of the three I bet on, you know. The other two sadly didn't finish, but you more than made up for the lost money there! I always—"

Ivan stepped sideways, cutting the man off as brilliant blue-white flares suddenly lit up the entire Great Hall.

"Jump flare," he hissed.

"Ivan, what the hell?" Charpentier demanded.

"Jump flare!" Ivan repeated, pointing up to where new stark-white pyramid shapes now hung in the darkness behind the line of racers. "That's a goddamn Navy squadron, Karl."

Their conversation partner looked up in horror. He wasn't alone as the entire room began to dissolve into chaos, and Ivan realized that someone *else* had been playing a very different game the entire time they'd been racing.

"Karl, to me," he snapped.

His friend obeyed, stepping over to him.

"What?"

"Hold my arms," Ivan ordered. *"Gently."*

Charpentier did so, linking his forearms with Ivan's and waiting.

Magic flared around them both as Ivan checked the calculations on his wrist-comp and *stepped*. The Great Hall vanished, replaced with the lit-up sensor screens of *Restoya*'s simulacrum chamber.

"Phew," Ivan exhaled. He released his friend and crossed to the simulacrum, using his left hand to carefully align his semi-motionless injured arm with the model. Around them he could see a dozen Royal Martian Navy starships maneuvering through the chaos, assault shuttles already in space and screaming toward *Stardust Dreamy* and the rest of the ships.

"Tell me you've got the money," Ivan demanded as he linked into the jump matrix.

"I've got the money," Charpentier replied. "Can you get us—"

Ivan wove his magic and *Restoya* jumped.

CHAPTER

SIXTEEN

"You bugged my ship."

Jessie Theodore laughed at him. Ivan had always liked her laugh—and it turned out to do fascinating things when the woman was wearing a skintight blue dress like she was tonight.

As promised, he'd taken her out to dinner at one of Serendipity's top restaurants. The price tag was going to hurt, but Charpentier had refused to keep *all* of the money he'd promised Ivan.

"I can neither confirm nor deny such an allegation," she told him with a smile, sipping her wine. "Not least of all, Ivan, you don't *own* a ship."

Ivan sipped his own wine while faking a fierce glare. He knew quite well that his angular features, a legacy of Ukrainian ancestors, made for an impressive glare.

"You know what I mean," he told her.

"And you know what I mean," Theodore replied, her tone suddenly serious. "*If* I had an encrypted radio transceiver installed on a certain ship, one that was recording and retransmitting every message that ship received, and *if* that transceiver had allowed a successful raid on the organizers of an illegal race, I would not be able

343

to associate that ship with *you*. You, my dear Ivan, are a perfectly innocent and honest Protectorate citizen, aren't you?

"What else would you be?"

She smirked at him over her wineglass, and he sighed and saluted her with his own glass.

"I see why you ended up a spy," he told her.

"I'm not a spy, Ivan," Theodore replied. "I'm an *administrator*. I sit in a quiet back office that doesn't officially belong to the Agency and run numbers eight hours a day, five days a week."

"And if some of those numbers happen to coordinate career-making raids on organized crime?" Ivan asked.

"Then the public credit goes to the officers in charge of the squadron," she said. "I may or may not get a healthy raise and promotion around the same time, but that would be *purely* coincidental.

"Nothing an analyst in a back office does could ever cause something of that scale, right?"

Ivan shook his head at her.

"I see. To things that never happened, then." He toasted her and they clinked glasses as she smirked at him again.

"I understand that Captain Charpentier's ship will not be seized after all," she told him. "A mysterious benefactor allowed him to come up with the money. Best for everyone, I think."

"You have some idea of what he's built on *Restoya* now, right?" he asked.

"We do," she confirmed. "I'll admit that we didn't until it drew eyes. I can't say much more than that. This isn't *supposed* to be a work dinner."

"Then what is it supposed to be?" Ivan said.

"A date, my grumpy-faced friend," Theodore told him. "You're currently a civilian, entirely outside of my chain of command. Even if we're both old enough to take things slowly, I prefer not to leave any illusions about my intent floating around."

Ivan chuckled.

"I appreciate the transparency," he told her. "I agree on taking things slowly, too." He raised his glass to her again. "Rushing into matters seems such a twenty-years-ago thing to do."

"Exactly. What are your plans these days?" she asked.

"A couple of weeks ago, I would have said I didn't know, and I'd have been telling you the truth," he admitted. "It was time for me to be done with the Navy, but leaving left me rather adrift."

"And now?" she said.

"I'll be staying in Serendipity for a bit. Probably home-basing here after that regardless, but..." He examined his wineglass. "I'm still making up my mind, I think."

"That's fair," Theodore admitted. "I went from the Navy straight into MISS with a transfer everyone signed off on and supported, and I still felt adrift for a few months."

She reached over the table and put her fingers on his.

"No one begrudges you taking the time to be certain of what you want, Ivan," she told him. "But if it helps...that raid we didn't talk about? Il Maestro Aquila was captured alive. He's heading for trial and already been denied bail.

"He's not getting out of jail anytime soon, if that helps your decisions."

Ivan captured her fingers under his free hand, ignoring his food as he met the woman's gaze.

"It might just," he admitted. "Thank you."

The warm touch of her fingers on his *also* helped his decisions, but she already knew that.

THE DOORBELL on Ivan's apartment sounded exactly six minutes and twenty seconds after it was supposed to. Despite his assorted misgivings about the Navy, he'd been an executive officer or a department head on various starships for fifteen years. If a subordinate had shown up that late for a meeting, he'd have told them off thoroughly—quietly and in private but thoroughly.

Karl Charpentier wasn't a subordinate, though. At this moment in time, he wasn't a superior or employer, either. Ivan had agreed to one voyage, one race.

That was done, but the future lay out before them, and Ivan had spent some time organizing his apartment to the standard he'd have expected of himself aboard a warship.

Now he poured coffee for them both and slid a mug over to Charpentier.

"Final documents are all signed and sealed," his friend told him. "I still owe ten million on *Restoya*, but that's payable over four years now that I'm back in good standing."

"That's good to hear," Ivan said. "What about the other debts?"

"Weirdly, I can't find anyone from la Cosa Nostra to try and pay them back," Charpentier said. "Aquila appears to have vanished and his people have gone to ground. I'm going to hang on to what I owe them for a while, just in case, but they're not around for me to pay."

"He is apparently in the gentle hands of the Martian Investigation Service," Ivan noted. "While he may not have turned on his people, I imagine the MIS got some of his junior hands who *did*."

"May they all receive their just deserts," his friend said prayerfully. "And hopefully never mention that we were there!"

"We'd be facing, what, a fine or a year in jail?" Ivan asked. "Worst-case scenario, we come out okay, I think."

He also suspected that any record that they had been present at the Black Pulsar Race was going to end up locked down in MISS files. Theodore may have used him and *Restoya*, but she had a solid sense of favors owed.

They weren't going to get caught up in that mess if she could do anything about it...and he suspected his new girlfriend was going to be able to do a *lot* about it.

"True enough, true enough." Charpentier drank his coffee. "It's been a hell of a few weeks, and I think you might still owe me an apology, but...we came out okay."

"I'm not sure apologies cut it for what I did," Ivan said calmly. "I am sorry I sold you out, Karl. I am. I just think I owe you more than words."

"You saved my life twice over," his friend admitted. "I won't call it even just yet, but I will call it forgiven. Fair?"

"More than," Ivan agreed. "Thank you, Karl. I still owe you one run, too. I promised to take you out to recruit Mages somewhere else."

"You did," Charpentier said. "Are you down?"

"Not today." The Mage chuckled. "Not tomorrow. But yes. I can do that for you. On the other hand, part of your recruiting trouble here was Aquila…and much of the rest was that you didn't have any Mages."

The other man finished his coffee and gestured the cup questioningly to the coffeepot.

"Go ahead," Ivan told him.

"You sound like you have a suggestion," Charpentier noted as he refilled his mug.

"Think of it as an offer," Ivan suggested. "I…I won't work *for* you, Karl. But everything looks handled to keep *Restoya* safe and back to just being another courier ship.

"I'll work *with* you," he offered. "I want a partnership in the operating company. I'll be your senior Ship's Mage, handle getting you the rest of the Mages—but we all take the two months you need to be here for Lyle off."

"Two months' vacation and a share in the company?" Charpentier asked. "That's…"

"You can consider my equity stake seven million dollars," Ivan said dryly.

His friend paused, then laughed.

"You're not wrong," he admitted. "And you're right; I have to be here while Lyle's out of school. I was thinking of that as a problem, not offering it to people as a guaranteed vacation every working year. Need to factor that we're only working ten months into the salaries…"

"Your *partner* and you could do that math easily enough," Ivan suggested. "Plus, with *Restoya*'s engines and acceleration couches, you can cut as much as twenty-four hours off any given courier run.

"That'll add up fast."

"It will," Charpentier admitted. "Twenty percent."

"Forty," Ivan countered. "My friend, you *need* someone with the shares, the patience, and the experience with you to yank you up short if you try and midlife-crisis at the crew again. I won't put up with that bullshit, and you can't afford to put yourself in a position where I follow Sonia."

That was a low blow, but he wasn't kidding. One screw-up of that scale could mean there'd be another. The best way to *avoid* that was for Ivan to be there to tell Charpentier when he was being an idiot.

His friend stood next to the kitchen counter, examining his coffee like it held the secrets of the universe.

"Done," he agreed. "We'll have time to do up the paperwork. Lyle's out of school in three weeks, so that first holiday kicks off right now."

"Good. We'll recruit toward the end of his break," Ivan said. "With me in place, I'm pretty sure we can fill our Mage slots easily enough. I'll keep an eye out for promising candidates, assuming we can put them on salary to wait for us?"

"At Mage salaries?" Charpentier said with a face, but it turned to a grin as Ivan raised an eyebrow. "No, that makes sense. I'll talk to the lawyer; we'll have the paperwork for the partnership in place before I grab Lyle and we head to a beach somewhere."

"Focus on him while you're away," Ivan said firmly. "*Restoya* isn't going anywhere and I'll keep an eye on everything else. We'll keep in touch, but your kid…your kid's important."

"I agree," his friend said. "Not the only place I fucked up, I know, but it's the one place I can *definitely* fix it."

ONCE KARL CHARPENTIER HAD LEFT, Ivan took a slow read-through of the quick and dirty memorandum of understanding they'd drafted and signed to cover both their asses.

It answered what one Ivan Halloway was going to be doing for ten months out of twelve for the foreseeable future. Forty percent of profits after costs would likely add up quickly once the ship was running—Charpentier's wife had put their son in a top-tier educational academy *and* kept up a mansion without straining his funds, after all.

Ivan wasn't entirely sure what had happened there and hadn't asked. He'd never even met Penny, so he refused to judge. His impression, though, was that his friend hadn't gone sideways until *after* the divorce.

Sighing, he shook his head and opened his messages to extract a contact code.

"This is the Royal Martian Navy Reserve, Xanth Station," a chirpy young Lieutenant answered the video call immediately. "How may I assist you?"

"Good afternoon, Lieutenant," Ivan told the young man. "I am Mage-Captain Ivan Halloway—retired, obviously. I need to speak to Sarah Tapiti.

"She's left me several messages over the last couple of months, and she and I need to discuss my Reserve status…"

MAGE-QUEEN'S THIEF

A STARSHIP'S MAGE UNIVERSE NOVELLA

CHAPTER
ONE

Bartholomew "Barry" Carpentier had fixed the problem less than five minutes after he'd crawled into the utility space. Buried underneath the pub in the Tau Cetan blocks, the compartment was cramped—but it was also the only access to the hardware he needed. His magic had swiftly guided him to the problem in the complex mix of power and network cables, allowing him to fix the issue with the Hawk and Rooster's data-management system before his initial software diagnosis had finished.

The lanky young man was a Mage by Right, one of the magically gifted youths discovered by the Mage-Queen's Royal Testers at the age of thirteen. Unfortunately, between one thing—a juvenile criminal record—and another—an inability to pass any kind of organized test for *any* reason—Barry was about as close to an unemployable failure as a Mage in the Protectorate of the Mage-Queen of Mars could be.

Even the electrician's license that allowed him to crawl around a pub's utility space was fraudulent. Not that anyone who'd hired him would ever realize that—or *care*.

"The blocks" were Tau Cetan social housing. Growing up there, Barry had seen the immense effort that was put into making sure they weren't the dead end such places had been historically.

But no one lived in the blocks and went to the Hawk and Rooster because their life was in a great place. That served his purposes. There weren't many Mages in places like this, which meant no one was looking for him.

And since the handful of businesses running in areas like this were desperately short on tradespeople, none looked too closely at his electrician's certificate. The only people who *officially* knew Barry was even a Mage were at his bank.

The Protectorate had a great deal of interest in making sure Mages didn't need to become criminals, after all, and he received a stipend directly from the Mage-Queen's government on Mars.

Even if he was completely useless to anyone as a Mage. He was a better electrician…but that wasn't what he *actually* did for a living either.

The diagnostic pinged complete at the same time as a message arrived on his wrist-comp. The PC was a cheap utilitarian thing, but it concealed better hardware than its exterior suggested.

The diagnostic was green—and the message made him chuckle.

I know you fixed the problem in the first five minutes. Get out here. We need to talk.

Alaina Waxer was officially "just" the Hawk and Rooster's senior bartender. In reality, she owned the place through a few layers of deception and a hired manager.

More relevant to Barry Carpentier, though, was her *other* role as a fixer for the Tau Ceti criminal underworld.

HE REENTERED the Hawk and Rooster's lounge and made a passing check of the holographic waiter's systems with his wrist-comp. The hologram's projector was older than he was—which, for the twenty-five-year-old electrician, wasn't saying much.

It was also probably older than the bartender, and Alaina Waxer was at least fifty. He'd never asked. Age was hard to judge, given the medicine of the twenty-fifth century, though he didn't *believe* Waxer had access to the literally magical class of top-end treatments.

"Barry, get over here," the jovially large woman bellowed across the room. There was a solitary customer sitting at the bar, who received a meaningful glance from Waxer and made themselves scarce.

Barry wasn't much of one for the normal day/night cycle of Deveraux, Tau Ceti *f*'s fifth largest city. Neither was Waxer, and it was a bit before four in the morning.

They were alone in the bar now and he claimed the stool the customer had vacated.

"Coffee?" the fixer asked.

"Black, no spices," Barry replied.

Tau Cetan cuisine could be described as the result of a French chef and an Indian chef having a fistfight in the kitchen. Coffee flavored with karha masala was one of the planet's favored drinks.

And Barry was allergic to key ingredients of the spice mix. Given the degree to which karha masala and other curry-style masalas ended up in things on Tau Ceti, he lived on a *very* bland diet compared to his friends.

Waxer knew that of old, and a plate of plain toast slid across the bar, accompanied by a plain white cup and a credit chip.

"For the utility room," she told him, then winked. "And the last chunk of payment for the Courvoisier."

Barry smiled as he tapped the chip against his wrist-comp. It was a hefty chunk of credits, enough to pay the rent on the low-profile townhouse he lived in for a while. He *technically* didn't live in the blocks themselves, after all, though few people regarded the other homes intermingled with the welfare housing with much warmth.

He doubted his was the only one with a hot tub and a high-end entertainment suite, though.

Waxer eyed him for a few long moments of silence, then sighed.

"Could you please turn off the game? I know it helps you, but..."

Barry winced and nodded, tapping a command to shut down the video game being projected into his left eye via an implant in his eyebrow. It wasn't a fast-paced thing—a turn-based economic strategy simulator based around fourteenth-century shipping routes—but it was almost always up while he was awake.

Focusing on one thing at a time was hard.

"It's off," he murmured, pulling the plate over to him. Eating would keep his hands occupied for a bit, he supposed.

"Marie was asking after you," Waxer noted.

"Feel free to tell her I died," Barry replied between bites of toast.

Marie was Alaina Waxer's daughter and had been Barry's girl-friend for an...*exciting* year. That had culminated in discovering that Marie Waxer had about the same attitude toward her personal promises as her mother had toward society's laws.

He wasn't even certain how many people she'd cheated on him with—and, he suspected, neither was the elder Waxer.

"Oh, *I* know she nuked that bridge from orbit, Barry, but she *did* ask," Waxer said.

He and Waxer had worked together before, during and after his relationship with her daughter. His impression was that his fixer thought her daughter was an idiot, but he would admit he was biased on that matter.

To himself, at least.

"You got work?" he finally asked. "The Courvoisier gig was fun, but I imagine there aren't that many interplanetary luxury shuttles we can get notes on."

The Courvoisier 2467 was a brand-new spacecraft model, built there in Tau Ceti, designed to carry the rich and lazy between planets in a star system in the lap of uttermost luxury and security.

Enough of the security on one of them, though, had slipped to allow Waxer to get her hands on the information of where and when it would be stored without crew on board.

Barry and his magical Gift had done the rest. Few pieces of software or hardware could impede him for very long.

"I know how much was on that cred-chip," Waxer said drily. "Planning on getting out of the blocks?"

He shrugged, finished the toast, and began to tap his fingers on the coffee cup.

"I don't like sitting still," he reminded her. "Fixing your bar's system-net connection isn't going to keep me busy for long. My license won't hold up to anyone with half a brain outside the blocks, so I need something to occupy me.

"And like I said, the Courvoisier was fun."

He could *feel* her gaze on his tapping fingers, but she swallowed whatever she was thinking and sighed.

"Fun and lucrative. Not many high-end shuttles get parked and left alone, though."

"I mean, I can steal whatever you can move," Barry pointed out. "Let me know where to drop things off and I can get to work."

"Do I *look* like I'm running a black-market shuttle dealership?" Waxer asked. "Moving in that kind of quantity draws attention, Barry. The wrong kind. One or two shuttles, even super high-end ones, can go missing and no one really cares.

"We start disappearing spacecraft in the kind of numbers needed to keep *you* from getting bored…"

"But you have work," Barry said. "Or you'd have let me sit in the utility closet and borrow your net-link for games till dawn."

"Aye." Waxer slid a second cup of coffee across the bar, this one accompanied by a datachip.

She knew him well, the last of his first cup vanishing as she passed him the new one. The chip went into his wrist-comp and he flicked his projector back on for something *other* than a video game.

"What is this?" he asked. It didn't *look* like a high-end shuttlecraft. The Courvoisier had stripes of literal gold in places. This one looked like a heavy-lift hauler. Big and efficient. Not *cheap* but common as dirt.

"Something far more special than it looks," his fixer told him. "Listen. I don't like to ask, but I know you *were* in a Jump Mage program. Can you jump?"

Barry clenched his fingers reflexively. Jump Mages were the elite of the semi-aristocratic Mages who ruled the Protectorate of Mars. They were key to crossing the gaps between stars, making them a core element of both the interstellar economy and the Mage-Queen's military.

Like everything else he'd tried in his life, he'd failed the exams. But…he ran the fingers of his right hand over his palm, feeling the stiffness where polymerized silver was permanently burnt into his skin.

Taking a silent sip of coffee, Barry eyed Waxer.

"Marie told you," he said quietly. It wasn't really an accusation.

"She *did* see you naked," Waxer said. "Frankly, Barry, every Mage I've ever known wore gloves, so I didn't know it was weird. But she mentioned the palm tattoos."

The big woman snorted.

"My girl isn't *dumb*, but she doesn't put pieces together the way she should, either," she noted. "She didn't realize you still had jump runes."

Barry stripped the tight glove off his right hand and held it up, palm toward Waxer. In the dim light of the bar, the delicate whorls of the magical rune that would allow him to jump a starship were hard to see, but he figured she knew what to look for.

"Not so much *still*," he replied. "But yes, I have the runes. I just can't actually *jump*. I failed most of my practical tests as well as my theoretical."

He shrugged.

"Give me enough *time* and I can make a jump, but I'm not good enough to be stealing jump ships, if that's what you want. And I don't see how any of that ties to an orbit-to-surface hauler."

"Because that's no hauler," Waxer said after taking a studious glance around the empty bar. "She's a custom job. Jump-capable."

Barry could control his wrist computer with eye movements tied to the projector implant. He dropped a ruler onto the image he was looking at to make sure he wasn't misestimating things.

"Nothing that small has a jump matrix," he observed. For a Mage to move a starship required a network of magical runes woven through the entire hull. Jump matrices varied in size, but they didn't come *that* small.

"So far as I know, nothing *else* that small has a matrix," the fixer said. "But I am assured that this shuttle does. A custom job, built—so far as I can tell—for Her Majesty herself."

Barry spun his coffee cup absently as he pulled more of the technical schematics from the chip.

"Not a lot of information here, but it looks like she's *mostly* a pretty standard X-Nine-Sixty-Five," he observed. "I know the hardware on the Nine-Sixty-Five backward and forward. Probably upgraded her, but I can open her up.

"But if she's what you say she is, she's got ten thousand times as much security as I can get through."

"You're underestimating it," Waxer said calmly. "Because while I have no idea where she *was*, I know where she *is*. She was delivered to *Extravagant Voyage* a few days ago. She's part of the shuttle complement for the Mage-Queen's personal traveling circus."

Barry's hand twitched, locking the coffee cup in place. For a moment, he said nothing, then he very carefully took a long sip of the drink.

Kiera Michelle Alexander, the Mage-Queen of Mars, had inherited her throne at a very early age. She was roughly his own age but had been Queen in her own right for five years.

She was also unmarried and her heir was her aunt. So, the young Mage-Queen had taken a tour of the Core Worlds a few years back to be introduced to all young Mages of a certain age.

And a certain class. *Barry* certainly hadn't been invited to the balls and parties where the system's upper class had paraded their sons past the Mage-Queen. Not then…and not now, when she was undertaking a second Grand Tour.

"I would love to know what you're thinking," he finally told Waxer. "Because while I can do a lot of things with security hardware, I'm pretty sure I can't hack and spoof my way aboard the personal cruise liner of the Mage-Queen."

"Do you think you can hack and spoof your way *around* said cruise ship?" Waxer asked.

Barry considered that. That was a very different question, he supposed.

"Probably," he said. "Might have to steal some code chips or whatever, but I can manage that."

He might not be a very *good* Mage by most standards, but he could manage pickpocketing someone with magic handily enough.

"If we get this ship, it's a game-changing score," Waxer told him. "My contact had heard rumors about our last few jobs and knew I had a good shuttle thief. This ship, Barry…you're right. There's nothing like her.

"The client figures the jump matrix is something new, modified to be smaller than ever before."

"Huh. How much?" Barry asked.

She told him and he blinked.

"Okay. That has my attention, but the job is still impossible," he admitted.

"Fifty/fifty split between us," she told him. "The usual spiel. I think we can do it."

"'We,' huh?" he asked absently. He'd brought up the publicly available information on *Extravagant Voyage*. Normally a cruise ship, carrying idiot tourists between the key sights of half a dozen star systems, she'd been commandeered to serve as the Mage-Queen's traveling court for her Grand Tour.

There was no information at all available on her security measures. The Mage-Queen's protectors in the Royal Guard and the Protectorate Secret Service were secretive groups that the system-net had little data on.

"I can steal the shuttle, but I think getting to it is impossible," he observed. "So, I'm curious to see how you plan on earning *your* fifty percent!"

There was a long silence.

"If you were anyone else, that phrasing might have got you in real trouble," Waxer told him. "But I guess I'll let it slide. This time.

"Because all I *need* to bring, Barry, is the person paying for the damn thing. But what I've *got* is your pass onto the *Voyage*."

A command sent the data windows overlapping on his vision away, and he focused his attention on Waxer.

"You're joking."

"No," she told him, a broad grin replacing her moment of anger. "It seems Her Majesty decided that a dozen or so of Tau Ceti's Mages are worth more extended consideration. They've been invited to join her on *Voyage* for at least the trip to their next stop.

"And thanks to some favors I'm owed and a few older-fashioned tricks, I can put you on the list. You'll need to avoid the Mage-Queen herself, of course, but…we can get you *onto Extravagant Voyage.*"

Barry blinked his projector back online and studied the shuttle.

"If you can get me onto the ship, I think I can steal the target," he told her. "And believe me, boss, I have no interest in being seen by the Mage-Queen of Mars! The moment she sees *me*, she's going to know I'm not one of her pretty noble suitors!"

CHAPTER

TWO

Kiera Michelle Alexander, Mage-Queen of Mars and Protector of Humanity, was bored out of her skull.

On Mars, the delicately built redhead was generally swamped. The Mage-Queen was more than a mere figurehead of state, even if her Chancellor ran most of the day-to-day affairs of the Protectorate. Meetings, reports, reviews and decisions ate easily half or more of her day, to the point where her staff specifically *scheduled* time for her to engage in hobbies.

Her Grand Tours, however, imposed sufficient separation from the Mountain of Olympus Mons and her government to force her to delegate all of that. Plus, well, her *job* on these Tours was to Be Seen.

And find a potential husband, but Kiera was about ready to give up on that and start considering wives—and unlike her late brother, Kiera's sexual preferences were quite specific.

Still, she'd been Queen for seven years since her father's death, and she knew how to put on the Queenly Mask when she needed to. The ridiculously overformal dinner the Governor of Tau Ceti was putting on was as much work as the industrial-planning meeting she'd had with the Royal Martian Navy's main shipbuilder earlier in the day.

It was also, despite the music, food and "adoring" crowd of potential suitors, a lot less fun.

"Thank you, Mage Rapallino," she told the young man who'd just finished giving an unasked-for lecture on the aquatic life of Tau Ceti *f*'s northern continent. The marine biologist was probably the oldest of the Mages by Blood—those born into Mage families—who had been introduced to her that evening.

He realized he'd accidentally shifted into teacher mode in response to her passing question about the fish dish and turned a delightful shade of embarrassed red that earned him a gentle smile from Kiera.

"Relax, Venkata," she told him softly, reducing her voice to a whisper. "That was *actually* educational, which puts it above most of the conversations I've had tonight!"

Venkata Rapallino might be the oldest of the Mages being presented to her that evening, but he was still only in his mid-twenties. His impromptu lecture on his passion was hardly the reason for Kiera's boredom.

If anything, his honest interest in the source of the fish Kiera had just finished eating was the *least* boring thing she'd dealt with tonight. The dark-haired scientist's flustered reaction to her reassurances didn't hurt. In a room full of self-confidence, there was a lot to be said for a man who'd admit a mistake.

"That's the third course," a voice murmured in her earpiece. "Time to swap tables."

"Got it," Kiera subvocalized back. She picked up her wine glass and rose to her feet, bowing slightly to the four men she'd shared the fish course with.

"Duty calls, it seems, and I must move on," she told them. "I hope the Governor's hospitality continues to impress everyone. Good night."

The four chorused back their own wishes, and an older woman in the crimson-red uniform of the Royal Guard seemed to materialize out of nowhere to guide Kiera away.

"Any thoughts on that lot?" Guard-Captain Shelly Lawrence murmured. Even standing next to Kiera, she was subvocalizing over their private channel.

"The butcher, the baker, the candlestick maker and the marine biologist?" Kiera replied wryly.

"Well, given that only one of those is an accurate description, I'm guessing Mage Dr. Rapallino made a more positive impression than I think *he* thinks," Lawrence said with a soft chuckle.

"I'd like to talk to him again," Kiera conceded. "But I don't think he's exactly a candidate for consort, either. He doesn't make the List."

The List was the very, very, *very* short set of names that Kiera was considering even a potential first date with. So far, there were ten names on it from Tau Ceti.

She didn't expect to add any more to it tonight, but the Governor had insisted on a farewell dinner. The ten names on her List were getting a better shot than anyone here, after all.

They got to spend a week on the hyper-secure cruise liner Kiera was flying around her Core Worlds on. If any of them impressed, they might even make it into her bed—that had *definitely* happened before, though it hadn't turned into more.

The whole process was organized, scaled, scored and measured. Kiera had *written* most of those scores and measures herself…but she was still starting to wonder if she was going about this the completely wrong way.

TWO HOURS LATER, Kiera had finished the seventh course of the meal and had been introduced to twenty-eight young men in total. They ranged from a trio of junior naval officers—on their finest behavior and completely suppressing anything resembling personality—to rich business heirs who merely happened to be Mages, to actors, to civilian Jump Mages, to cops, to a few scientists like Dr. Rapallino.

As Kiera made her getaway from the dessert table, she paused at the edge of the ballroom to survey the entire affair. The Governor had put a massive amount of effort and money into organizing the farewell party, but, as usual, the Mage families had turned it into another opportunity to parade young men past the unmarried Queen.

"Well?"

Shelly Lawrence probably shouldn't, in Kiera's opinion, speak to her Queen like an exasperated mother dealing with a wayward daughter. On the other hand, Kiera felt she had to give a *bit* of leeway to the people tasked to die in her defense.

Lawrence was also a powerful Mage in her own right and, like every member of the Royal Guard, a veteran of the Royal Martian Marine Corps. Three hundred of the deadliest Mages in the Protectorate guarded Kiera, her aunt and her Chancellor, Damien Montgomery.

And Montgomery's twin toddler daughters, who were third and fourh in the line of succession. Like their father, they were Rune Wrights, Mages with the Gift to see and control the flow of magical energy in a more direct and explicit fashion.

Including the two toddlers, there were only five known Rune Wrights in the galaxy. That was part of why Kiera was under pressure to find a partner and have kids. That Kiera *wanted* kids was also a motivating factor.

She just hadn't found a partner worth getting a sperm sample from yet.

"Let Driessen know we're coming back aboard the ship," Kiera decided aloud. Lakshmi Driessen was her head of household staff, a man originally hired to lead her *mother's* team thirty years earlier.

"You may want to at least *speak* to the Governor before we abandon the party," Lawrence noted mildly.

"*Want* is a strong word," Kiera replied. "But you're right. Get the shuttle ready for us to head back into orbit. I will speak with Governor Antonov and then I will head back aboard *Extravagant Voyage*."

She glanced around the room, packed with officials, diplomats, soldiers—and a collection of potential suitors tasked to make a good impression under the worst possible circumstances.

"No one made the List tonight," she admitted. "But I'll make sure Driessen has the pieces moving to get them invited aboard the ship. You'll want to run background checks, I assume."

"My Queen, you are sensible and intelligent, and you know damn well I already ran full checks on every person you met on this planet,"

Lawrence said calmly. "But yes, I will be running further checks on your invitees. I doubt I'll be blocking any of them, though.

"If there was going to be *that* level of problem, someone would have known by now!"

Kiera nodded silently and inhaled a deep breath. She'd speak to the Governor and then retreat to *Extravagant Voyage*. The cruise liner had its own issues, but at least there she didn't feel like an entire planet was conspiring to run her through a meat market!

CHAPTER

THREE

Extravagant Voyage was, in Kiera's considered opinion, a gaudy mess. A testament to the lack of taste of the Protectorate's upper classes. If the choice had been entirely hers, she'd have undertaken her Grand Tours aboard one of the squadron of destroyers flying escort on the big liner.

But she needed to entertain and impress and, at least theoretically, enjoy herself. So, her Cabinet had talked her into leasing the entire four-million-metric-ton passenger ship and allowing her security detail an unusual amount of luxury for the trip.

Extravagant Voyage was a flying transparent dome, three hundred meters across and fifty high. A forty-meter-thick "base" held the engineering systems for her life support and engines, but most of her volume and mass were dedicated to the garden in the dome and the small resort it held.

There were certain efficiencies to the design, Kiera had to admit as her shuttle approached the mobile monstrosity. Like warships, she was built with her floors aligned to the direction of thrust. That allowed the ship's Mages to maintain fewer layers of the powerful gravity runes that magically offset the engines and kept the entire ship at a comfortable half Terran gravity.

It was still a park someone had built a dome over and launched into space, designed to haul two thousand of the Protectorate's more profligate citizens between systems as fancy tourists.

Kiera's main hobby was building ship models. She'd long since left behind the official models that could be built and had mastered both computer-aided design and small-scale fabrication-printer programming to build herself new kits.

While she wouldn't claim to know shipbuilding *well*, she was more familiar with ships than many people would expect—and her focuses meant she was more familiar with *warships*. That practice meant she could pick out the fact that *Extravagant Voyage* was also built to protect her cargo. Two dozen rapid-fire laser antimissile turrets were positioned around the base, covering the ship from incoming missile fire.

Against any normal threat, that would be enough. Against the kind of extraordinary threat that might come after the Mage-Queen of Mars, there was an entire squadron of the most modern destroyers of the Royal Martian Navy arranged around the ship and the orbital station she was currently docked with.

"Invitations went out while we were on our way up," Lawrence told Kiera, the Guard stepping into her compartment. "I'm sure everyone is vastly shocked and surprised to find out that all your young men have already eagerly accepted your invitation to join them aboard *Extravagant Voyage* for a more extended introduction."

Kiera chuckled.

"Will they feel the same way after your people have stripped them naked and cavity-searched them before allowing them aboard?"

"Please, Your Majesty, we are hardly limited to such…*brute-force* methods," Lawrence purred. "I am here to guarantee your safety. Driessen is here to guarantee your comfort. Commodore Courtemanche is here to guarantee *everyone's* safety."

The Mage-Queen of Mars sighed.

"Fair. I'll check in with Driessen and then Captain Salonen once we're aboard," she promised. "That should get everyone moving in the right direction. I want to be on our way by tomorrow night.

"*With* the only people of actual interest this system apparently had to offer aboard!"

~

Captain Abhishek Salonen made no pretense of being a military officer. Kiera had met civilian captains who leaned heavily into the role of "Captain" with drama and grand uniforms and so forth.

Salonen possessed some truly glorious dress uniforms that he'd produced for events Kiera had held on his ship, but he only produced them when dealing with his passengers. Most of the time, the old Mage was in his simulacrum-chamber bridge—the one thing his ship shared with warships—wearing a standard crew shipsuit, with the only marker of his rank being that both his shoulders bore a hyper-detailed image of *Extravagant Voyage* in gold.

"Your Majesty," he greeted her as she stepped onto the bridge. The simulacrum chamber was suspended at the exact center of every star-ship and held the simulacrum itself: a semiliquid silver model of the ship integrated into the runic jump matrix.

Without the simulacrum, the jump matrix was incomplete. Without the touch of a fully trained Jump Mage, with the interface runes inlaid into their palm, the simulacrum was incomplete.

Complete, the setup would allow a Jump Mage like Abhishek Salonen to teleport his ship a full light-year in the blink of an eye. Incomplete, it was fancy silverwork throughout the ship.

"Will we be ready to depart tomorrow?" Kiera asked without preamble, looking around her at *Voyage*'s unusual bridge.

For a simulacrum chamber to work, its walls had to receive a direct optical feed via fiber-optic cable from the exterior of the ship. A Mage had to be looking at real light, not a digital duplicate, for the jump magic to work.

But to put the simulacrum chamber in the exact center of *Extrava-gant Voyage* had required building a tower at the center of the ship. The decorated spire did dual duty as a support strut for the dome itself and suspended the simulacrum chamber five meters from the floor of the main dome.

At that moment, while *Voyage* was docked with a space station and hours at least from jumping, the fiber-optics had been redirected. Instead of displaying the outside of the cruise liner, they displayed the outside of the spire, simulating the bridge being even higher up the central tower and allowing the bridge crew to survey the park around them from above.

Kiera had to admit that *Extravagant Voyage*'s designers had known how to lean into the ship's advantages. She was as extravagant as her name, but she wore it well.

"If you really needed us to, we could leave in…hmm…ninety-six seconds," Salonen observed brightly. "I imagine *f*-Signs would rather prefer we actually let them retract and store their umbilicals and such, but we could sever them, break free and jump in about a minute and a half."

"I am not quite that desperate to flee Tau Ceti," Kiera replied, but she smiled at the Captain. He was a grandfather with a daughter her age and she appreciated his sense of humor.

"There are still a few supplies we are pulling aboard," he admitted. "If you wish it, we could depart safely and fully loaded in about two hours. Tomorrow will not be a problem."

"We'll stick to the schedule. We're not due in Eridani for a week. There's no rush."

"Of course, Your Majesty." Salonen observed her for a moment in silence, then turned to look out over his spaceborne domain. "I understand we are picking up new guests?"

"A few. Not many," Kiera admitted. "The ones who appear worth giving the time to make an actual impression."

"I don't envy you this," he told her. "My daughter went through *eleven* partners she was dating for at least six months before settling with her wife. This whole affair makes *sense*, but it's stressful to even watch!"

"In all honesty, Captain, this is probably the least stressful task I've taken on in at least two or three years," Kiera replied. "It's just…frustrating."

For her purposes, she was sure she'd have been better served going to university and meeting people there. But the Protectorate needed their Queen.

CHAPTER

FOUR

In years of working together, Alaina Waxer had almost always come through on her promises. She was clear on risks, clear on her limitations, and knew her connections. No one was perfect in Barry's experience, but her mistakes had been few and far between.

As he shifted uncomfortably in a brand-new suit that had been tailored close enough to make his skin crawl, every one of Waxer's previous errors was running through his mind on rapid replay.

He was carrying an invitation written on actual *paper*—matched to a digital file—and he had no idea how Waxer had managed to get him onto the list of people allowed aboard *Extravagant Voyage*. The suit meant that he didn't look horribly out of place as he approached the boarding tube, but nothing about the situation felt right to him.

The faceless gazes of the Royal Guards in their massive suits of blood-red exosuit armor were *not* helping his mood. Four were arrayed on either side of the door, while a ninth was checking the identity and paperwork of everyone coming aboard.

Barry was grimly certain that there was no way that Waxer could have put together false paperwork that could get him through this. But she had told him she had, and he trusted her, so he swallowed his fear and walked up to the suit of armor checking IDs.

"Invitation, huh?" A surprisingly gentle feminine voice emerged from the two-meter-tall suit. "May I see it?"

He held the paper out. It floated out of his hand, a stark reminder that every member of the Royal Guard was a Mage.

The suit was bad enough. The fact that Barry was wearing his Mage medallion, the gold coin at his throat that marked him as one of the Protectorate's elite, *chafed*. Plus, everything on the medallion except the coin itself was false.

He wore the three stars of a Jump Mage. But like he'd told Waxer, while he could theoretically make a jump, he'd failed all of his testing. He had no right to those stars.

Keeping his attention on the matter at hand was *hard*. Even knowing that if Waxer's false paperwork failed, he was in more trouble than he could possibly imagine, it was hard for him to focus—and he had his economics game up on his projector without even consciously deciding he needed the distraction.

"Everything checks out, Mage Guidi," the Guard told him. It took Barry a moment to remember that was him, but his general distraction covered it. "Is everything all right?"

"Sorry, I'm nervous," he said with complete honesty.

The Guard chuckled.

"That you're on this List, kid, means you were more interesting than about two thousand other people Her Majesty met," the woman told him. "There'll be a member of the ship's crew waiting for you on the other side to show you to your room.

"You're still more likely to muck this up than not," the Guard concluded, "but hey, how many people can say they even got to spend time with the Mage-Queen of Mars? Behave, and it won't end *badly*."

Barry nodded in acknowledgement, even as his eye-twitch ordered two more factories built in Luxembourg.

He was *quite* certain that his plans aboard *Extravagant Voyage* weren't going to count as "behaving."

❀

A GORGEOUS WOMAN in her late thirties met Barry at the other end of the boarding tube. She was wearing a decorated shipsuit, with an image of the cruise liner emblazoned across her chest.

"Mage Guidi," she greeted him. "I'm Steward Trammer. If you'll walk with me?"

Barry nodded and fell in beside her.

"Guides instead of a map?" he asked. He'd paused his game as he entered the ship and had the publicly available information on *Extravagant Voyage* running through his projector implant.

"Aboard *Extravagant Voyage*, we value the human touch, Mage Guidi," Trammer replied. "I can send you a download of the ship's details, but I'll show you to your room and give you the rundown either way."

"Please do," Barry asked. "I don't like to impose on other people if I can avoid it."

"We are here to support Her Majesty's people and her guests," Trammer told him as she led him into an elevator. "If you have any concerns at any time, please feel free to stop and ask anyone wearing the ship's emblem.

"Her Majesty's security are present throughout the ship, and they should also be able to help, but they have other priorities," she added. The elevator moved so smoothly that only Barry's vague sense of what machinery around him was doing allowed him to know it *had* moved.

As the elevator stopped, the projected screen on his eye told him he'd received the download she'd promised. He wasn't sure what type of data-management system Trammer was using, but there were either implants or something else invisible in play.

She hadn't touched her wrist-comp to have the files sent. From her expression as she glanced over her shoulder, she'd realized he hadn't touched his to open them.

"That's an unusual implant for a Mage," the steward noted. "I think one of our engineers has a similar one, but I don't think I've ever seen it on a Mage."

The corneal projector was more of a tradesperson's tool or a hobbyist's toy than anything else. It allowed for an artificial heads-up display over the world, but the military tended to prefer visors and helmets.

Barry had seen enough hesitant or outright hostile reactions to recognize that personal implants were unpopular in the Protectorate. The fact that the secessionist Republic of Faith and Reason, the loser of a still-recent civil war, had leaned heavily into cybernetics for their soldiers and personnel didn't help.

"It serves my needs," he told her with a smile. "The overlays are handy."

As the elevator door opened, he was moving files around to link the map he'd been provided to a location-tracking program he used. It would take a few minutes to map his location against that map, but it would guide him around the entire ship once it did.

"Of course; that's why the engineers I know use it," Trammer agreed. "This way, Mage Guidi."

He followed her out of the elevator and then had to pause. Blinking away his projected map, he just *looked* out at the main dome of *Extravagant Voyage*.

The gravity holding him down was weaker than he was used to, and he could *feel* the ship's systems humming around him. Even with all of the indicators, it still managed to feel like he'd stepped into some kind of manicured estate or resort.

The elevator emerged into a glass-roofed lobby open to the air of the main dome. There were a dozen or so other doors behind him, suggesting that this was the endpoint of an internal transit system, but his attention was out the open sides of the lobby.

Paths swept away in several directions, each lined by carefully manicured trees and bushes. Everywhere he glanced, things were green, growing and alive. It had been arranged to give the illusion of distance, helping to disguise the fact that the closest set of resort-style condos were less than three meters away.

He could hear the soft burble of a water feature, though he couldn't see it—and suspected the noise might be artificial.

Still, it made for a gorgeous—if very *managed*-feeling—garden floating through space. Tau Ceti *f* hung in the sky "above" them, and Barry spent a few seconds looking to see if he could pick out Deveraux.

"She's impressive on first sight," Trammer told him after a few seconds.

"Sorry, we can be on our way," Barry murmured.

"Please, Mage Guidi, I *want* people to admire the ship," she said with a chuckle. "My colleagues and I put a lot of work into making *Extravagant Voyage* look her best, and we appreciate the people who appreciate her."

"She's a wonder," he told the woman. "I can see why the Mage-Queen picked her."

"Security is also a factor," Trammer admitted, gesturing for him to follow her again. "While our own security people have surrendered their control systems to the Secret Service, we're working with Her Majesty's people."

"With Her Majesty aboard, I'd hope security was tight," Barry said. "I like my privacy, of course, but I assume all the concourses are monitored?"

"The private rooms aren't," she said. "But yes, there are concealed drones throughout the dome that keep track of all movement. If you're ever in trouble, stop where you are and yell help three times, loud as you can."

"What's the response time to that?" he asked.

"Oh, about forty seconds usually," Trammer said with a chuckle. "I think Her Majesty's people might have it down to *fourteen*, though. For some reason, they're very, very twitchy."

THE "ROOM" Trammer led Barry to was the size of his apartment in Deveraux and even better appointed. The only thing missing was a kitchen of any kind, though he at least had a fridge.

"Your wrist-comp should be on the ship-net," Trammer told him. "Room service is included in your package. There will be no costs to you for the trip, of course."

"Of course," Barry murmured, looking around the suite. It was only two rooms—a luxuriously appointed bedroom he didn't expect to be on the ship long enough to use and a glass-fronted sitting area that looked out toward the central spire of the dome.

"Thank you, Steward Trammer," he told her. "This is incredible."

She bowed her head slightly.

"You should have a schedule and itinerary in the email I sent you," she told him. "I believe all of Her Majesty's guests are scheduled for a dinner in the Scarlet Dining Room at nineteen hundred hours Olympus Mons Time."

Barry checked how far away that was. That was a few hours behind Deveraux local time, which meant his lunchtime arrival was midmorning by OMT. He'd have seven hours before he was apparently supposed to meet the Mage-Queen.

Since he wasn't actually on the Queen's list of guests, he figured he could miss the dinner without drawing too much attention. Still, he wasn't going to try and abscond with a shuttle while they were in orbit of Tau Ceti *f*, with all of the ships and patrols and sensors that entailed.

"Do you know when we'll be leaving orbit?" he asked.

"I don't believe that has been decided yet," Trammer told him. "That will be available on the ship-net once it is.

"Is there anything else you need immediately, Mage Guidi?"

"No," he conceded. "Assuming, at least, that there's water or coffee in here somewhere?"

"There's a machine in the counter. Let me show you."

CHAPTER

FIVE

The very first thing Barry did once Trammer left the apartment was fill the largest mug in the cupboard with black coffee and then fill several glasses of water, lining the drinks up on the work desk in the suite.

Luxury vacation ship or not, *Extravagant Voyage* played host to the kind of people who would always do at least *some* work. The desk had a link to the ship-net and a semi-capable built-in console.

The second thing Barry did was confirm that, whether by ignorance or intent, Steward Trammer had lied about the surveillance in the room. They weren't even bugs inserted by the Mage-Queen's people— there were concealed cameras built into all four corners of both rooms.

Most likely, it would take a direct order from the ship's captain or a judge to open up the recordings, but Barry had no intention of leaving *any* evidence behind. His wrist-comp linked into the ship-net even as he wove magic through the systems in his room's walls.

The cameras weren't, of course, linked to the same network he'd been given access to. He hadn't expected that. Between the *highly* illegal hypersensitive network sniffer hidden in his wrist-comp and his magic, though, he was able to locate the network they were running on.

He'd been given automatically generated credentials for the main ship-net. Those *shouldn't* have worked on the security network, but Barry had long ago learned how to get around that kind of minor obstacle with his magic.

He logged into the main net with them, using the sniffer and his magic to learn what the local system's positive responses should look like, then poked at the security network. It took him two tries to break into the hardware of the cameras in the room—and that gave him access to the network feeding their data back to the main security system.

The first thing he did was erase any record of him being in the room. It had been empty for several weeks before he'd come aboard, and producing a loop of an empty room was easy. A few wires twitched with magic, a few instructions given in regular code and then concealed in the software with more magic...and then Barry had never been there.

It took him most of an hour to piggyback from his access to his room's security systems to finally break into the main surveillance suite. There wasn't *too* much he could do there, but it was fascinating for him to go through all of the drones and get a good view of what *Voyage* really looked like.

While the brook he'd heard on the way in had clearly been a speaker, there *were* two faux-lake-style pools in the dome. Both were attached to large villas tucked back from the main condo suites—presumably the true high-end quarters for the most important guests.

Barry spent a few minutes linking his new access into the console in the room. As he did so, he continued to skim through the drone feeds —until he found himself half-distractedly watching a gorgeous redheaded woman emerge from one of those faux lakes in a one-piece swimsuit.

The arrival of the exosuited guard passing the woman a towel shook him into awareness of what he was doing—and of just *who* he was watching. With a surprised shiver, he shut down the feed watching the Mage-Queen of Mars and tried to focus his attention as much as he ever did.

He needed to get a daemon into the network to erase his presence as he moved around the ship. There was too much surveillance for anything except a live program to keep his face off the records.

A different face stuck in his head as he did so—but Barry was *always* distracted, so the only thing that had changed was *what* he was focusing past.

~

UNFORTUNATELY FOR BARRY, the ship's systems had multiple layers of security. He could circumvent a lot of it via his coding and his magic, but he needed direct access to something *on* a given network to use his magic.

The ship's surveillance systems all ran on the same network, with subdivided security that failed to slow him down. He got his daemon up and running, and tried to see if he could get into the overall security control.

The encryption and security protocols available to the personal guard of the Mage-Queen of Mars proved insurmountable, and he glared at the console's screen. His magic had been enough to extricate his software probe without triggering an alarm, but it was closer than he was used to.

"Okay, so, *that* isn't working," he murmured aloud. Leaning back to think, he considered the map on his projector and the access he had. The ship should have a listing of shuttles and so forth aboard. That wasn't likely to change now that they were leaving.

Speaking of. It took a quick search through the public ship-net to confirm that a departure time *had* been set—in the middle of the Mage-Queen's scheduled dinner.

The course he found suggested that the plan was to take the ship through a pattern that would create an incredible view while she departed. The Mage-Queen and her would-be paramours would get a show.

Barry was a decent shuttle pilot—his "job" required it. He could make sense of the course that was plotted for the starship, even if actually plotting a course for a multimegaton cruise liner was beyond him.

The ship would be accelerating at two gravities—he figured the gravity runes would keep them all safe and comfortable while she did that—for about sixteen hours before she was clear to jump. That would put them about two light-minutes away from the planet.

Plenty of distance to hide from local law with his stolen shuttle. He'd need to avoid the escort—he could make the shuttle vanish from *Extravagant Voyage*'s sensors, but he doubted he could fool the computers aboard Royal Martian Navy destroyers.

The best timing, in fact, would be for him to flee *Voyage* just before she jumped. Then he could make his way back toward f and his rendezvous with the buyer without worrying about the Queen's ship or her escort destroyers.

Of course, the value of his target meant that its absence would be noticed. Eventually. Even a shuttle that could jump, after all, was unlikely to be used while they were in deep space.

A few queries told him that his access didn't stretch far enough for him to pin down the listing of shuttles. He needed to access the working sections of the ship and get into the administrative systems.

Fortunately, he still didn't think anyone was going to miss him at dinner. He had time.

CHAPTER

SIX

K iera was aware that her opinion of *Extravagant Voyage*'s style of luxury was shaped by the fact she'd grown up in Olympus Mons. Her quarters in the royal palace as a child, let alone now, had been filled with things that cost as much or more than the luxuries that surrounded her on the cruise liner.

But all of that furniture, glassware, fabric—everything, in fact, except the electronics and clothing—had been decades old. Centuries, in some cases, with some items of furniture and even cups and plates dating back to the first Mage-King of Mars two centuries earlier.

Everything on *Extravagant Voyage* was expensive and looked it, with highly paid designers not only attempting to make the objects functional but also gorgeous. The point was not only to be luxurious but to *feel* and *appear* luxurious.

Everything in the royal palace in Olympus Mons was expensive and *didn't* look it. Function, endurance and comfort had been the priorities. The point had been to create objects that would last forever and become part of tradition.

Still, Kiera couldn't help but feel a touch of disdain at the intentional broadcasting of luxury present throughout the villa she was staying in. There was only one thing on the entire cruise liner that

383

didn't trigger that vague displeasure and discomfort—and that was her pool.

The rocks that made up the false pond were real. She wasn't sure which planet they'd been hauled up from, but she was guessing Earth. The water was clear and kept at the perfect temperature, and the space was concealed behind a wall of trees to leave her a sensation of privacy.

Of course, Kiera Alexander was the Mage-Queen of Mars. Any privacy was merely an illusion, and she *knew* there were half a dozen exosuited Royal Guards concealed in those trees. Her swimsuit was incredibly conservative by the standards of Martian aristocracy, but there were limits to her comfort with her security.

"Enjoy your swim, Your Majesty?" Lawrence asked, the Guard passing her a towel. "Driessen has laid out an outfit for you inside."

Kiera sighed as she took the towel.

"Are we at that point already?" she said. "Dinner isn't for another few hours."

"He's *your* batman," Lawrence pointed out. "If you want him to stop picking clothes for you, I'm sure all you have to do is ask."

Normally, reducing the number of decisions Kiera had to make was a *good* thing, one that resulted in the Mage-Queen running around in versions of much the same outfit day to day. Having Driessen and the rest of her staff pick outfits for her more formal outings was a godsend.

Aboard *Voyage*, however, Kiera was reduced to daily briefings via the Link communicators from Mars. There was a limit to what she could do.

"No, he's probably right," she sighed. "I need some…not-fresh air."

Her bodyguard chuckled.

"Engineering?" Lawrence asked. "I'm sure you can get Officer Chateaux to give you a lecture on any part of the ship you want!"

Kiera grinned back at her bodyguard. Lawrence had been present when the cruise liner's chief engineering officer had realized that his monarch actually *was* interested in the ship she was flying aboard. The ensuing forty-five-minute lecture on *Extravagant Voyage*'s power systems had been fascinating to the young Queen.

Her bodyguard had been…less enthused.

"Shuttle bay, I think," she decided. "Let's go look at fast, pretty things, shall we? I'm sure at least one of our guests has been sent up in something shiny by their family."

There were advantages to the fact that nine of her ten guests were members of Tau Ceti's First Families. Their families' magical Gifts and involvement in the original colonization had left them all wealthy, which meant the families could have private shuttlecraft.

And at least three of the young men she'd invited aboard had earned her interest by engaging her in serious conversation on shuttles and interplanetary spacecraft.

EXTRAVAGANT VOYAGE's shuttle bays were inside the dome's thick base layer. Normal passengers would only see the working spaces of the ship on their way in—and the corridor between the main shuttle bay and the dome were better decorated than the *rest* of the lower layer.

Kiera, on the other hand, had spent time aboard the warships under her theoretical authority. Even the "undecorated" parts of *Voyage*'s interior were at least equal to the living and working spaces aboard those warships. The cruise liner's crew might not live in the luxury that their passengers enjoyed, but they were hardly scrabbling in the dirt, either.

She was still working on building a mental map of the lower reaches of the ship. There was a map loaded into her wrist-comp, but she attempted to find her way to the shuttle bay without it—along a shortcut that passengers shouldn't normally see.

Guard-Captain Lawrence accompanied her the entire time. Kiera figured the Guard had the map up on the display of her exosuit helmet, but she remained silent as her Queen got herself ever so slightly lost.

It was only when Kiera finally stopped and sighed that her bodyguard finally said anything.

"I think our shortcut has gone a bit astray, hasn't it, Your Majesty?"

Kiera gave Lawrence a dirty look.

"Why is it that you only call me that when you think I'm being silly?" she asked.

"Because sometimes I have to remind the young woman I am charged to protect that she is *also* the ruler of basically every human being alive," the Guard said calmly. "Some silliness is required for you to be *human,* but we need to avoid risks."

Kiera snorted and brought up the map in a holographic projection above the wrist-comp. Tracing her route with her other hand, she sighed.

"Missed the turn here." She tapped the spot. "We're under one of the condo terraces, at least fifty meters in the wrong direction."

"Okay. A bit more of a walk, then. Can we keep the map up this time?" Lawrence asked.

"Sure," Kiera conceded with a chuckle. A green line flashed into existence on the display, marking her route toward the shuttle bay. "We have time, but I didn't plan on getting lost."

Lawrence, in what Kiera recognized as a great feat of patience, said nothing.

THE CORRIDORS they were traversing weren't empty, but there were few enough people moving through the workspaces of the ship that Kiera had the opportunity to place each one as they passed.

She knew all of the Royal Guard and other Mages on the ship by face and name, and knew most of the crew and her security detail by face at this point. She'd put a lot of effort into building that skill over the years.

Kiera's title came with power and authority, but all of that only mattered so far as the people around her supported her. As a Rune Wright, she had Runes of Power inlaid across her body that dramatically expanded her magical power—but even her magic only meant so much.

To be the Mage-Queen of Mars, she needed people she trusted and who trusted her. More, she needed people who encountered her to come away with a positive impression, the feeling that their Queen respected and valued them.

That the cold-blooded strategy inherent in that lined up perfectly with her natural inclinations was handy.

Still, she had a moment of surprise when a stranger stepped around a corner and her Gift instantly identified them as a Mage. But she didn't recognize the lanky young man. He was wearing a crew ship-suit and vanished around another corner almost before she was sure she'd seen him, leaving her staring after him for a few seconds.

"Kiera?" Lawrence said. "What is it?"

"I thought I knew every Mage on the ship," Kiera replied, focusing as she locked the stranger's face into her mind. "But I just saw a Mage member of the crew that I don't think I've even met."

It was a nice face, she noted absently as she completed the not-quite meditative trick that stored the face in her memory palace. But if he was a Mage, she should have known him.

"Security breach?" Lawrence asked, her tone soft and concerned.

"I don't think so?" Kiera said. "Feel free to double-check things, of course, but I think he's crew. Just…Captain Salonen made a point of introducing me to his Ship's Mages, and I didn't think there were any other Mages aboard."

"Entertainer? I'll have someone check the crew list," Lawrence said firmly, then chuckled. "Of course, there is another possibility, my Queen."

Kiera glanced at her companion, realizing she'd stopped in the middle of the corridor.

"What do you mean?"

"Your Testers used runic artifacts designed by your great-grandfather to identify Mages," Lawrence murmured. "But they are an attempt to duplicate your natural ability as a Rune Wright. It's possible that you have sensed someone as a Mage who the Test missed."

Kiera whistled softly.

"That's a headache I hadn't thought of," she admitted. "If the Test is missing *any* Mages, though, that's a problem." She shook her head. "I'll think on it. Check that list.

"For now, I still want to go look at shinies!"

In hindsight, she was realizing that putting all ten of her suitors into a single dinner *might* have been a foolish idea.

CHAPTER

SEVEN

Barry was well aware that the last thing he needed was to run directly into the Mage-Queen of Mars. If someone put together the fact that the Queen didn't know who he was with the fact that he was supposedly aboard as one of her guests, he'd be in serious trouble!

He hadn't been expecting her to be slumming it down in the working sections of the ship, though, and had relied on a uniform stolen out of a storage locker to avoid attention.

Long practice and repeated success told him that the best way to move through any workspace was to dress like a low-level laborer and look busy. His stolen shipsuit would get him most places in the base of the ship, though his need to hack through security doors would draw attention if he wasn't careful.

Trying to slow his breathing and focus on the task at hand, he ducked into a quiet supply closet. Blinking away the moment, he checked the burgeoning Empire of Greater Luxembourg in his game. A few commands assigned resources to stabilizing the western front, where the English were trying to retake their French holdings from his mercenary armies—and helped calm his nerves.

His map told him that he was close to the main shuttle bay. Unless he was mistaken, though, that was where the Mage-Queen and her terrifying red statue of a bodyguard had been headed. Maybe she was meeting one of her guests?

Barry didn't know. He *did* figure that trying to hack into the flight-control center of a shuttle bay while a Royal Guard was standing *right there* ranked somewhere between suicidal and just phenomenally stupid.

Fortunately, *Extravagant Voyage* was designed to not need access to an orbital. She was currently docked with one, with both personnel tubes and cargo umbilicals linking the spacecraft to the *f*-Signs space station, but the design criteria meant she actually had *six* shuttle bays. Two major ones, at the "north" and "south" compass points of the circular ship, and then four smaller ones equally offset from each other around the rim.

The one closest to him was right next to the station, which *should* mean that it was shut down and quiet right now. For his purposes, that was perfect.

THE SHUTTLE-BAY DOORS were open when Barry reached them, which was sufficiently odd that he tucked himself into a corner to try to get a decent look at what was going on. He could hear faint conversation in the hangar area, but it sounded like the speakers were at the far end.

There might be people *there*, but it was still quieter than the main shuttle bay and remained his best option. A touch of magic swirled around him, drawing the shadow with him as he darted through the open bay doors and into a corner of the space.

The two big shuttle bays easily filled the full forty-meter height of the base, basically taking the form of forty-meter-wide caves a third of the ship's diameter deep. The secondary bays, like this one, were far smaller structures. The entrance was a fifteen-meter square on the outer hull, and the shuttle bay held those dimensions for its full thirty-meter length.

It was enough space to hold two or three smaller standard shuttles and still allow for one to land. There currently weren't *any* spacecraft in the bay, but several cargo containers—the smaller standardized units that fit inside the big interstellar shipping units—were stacked up neatly in the middle.

"Any problems?" a voice said, clear now that Barry was inside the hangar bay.

Also clear, he realized, because the speaker was *new* and had just entered the room behind him. With a shiver, he pulled his magical shadow tighter around himself as he realized just *who* was speaking.

The man who'd followed him in wore the uniform of a Royal Martian Marine Corps Mage-Major. A fully trained Marine Combat Mage likely wouldn't even *register* the amount of effort it would take them to kill or capture Barry himself.

Four other men, in the same crew shipsuits Barry wore, were maneuvering a new container in to join the rest.

"None," one of them said. There was something ever so slightly off about his voice to Barry. "Your local contacts delivered the container as promised. We'd already temporarily disabled the detectors, so no one who wasn't in the loading tube even knows the container came aboard —and we're the only ones who were there."

Someone was *smuggling* something aboard the Mage-Queen's transport? That sounded like a terrible idea to Barry, though he assumed that the presence of a senior officer of the Mage-Queen's detail meant it was only *so* underhanded.

"Good." The Major strode forward, running his hand through close-cropped black hair as he studied the four longshoremen.

"Take this." He produced four sheets of paper. "They show where to put the cargo throughout the ship. Once you're done, destroy the paper. Return to your quarters and take these."

The Marine handed out something Barry couldn't see from his vantage point.

"Your service to humanity will be remembered," he told the four crew. "Let's get to work."

The crew got to work opening the container they'd just brought in, and the Major stood watching them.

Barry found himself walking a razor's edge between being terrified of being discovered—ending up in the hands of the Martian

Marines would *not* end well for him right now!—and his inability to just *wait*.

He cast his attention around the shuttle bay, looking for his original target. The main flight-control offices were in the two main hangars, but even this space needed... *There.*

It was more of a cubby off the side of the hangar than an actual *office,* but it would have a console with a hard connection to the flight-control network. He didn't really need the *flight* side of things—not yet, anyway—but it would also tell him which shuttles were where.

On top of letting him find his target, combining access through the surveillance network with access through the flight network would almost certainly give him enough vectors to break in to the main administrative system.

He wouldn't have *control* of much—he needed to be right on top of things to make his particular combination of coding and magic work to break security—but he'd be able to observe everything.

Right now, though, he realized he was already plotting a path across the shuttle bay that would get him into the cubby without entering anyone's line of sight. His shadow cloak wouldn't do much to conceal him in areas that, well, didn't *have* any shadow.

When the Marine officer finally made an approving noise and turned crisply on his heel to exit the bay, Barry sighed in relief. He hadn't been able to route around the Mage, and the Mage was the *last* person he wanted to spot him.

Keeping his magic wrapped around him, he began the painfully slow process of sneaking across the bay. It was straightforward enough, helped by the fact that the four laborers working on the cargo seemed oddly oblivious to everything around them.

As he reached his destination, he glanced back to see just what they were smuggling aboard the ship. The container was only about half-full, but the four boxes the crew were maneuvering were still large enough to be awkward.

Barry's curiosity forced him to creep back a few steps as the first box slid onto a transport pallet. It was roughly the size of four coffins bundled together, a solid-looking secured transport crate.

There was no company name or logo on the crates. There had been some kind of label, but someone had painted over it. Whatever the containers held, someone had wanted it to be unobtrusive.

If he hadn't just seen a Marine taking charge of the delivery, Barry's moment of concern would have been stronger. He could think of four or five different ways he could draw attention to the crates without getting caught—but they weren't without risk.

And since the Mage-Queen's people clearly knew what was going on, he focused on what was in front of him.

Tucked behind the console where no one entering the shuttle bay could see him, he used his magic to connect a cable from his wrist-comp to the console. He'd set up a wireless link later, but wires were always easiest to start with.

For whatever reason, it was a lot easier for him to magically influence technology through a wire than a wireless network.

BY THE TIME Barry had carved his way through the security protocols on the flight-control network, the four crew had departed, each pushing one of the big crates on a portable pallet jack.

Finally alone, he dropped his cloak of shadow and pulled the data up on the console. As he'd already figured out, Shuttle Bay Charlie was serving as a main cargo-access point with a heavy umbilical connected to *f*-Signs.

Shuttle Bays Alpha and Bravo both had lists of shuttlecraft stored aboard. Alpha was what he expected—luxury shuttlecraft, smaller versions of the Courvoisier he'd stolen for Waxer last time.

Bay Bravo, though, had clearly been taken over by the Queen's detail. The security codes that tried to keep him from seeing what was there barely slowed him down before he pulled the list. Every occupant of Bay Bravo was military, assault shuttles with the gear to drop from orbit and take out armored bunkers before delivering exosuited solders into the wreckage.

"That's not a bad fallback," he murmured to himself. It wasn't often that assault shuttles were in civilian areas, and he'd never even had an opportunity to test his skills against military hardware.

He was confident that he *could* break open the security on even the brand-new Model Twenty-Four-Sixty-Five assault shuttles in *Extravagant Voyage*'s hangar. But while they were valuable, they weren't his target, and he quickly pulled the lists for Bays Delta, Echo, and Fox.

Between the console and his corneal projector, he had all six shuttle lists up, and he stared at them grimly for a few seconds.

Charlie, as he could see with his own eyes, was empty. Delta held a pair of medium-lift cargo shuttles—not the big craft that hauled interstellar shipping containers to and from planetary surfaces but solid utility ships with internal cargo bays. Echo, like Charlie, was facing toward *f*-Signs and had been emptied.

Fox held a trio of lighter personnel shuttles that looked like they didn't even have the legs to make it to a planet and back. Literal touring shuttles, he realized, intended to take the passengers close to interesting sights and places.

What *wasn't* on any of the lists was a modified heavy-lift utility hauler. The ship he was looking for was the type that hauled ten-meter-by-ten-meter-by-hundred-meter interstellar shipping cargos to and from planets.

It would fill most of one of the secondary shuttle bays. It *definitely* wasn't in Charlie.

So, either it wasn't aboard the ship…or it was in Echo. And *Echo*, it looked like, was right next to the secondary security hub that ship's security had been exiled to.

They would *love* to catch someone the Mage-Queen's security had missed. He needed time to put together a plan of attack.

Plus, whether he was stealing the jump shuttle or an assault shuttle or even one of the luxury craft in Bay Alpha, he needed to wait until *Extravagant Voyage* was clear of Tau Ceti *f*.

Sixteen hours from when they powered up the engines until they jumped. He figured he needed three hours to make sure everything was the way he needed.

Dinner and departure were in two hours…and that meant that Barry had at least twelve hours to sort out his plan of approach.

CHAPTER

EIGHT

K iera was not *consciously* obsessed with prestige and presentation. She was capable of using them as tools when she needed to, but she tried to keep herself grounded and use simpler tools and places where she could.

Of course, everyone *around* her had extremely solid opinions of what was fitting for a person of her eminence. And she was far from immune to the attractions of luxuries and views.

All of which combined to put her first-night dinner with her selected suitors in the Diamond Room, a transparent-walled private dining area at the absolute peak of *Extravagant Voyage*'s central spire.

From there, they could see all of the dome with ease and could look up to see Tau Ceti *f* hanging above them. It was an incredible view, especially as *Voyage* began her journey away from the planet.

The Tau Ceti System had a lot of loose debris, the result of some ancient cataclysm or failure to form. Both habitable planets had fortress formations positioned ahead of them in their regular orbits, the Impact Defense Platforms tasked with keeping Tau Ceti's people safe from meteors and asteroid impacts.

But those diffuse clouds of debris and chaos created a glorious mix of light and not-quite-smoke scattered across the skies.

The view was amazing. The food was incredible.

Unfortunately, all ten of Kiera's dinner companions appeared to have been struck dumb by the prospect of eating a full meal with her. None of the ten had been this quiet during the thirty-minute introductions she'd first met them in, but all seemed intimidated by the more intimate setting.

As the main course was cleared away, she glanced around the room, inspecting her guests. None of the ten Mages in the room were lacking in confidence, she was certain, but something about *this* setup was intimidating them.

"Was there a memo I missed about not talking in the Diamond Room?" she asked with a soft smile. "I don't *think* I grew any extra heads since I met each of you on the surface, but everyone has been very, very quiet."

She got some chuckles and sheepish looks in response to that, but it still took a few moments before any of them spoke up.

The one who did was the only Mage by Right in the room. Upton Ayaan Meical McGregor's parents must have been absolutely *delighted* when their second son tested as a Mage as a pre-teen.

The McGregors were fabulously wealthy entertainment tycoons who, among other things, ran the water, land, air, and space race industry in Tau Ceti. Of their four children, only Upton was a Mage—one of those flukes of genetics that came along every so often—and he'd thrown himself into being as skilled a Mage as his elder brother was an engineer and manager.

And all four of the younger McGregors were racers. Upton McGregor had flown himself to *Extravagant Voyage* aboard a custom-built interplanetary racing shuttle. Now the blond-haired and blue-eyed Mage shrugged away his own sheepish expression and met Kiera's gaze.

"None of us, I suspect, are quite sure of the parameters," he told her. "The...rules of engagement, so to speak. I only know Brandon over there"—he gestured toward another of the Mages—"but that leads me to suspect that *no one* you picked to be here is the type to want to undermine others.

"But, frankly, we all know that this is a competition and that it's quite unlikely you're planning on keeping *all* of us," McGregor concluded. "I mean, no one is going to argue if the *Mage-Queen* wants a harem, but I imagine you're planning on dropping at least some of us off in Eridani."

"So, I guess we're wondering what you're expecting from us," one of the others murmured. "McGregor has the right of it. I don't want to start any fights here, but if we're expected to impress…"

"Fair," Kiera told them. "I appreciate your honesty."

McGregor being the first one to speak had certainly earned him some brownie points. She didn't exactly have a scoring matrix going. This was something she felt should be done by…emotion and gut feeling, not logic and math.

"Honestly, I have no idea," she continued with a chuckle. "This is the second time we've done this, and the last time was a bust."

Literally, in the case of the last "gentleman"'s arm when he'd taken the fact that she'd slept with him as a sign that he'd "won." Things had gone…very downhill from there, helped by a few mistakes of Kiera's own.

Eventually, she'd thrown him into a wall. She still felt bad about that—but she was *also* moderately sure that Lawrence had been about to kill the man.

"From where I stand, I spoke with about two hundred and thirty young men on Tau Ceti," she reminded them. Despite her people's snark, she hadn't met *every* one of the two thousand or so Mages in the right age bracket. "You guys were the ones who intrigued me the most, that I wanted to get a chance to get to know better.

"This is that chance. There's no need to impress or rules or competition." Boys would be boys, she was sure, which meant there *would* be competition. But hopefully it would stay…genteel.

"My staff are sorting out a schedule for the days we're in transit, and I will be spending at least a few hours with each of you," she continued. "The point is to get to know each other. The *hope* is for me to find a husband, yes, but I feel like holding that up as the goal is going to warp things."

She smiled.

"Does that work for 'rules of engagement' for you all?" she asked sweetly.

None of the men she'd picked were stupid enough to argue with that.

~

PUTTING ALL of them in one room had served one purpose, Kiera supposed as she entered the office in her villa. She'd confirmed that none of the ten Mages she'd chosen to bring with her were the type to sabotage each other.

That, and apparently proving that McGregor-of-the-too-many-names had both solid insight into others and some courage. None of the rest had been willing to speak up until he had, and even then, most of them had been quiet afterward.

Kiera wasn't going to make any decisions based on one action, but she'd admit that McGregor now had a small lead over the others.

"Need anything, Kiera?" her batman asked. "A drink?"

She glanced up at the graying man who ran her household and was doing most—if not all!—of the work of taking care of her as she flitted between star systems.

"I need to go over Damien's messages, see where we're at," she told him. "Have you put together the schedule for our guests over the next few days?"

"I've got tomorrow sorted out," Driessen confirmed. "We'll probably want to talk over the rest of the trip at some point. I've got you marked for an hour, roughly, with each of them tomorrow. A busy day."

Kiera chuckled.

"Self-inflicted problems," she noted. "I'm hoping you have more planned than for us to just sit and stare at each other?"

"This is a flying resort, Kiera," her batman chuckled. "I've arranged activities for each of them."

"Thank you."

She realized he hadn't waited for her to *say* if she wanted a drink when he slid a mug of hot chocolate onto the desk.

"Do you need me for anything else, Kiera?" he asked. "I'd suggest you not work *too* hard on the updates from Mars, but I know you."

"You've looked after me since Dad died," she agreed. "Thank you. It means a lot to still have you here."

He nodded, an odd stiffness to it she couldn't quite place.

"I'll leave you to your mail," he said brightly. "We'll talk in the morning—unless you *do* need me for anything else?"

Kiera took a sip of the thickly sweet beverage and smiled.

"No, Lakshmi," she said. "I'll be fine."

He bowed his way out of the room, and Kiera waved the holoprojectors and wallscreens to life. Her wrist-comp connected to the console, engaging in a complex series of electronic call-and-response to decrypt the information sent over the FTL Link communicator.

Kiera knew that her Prince-Chancellor was limiting how much detail was coming to her while she was on her Tour. That was how he was keeping her as widely informed as possible—she heard about everything she normally would hear of but at a much higher level than usual.

She trusted Montgomery's assessment of what she needed more info on, mostly, and could ask for more information on anything and get it in minutes. It was a decent compromise, considering that her focus was supposed to be elsewhere.

Taking another sip of the chocolate, she opened the initial daily precis. Eighty-six major items, seventeen of them marked as critical by Montgomery.

Ruling a hundred worlds was hardly simple, but Kiera and her Chancellor knew the drill by now. She reached out to open the first of the critical messages…and missed the icon on the touchscreen.

Blinking at her unusual clumsiness, Kiera found herself staring blankly at her hand for a moment as she held it in the air in front of her. It blurred in her vision and she swallowed against a sickly sweet aftertaste that she'd *thought* was the hot chocolate.

She'd been drugged—by Lakshmi Driessen?! That made no sense… but the hot chocolate he'd given her was the only vector she could think of through the fog filling her mind.

Then the fog turned to darkness and she fell into the void.

CHAPTER

NINE

A few hours of poking around *Extravagant Voyage*'s systems left Barry with more questions than answers. Not only was the shuttle Waxer had sent him to steal missing from all of the listings of parasite craft aboard the ship, there was no record of it ever coming aboard.

Thanks to the client, he not only knew *when* the shuttle had landed on the cruise liner but even had the footage from *f*-Signs' external sensors. Comparing the two sets of records was fascinating—because everything *else* matched, but so far as *Extravagant Voyage*'s computers were concerned, the jump shuttle didn't exist.

Shuttle Bay Echo was out of the way of most of the work going on aboard the ship, not least because records showed it had been shut down before they'd reached Tau Ceti *f*. The crew had flagged that Echo would be blocked by the station they were docking at, and transferred the shuttles. According to the liner's own records, the hangar was empty.

The only active part of the ship near Echo was the security station, but Barry figured he could slip by that without issue. The whole situation was strange—though he supposed it was going to be a lot easier to steal something no one seemed to know was aboard!

401

One way or another, he wasn't coming back to the suite he'd been staying in. He spent five minutes sweeping the room with a set of digital, magical and chemical tools to make sure there were no fingerprints or DNA left to identify him.

When he stepped out of the suite, there was no sign anyone had been in it at all. It was late by the clock of the far-distant mountain on Mars, which seemed to be calming most of the ship's crew. He suspected the true "day" of *Extravagant Voyage* was "the Mage-Queen is up," but since she was clearly running on Olympus Mons Time, it matched handily.

His wrist-comp said that the Mage-Queen's dinner would have wrapped up two hours earlier. Thirteen hours to jump. He only *needed* three or four hours, but the sooner he was in place, the less likely it was that any problem would keep him from getting away.

It was time to get to work.

ONCE AGAIN WEARING his stolen crew uniform, Barry found a currently unused parts cart and began to make his way to his destination. He was doing his best to remain unobtrusive and not *obviously* avoid people, but when he heard voices ahead, he pulled the cart against the wall and started going through its contents as if cataloging or searching for something.

"We need the coroner to crew quarters four," one of the voices said loudly. "A couple of our security guys, too."

"Captain doesn't want the Mage-Queen's people to know?" a woman replied. "What happened?"

"That's what the coroner's supposed to sort out, isn't it?" the first said. "But from what Jake said, one of the junkies in cargo handling decided to shoot up the entire stash they picked up on the planet. So, we got a corpse instead of a coworker."

"Show some damn respect, Hal," the woman snapped. "Who was it?"

"Dunno, but Captain sent me to go get Doc Lyle. Can I get you to round up a couple more of the sec team?" Hal didn't *sound* any more respectful to Barry.

"Yeah, yeah." The woman paused. "You're a *dick*, Hal."

"Maybe, but I'm not the dumbass that just ODed!"

Footsteps faded away into the distance, and Barry glared at the tools in front of him. He'd met people like Hal before, the type who didn't understand what caused someone to get addicted.

Barry had spent too much time in the blocks to think that it was only a matter of being weak, after all. And something about the situation didn't sit right with him—not least the hiding it from the Mage-Queen's security retinue.

There were more secrets being kept on the ship than *he* would be happy with if he was her. On the other hand, he was planning on being off the ship before they jumped out of Tau Ceti, let alone before those secrets came home to roost.

With the footsteps fading, he got his cart moving again toward his destination. His route kept him around corners and out of view from the security station itself, and he seemed to avoid any attention until he was practically at Shuttle Bay Echo.

He never even *heard* the Marine before the man appeared in front of him. It was the same Major he'd seen checking over the cargo in Bay Charlie, a Mage with similar height and build to Barry's own bean-pole-esque frame.

"Hey, spacer," the Mage barked as he spotted Barry. "You got coms, right?"

The stranger was *trying* to sound like he was concerned, but a layer of smug self-satisfaction slipped through. He was very pleased with himself about something.

He was also trying to hide it, which only reminded Barry of his conviction that this ship had too many secrets.

"I have the administrative ship-net, sir," he confirmed in his most obsequious voice, keeping his face slightly turned away from the Marine.

"I don't have access to the maintenance listings," the Marine said. "There's been some kind of systems failure down by Shuttle Bay Echo.

Looked like a coolant pipe busted and opened up some electrical wiring on the way.

"Can you flag the place as a hazard? We don't want anyone stumbling through it before Officer Chateaux can get some of your people together to fix it."

"Of course, sir," Barry said, still sounding as small and cooperative as possible as he considered the man's words. "I'll put it up and see if any of the repair teams are nearby. That sounds serious."

"Just make sure Chateaux knows, son," the strange Mage told him. "There's nothing in Bay Echo, so there's no big rush, right?"

He slapped Barry on the shoulder and strode off purposefully.

Barry carefully didn't look after the stranger...and also decided he was going to go *check* on this supposed coolant leak before he tried to get into the maintenance network.

And if he found what he expected to find, he was going to be leaving some time-delayed emails in the ship's systems. He knew he could get one to the Captain, and he figured he might even get one to the Mage-Queen.

The mess on *Extravagant Voyage* wasn't his problem. But he'd seen and heard too much over the last day or so to not think that something was rotten in the state of Denmark—and he had enough of a sense of responsibility to not want to leave that hanging.

CHAPTER

TEN

The lack of an electrified coolant leak only solidified Barry's certainty that something was very wrong. As he approached Shuttle Bay Echo's main hatch, though, he realized another factor that was almost as concerning.

It wasn't clear when accessing the system from anywhere else on the ship, but Shuttle Bay Echo was completely disconnected from *Extravagant Voyage*'s systems. Whatever was in there, someone had gone to a great deal of effort to conceal it—to the point where the half-casual instruction to report an incident seemed out of character.

That deception would only hold up for a few hours at most. By the time they were supposed to jump, Barry figured it was *guaranteed* that someone would come looking to fix the leak. That would draw attention to both the shuttle bay's system disconnection and the Marine who'd told him to look for it.

Something stank. Still, Barry had his own reasons to be there, and Echo being a hidden section of the ship worked for him. A gesture unscrewed the access panel next to the secured hatch, and he moved the cart to block anyone else's view of the exposed wiring.

A wire unrolled from his wrist-comp as his corneal projector overlaid a schematic on the open panel. He gestured, directing the wire to the right connection. This was all standard enough. There wasn't even any sign in the hardware of the fact that the shuttle bay had been severed from *Voyage*'s systems.

A few seconds after making the connection, though, the security software on his wrist-comp started freaking out. Multiple alerts blazed across the corneal implant, and Barry refocused his attention. *His* wrist-comp, at least, had been customized for easy manipulation through his magic.

It only took him a few seconds to secure the device against the virus that had tried to counterattack his intrusion. Still…that was *not* standard civilian security on a jump ship. He'd never seen anything like it before—and while he'd never dealt with military hardware, that seemed oddly aggressive even for military security.

A few gentle software probes into the network confirmed what he was expecting. The hatch was running on independent software *and* hardware. It wasn't obvious from the wiring he could see, but tracing the flow of data, it looked like everything in the door had been rerouted back into the hangar itself and then fed into entirely new hardware.

Hardware not just unconnected but *unrelated* to anything on the ship. The only reason Barry could think of to do that was if someone was worried about back doors in the hardware or firmware.

Like the person who'd secured Shuttle Bay Echo had been worried someone was going to show up with firmware overrides to get past his security. Barry had heard…rumors of such things, in the hands of the Mage-Queen's top agents.

He supposed if there was anywhere to be worried that people with the Mage-Queen's personal magic keys might go poking, it was around the ship *carrying* the Mage-Queen of Mars.

Unfortunately for whoever had set this up, Barry didn't have said firmware keys. He just had his usual bag of tricks, which meant that while it was going to take him a few minutes, nothing they'd set up was actually going to stop him.

∾

WHOEVER HAD PUT TOGETHER the security modules and code that had Shuttle Bay Echo locked down was *good*. Barry had never before met a door that could hold him up for more than about ten minutes—though he would freely admit that he hadn't, for example, tried to crack bank vaults.

He was a *shuttle thief*, after all, and shuttles had very different security protocols—including physical-part lockouts.

The systems that had been rigged up to secure the hatch, however, were closer to the systems he was used to on high-end aircars and shuttles than on any door he'd ever seen. It took him over thirty minutes to break through the door's systems—long enough that he was worrying about who was going to come through behind him and was considering using his magic to brute-force the door.

Somehow, though, Barry figured that cutting the door open with his magic was *definitely* going to trigger some alarms. So, he stuck with it and breathed a sigh of relief when the hatch finally slid open enough to let him through.

The *second* relieving piece of news was that he was definitely in the right place. He'd been pretty sure, but it was still a reprieve to actually *see* the utility hauler he was looking for. The ship didn't *look* special—but the fact that she was inside a secured shuttle bay that had been cut off from the ship's networks told Barry everything.

The jump shuttle was an ugly thing, all fuel tanks and extendable gantries wrapped around a personnel pod barely big enough to provide the two-person crew a place to sleep. She was a working spacecraft, one that no one would take a second look at.

But even a momentary glance at her serial numbers confirmed she was the one he was looking for. If this shuttle wasn't actually the jump shuttle—somehow—she was still the one the client had asked for.

So, she was the one Barry would deliver.

He looked back at the hatch behind him and considered the situation. It was still almost half a day until the jump, and he didn't want to leave with his prize much before then. Except...he was pretty sure the Marine Mage-Major would be back inside that time. There was *something* going on there.

But…if something secretive was going on, that would also limit the Mage-Major's ability to ask for *help*.

Between rejiggering the aftermarket security modules and a little bit of magical welding, it only took Barry about five minutes to *permanently* seal the hatches into Shuttle Bay Echo.

That left him alone with his prey, and he took a few minutes to just pace around the gangly-looking spacecraft. At first glance, there was no sign that she was magical beyond a faint buzzing sensation in his teeth that he'd never felt before.

Examining her, though, the truth slowly became obvious. The problem the people upgrading her had encountered was that large chunks of a utility hauler were open to space for ease of maintenance and operation.

Those pieces of the shuttle had still needed to be included in the jump matrix, but they weren't easily concealed. The Rune Scribes who'd modified the ship had done an impressive job, but Barry was *looking* for the runes.

And he found them. Someone had turned one of the most ubiquitous midrange in-system craft in the Protectorate into an interstellar jump ship.

He wasn't sure *why* someone would have done that—but he did know that someone else was prepared to *pay* for it.

WITH THE HANGAR sealed behind him, Barry took his time opening up the shuttle itself. It was this layer where people tended to hide the most…*active* anti-intruder devices. Anything more than locks or an alarm was supposed to be illegal for anyone outside the military, but someone *always* thought they were above such rules.

Given how unusual the shuttle was, he wasn't surprised to locate a few bits of nastiness. The pair of fully automated turrets set to activate if the wrong security codes—or even wrong security *connections*—were used was special, though.

There was an entire false access setup that needed a physical key to open. Barry spent longer finding the hidden keyhole than he spent picking the lock, though, and the system behind it was extremely familiar.

He'd just cracked its twin to get into the hangar. The pass phrases and codes might have been different—but it wasn't like Barry was *using* the usual unlocking methods.

Resetting the system and activating the same sequence that had opened up the hatch took him about a minute. All told, it took him less time to breach the shuttle than it had taken to breach the hangar itself.

"Good sign, good sign," he murmured to himself. Schematics for the base shuttle type appeared on his corneal projector, but moments after he'd opened them, he realized they were useless.

The hatch was supposed to lead into one of four compartments, stacked two on top of each other in a line. The forward two compartments should have been shorter, the lower acting as the airlock, and what limited passenger space the craft contained and the upper half as the cockpit.

The back section would have been the minimal living quarters and the internal engineering spaces.

Instead, the entire lower section had been opened up and reduced in height. Instead of entering through a two-point-five-meter-square meter-thick airlock into a roughly two-and-three-quarter-meter-wide space four meters long, Barry discovered that the inner door of the airlock was partially blocked.

The interior hardware of the shuttle had clearly been heavily reorganized, giving up the onboarding and passenger space and lowering the ceiling to barely two meters. The airlock opened directly into the squashed and extended engineering space.

Barry's eye implant was a display, not an actual neural link. He couldn't feed the systems he was looking at into the computer to assess them, but he could tell glancing around that these weren't the systems that would be mounted in a utility hauler.

The engines more closely resembled what he'd have expected to see in one of the assault shuttles belonging to the Mage-Queen's security detachment. Despite the clear attempt to keep the exterior ordinary-seeming, this shuttlecraft was clearly packing a great deal more engine power than it should have.

Despite all of the changes, however, Barry quickly confirmed that the access up to the cockpit was still where it should have been. Scrambling up the ladder in *Extravagant Voyage*'s reduced magical gravity, it was quickly obvious what the engineering space had been modified to create.

No utility hauler had the space to put a magical simulacrum at the dead center. Everything on this one had been moved around to make the inclusion of the simulacrum possible. Most of what should have been the cockpit was taken up by an additional computing center managing bundle after bundle of fiber-optic cables that split out to cover a bulkhead with a hatch barely large enough for Barry to duck through.

It had been a long time since he'd set foot in the simulacrum chamber of a starship—and even that had been on the rundown ships used for Jump Mage training. If nothing else, this was much, *much* smaller.

The simulacrum in the center of the ship was less than twenty centimeters across. There was no question what it was, though, and the new control space had been set up around it. The pilot's chair was inverted, with additional runes around it that Barry realized had to be gravity magic.

He could move around the area of inverted gravity toward the hatch he presumed led to the quarters, but the zone around the chair and the simulacrum had the opposite pull to the rest of the ship. A test with his hand confirmed that the shuttle's magic overpowered *Voyage*'s in that small area.

It was a clever use of space—though it still meant that the living quarters were smaller than the cockpit had originally been. This was very clearly intended to be a *one*-person spacecraft now.

With a deep breath and a careful assessment of the position, Barry stepped *up* into the gravity well around the chair, grabbing a bar that he realized was at the perfect height for him to do exactly this, and rotated himself down into the seat.

The height of the bar told an interesting story. It looked like it might be adjustable, but it was locked in the right position for Barry—which suggested the Marine Mage-Major he'd seen, who was of a height with him, was the likely owner of the ship.

He'd figured that.

"The problem, Barry," he addressed himself aloud, "is that a pissed-off Marine Mage is going to go through that hatch like it isn't there. So, let's get everything moving, shall we?"

CHAPTER
ELEVEN

The biggest surprise to Barry was that the security around actually *flying* the shuttle was "merely" a third iteration of the same specialty encrypted cipher modules that he'd run in to on the hangar access and the shuttle entryway.

They were capable and clever bits of hardware, but to *him*, they were even less of a barrier the third time than they had been the second. He was still going to have problems convincing all of the systems to talk to him—and the jump computer was a fully stand-alone installation, he judged—but he had flight controls and communications thirty minutes after settling into the seat.

It was an extremely comfortable seat, too, the kind that adjusted to his body and even did intermittent massage on key points as his muscles started to lock in place. He had a very similar one in his computing setup at home—and it cost almost as much as a quality aircar.

Once he had control of the shuttle's communications, he carefully linked in to the network for *Extravagant Voyage*. None of the daemons he'd left in the systems reported issues, and he considered his situation.

Barry couldn't access Shuttle Bay Echo's systems from the main ship network, but even if he had to go physically access the consoles, that wouldn't take him long. Between the various stages of the process, he'd spent the three hours he'd flagged as the minimum to secure control of the shuttle.

It would have taken him longer if the shuttle's master hadn't used identical security systems for access and control—and then set a third copy of the same to secure the shuttle bay.

In fact, he suspected… A few commands opened the link to Shuttle Bay Echo's local flight control, and he chuckled in amusement. Assuming that Mage-Major was the shuttle's pilot, the man had possessed a great deal of faith in his custom cipher modules.

The actual flight-control systems for the hangar were locked to the shuttle. Barry could have undone that with access to the console, but since he controlled the shuttle now, he didn't need to. Whenever he was ready to go, he could easily open the hangar and get out into open space.

The problem *now* was the limited feed he was getting from the cruise liner's exterior sensors. Barry was confident in his ability to outrun, confuse and evade regular police and High Guard craft. He'd back his skills and tricks against the Tau Ceti System Defense Force, though he knew the edge was a lot thinner there.

He wasn't going to try to convince half a dozen Royal Martian Navy destroyers that he was innocent, and he *knew* he couldn't evade their sensors or outrun them. A single assault shuttle in competent hands could end his heist within minutes of his leaving *Extravagant Voyage*—let alone the six million-ton-plus warships on the screen.

But even as he was considering the ships on the screen, a half-forgotten sensation rippled through him—and the sensor screen flickered.

Blinking away the sudden disorientation, he realized the warships were gone. So was the Tau Ceti System.

They hadn't been supposed to jump yet. By the clock he was following, they were still over ten hours away from their planned jump point—and there was *no* reason to jump the big cruise liner without taking the destroyers with her.

"That is *not* right," he whispered. "And whatever is going on, I don't want to be anywhere near this."

He jumped into motion. He'd already got halfway through setting the shuttle up for launch, and now he finished the work. The shuttle had been *physically* prepped for this, he observed. He hadn't had time to check fuel status and whether the lines had been attached or anything yet.

Now the check lights for those items flashed green. The shuttle had been ready to go, he realized, and that fit a very ugly pattern taking shape in the back of his mind.

It wasn't his problem. He repeated that to himself as he ran through an abbreviated safety checklist—and then ordered Shuttle Bay Echo to open its doors. The entire bay acted as an airlock around him, alarms warning anyone who'd somehow sneaked past the sealed doors to get the hell out.

Whatever was going on aboard *Extravagant Voyage* was not Barry Carpentier's problem, he repeated to himself. There were Marines, Secret Service, even *Royal Guards* aboard the ship to make sure that the Mage-Queen of Mars and her guests were safe.

Given all of that security firepower, he was surprised that he managed to prep for launch and open the bay door without any challenge from the cruise liner's crew. There was dead silence on the general channels.

Not even anyone asking where their escorts had gone.

That silence only accelerated Barry as he brought the shuttle's maneuvering thrusters online and flung her out of the ship. Once he was clear, he began the staged process of bringing up the more powerful engines to get clear of the mothership.

That should *definitely* have drawn attention. The miniature simulacrum chamber had the same direct-optic-link exterior view as the larger version, and he turned a baleful glare on *Extravagant Voyage*.

"What the hell is going on?"

Barry was sufficiently engrossed in the weirdness of the situation that it took him three whole seconds to realize *he* wasn't the one saying that.

THE LACK of response from the cruise liner was of significantly lower importance than someone being aboard Barry's stolen shuttle. It took him a moment to realize that the person had to be in the quarters that he hadn't yet entered—though the sudden stream of angry swearing certainly helped locate her!

Locking the shuttle into a course directly away from *Extravagant Voyage* at a thrust her gravity runes could absorb, he flipped around the useful bar again and strode to the hatch to the last compartment.

Flinging open the door, he found that the living quarters had seen the same level of reconfiguration as the rest of the ship. Where there once would have been two sets of bunk beds, there was now a comfortable-looking single bed on one side, with a kitchenette replacing the second set of beds.

Still on the bed and struggling to get herself upright was the absolute worst possible individual to be aboard the shuttle craft. Even Barry had *no* problems recognizing the slim redheaded royal trying to wriggle herself off the bed.

He had no idea *why* Mage-Queen Kiera Alexander was on his stolen shuttle—let alone why she was cuffed in the shuttle's single bed! —but he doubted it was anything good for him.

"Who the fuck are you?" Kiera snarled at him. "If you think you're going to get away with this, you are very, *very* wrong!"

The fact that Barry was still breathing told him *something* was going on—and he realized what Alexander had clamped around her wrists.

They weren't merely manacles solid enough to hold a cyborg. They were *Mage-cuffs*, built with materials that drew magic away from the prisoner and then augmented, as he understood it, with runes that did even more of that.

He wouldn't have expected them to hold the Mage-Queen of Mars, but what did *he* know?

"If I help you stand, will you at least promise not to murder me immediately? I'd like to work out what's going on myself?" he asked.

"You got Driessen to drug me and kidnapped me," she growled. "Why would I trust you for a damn second?"

"Well, frankly, because I didn't do that," Barry said dryly. "*I just stole a shuttle, which seems to have come with an extra passenger that I *really* don't want to deal with."

He glanced around the quarters.

"I wonder if the escape pod is in the normal place," he murmured.

"You have got to be *fucking* kidding me!" Alexander shouted. "If you're not my kidnapper, let me out of these damn cuffs."

Barry wasn't going to do *that*—he liked breathing, and he suspected being around the Mage-Queen in her current level of anger *without* her power being restrained was a terrible idea.

He did at least help her to stand.

"I think I'm leaving the cuffs on for now," he admitted. "I would like to live through this spectacularly fucked-up situation. Right now, I'm thinking that involves stuffing you in the escape pod for your people to pick up."

"Are you *kidding* me?" she repeated. "Look, if you give up now and let me ping my security, I'll rig a deal where you walk free if you give us your conspirators. I doubt you got this far on your own."

"Your Majesty," Barry replied, hoping that his sarcastic edge didn't drip on the floor *too* hard. "I'm here to steal a shuttle, not get involved in Protectorate politics. Plus, *my* conspirators have nothing to do with kidnapping you."

He half-led, half-pulled her behind him as he headed toward the front of the shuttle, where the escape pod should be. For her part, Alexander stopped dead once they were in the simulacrum chamber.

"What the hell is this?" she snapped.

"A shuttle rigged with a jump matrix," he told her. "I figured it was yours."

"I didn't think that was possible," Alexander said slowly. "But if this is a simulacrum chamber, we're in space. And I don't see the rest of the flotilla, so what game are you playing?!"

Barry sighed and tapped a command on his wrist-comp, highlighting and zooming in on *Extravagant Voyage*.

"No one on *Voyage* seems to have noticed this shuttle leaving," he said. "And I have no idea where your escorts are, because we jumped just before I took this shuttle and ran."

"You're not helping any sort of case here," she told him coldly. "Look, fine. If you *didn't* kidnap me, let's go back to the ship. You tell Guard-Captain Lawrence and me everything you saw and encountered leading to this, and we forget you stole this shuttle."

"Or what?" he asked. "No offense, *Your Majesty*, but I'm not overly impressed with monarchs offering deals. We're going to the escape pod. Once I'm ready to jump this ship back home, we're going to fire you off toward *Voyage* and your people will find you.

"Everybody wins."

"You have a very strange definition of 'win,'" she growled.

"The only win I care about," he admitted, "is my getting out of here with this shuttle and getting paid. Beyond that, I have no interest in causing any *other* harm, and I would very much prefer *not* to get involved in any *political* mess."

"I suspect it is way too late for that, Mister…"

"Please, Your Majesty, I am *not* fucking stupid enough to give you my name," Barry told her. There was no way he could pretend to not be a Mage, but the fact that there was no record of his face aboard *Voyage* should keep him safe.

With a gesture, he used his magic to open the access to the forward computing center. The escape pod *should* be the—

A brilliant blaze of light interrupted his thoughts and schemes, the simulacrum-chamber systems automatically darkening the feed to protect their eyes as the ship he'd zoomed in on vanished in a ball of pure-white nuclear fire.

And any *easy* solution to Barry's situation vanished with it.

CHAPTER

TWELVE

Kiera *knew* she was groggier and duller than she was pretending to her...not-captor? She wasn't entire sure *what* the beanpole of a Mage who'd been about to shove her into an escape pod was.

Well, she knew *one* thing about him: he was almost as shocked as she was to watch *Extravagant Voyage* die in a ball of flame. Both of them just stood in the shuttle's simulacrum chamber, staring at the fading light in horror.

There had been roughly two thousand people on that ship, Kiera knew. One way or another, *all* of them had worked for her. The only people who hadn't either been her security, her staff or the ship's crew had been the poor bastards she'd brought along to get to know better.

"That...that..." The words *that isn't possible* couldn't quite clear her lips. She couldn't argue with reality. Any tendency toward *that* had been drilled out of her by her father.

A monarch could afford no illusions.

So, Kiera faced her situation as squarely as she could and tried to establish what was happening. She couldn't allow herself to grieve. She had to focus on the task at hand.

That certainty lasted all of about fifteen seconds before a mixture of remembering Driessen handing her the drugged hot chocolate and Guard-Captain Lawrence's gentle teasing hit her at the same time, and she collapsed against the bulkhead, sucking in deep breaths.

Then the stranger was there, his hand on her shoulder as he looked down at her.

"You need to sit down," he told her. "Come on."

Kiera barely registered being moved back into the living quarters and eased onto the bed. Her not-captor searched for a moment and then found a chair.

"I have to stop our engines," he told her as he stared at the folding furniture. "I'll be right back."

Kiera stared blankly at her hands, trying to keep her grief to something quiet. She had made a *point* of knowing her entire retinue to one degree or another. And now they were gone. All of them.

"What the *hell* happened?" she asked the air. As if in answer, the rumble of the fusion engines cut out.

Rubbing unshed tears from her eyes, she managed to find some semblance of calm by the time the Mage returned.

"Well, either this is a very clever plan or you're as much in the dark as I am," she told him. "What the hell is going on?" she repeated.

"Damned if I know," he admitted.

She realized now that he was the unknown Mage that she'd seen in crew uniform. It seemed that he hadn't been some statistical fluke at all. Just a liar.

"Your honesty is somewhat in doubt here," Kiera warned.

"Look, I stole a shuttle," he conceded. "I have a rendezvous to sell said shuttle. I have a rep to maintain, and if I don't deliver the shuttle, some quite-nasty people are going to start wondering whether I'm still useful enough to them to be worth the secrets in my head.

"So, my priority—until someone killed a couple thousand people— was to finish the job and get paid."

"And now?" she asked. He didn't strike her as nearly as callous as he said he was. Someone *that* callous wouldn't have dealt with her grief before slowing the shuttle to preserve their fuel.

"Right now, my priority is surviving. The first part of which is going to be working out just where in the void we even are."

"At this point, we're better off if we work together," Kiera pointed out. She still wasn't sure if she could trust this man, but she knew she'd be a *lot* more trusting if she wasn't currently Mage-cuffed.

For that matter, regular Mage-cuffs shouldn't have been enough to contain her power. The Runes of Power inlaid in her flesh should have been more than enough to overwhelm the runes and silver alloys of a standard set of Mage-cuffs. For this set to work, someone had put true Runes of Nullification on the inside of the cuffs, where they pressed into her skin.

The stranger—he *still* hadn't given her a name—was studying her in silence, and his gaze flicked to where her hands were cuffed behind her back.

"Don't take this the wrong way, *Your Majesty*," he told her, "but I am quite certain I can get us out of here on my own. At which point I have every intention of falling back on my *throw you in an escape pod* plan."

He shook his head.

"Look, rest," he instructed. "Your day appears to have gone better than it might have, but it's still been rough on you. Being drugged out like that doesn't give you any actual *rest*. Trust me."

Something in his tone suggested that was from bitter personal experience.

"Treating me like your prisoner is not really serving your argument that you're *not* my kidnapper," Kiera said archly.

"No, I can see that. But it turns out that I have a problem with authority, and I am *well* aware that taking those cuffs off would mean you can kill me with your brain," he told her. "So, I'm going to solve this problem myself, *Your Majesty*."

The sharp tone he put on her title made her want to throw things at him. But the truth was that with her hands locked behind her back and her magic contained, unless this *idiot* released her, there wasn't much she could do to help him.

Even if he was kind of cute.

CHAPTER

THIRTEEN

Being in close proximity to Kiera Alexander did not, Barry was realizing, make the woman any *less* distracting. She terrified him in about six different ways, and he was *not* okay with taking the easy way out and leaving her cuffed.

He just didn't see an option that didn't leave him trapped in a ten-meter-long crew pod with the most powerful Mage alive while she was utterly, homicidally pissed the fuck off.

It was easy and it was dangerous and it was probably going to screw him in the end—but he *didn't* trust her not to immediately reverse the tables, magically bind him and hand him over to her troops for an interrogation that wouldn't help *her* at all.

Since Barry had no illusions about his ability to withstand modern interrogation techniques, he was reasonably sure that interrogation would help the Mage-Queen break a few low- and mid-level players in Tau Ceti's organized crime, including Alaina Waxer.

The universe would probably be better off if a few of the names he could name went away—but he knew that whoever named those names would probably *also* "go away."

It would confirm that he wasn't involved in her kidnapping, but he'd be completely screwed either way.

423

Plus, while he hadn't admitted as much to the young woman he was trapped with, he was reasonably sure he *couldn't* unlock the Mage-cuffs. He didn't know much about them, but he understood that they were almost as resistant to external magic as to their captive's power.

And Barry couldn't actually pick locks without magic.

Sighing, he stepped through the forward hatch and examined the navigation computer. The shuttle's regular systems wouldn't have the databases or algorithms necessary to map out the stars around them and locate where they were.

Just standing in the simulacrum chamber told him as much as using the main system would: they were in the deep void. Anywhere up to a full light-year away from Tau Ceti—and he couldn't easily pick the star out from the rest of the universe, which he figured meant they were at least a few light-months out.

He ran a set of wires from his wrist-comp into the nav computer, setting his antivirus software to maximum sensitivity first. Unsurprisingly, the software reported that the nav computer attempted a complex software handshake he didn't have the protocols for.

And as soon as his system missed those, it dumped an entire series of hostile software back over the link. Since Barry had been expecting that, it was all isolated, and he took a few minutes to poke at its code.

Thankfully, it looked like the computer wouldn't do anything drastic—like wipe itself, for example—without receiving some kind of message from the attack software. Whoever had coded the viruses hadn't expected quite as effective a lockbox as Barry had constructed, which bought him some time.

Potentially not much, though, and he warmed up his software tools while his magic searched through the nav computer for the now-familiar cipher modules.

Given everything else that the shuttle's master had used the cipher modules for, Barry figured they'd used them for the computer as well —and he was right. There they were. There was an extra layer of security with the viral counterattack, but that had been present in one of the setups before.

Complicated and effective as the cipher modules were, he had their number now. It still wasn't a fast process, but it was straightforward enough.

❧

IT TOOK a lot for Barry to focus on something without distraction—but even with distractions, he often wasn't fully aware of what was going on around him. He didn't realize until he'd successfully unlocked the nav computer that he was being watched.

Alexander was standing in the hatch to the simulacrum chamber, her hands still cuffed behind her, watching him with an odd expression.

"I was going to offer to help," she told him. She pointed her chin downward at a chain she was wearing around her neck. "I'm wearing a version of a chip we give my Hands that contains root-level overrides for all Protectorate computers."

Barry's gaze followed the chain down from her neck and rather farther than he should have. He realized he was tracing the chain into her cleavage and immediately snapped his gaze up to her face, trying not to flush.

From the flash of a mischievous grin that crossed her face—before fading back into a worn expression of stress and grief—she had definitely noticed.

"It wouldn't have helped," he admitted. "Though knowing that particular rumor is true explains some of the oddities on this bird."

Alexander tried to move her hands, sighed, and then settled for a half questioning head-tilt, half-glare.

"All of the security is based around completely nonstandard physical modules," he told her. "I've got their number and I can break them pretty easily now, but I was wondering why they had something *so* unusual and kept using it."

"If they knew about the overrides..." Alexander shook her head. "I'd say no one is supposed to, but as you said... Rumors. My Hands use them often enough that they're not a well-kept secret."

The Hands of the Mage-Queen of Mars. That was a name to send shivers down Barry's spine. In some ways, the *Hands* scared him more than the Mage-Queen herself did. *She* was a monarch, a font of authority, but basically a politician raised to the job.

The Hands were troubleshooters. Emphasis, from the stories he had heard, on *shooters*.

"But if you don't have any kind of override…" She glanced past him at the computers. "Nonstandard hardware architecture. I'm guessing at least partially nonstandard software architecture. It would have to interface with the standard wrist-comp OSes, but the parameters for that are well established.

"Still, nonstandard soft-, hard-, and firmware… How are you getting into their system?"

"Magic," Barry said with a chuckle. He figured that the Mage-Queen of Mars would have guessed that.

There was a surprisingly long silence.

"You're not being metaphorical, are you?" she asked.

He blinked.

"No?"

"I have studied every type of magic known to humanity," Alexander told him quietly. "I have read documents and gone through research that I would have to imprison anyone else looking at. I wield a particular magical Gift that is shared by less than ten living human beings. I know as much about *alien* magic as any living human.

"I have never heard of anyone using magic to directly influence technology."

Something in how she was looking at him made him very uncomfortable.

"That's…strange," he replied. "And now I feel like I'm going to be vivisected if I let you get me into your people's hands. No offense, Your Majesty, but I think I'm going to lock you in the living quarters now.

"Calculating the jump is going to take a while, even once this thing gives me our coordinates."

"I can calculate the jump for us," she said sharply. "And I think, sir, that you should give me a *bit* more credit than to think that the man who appears to have saved my life, however accidentally, is heading for a laboratory table!"

"Maybe," he conceded. "But while you seem sane enough, you are the Mage-Queen of Mars—and I am a thief. You will have to excuse my paranoia, I'm afraid. I *will* get you to safety. But I will look to my own survival first."

Sort of. He was surprised when his brain gave him *that* thought. Something about the young woman was more distracting and unsettling than anyone else she'd ever encountered.

She did, at least, let him lead her back to the living quarters and lock her in.

One of them, at least, should get some rest.

CHAPTER

FOURTEEN

Kiera wasn't getting any rest. Even locked in the living quarters, she found herself pacing the narrow slip of space between the kitchenette slash eating counter and the bed. There was enough equipment to cook properly in the tiny space—possibly even for two people—but there clearly wasn't enough space for more than two people to eat.

And one would be sitting on the bed.

With her hands locked behind her, she couldn't even *examine* the Mage-cuffs. That was, she conceded, part of the *point*—but it was frustrating as all hell. She could still see and feel the magic around her. Even the Runes of Nullification on the upgraded cuffs couldn't seal that part of her Gift.

She suspected that if she could *see* the cuffs, she might be able to shuffle them around enough to separate some of the nullifiers from her skin. If she reduced that effect enough, she could potentially salvage enough of her magic to break free.

Then she would be able to have a more-level conversation with the frustratingly unique cute idiot currently taking way too long to calculate a jump. There was no way they were more than a light-year from

Tau Ceti, which meant it should only take an hour or so at most to calculate the jump back.

If she was being honest, it would take *her* longer than that to do the calculations. But while she wasn't sure how long it would take her not-captor to do the math, she had the distinct feeling that he was *far* from a fully trained Jump Mage.

She turned on her heel for the ninth or tenth time and glared at the hatch. *No one* could use magic to influence hardware and software. It wasn't…outside the realm of reason, she supposed, but most of what Mages could do was variations on changing the energy levels of things.

It would take a very specific and very targeted change of energy levels to do anything inside a computer. To be fair, a lot of spells involved similarly focused changes—but usually in more-resilient targets than computer hardware.

The Mage in the pilot's seat was unusual. Unique. Also uniquely frustrating. There was no reason she would turn on him. She believed him when he said he wasn't involved in her kidnapping—which meant that her kidnappers, including Lakshmi Driessen, had died aboard *Extravagant Voyage*.

That particular betrayal was like a sore tooth. She couldn't stop poking at it. Lakshmi Driessen had been working for the royal family since before she was born. He'd served Kiera's mother until her death, then her brother until *his* death.

He'd entered Kiera's own staff as the deputy head, but her previous head of staff had retired a few years later. Driessen had stood by Kiera's side for half a decade—and he'd helped change her diapers as a baby.

His betrayal made *no sense* to her. She couldn't even be glad that he'd died in the mess that her thief had made of the kidnapping attempt. She wanted Driessen alive so she could ask him questions!

And that would never happen now. The strange part was that she didn't see how her batman had been planning on making it off *Voyage* before the explosion—he was neither a Mage nor a pilot, so there was no way this shuttle was his.

Someone else had been planning on flying her away from *Extrava-*

gant Voyage, and there wasn't enough space on this shuttle for Driessen. Or any of the other traitors inevitably involved in the bombing.

Guard-Captain Lawrence and her people had been the best in the galaxy. Kiera wasn't sure *how* her attackers had got around them, but she had a grim suspicion of who. Only one organization out there knew enough about the high levels of Martian government to have specialty-built hardware to offset the override codes.

The same people who'd killed her father and brother.

Nemesis.

Remembering that name made her snarl at the air, and she half-consciously slammed her shoulder into the hatch—and was surprised when it clicked open and allowed her back into the simulacrum chamber.

Her thief looked up/down at her from the chair on the roof and shrugged sheepishly.

"So, it turns out there are no interior locks on this shuttle," he admitted. "You really *should* rest, though. I will guarantee your safety, Your Majesty."

That was the first time he'd used her title without adding enough acid sarcasm to risk the shuttle's hull integrity—and there was a strange, distracted confidence to his promise, too. Like he wasn't quite thinking about what he was saying, and that made him mean it more.

"The vast majority of the people who have been around me for the last half-decade just died," Kiera told him quietly. "I don't think sleep is going to come easily."

The Mage met her gaze.

"I'm still working through the jump calcs," he admitted. "Take the passenger seat if you want. There's not a lot of space in this ship."

SETTLING into the chair as comfortably as she could, Kiera spent the first few minutes just trying to be covert about studying her not-captor. He was slightly taller than her, with both of them tending toward a lanky frame readily described as "beanpole." His skin was pale and his hair was a dark brown, almost black—the shade of freshly brewed coffee.

It took her a few minutes of observation to realize that he had a visible strip of metal on the underside of his left eyebrow—and once she was looking at it, she saw the lights from the projector dancing across his eye.

She wasn't sure what he was looking at on the implanted display, because the calculations for the jump were displaying all over the simulacrum-chamber walls. He was working through them. Slowly. Laboriously.

Incorrectly.

She stared at the error for about ten seconds, then settled on a solution. She *scoffed*. Loudly and derisively, while being *very* obvious which chunk of his math she was looking at.

She met his glare with a winning smile—one that sharpened as he went back to that section of the math and reviewed it. Despite being an idiot, her thief wasn't stupid. He found the error and fixed it once she'd hinted at where it was.

This wouldn't be as fast as her doing the math herself—but, on the other hand, irritating the hell out of her unnamed new acquaintance was worth something in itself.

As a distraction for her, if nothing else.

CHAPTER

FIFTEEN

Kiera didn't remember falling asleep. She was only aware she *was* asleep when a gentle hand shook her shoulder and she started awake.

At that point, of course, she rediscovered that she was bound. Her magic was gone. Her friends and personal staff were dead. And she'd wrapped her arms around the back of the seat in a way that, in the clarity of hindsight and pain, had been a terrible idea.

"Your Majesty," the Mage greeted her. "I'm sorry to wake you. You needed the rest, but we may have trouble."

She blinked her fatigue away, trying not to lose herself in the man's dark eyes as she moved her arms. He spotted her problem and raised an eyebrow.

"May I help?" he asked.

"Please."

With a bit of assistance from the stranger, she got her arms unwrapped from the chair. Pins and needles rippled along her limbs as the blood rushed back to them, and she winced as she nodded gratefully to him.

"You said 'trouble'?" she finally asked.

"How quickly would you be expecting a rescue?" he asked. "Because my jump math is not done yet, and a ship just showed up.

"We're twenty-nine light-weeks out from Tau Ceti," he continued. "No one is going to show up here by accident. They knew where we'd be."

Kiera grimaced against the pins and needles, wishing she could rub her arms.

"*Theoretically*," she said slowly, "if one of the Trackers was in Tau Ceti, they could have tracked the jump and put together a rescue contingent. But the nearest Tracker is…days, at least a week, away."

She shook away the last of her fatigue as fear stabbed into her.

"No, thief. If there's someone out there, they were working with the people who tried to kidnap me. Show me the ship," she instructed.

He didn't visibly move, but she realized he'd interfaced whatever control mechanism his projector had with the ship. His eye twitched in an odd-looking pattern, and a section of the simulacrum chamber's optical feed was replaced with an overlay screen.

The ship in the image looked innocent enough. It wasn't a warship or anything of the sort. It was, in fact, *Extravagant Voyage*'s less-extravagant younger cousin in many ways.

Lacking the gorgeous dome of the luxury liner, it was a more-economical passenger transport. Under a million tons, no massive false ecosystems or anything of the sort. Just a ship designed to move five or six hundred paying passengers between systems at a slow but acceptable pace.

Except that Kiera Alexander built starship models as a hobby and had built a model of the exact class that the strange ship was pretending to be.

"That's not right," she said aloud. "They're *pretending* to be a Hyperion X-Ray Seventeen. Passenger liner, five-hundred-fifty thousand tons dry. Carries six hundred passengers, four hundred crew."

Her thief was waiting for the other shoe.

"'Pretending'?" he asked softly.

"They've got bits on there that are from the X-Ray Sixteen, the Nineteen, and what looks like a Rodriguez Orbital Guard corvette,"

Kiera told him. "And those blisters…" She nodded toward part of the ship.

"Those aren't part of the Hyperion X-Ray design at all. Those are heavy laser emplacements. And those points there and there"—she gestured again—"aren't shuttle bays. They're trying to look like it, but they're too small if you know the proportions of the ship.

"Those hatches are almost certainly covering missile launchers."

She exhaled a long sigh.

"Four battle lasers," she concluded. "Likely on the lighter side, but… Probably concealed antimissile defenses, too. Those two hatches probably cover three to four missile launchers each."

"This is a utility hauler, Your Majesty," her thief told her.

"So, unless you know a way for an unarmed shuttle that masses about fifteen hundred tons to fight off a pirate ship massing almost *six hundred thousand* tons, I really suggest you release me," Kiera murmured. "I promise you, my thief, that you are *not* going to end up in a jail cell."

There was a long silence.

"Turn away from me," he instructed. "I don't actually know if I can undo these, but I can sure as hell try."

Even realizing that he'd used magic on the computers, she'd expected him to try and undo the Mage-cuffs with a key. It had never even *occurred* to her, despite everything, that he almost certainly didn't *have* the key.

Instead, she could feel his magic working behind her, dueling with the magic of the Mage-cuffs as he tried to work on the technology without interfacing with the cuffs' magic.

It shouldn't have worked. Even *Kiera*, with five Runes of Power inlaid into her skin, would have exhausted herself overcoming a normal set of Mage-cuffs, let alone the Rune of Nullification–enhanced ones her captors had prepared for her.

But she could *feel* him thread the narrowest of gaps to insert his magic into the combined electronic and physical lock. She sucked in a breath—and then released it as the cuffs finally clicked free.

"To be completely honest, Your Majesty," he said quietly as he pulled the cuffs off her arms, "part of the reason you were still in those was that I wasn't sure that would work, and I was worried that Mage-cuffs powerful enough to contain you would somehow screw up my magic."

Kiera nodded as she exhaled, feeling the blood rush into her arms and her magic flood back into her system. She turned back around, meeting the gaze of the young man who—however frustrating he'd been about it—was now half of their chance of getting out of there alive.

"Call me Kiera," she instructed. "I think we're there."

He snorted.

"Call me Barry," he replied. "You're right. What happens to me is… in your hands now."

She looked at the ship on the screen and shivered.

"No, Barry," she told him. "I think it's going to take both of us to get out of this alive."

CHAPTER

SIXTEEN

Barry wasn't entirely sure what had convinced him to trust the Mage-Queen. Part of it, he suspected, was that she had apparently trusted *him* enough to fall asleep in the observer seat. Part of it, he also suspected, was just how peaceful and adorable she had looked sleeping.

He cursed himself for a fool. However nice she might seem and however pretty she was, Kiera Alexander was still the *Mage-Queen of Mars*. There was no way the monarch of humanity was going to play fair. She couldn't. That wasn't how politics *worked*; even Barry knew that.

But right now, she was entirely correct. He was relying on their engines being offline to conceal them from the unknown ship, but that wouldn't last for long. They might not have been firing off a miniature star, but the shuttle was still warmer than the rest of the empty void.

With his hands on the simulacrum, he could *feel* the space around the ship through the jump matrix. It wouldn't let him augment his magic—only the actual jump spell could work with the runes to do that—but it gave him a decent sense of his surroundings.

He could feel the heat they were venting into space and tried to smother it with his magic, directing it away from the strange ship.

If he succeeded at all—and Barry was not at all sure he *had* succeeded—it was already too late. The shuttle's communications systems beeped with an incoming transmission.

"That's, what, a minute coms delay?" Kiera asked.

"About half that," he told her. "A bit under nine million klicks."

He flipped the message up on the pilot's display. The interior of the transmitting ship's bridge made much less pretense of innocence than the exterior. It was very clearly a warship bridge, with the Captain looking at the video pickup over the silver simulacrum of his ship and multiple stations positioned around the sphere of the simulacrum chamber.

"Crux, what the hell are you doing?" the pirate commander asked. "You're supposed to have been back in Tau Ceti hours ago. I didn't think we'd *need* to know where you jumped the damn liner to.

"Report in. You know the time limit we're under."

"Crux," Barry assumed, had been the Marine Mage-Major who appeared to own this shuttle. The corvette's unnamed commander clearly knew about the whole plan that Crux had executed—which almost certainly meant that they knew the Mage-Queen was supposed to be aboard.

He glanced over at Kiera. He'd played the message openly enough that she'd clearly *heard* it.

"I'm going to try lying to them," he told her. "But they're already headed our way at twelve gees."

"And they may well have a second Mage aboard for a microjump," she replied. "If they get close enough, I can make them regret that, but…not at eight million kilometers. And if they have military missiles on that ship, they…"

She swallowed hard, and Barry fought the impulse to try to hug her to reassure her.

"They *will* destroy this shuttle if they realize I'm unrestrained, well before they let us into a distance where I can affect them with my magic," she said quietly. "Even *I* need an amplifier to affect a warship at any real range. With just a jump matrix…"

She trailed off thoughtfully.

"Right. Lying to them," he repeated.

Keeping the position of the incoming ship on his corneal projector, he pulled up the coms suite and considered his approach. Settling on *panicked and uninformed*, he activated the video pickup.

"Sir! I'm glad to see any help out here," he said quickly. "Something went badly wrong on *Extravagant Voyage*—I don't know what! Mage-Major Crux ordered me aboard this ship and clear while he went back to handle something aboard the liner.

"But then she *blew up*. I...I think the Major is dead, sir! Please advise!"

The recording shot across space, and Barry felt like he had stones in his stomach as he waited for the response.

Sixty seconds passed. Enough time for a response, but only silence answered him—and the pirate corvette continued to close at high acceleration.

Even assuming they were planning on blowing past the shuttle without slowing, they were over two hours away. But Barry had no illusions about his ability to complete the jump calculations in two hours. He was at least three or four hours away from being able to jump still—and despite Kiera's "assistance" before, he had the suspicion she wouldn't be *that* much faster.

Finally, the coms suite chirped another message receipt, and the stranger in the unfamiliar uniform appeared on the screen again.

The Captain wore an amused smirk, as if Barry's communication had been a great joke and not informing him that thousands of people were dead.

"You lie like crap, kid," he told Barry. "So let's try this again. I am Mage-Captain Edmund Stanford Kron of the Protectorate Special Covert Operations Service. My colleague, Crux Aloysius, was aboard *Extravagant Voyage,* carrying out critical operations.

"You have his ship, so I suspect that Major Aloysius is dead. I sincerely doubt you killed him, but I suggest you come clean very quickly."

A threat indicator on Barry's console flashed red, and Kron smiled coldly.

"If you are unfamiliar with the systems on your borrowed spacecraft, the indicator that just turned on is informing you that my people just locked you in with active radar. Talk quickly, son, because if I do think you killed my friend, well...missiles aren't *that* expensive."

Barry winced as the recording ended, and he checked the console. Unsurprisingly, Kron was not bluffing. The red icon flickering at him was a threat-detector system, saying that they were being hit with sufficient radar to lock them in for targeting.

"At least they can't hit us with the lasers from this range," Kiera told him. "If you're willing to let me at the simulacrum, I can probably stop the missiles they can throw. But..."

"But what?" he asked.

"Never mind," she said. "Focus on the task at hand. What are you going to tell them? As the man said, you can't lie for shit."

"Then I try not to lie," Barry said. He closed his eyes and exhaled, considering his options. Finally focusing on the video pickup again, he activated it.

"Look, Captain Kron," he told the stranger. "I don't actually know *anything*. I stole this shuttle, realized I was in the middle of nowhere and then watched the ship my fallback plan relied on vaporize itself.

"I don't actually know your Crux; you're right. I'm guessing he was on *Voyage*. I wasn't. I'm also guessing, though, that you know about the passenger I have locked in the bedroom."

He sent the message before he could reconsider that, and glanced back at Kiera.

"Two truths and a lie?" he murmured. "Or something like that."

"Pretending I'm still a prisoner, huh?" she asked. "Dangerous."

"Right now, Kiera, you're the only chance I see of getting out of this without them killing us both," he admitted. "From what you said, so long as they think you're still restrained, we have a chance."

"And the moment they realize you've freed me, Kron is going to start finding out how many missiles two Mages with no practical experience in antimissile defense can stop," she conceded grimly. "Let's see what they have to say."

Her gaze meeting his was fierce, and Barry consciously drew on some of her fire to support his own determination.

"I'm not turning you over to them," he said softly. "But I'd really like to not die here today."

Kiera reached out and touched his shoulder, sending a shiver of warmth through him. She was still standing on the floor as he sat on the ceiling, making it weird to meet her gaze.

"Neither of us has eaten," he pointed out. "Can you check the kitchenette and see if there's like…I don't know, sandwiches or premade meals or something?"

She laughed at him.

"I'm sorry, did you just ask the Mage-Queen of Mars to make you a sandwich?"

Despite everything, he found himself laughing along with her. Her giggle was absolutely *delightful*—and given how much darkness he knew she had to be facing right now, it was good to hear.

"No," he finally corrected. "I asked the Mage-Queen of Mars to make *herself* a sandwich and *maybe* find me one at the same time."

She grinned at him for a few more seconds before the humor faded into her previous stress lines. But she nodded anyway.

"Yeah. It's a good plan. Let me see what I can find."

She disappeared back into the bedroom slash kitchen, and Barry stared blankly at the pilot's controls and screens around him. He had his corneal projector linked into the system as well, trying to track everything going on around them.

Not that there was much. He *should* continue the jump calculations, but it was difficult with their lives in danger. Right now, there was their stolen shuttle, the pirate corvette, and a debris field that *had* been two thousand people.

The coms suite chirped at him, and he realized that, however unintentionally, he'd sent Kiera away while he received the pirates' response.

"All right, son," Captain Kron told him levelly. "Your honesty is noted and probably buys you your life. If you knew enough and were equipped enough to steal the shuttle, I'm assuming you have a client waiting for it and you're in this for the money."

He smiled, showing a set of too-perfect, too-white teeth.

"Believe me, my little thief, I have money to burn. Bring me that shuttle and its 'passenger.' I will deliver you to a safe system of your choosing with ten million Martian dollars in cash chips.

"Don't… Well." Kron shrugged. "I need that passenger. Do not underestimate me, little thief."

The message ended, and Barry stared off into space for several seconds, his brain in about nine different places. Frustratingly, one of said places was Kiera emerging from a swimming pool, dripping wet.

That hardly reassured him on his level of logic with regards to her. On the other hand…when it came to refusing giant bribes, *logic* was rarely the main push.

He smiled. He needed time and there was an easy way to get that.

A few commands later and he was looking straight into the camera again.

"Make it twenty million, Captain, and I'll think about it."

CHAPTER

SEVENTEEN

Kiera knew she'd missed something when her thief—*Barry*—entered the tiny living quarters with a tired expression on his face. She hadn't gone so far as to make sandwiches, but she'd found a couple of standard RMN self-heating rations.

"Eat," she told him, sliding one toward him.

"We don't have a lot of time," he said, but he took the ration and stared down at it. "What *is* this?"

"The packet said butter chicken. I'm not sure the cook had been to Tau Ceti, let alone India," Kiera observed. "But it's edible."

"They know you're aboard," Barry told her, still staring at the food. "They offered me ten million to deliver you to them."

"I feel undervalued," she replied automatically, before she even considered the situation. As the reality sank in, she took one last bite of the faux curry and slid it to one side.

"I mean, ten million dollars for the Mage-Queen of Mars? I'd think I'm worth more than that."

"I asked for more money to buy time," he admitted. "But..."

He shook his head and dropped the fork back into the ration box. She didn't think he'd even taken a bite.

"We can't trust them," he told her. "And…" He stared down at the food, then finally lifted his head to look at her face.

Something in her thief's expression sent a wriggling sensation through Kiera's stomach. It wasn't fear, but it was a close cousin in some ways.

"It's not just about money. It usually is, for me and the folks I live and work with, but it can't *just* be about money," he said levelly. "A couple thousand people already died today. I'd like to get through this mess without anyone *else* dying—but I'm not handing you over to anybody you don't tell me is okay."

If Barry thought Kiera needed protection, he was *adorable*. On the other hand, all he'd needed to do was not tell her about their offer and fail to run, she supposed.

"What are our options?" she asked.

"They'll reach us before I can calculate the jump," he admitted levelly. "And I'm discovering that there's a level of distraction that wrecks my ability to do high-order multivariate mathematics, even with computer assistance.

"How fast can you finish the jump?" he asked.

Kiera grimaced.

"Jump calculations are…" She sighed. "I'm not sure I could pick up your calcs halfway through; I'd have to start from scratch or close enough to make no difference. Couple of hours. I haven't jumped often."

"We're losing time," he admitted. "They're coming for us at twelve gees, and the base velocity vectors were in their favor to start. If we match speeds, it will take a few hours…but if they decide to end us or microjump… And it sounded like Captain Kron had a plan for if I decided to play games."

"So, we play a different game," Kiera said, reaching out to take his hand. His fingers were warm against hers, and she felt him shiver. "Tell them you've got me locked in the bedroom and you'll take their deal. You're not sure you can get me out on your own, so you'll need help, but they'll hopefully plan to bring you aboard.

"And that, Barry, will get them into my reach." She smiled. "And it has been demonstrated, I believe, how foolish it is to let a member of my family loose near a spaceship you'd like to keep."

❧

KIERA DIDN'T REALIZE she was still holding Barry's hand until he had to let go to rotate up into the pilot's chair. There'd been no discussion of their shared grip, only a reassuring strength shared between them.

She settled back into the observer seat, scanning the information on the ship as Barry tapped the command to receive the newest message.

"You've got some backbone, I see," Captain Kron declared. "And while your negotiating position is weaker than you think, you have some idea of the value of your passenger."

He paused, then chuckled.

"Very well, little thief. Twenty million. You'll find a course attached to this message. Once you're done thinking and have made the correct decision, let us know and adopt that course."

The message ended and Barry met her gaze.

"There aren't many choices left to us," she told him. "Though I'll need that chair before we're done."

"Can you fly?" he asked.

"Nope," Kiera admitted. "But I need the simulacrum if I'm going to be able to do anything useful. So, you fly us, but once we're there…"

There wasn't enough space in the shuttle's simulacrum chamber for her to interface with the simulacrum chamber *without* being in the inverted pilot's chair. Not without getting very cozy with Barry, anyway.

In a physically awkward way, she firmly informed the part of her brain that said that would be fine. What was *wrong* with her? He hadn't kidnapped her himself, but he'd certainly left her in the Mage-cuffs for hours—and he was a thief!

A thief who'd breached the security around her and stolen a shuttle from her ship… A shuttle which, to be fair, hadn't been supposed to be there and had been in the service of the people who *had* tried to kidnap her.

She shook off her momentary distraction and gestured to Barry.

"Tell them you'll take their money, Barry," she instructed. "And then match their course. How long will it take?"

"Let me see," he replied. The numbers were flashing across his eye as he did the math on his odd implant, and then he sighed.

"Well, it took us forty-ish minutes to get this far, and now the time to zero-zero rendezvous is what their time to catch up to us at full speed was," he observed. "Two hours, forty minutes. An hour of both of us accelerating toward each other, and then a hundred minutes of shedding velocity."

"How fast can this thing go?" Kiera asked.

"According to the controls, her standard is eight gravities. Not sure if that's the engines or the gravity runes, but I'm figuring that should be safe enough."

He put his finger to his lips for a moment and then looked into the video pickups.

"It's a deal, Captain," he told the stranger. "I'm bringing up my engines and vectoring along your course. I make zero-zero in one hundred sixty minutes."

~

"TURNOVER."

Barry's soft words woke Kiera from a fitful doze. Given her fire-filled nightmares, she didn't really mind, and she looked up at him in his inverted seat.

"We flipped? I didn't feel it," she admitted.

"The gravity runes are fully charged," he told her. "Crux, whoever he was, took good care of his ship. The eight gees the controls call our standard thrust is more about the engines than the runes."

"Makes sense," Kiera agreed. "Most gravity runes can handle up to ten gravities—and the military version that handles fifteen just requires more maintenance. It's not classified or anything."

"A hundred minutes now," he told her. "How close do we need them to get?"

She grimaced.

"My aunt took out a battle fleet with her magic once," she told him, thinking back to what she'd been told about *that* mess. Her aunt was Mage-Admiral Her Highness Jane Alexander—and Kiera also knew Mage-Admiral Alexander's then–Flag Lieutenant well. She'd heard a lot about their ugly skirmish to escape enemy captivity.

"But that was literally inside planetary orbit," she admitted. "I think…well, the closer the better. But fifty thousand klicks is probably the best I'm going to manage."

"Well, so far, everything looks…"

The silence trailed on for a few seconds until she cleared her throat. "Barry?"

Her thief shook himself and refocused his attention back on her, not on whatever items had stolen his concentration. Kiera was already learning that her thief didn't so much have a train of thought as a herd of sheep. They mostly moved in the same direction, but there were always *some* going astray.

"I didn't expect him to actually pay me, no matter what, but it looks like we might have convinced Captain Kron less than we thought," he told her softly. "On the other hand, he clearly doesn't realize how much control I have of Crux's ship."

Four new icons appeared on the display, bright green triangles arcing away from the unnamed pirate corvette toward them.

"Our sensors see nothing," he continued. "Not even the slightest blip to suggest there's anything else out there.

"Except that I have *full* access to this ship's communications and networking. And it turns out that our friends didn't think to cut her out of what I think is their background tactical network."

"Meaning…we're getting telemetry from their hidden ships?" Kiera asked. "Magically concealed, I presume?"

"I don't know," he admitted. "All I can tell you is that, yeah, I'm getting low-energy omnidirectional location beacons for four small craft they just launched. They're encrypted frequency-hopping low-energy signals, designed to avoid attention.

"Except that we *have* the protocols to receive them and the computer got them automatically."

"Any idea what they are?" Kiera asked.

"Like I said, our sensors don't see anything," he admitted. "But they're moving too slowly to be missiles—and to hide like that, I'm assuming they have to have Mages aboard?"

"They have to," she agreed. There were stealth ships in the arsenal of the Protectorate of Mars, but they were closer to the size of the pirate corvette. They certainly weren't small enough for the corvette to have launched four.

"Shuttles of some kind," she concluded. "Can we interrogate that network for more data?"

"I don't know," Barry admitted, then smiled. "I'm betting that it isn't *designed* for that…but I'm also betting that I can make it do things it's not supposed to."

His focus wandered again, and screens began to appear and disappear around him as he got to work.

Kiera could *feel* his magic working, filtering into the computers and —in a sensation that she'd *never* encountered with magic before!—very clearly going out in the transmission packets.

It took him five minutes—five minutes in which the oncoming spacecraft settled into a clear ten-gravity acceleration directly toward them. Her experience said that Mages couldn't hold that kind of stealth magic for particularly long—but at that pace, the shuttles were only an hour away.

Their Mages could almost certainly hold the stealth spell that long.

"Who even *are* these people?" her thief asked.

"Nemesis," Kiera said flatly. "They're the people who murdered my father. We smashed their organization after that, but clearly, we didn't do as thorough a job as we thought. They know all of our secrets, and they have plans of their own that we haven't caught up with.

"And I really did think we'd wiped them the fuck out."

"Could be…" He snorted, as if even he wasn't sure he believed what he was trying to say. "Who am I kidding? It sounds like you know exactly who was trying to kidnap you. They certainly don't seem particularly 'smashed' at this moment."

"No. Any idea what those shuttles are?"

"Yeah. Model Twenty-Four-Sixty assault shuttles," he said, his gaze moving away from the screens to look at her. "I can't get a lot of detail out of them, since I'm still using the low-energy beacon as the carrier wave and the bandwidth is basically nonexistent. But they're RMMC assault shuttles."

"I don't suppose the beacon is accurate enough for targeting?" she asked.

"No," Barry said flatly. "Well, not accurate targeting, anyway. When they set it up, they thought of that. I *might* be able to convince them to send a more-powerful transmission, enough to short-circuit their magical stealth, but..."

He sighed.

"The moment I do *that*, they know what's going on and are going to cut their beacons. And probably shoot at us."

Ten minutes since turnover. Everything was still over ten light-seconds away, but even while the corvette and *their* shuttle were decelerating toward rendezvous, the assault shuttles were increasing their speed.

"At the range I can hit them..." She swallowed. "I don't remember the specs on the Twenty-Four-Sixty perfectly, but I know they carry missiles and light railguns. The missiles are toys against a warship, but they're *designed* to shoot down shuttles. At about six, seven hundred thousand kilometers."

"If only..." Barry was silent again, staring at the displays, then looked back at her. "Overrides."

"Overrides?" she asked—and then she caught up and started fishing her necklace out of her shirt. Where her Hands concealed their chip in a golden medallion in the shape of a closed fist—the symbol of their office—*she* wore what looked like an obsidian arrowhead.

It had been carved out of obsidian from *Olympus Mons* itself before Kiera was born. By her mother. The artisan who had installed the security chip more recently had been utterly *terrified* of damaging the precious gift.

She held it in the palm of her hand and shivered.

"This was my mother's," she admitted. "Be careful?"

Their inverted positions made his outreached hand look awkward, but she saw his gentle smile and his nod.

"I...I am honored by your trust," he whispered as she placed it in his palm. "Genelocked, I see, but you've already released it. Let's see…"

It took Kiera several seconds to realize that he wasn't even *touching* the arrowhead. It was floating a millimeter above his palm as he wrapped it in a bubble of protective magic.

He landed the arrowhead on a scanning pad and waited.

"Okay," he said. "I've pulled codes that should work. Now…give me some time."

"What are you doing?" she asked, her gaze switching between him and her mother's gift.

"I can't get much data *out* of them," he admitted. "But if I find the right pieces of code and power, wrapped in your override codes… They can't have changed out enough of an assault shuttle's computers to negate your authority, not without doing enough work that they might as well have built an entirely new shuttle."

"And when you're ready?" she whispered.

"Then we need to be very ready," Barry said. "Because we're going to get one shot at this, Kiera, and if we get it wrong, they're going to kill us."

She swallowed and looked at the displays around her.

"Then I think it's time for us to switch spots," she told him quietly. "Because I need to sort out how much I can do from this simulacrum."

Unfortunately, while it was *possible* to convert a jump matrix to an unrestricted amplifier, *this* jump matrix was mostly outside in vacuum. And while there were probably vac-suits aboard the shuttle, Kiera wasn't actually trained in EVA—and at eight gravities of acceleration, any attempt at extravehicular work was basically suicide anyway.

They had what they had and they could do what they could do with it.

CHAPTER

EIGHTEEN

Barry wasn't sure *what* Kiera would be able to do from millions of kilometers away. He understood the theory that the Royal Martian Navy's Mages could strike down hostiles at ten light-seconds with their magic—but that was as much a function of the ships as anything else!

He had no illusions about what he might be able to pull off. With root-level override codes and his magic, he thought he had a decent chance at short-circuiting the assault shuttles. He had *no* idea what could be done about the corvette.

Especially because putting together the kind of packaged magical software bomb he was assembling took time. Ten minutes passed. Fifteen. Twenty. *Thirty.*

And then everything seemed to pop together into place, his magic weaving through override code and virus segments to tie it all together into a terrifyingly deadly gift basket.

"I don't know for certain that this will work," he told Kiera. He stood from the observer chair, stretching to try to relieve muscles strained by sitting and focusing.

"Would five more minutes help?" she asked.

"Probably not. An hour might."

"Well, in five more minutes, the assault shuttles are basically going to be on top of us," she reminded him. "And the corvette won't be long behind. I don't know what they're planning, but I doubt it's going to be an unexpected delivery of tea and fucking cookies."

Barry chuckled softly.

"Are you ready, then?" he asked. He looked at the Nemesis corvette on the displays. "She's seven light-seconds away. Are you sure you can do something?"

"Are you sure your virus is going to take out the shuttles?" Kiera replied.

"No. I just don't see any other choice."

"Exactly," she agreed, her face sinking in a way that made him want to tell her it was fine, she didn't need to push herself.

Barry had only the vaguest idea of what overstretching magic could do to someone. It had been covered in his courses, but he didn't really *remember* his classes. He definitely wasn't sure what would happen to the *Mage-Queen of Mars* if she stretched beyond even her extraordinary capabilities—except that he knew he didn't want to see Kiera get hurt.

They had no choice. He exhaled and nodded to her.

"Ready?"

"Do it."

He pressed the command on his wrist-comp. His virus was already in the coms suite's buffers, shivering with the power he'd forced into it. All the digital button did was unleash it.

He couldn't really feel magic, not even his own—but he *felt* the moment the energy left their shuttle's buffers. He'd concentrated a *lot* of his energy into those programs, and transmitting them pulled the last dregs out of him.

He wavered on his feet and collapsed back into the chair, watching. Two seconds for the transmission to cross the distance. Two seconds for him to see whatever happened.

Plus some seconds for his code to override its way into the shuttle's systems, unpack itself, and execute. The "good" news was that it was going to be very obvious when—

"Fuck me," Kiera whispered.

What had been empty pieces of space now lit up with the blazing torches of fusion rockets opened up *far* wider than was wise. All four shuttles were suddenly spinning away from them at over fifty gravities.

It didn't *matter* if they had gravity runes at those thrust levels. Everybody aboard the shuttles would have died in the first few seconds—and the magical cloaks collapsed with the Mages conjuring them.

The shuttles themselves wouldn't last too much longer, Barry knew. At that kind of throughput, the engines were going to fail and explode. With their crews dead, they weren't a factor anymore.

He buried the realization that he'd probably killed at least sixty people underneath his fatigue and activated the evasive-maneuvering program he'd set up. It wouldn't buy them much, not once the seeking missiles launched, but it would…

"It's done."

Kiera's words hung in the simulacrum chamber, wrapped with an exhaustion even more bone-deep than his own.

"What?" he asked, glancing at the screen showing the corvette.

"Seven seconds, Barry," she told him, and he realized she was slumped back into the pilot's seat, her hands slipping away from the simulacrum. "You'll see about…now."

Starships had enough "body language," so to speak, for Barry to be absolutely certain of the moment when Mage-Captain Kron and his people had seen the fate of their shuttles. Engines flared to additional power as the corvette began to twist into an evasive maneuver of her own.

An evasive maneuver she would never complete as a shivering web of superheated plasma twice as wide as the corvette was long appeared out of nowhere and crashed in on the Nemesis ship.

Lines of magical starstuff crashed into the Nemesis ship like it was a toy built of papier-mâché. Whatever defenses it had, they weren't enough to hold off its fate. Fifteen seconds after Kiera had instructed "*Do it,*" they were alone in the deep void.

And Kiera Alexander, he realized, was flagging fast. He didn't have much energy of his own left, but he managed to magically release her from the straps and pull her down to him.

Catching her in his arms, he was almost surprised by how delicate she was. Like him, she was too lightly built for her height.

"I'm…okay," she whispered as she curled into his grip, nestling her head on his shoulder. She wasn't resisting him holding her. "No burnout. No bleeding. Just…I'm not jumping us for a bit."

"Me either," he whispered back.

"Bed, Barry," she instructed. "I need to rest. You need to rest."

"We can take turns," he said, slowly guiding her back toward the single bunk. "There's only one bed."

"I am aware of the number of beds on this shuttle, Barry, and if you don't come hold me in the one bed we have between us, the only thing saving you will be my complete exhaustion."

She was basically *nuzzling* his neck now.

"We're alive," she murmured, her breath warm against his skin. "We'll get home, once we've rested. And then, Mr. Barry, you and I are going to talk about what comes next."

He wasn't *entirely* sure what she meant…but he had the distinct impression that he wasn't going to object to whatever she had in mind.

JOIN THE MAILING LIST

Love Glynn Stewart's books? Join the mailing list at

GLYNNSTEWART.COM/MAILING-LIST

Be the first to find out when new books are released!

ABOUT THE AUTHOR

Glynn Stewart is the author of *Starship's Mage*, a bestselling science fiction and fantasy series where faster-than-light travel is possible–but only because of magic. His other works include science fiction series *Duchy of Terra*, *Castle Federation* and *Vigilante*, as well as the urban fantasy series *ONSET* and *Changeling Blood*.

Writing managed to liberate Glynn from a bleak future as an accountant. With his personality and hope for a high-tech future intact, he lives in Canada with his partner, their cats, and an unstoppable writing habit.

VISIT GLYNNSTEWART.COM FOR NEW RELEASE UPDATES

CREDITS

The following people were involved in making this book:
    Copyeditor: Richard Shealy
    Proofreader: M Parker Editing
    Cover art: Roman Chalyi
    Typo Hunter Team
    Faolan's Pen Publishing team: Jack, Kate, and Robin

facebook.com/glynnstewartauthor

OTHER BOOKS BY GLYNN STEWART

For release announcements join the
mailing list or visit **GlynnStewart.com**

STARSHIP'S MAGE

Starship's Mage
Hand of Mars
Voice of Mars
Alien Arcana
Judgment of Mars
UnArcana Stars
Sword of Mars
Mountain of Mars
The Service of Mars
A Darker Magic
Mage-Commander
Beyond the Eyes of Mars
Nemesis of Mars
Chimera's Star *(upcoming)*

Starship's Mage: Red Falcon
Interstellar Mage
Mage-Provocateur
Agents of Mars

Starship's Mage Novellas
Pulsar Race
Mage-Queen's Thief

DUCHY OF TERRA

The Terran Privateer
Duchess of Terra
Terra and Imperium
Darkness Beyond
Shield of Terra
Imperium Defiant
Relics of Eternity
Shadows of the Fall
Eyes of Tomorrow

SCATTERED STARS

Scattered Stars: Conviction
Conviction
Deception
Equilibrium
Fortitude
Huntress
Prodigal

Scattered Stars: Evasion
Evasion
Discretion
Absolution

PEACEKEEPERS OF SOL
Raven's Peace
The Peacekeeper Initiative
Raven's Course
Drifter's Folly
Remnant Faction
Raven's Flag *(upcoming)*

EXILE
Exile
Refuge
Crusade
Ashen Stars: An Exile Novella

CASTLE FEDERATION
Space Carrier Avalon
Stellar Fox
Battle Group Avalon
Q-Ship Chameleon
Rimward Stars
Operation Medusa
A Question of Faith: A Castle Federation Novella

Dakotan Confederacy
Admiral's Oath
To Stand Defiant
Unbroken Faith *(upcoming)*

AETHER SPHERES

Nine Sailed Star
Void Spheres *(upcoming)*

VIGILANTE
(WITH TERRY MIXON)

Heart of Vengeance
Oath of Vengeance

**Bound By Stars: A Vigilante Series
(With Terry Mixon)**
Bound By Law
Bound by Honor
Bound by Blood

TEER AND KARD

Wardtown
Blood Ward
Blood Adept

CHANGELING BLOOD

Changeling's Fealty
Hunter's Oath
Noble's Honor
Fae, Flames & Fedoras: A Changeling Blood Novella

ONSET

ONSET: To Serve and Protect
ONSET: My Enemy's Enemy
ONSET: Blood of the Innocent
ONSET: Stay of Execution
Murder by Magic: An ONSET Novella

STAND ALONE NOVELS & NOVELLAS

Children of Prophecy
City in the Sky
Excalibur Lost: A Space Opera Novella
Balefire: A Dark Fantasy Novella
Icebreaker: A Fantasy Naval Thriller